I0738065

# FORESEEABLE FUTURE

---

## The SEEDER Series

---

### HOWARD LIBES

HAPPY MISTAKE PUBLISHING
*Eugene, Oregon*

*In memory of George Krauss*

# MAR

A fist pounded on the front door of the bungalow, startling Mar.

"Mar Jeps, you know who this is," said the man with the scars on his hands. "I'm here with a platoon of Global Guards. I've been ordered to give you the courtesy of a twelve-count to come out, then we'll batter your door down."

Mar gulped an entire glass of Malrap from the half-full bottle she recovered out of the kitchen trash, then leaned back in the cushions of the couch she'd purchased with Rajer. They'd spent many days entwined here, watching a vid, talking about their day or silent.

"We know you're in there, Mar," the man said. She hated how he said her name, singing it out as opposed to the terse way he said the other words. "We tracked you here. Make this easy and surrender peacefully."

*Peacefully*, Mar thought. *That's a joke.*

Just a short time ago, in the Arena filled with 200,000 Kodans, a woman had taken aim at her son with a gun. Then Rajer appeared out of nowhere, tackling the woman and tumbling off the ramp out of sight. In a state of shock, Mar wandered away from the Arena with the agitated crowd. The people on the Plaza were chanting, "When All Else Fails…When All Else Fails…When All Else Fails," some climbing surveillance-cam poles and toppling them. As she headed down an avenue in the Old Quarter, troop carriers pulled up behind her, blocking off the Old Quarter from the Plaza. Global Guards poured out of the carriers wearing riot gear, and Mar hurried to the rail-car station.

At home, behind the new front door installed while she was at the Arena, she discovered an envelope. She cracked open the seal, removing a large stack of paper. She read the first two paragraphs of the cover page, then felt something stuck at the bottom of the envelope and turned it open-end down. A memory wafer slid into her hand.

Now, she sat on the couch and inserted the memory wafer into her viewer. On the vid start-up screen, Yor's smiling face stared out at her. She leaned forward and pressed play and sank back into the cushions. "Hello, Mother," Yor said. "By this time, the Breeze Celebration events have unfolded. If everything went as planned, then Mado and myself lifted off in the WAEF and are hiding in an undisclosed location. As we've discussed, in the envelope are the legal documents making you CEO and majority shareholder in trust of Prevor Industries. Mado's people should have swapped out the old bungalow front door for a newer, more secure model and reinforced the walls around the door. Global Guards will be descending on the bungalow soon. The door should keep them out for awhile. I'm assuming you and Rajer have packed your bags." Then Yor turned and was listening to someone offscreen. She assumed it was Mado. Yor continued, "Oh yes, turn the bungalow Active Glass to opaque so they can't see inside, then get your bags and stand in the kitchen. A cruiser from Prevor Industries will be coming for you two and you don't want to be in the living room when they arrive. Don't forget to take the envelope and its contents with you, including this wafer. Be safe. I love you." The vid reset to Yor's smiling face. Mar felt herself about to cry but fought back the tears. She removed the wafer from the viewer and put it in her pocket.

"All right, Mar. So be it," the man said. "One…"

Mar hurried to the bedroom and grabbed her overnight bag. Reflexively, she reached for Rajer's bag, too, then simply stared at it.

"Two…"

A sense of loss washed over her. She fought back tears again.

"Three…"

Mar had to believe Rajer was alive.

"Four…"

Mar hurried to the living room, stuffed the documents back in the envelope and into the outer compartment of her bag.

"Five…"

She picked up her bag and the viewer and ran into the kitchen.

"Six…"

Outside, the bungalow was surrounded by Global Guards.

"Seven…"

The man stood at the front door; two Global Guards waited behind him, holding the cylindrical metallic pillar of a battering ram between them.

"Eight…"

A few of the Global Guards noticed her in the kitchen window and alerted the man, who peered at her with disgust. Mar realized she'd forgotten to turn the Active Glass opaque.

"We see you there, Mar," the man said, pointing at her. "You're only delaying the inevitable."

She dropped the bag and placed the viewer on the counter, then ran to the bungalow control panel and adjusted the Active Glass to opaque.

"Nine…"

As she returned to the kitchen, she felt a twinge in her head and her legs became wobbly.

"Ten…"

She wondered if she should grab fotos or keepsakes from the living room. After today, she'd never return here again. She thought about how this place had been her family's home for so many years. There were so many memories here.

"Eleven…"

She attempted a step forward, but her legs didn't respond.

"Twelve…" the man said. "Last chance, Mar. You can walk out, or we can drag you out."

A moment passed, then the battering ram struck the front door. Mar was startled at the impact and her heart raced.

The battering ram smashed against the door over and over until Mar distinctly heard the doorframe cracking. She felt another twinge in her head and sat down on the floor as she became dizzy and her vision began to blur.

The battering ram sounded far off in the distance now. She took deep breaths, attempting to remain conscious. The battering continued relentlessly and she felt herself on the verge of passing out when a crash emanated from the living room.

Light streamed in, then a Global Guard was standing over her, wearing full commando gear and a helmet enclosing his entire head, calling out, "Mar Jeps…Mar Jeps…" sounding more machine than human. The Guard bent down so his face was at the same level as hers and flipped up the helmet's visor. His eyes looked less angry than concerned. "She's in sonic shock," the Guard said. He flipped down his visor then lifted her from under her armpits and tossed her over his shoulder as if she weighed nothing.

*At least I'll see Rajer soon*, she thought.

She was carried into the living room where a Guard in similar gear stood beside the couch. The battering ram struck again and again, then the front door burst open and fell to the ground. From Mar's upside-down vantage point, she saw the man with the scars on his hands, flanked by two Global Guards.

"Halt!" the man yelled. "Halt or we'll fire."

The Global Guard carrying Mar kicked aside the low table in front of the couch. The other one reached for the bottom of the couch and tipped it over so it lay on its back. Mar was lowered to the ground behind the couch and the Guards stooped down beside her. She was paralyzed. She was confused. *Why are these Global Guards fighting among themselves?*

"Open fire!" the man with the scars on his hands yelled, then the sound of discharging stun weapons rang out.

The couch shielded them as its foamy white innards exploded into the air, then began floating down like snow as the weapons fire continued unabated. Mar was frightened and she couldn't move. Beside her, the Global Guard who had raised his visor wasn't shaken at all. He calmly detached a sonic grenade from his belt and pressed the button on top.

"Cover your ears," the Global Guard said to Mar. He watched Mar as she attempted to raise her arms. She only managed to raise them a few centimeters before they fell to her sides. The Guard tossed the grenade over the couch and pressed his gloved hands tightly over Mar's ears.

Mar blacked out, then in a dazed state found herself being lifted up, into the light, toward the roar of engines. She was placed in a seat and a door slid closed. A voice said, "Let's get out of here." Her head was beginning to clear as engines powered up. She was in a cruiser, hovering above her neighborhood. There was a hole in the roof of her bungalow, which was surrounded by Global Guards looking up at the cruiser. Maybe half a dozen lay on the ground by the front door. She attempted to lean forward, but couldn't budge and realized she was strapped in. Then she was pinned to her seat by the acceleration of the cruiser.

Her bag sat in front of her legs and she was flanked by the helmeted Global Guards. The one on her left had raised his visor again, then removed his helmet. He was older than the average Global Guard. Maybe Rajer's age.

He had short, dark, closely cropped hair with some grey in it. Square-jawed.

"Are you taking me to the Detention Facility?" Mar said. Below, the city raced by. "You have no grounds to arrest me."

The Global Guard laughed. "You were more disoriented down there than I thought. Did you hear half the things I said? Do you know who I am? Where you're headed?"

"You're a Global Guard. I assume the Detention Facility."

"I should probably start from the beginning, then. My name is Wel Warver. I'm head of security for Prevor Industries and I'm here—we're here to take you to the Prevor Industries Complex," Warver said, then pointed to the man on her right. "This is Kush Suron, my second-in-command."

Mar turned to the other Guard who now had his helmet off too. He was younger than Wel Warver. He had the same haircut and no grey in his dark hair. He was observing Mar as if taking the measure of her.

Mar said, "I guess I was semiconscious down there."

Warver said, "The Guards activated a sonic cannon before they began their assault. They weren't taking any chances after what happened at the Arena. Only standing behind the cannon or wearing one of these helmets helps." He tapped the helmet on the seat beside him. "Fortunately for us, the Guards outside your door didn't think they'd need these helmets when arresting you."

"But how did you get by those Guards at my door?"

"You were definitely out of it," Warver said and chuckled. "We blew a hole in your roof to get in, then I used a sonic grenade for cover and evacuated you up into the cruiser. We disguised this cruiser as one of theirs and dressed like them, then when they realized our trick, they didn't fire on the cruiser because regulations dictate that inside the dome, nobody shoots at an object overhead. We also jammed their comms, so we'll be at headquarters before they can scramble a cruiser to give chase. Please excuse me for a moment." Wel Warver leaned forward between the pilot and copilot and said something Mar couldn't make out over the din of the engines.

"What's happening?" Mar said as loudly as she could over the engines so Wel Warver would hear her, then he turned around and pressed a few buttons on a control panel in the cruiser's ceiling and a small viewing screen descended.

"This is a message being broadcast on every Global Assembly channel both vid and aud," Warver said, reaching out and tapping the pilot who pressed a few buttons on his control console.

A light-blue orb, the Prevor Industries logo, appeared on the screen. Mar's head was aching. Mado appeared wearing a blue suit the same color as the orb, standing on the balcony of his lab. His arms were crossed over his chest and he had a stern look on his face. "Hello, I'm Mado Prevor," Mado said, as if this were some industrial-info vid. His voice was emanating from speakers in both side doors. "By now you've experienced disturbing events, running counter to the Global Assembly's agenda, and no doubt you are searching for Professor Vanderlord. First off, you'll stop searching for him, and second, you'll take no actions against Professor Vanderlord's family or Prevor Industries. Why would you agree to such demands? One word: power. You have no idea how to reenergize the domes' power generators. When you signed the agreement for Prevor Industries to provide power for the domes, you gladly left the ability to reenergize them as a Prevor Industries corporate secret, and by my estimation there are sixty-five days left before the generators run out. And don't go arresting my employees for the secret. I'm the only person who knows how to reenergize them. Two more things. First, anyone arrested on suspicion of being involved in today's events— and I'm talking about suspected without concrete evidence of involvement—will be released from the Detention Facility in any dome where they might reside. Also, you will not create any negative propaganda regarding Professor Vanderlord, myself, or my corporation for the viewing channels or digi-media outlets." Mado uncrossed his arms and pointed at the cam. "This is not an idle threat. If you think your internal approval polls have seen a downward trend with today's events, then ponder how they'll be affected by the powering down of the generators in every dome, after which the air circulators will cease to operate. It would be foolhardy on your part to let things go that far. Do not test me. You don't know me as well as you may think. Happy Breeze Celebration." The blue orb appeared again, then the viewing screen went black.

Mar was surprised by Mado's message. It seemed to put his corporation in a vulnerable position.

Warver reached up and pressed a few buttons on the ceiling control panel again and the screen retracted. Mar heard the engines power down a little and felt the cruiser descending. They were approaching the Prevor Industries Complex.

"Any further questions, boss?"

"Please call me Mar."

"That's a little informal for me. How about if I call you Mar Jeps?"

"If that makes you comfortable. What shall I call you?" Mar said as the cruiser slowed and hovered over a landing zone inside the Complex, then began descending straight down. "And what's the plan after we land?

"Warver is fine, and Mado Prevor's admin will orient you to your new position. If you need me, I'll be nearby," Warver said. "But for now, please stay in the cruiser until I tell you we're all clear to disembark."

Before the cruiser touched down, Warver slid the door open and jumped out with a stun weapon in hand. He checked the perimeter around the cruiser as the wheels hit the landing pad. Suron exited the cruiser as well and dashed out of sight.

The engines continued humming. Mar detached her shoulder harness as Warver leaned into the pilot's window and discussed something that appeared to concern him.

Mar moved forward between pilot and copilot and said, "Is everything all right?"

The pilot said, "A company of Global Assembly soldiers haven't withdrawn from the front gates yet."

Warver said, "Mar Jeps, we have a backup location in

case Mado Prevor's message isn't heeded. Please put your harness back on. If I get a signal from Suron, then we may need to lift off."

Mar sat back down and secured the harness. Then she thought about Rajer, what he'd done for Yor at the Arena, and how he might not have survived. She felt sad and guilty she'd done this to him, although part of her grasped that the incident wasn't her fault. She attempted to control herself, but there was no stopping the tears welling up in her eyes. She put her hands over her face as the tears streamed down. She was surprised she'd held herself together this long. *This is no way for the CEO of a corporation to act in a time of crisis*, Mar thought. But that thought only made it worse. She couldn't hold back the grief and sobbed.

Somebody touched Mar's shoulder and she removed her hands from her eyes.

Warver squatted in front of her and said, "Everything will be fine one way or the other, Mar Jeps. We've got you covered." He offered her a handkerchief.

That only further exacerbated how she felt and she covered her eyes with her hands and wept once again. After a while, the wave of emotion subsided. She wiped her eyes with the handkerchief and composed herself. Warver was now standing guard outside the closed cruiser door. The pilot and copilot remained in their seats, running through a checklist and flipping switches. Mar knocked on the cruiser door. Warver turned and slid it open.

Mar said, "What's our current situation?"

"Global Assembly forces are withdrawing, but we're still waiting for the all-clear. Shouldn't be long." Warver slid the door closed, then headed back to the pilot's window and began chatting with him.

So Mar waited. She stared out the window at the Complex's buildings and the cruisers parked in the landing area. She looked around for her viewer, then realized she'd left it at the bungalow. Warver had walked away and was nowhere in sight. She listened as the pilot and copilot talked about their lives. She wondered what the future held for her. She sat patiently for what felt like a considerable amount of time. Then she closed her eyes, took a deep breath, and thought, *I can't sit here anymore.* She unbuckled her harness, slid open the door, stepped out of the cruiser, and headed toward the nearest building.

Warver called out, "Mar Jeps, please return to the cruiser."

Mar looked around but couldn't spot him, then there was a screeching sound overhead and she was tackled to the ground from behind. Somebody draped their body over hers, and there was an explosion about ten meters away. Debris showered down.

Mar got to her knees. Her ears rang.

Suron appeared in front of her and grabbed her arm, lifting her to her feet. He yelled at her and pointed, "Run to that building. Run. Now!"

Another volley screeched overhead and exploded nearby.

Mar sprinted to the building's open door where a pasty-faced, short, middle-aged man was standing.

Mar slammed the door shut, out of breath.

The man said, "That was close. Are you all right?"

"What was that?" Mar's ears were still ringing.

"I assume the forces outside the gate lobbed artillery our way," the man said. "Are you all right?"

Mar placed her hands on her head and checked them for blood, then gave her body a quick inspection for injury. "It appears so," she said. "Thanks for asking. I'm Mar."

"Yes, I know. I'm Tovar Gols. People around here call me Gols, although it's your prerogative to call me whatever you prefer."

"Gols is fine," Mar said.

"I'm your lead admin here at Prevor Industries," Gols said. "I've come to escort you to your residence."

"I forgot my bag," Mar said, pushing at the door, which wouldn't budge.

"The door is locked for security purposes," Gols said. "I don't advise going out there."

"Everybody has lots of advice for me today."

Mar pushed at the door again.

"Please, don't worry about it. The bag will be brought to your residence."

She examined Gols. He wore a cheap knockoff of an expensive suit with the emblem of Prevor Industries corporation over the right breast of the jacket. He was clean-shaven, and his hairline receded halfway up his scalp to meet what remained of a thick, curly mop of grey and black hair. She noticed a thick envelope like the one at the bungalow in his hand. Something about this man made her believe he had her well-being in mind.

"Well, then show me the way, Gols," Mar said. "I should probably clean myself up."

"I suspect you haven't seen yourself in a mirror lately. You're looking tousled."

Mar chuckled. "I like your honesty. I'm feeling tousled. It hasn't been an easy day."

They entered a nearby lift. Gols pressed the button for the top floor and the doors closed. He turned to Mar, forcing a smile as the car ascended, then faced forward. When the lift halted and the doors opened, it appeared she'd been transported home and was standing at the entrance to her bungalow. As she entered, the symbol for peace from the bungalow's front door was posted on the right-hand wall.

While Gols stood by the open lift doors, Mar walked around the living room. It was an exact replica of her bungalow in layout and furnishings. There was the couch, and the old cabinet with the compartment and fotos. In the kitchen, the drawers were filled with her chosen eating and cooking utensils, and the same pots and pans hung from the same hooks by the stove. The cabinets and cooling chamber were stocked with her preferred foods. She almost expected the cabinet drawers in the bedrooms to be filled with her and Rajer's clothing but they were empty, although the beds were made with the same bedspreads and pillowcases. Mar recalled Yor capturing detailed fotos of the bungalow and when she asked what he was doing, he said, "A project with Mado," and she never gave it another thought. Now that made sense. The home control panel looked identical to the bungalow's and when she switched the kitchen Active Glass to transparent, the view looked out over the Prevor Industries Complex to the dome boundary.

One noticeable difference was a door with an opaque Active Glass window in the living room. Mar tried the door, but it was locked. Gols still stood by the lift with an awkward smile on his face, watching her.

"What's this door, Gols?"

Gols' reply was so soft-spoken that Mar couldn't hear him.

Mar said, "Why don't you come over here?"

Gols scurried across the room in quick, small strides. "Please excuse me, Mar Jeps. I'll speak louder next time," Gols said, his voice quaking. He looked sincere but scared. His hands were shoved into his pants pockets and he kept fighting between slumping his shoulders and standing straight.

"Why are you so nervous all of a sudden?" Mar said. "I find it counterproductive and I'm the one who should be the nervous wreck around here."

"Sorry, Mar Jeps. My apologies. I just want you to be happy. I'm concerned about keeping my job. I worked for Mado Prevor for years and he was good to me."

"If Mado kept you as his admin and assigned you to me, then you must be good at what you do, so relax. I'm sure this relationship will work out fine," Mar said. "And please please please call me Mar. I need someone to talk to me on a first-name basis around here."

"If that's your wish."

"It is," Mar said. "Now, what's this door and why is it locked?"

"One moment." Gols took out his comm, pressed a few buttons, then engaged in a conversation while he walked over to the control panel and stood by it. He waved at Mar and nodded as he listened to the person on the comm, then pressed a few buttons on the panel. Mar saw the window in the door clear and heard the lock disengage. Gols approached her.

"Who was that?" Mar said, pointing at Gols' comm as he placed it back in his pocket.

"I was speaking with Commander Warver. He gave me explicit orders not to open the door until I received the all clear."

"Commander?"

"Yes. That's what I call him. He's a retired commander in the Global Assembly forces," Gols said, sliding open the door. "Please, you first."

Mar stepped onto a terrace where she could view the Capitol City skyline. The Royal Quarter and the Plaza were the tallest buildings in the distance. Black smoke rose from the Plaza. She had to admit that as much as she hated the tactics and policies that had erected it, from this vantage point, the dome was magnificent in its scope and achievement.

"Spectacular," Mar said, walking up to the railing. She turned around to find Gols standing inside the doorway. "Please come and join me," she said to Gols.

"I'm not fond of heights, but people say it's pretty," Gols said, taking one step onto the terrace. "Do you like the terrace furnishings? Mado Prevor salvaged them from the Vanderlord estate."

Mar immediately recognized the antique chairs with their flowery cushions from the estate's back porch overlooking the lake. They seemed out of place here.

Mar patted the cushion on one of the chairs and said under her breath, "Still here, old man."

"What was that?" Gols said.

"Nothing." She sat down and sank into the cushions which embraced her like an old friend. "Please come and join me."

"Gols has other things to attend to." Wel Warver was standing beside Gols, towering over him. "Don't you Gols? Mar Jeps and I need to talk privately."

"That's fine. I need to make sure the office is prepared for our new CEO," Gols said, waving the envelope. "Your bag has arrived. I'll leave this envelope on the table by the couch. Comm me when you'd like to see the office and you're ready to take in the details of your new position." Gols handed Mar a comm.

Mar checked her pockets for her comm and realized that she'd left it in the bungalow. She took the comm from Gols. "Is this my old one?"

"A new one, and nearly impossible to track or tap," Gols said. "It has my comm and Commander Warver's contact info in addition to all your old contacts."

"How do you have my old contacts?" Mar said, then cut off Gols before he could answer. "Let me guess—Mado?"

Gols smiled sheepishly and nodded. He obviously admired Mado. "If you need anything else or when you're ready for business, you know how to contact me. I'm off." Gols exited the terrace.

Mar said, "So, what can I do for you, Commander?"

Warver strode in front of Mar's chair, standing over her. She hadn't noticed earlier, but he was larger, wider, and taller than the average Kodan male. His form-fitting pullover shirt revealed taut muscle hidden by his combat armor before.

"This is awkward," Mar said. "Please sit."

"If that's what you'd like?"

"Please. It's been a long day and I'm enjoying this chair. Try it."

Warver lowered himself into the other chair and the antique wood creaked under his mass until he finally settled into the cushions. "This is nice," he said.

"This day has been insane, but somebody once told me, when life gets crazy, you should remind yourself to breathe."

"That would run counter to my job," Warver said. "I do have something to discuss with you, though."

"Yes, we do…Commander?" Mar said. "You have some explaining to do."

"I wasn't trying to hide anything, Mar Jeps," Warver said. "I thought that in the heat of rescuing you from the Global Guards and while you were recovering from sonic shock, it probably wasn't the best idea to bring up my previous vocation."

"Understandable," Mar said. "But no secrets from now on. I've had enough secrets for a lifetime."

"Duly noted."

"What would you like to discuss?"

"It's actually more of a request."

"All right. What is it?"

"When I ask you to stay somewhere, please stay there. I understand you're my superior, but my job is protecting you and the interests of this corporation. With all due respect, what you did out there was reckless. Both you and Suron could've been killed."

"You're correct on all counts," Mar said. "I promise to follow your lead from now on when it comes to security, and please thank Suron for his protection."

"That's his job, but I'll pass it along."

"Now, about your previous profession. I presume Mado hired you knowing the duplicitous nature of the Global Assembly as well as I do. So I'm wondering why he would hire you?"

"You mean why would a commander in the Global Assembly forces work for the person who just revealed the Global Assembly for the charlatans they are?"

"Took the words right out of my mouth."

"If you don't mind, let me tell you the short version," Warver said, leaning forward in the chair.

"Please go right ahead, although now that I think about it, I do recall hearing your name before."

"More than likely," Warver said. "During the Separatist Revolts, we were assigned to the Shamban region on a relief mission. We were told by the higher-ups to hold off on treating and feeding the refugees until the aid station reached maximum population, which was in the tens of thousands. When we reached capacity, we were ordered to eliminate the inhabitants as hostiles. These were sick, injured, and starving civilians. Families. Women and children. Unarmed. I refused the order and was locked up along with others under my command, but the order was eventually carried out by cowards and criminals. I was court-martialed for insubordination by a military tribunal.

"When I interviewed for the head of security job here, Mado Prevor knew exactly who I was. He confirmed my story and asked me if I'd like to work for the other side."

"I trust Mado," Mar said. "I trusted him with my son, for Powers-That-Be sake, so if he cleared you for the position then I'm completely fine with it. I can see you're good at your job. Would you prefer I call you commander?"

"That part of my life is behind me and I'd rather not be associated with the Global Assembly anymore. I indulge Gols because I know he gets a kick out of it. You can just call me Warver." He rose from the chair, which creaked as he vacated it, walked over to the terrace railing, and gazed at the city.

Mar began to rise out of her chair but flopped back down, feeling dizzy.

Warver turned to her. "You got a heavy blast from the sonic cannon. Your equilibrium is still adjusting. Best to stay put."

"That's fine by me."

Warver walked toward the terrace door and stopped before entering the building. "Your viewer from the bungalow is by your bag. I stashed it in my pack before we ascended to the cruiser. That thing is a security risk—you should have Gols install some jamming software on it. If you don't need me for anything else, may I be dismissed?"

"Yes, and thanks for saving me."

"My job and my pleasure," Warver said, smiling. He was satisfied by his work. "Before I leave, I wanted to say that your partner and your son acted bravely and selflessly today. You should be proud of them."

"I am," Mar said. "By the way, I'm curious—what's the black smoke over by the Plaza? Looks like it's getting worse."

"That's your son's doing. The citizens heard his message. Whether they can sustain it against the Global Assembly forces is another thing entirely. Happy Breeze Celebration," Warver said, and exited the terrace.

# MADO

Mado undid the harness which had been restraining him in the pilot's chair since the WAEF launched from the Arena and he immediately experienced the ship's artificial gravity. It felt like home. Yorlik would have understood, and now that he was back in space, Mado missed his friend more than ever. He gazed up at Yorlik's foto mounted above the control console. It didn't feel right being out here without him.

Then Mado peered out the control-room window at the mostly brown planet they were orbiting. Since he first approached Koda twenty-four years ago aboard the WAEF, the difference in the view from up here was striking. On the side lit by the nearby sun, more of the ocean had engulfed the continent below, eliminating a large portion of its previous landmass. The difference on the dark side was notable, too. Years ago, Koda's dark side was awash with the lights of countless cities which had survived the first onslaught of the environmental crisis. Now, the nine domes and a few of the surviving non-dome cities were lone beacons spotting the dark landscape.

"We did it," Mado said to the foto. "It happened sooner than we planned, and there were a few glitches along the way, but we made it. Now it's up to them."

"Talking to my great-grandfather?"

Mado turned to Yor. He hadn't heard him enter the room.

"You don't need to be embarrassed," Yor said. "I've done the same…many times."

Mado ran through the readings on their orbit and made a slight course correction with the thrusters, then rose from the pilot's chair and joined Yor, who was staring out the window.

"What do you think?" Mado said.

"Speechless," Yor said, continuing to gaze out the window. "I had no idea you'd prepped the ship for space."

"You had your tasks and I had mine. I did the best I could with the time available," Mado said. "I wanted to make sure we had this option and the WAEF would've needed to do this soon enough anyway."

"What do you mean?"

"How did you think I was getting back to Prevor?"

"I haven't really thought about it. There seems to be plenty ahead of us before that happens."

"True," Mado said, walking back over to the console and rechecking the course correction. "I'm enjoying being out here, though."

"When do we head back?" Yor said. "Our people in Shamba are probably wondering where we went."

"Probably not."

"Why? Have you commed them?"

"No."

"I thought you were going to handle it while I was resting."

"I was, but I intercepted a viewing-channel news transmission that may change how we proceed."

"Is my mother all right? Rajer?"

"Your mother is fine. My head of security sent a message that she's safe. I have no word on Rajer or Insol or anyone else," Mado said. "This transmission is about us and it'll influence what we do next."

"About us?" Yor said, turning to Mado. "What's happening down there?"

"The report I received says rioting has broken out in six of the nine domes. We always knew a few would keep supporting the Global Assembly. The Shamban dome government is the only one completely overrun. Global Assembly forces are fighting back across the planet and they're not using sonic weapons, so losses are high. The Global Plaza is on fire. No word on the extent of the damage. According to the viewing-channel propaganda, this is just a fringe anti-government effort that'll soon be suppressed."

"How does all of that change our plans?"

"There's more to it." Mado suggested they go to the living chamber so they could watch the intercepted broadcast together, and he could prepare something to eat.

When Mado's meal was ready, the replicator beeped six times and Mado removed the steaming tray. The day before Breeze Celebration, he had programmed the replicator for Prevorian delicacies.

Yor pinched his nose and said, "What's that smell?"

"That's deliciousness," Mado said. He carried the tray containing a half-dozen finger-length reddish portions over to the table beside where Yor was sitting in a recliner. Mado sat next to him. "I love these Gleckos. They're my favorite, but your great-grandfather had the same reaction to them as you."

"I'm not going to ask what they're composed of, but they smell horrible. I assume your people lack sensitive olfactory organs?" Yor unpinched his nostrils.

"No, the opposite," Mado said, popping one of the Gleckos into his mouth. With the first bite, images of life on Prevor—the oceans, his family and friends—rushed through his mind. His brain tingled. A look of disgust spread across Yor's face. "That doesn't help while I'm eating."

"Sorry," Yor said. "Let's see this vid."

Mado pressed a few buttons on the armrest of his recliner and a viewing screen rose out of a counter in front of them. "As I said, I uploaded this earlier."

The viewer activated, and displayed in the middle of the screen were large red words outlined in black—"BREAKING NEWS, SPECIAL REPORT—ATROCITY AT THE ARENA"—accompanied by the Global anthem, then an announcer appeared, wearing a white button-down shirt fastened all the way up to his collar and a blazer in Global Assembly colors.

"Citizens," the announcer said, "we have breaking news on the Atrocity at the Arena…" The vid cut to an aerial shot of a smoking crater in the mountains. "… When All Else Fails has been shot down by the glorious cruisers of the Global Assembly. Due to the treacherous elements in the Mlimoan mountains, it may take rescue teams more than a few days to sift through the wreckage for the body of the traitor Yor Vanderlord." Then the vid cut back to the announcer. "We'll be back soon for more breaking news regarding the Atrocity at the Arena. Until then, may the Powers-That-Be bless our global union, and we return to our regular programming." Then the vid went to static and black.

Mado pressed buttons on the recliner and the viewing screen descended into the counter. Yor was silent, features frozen on his face, nodding his head. Mado thought if Yor's brain were made of mechanical parts, he would hear gears grinding.

"Thoughts?" Mado said.

"Looks like the WAEF crashed and I'm dead."

"Would seem so."

"You weren't mentioned at all."

"You noticed that," Mado said. "If you recall, one of the goals of my Global Assembly message was to convince them I wasn't on the WAEF so I'd have the option of returning to Capitol City from Shamba. Your breaking with the plan by going to the Library early and alerting the authorities caused us to head out here, removing that option."

"Right, and wasn't your message supposed to stop anything like that vid?"

"My broadcast probably put some fear in them, but not enough to stop that stunt. They're taking a calculated risk that propagating this disinformation to remind the citizens they're in control won't put Kodans in jeopardy because I care about them. Your mother might be upset, though."

"Yes, we need get word to her immediately."

"Don't worry. I'll take care of it."

"Please. As soon as possible."

"As soon as we're done talking."

"So what's our next move? I understand we're in unplanned territory. Are there any options that involve returning to Koda sooner than later?"

"None right now. This ship has no defensive or offensive capabilities. We can outrun any cruiser in the Global Assembly fleet, but we'd eventually have to land and Harmin's virus was a one-shot deal. I bet they're tracking us right now, waiting for our reentry. We're stuck out here, plain and simple, only because the virus didn't cover our escape."

"That time limit—"

"That's history. We made it out safely and that's what counts."

"But they still have no reason to believe you're on the WAEF. That could work to our advantage."

"Or it could be a disadvantage, causing problems for your mother."

"How would it do that?"

"I can think of a few ways, although I'm not sure what we can do to make it better before we leave orbit and head out into space. But this is all hypothetical."

"Leave orbit?"

"Yes, follow me to the control room and I'll explain. Just keep an open mind."

"Look where we are," Yor said, throwing up his hands. "I believe my mind is fully open."

"Get something to eat, it'll take time to warm up the holo-device and upload the charts," Mado said. "I have Gleckos left over—they're all yours." He slid the tray in Yor's direction.

"As delicious as that sounds…and smells," Yor said, pushing the tray back in Mado's direction, "I'll prepare something else."

"You just said your mind is fully open."

"I didn't say my taste buds were fully open."

"Your loss," Mado said, carrying the tray to the food-recycle unit. "They can't be reheated."

"I'll survive," Yor said, following Mado to the food-prep area and flipping through the menu.

In the control room, Mado activated the holo-device. He unlocked the drawer underneath, removed the cylinder and inserted it into the device, then he sat down in the pilot's chair and looked over at the foto of Yorlik.

"I know," Mado said, "he's not you and I shouldn't expect him to be like you. I know he's more sensitive than you. I'll lay out the options and let him decide what he wants."

"Still talking to him?" Yor said.

"Have you eaten already?"

"I looked through the menu and decided to eat later," Yor said. "Second time I've caught you talking to Great-grandfather."

"I didn't realize how much I missed him."

"My great-grandfather was lucky to find someone like you. Not many would've taken on what he asked."

"We were together so long, and he was an extraordinary being."

"Without a doubt. I'm here because of him, too. I guess we're figuratively and literally in the same boat."

"That's a funny one," Mado said, standing up from the pilot's chair and walking past Yor to the holo-device. "Especially knowing your great-grandfather." Mado uploaded the necessary files and the holo-device stitched them together, then the lights in the control room dimmed and the stars appeared above the table.

Yor said, "So what are we looking at?"

"Your great-grandfather called it Terminus A-1." Mado punched a few more buttons on the device and an orb turned brown. "I call it A-1."

"That was the name of the first base of operations for the SEEDER program. It was never developed into a permanent transit point, but it was used by later expeditions as an outpost for resupplying before traveling further into the universe. That was before the program built replication devices and oxygen generators, of course."

"That's it. I should have assumed you possessed that knowledge. Well, one thing you don't know about A-1 is that your great-grandfather decided to use it as a staging area and storage facility on the way back to Koda. He thought it was the perfect place because of its proximity to a red dwarf star," Mado said, pointing to the star near the planet. "The side of the planet with the way station always faces away from Koda, so we could sneak onto the planet without Koda's telescopes catching us by flying behind the star.

"We stopped there for a hundred and eighty days or so while we stripped the WAEF of my engines, the shield generator, and a few other items we didn't want to fall into the hands of the Global Assembly, then restored the WAEF to the spaceship that left Koda over a century before. When we were done, we launched and Yorlik made his famous transmission saying he was alive. I'm assuming those items are still where we left them. It shouldn't take us more than a hundred and thirty-four days to arrive there."

"So, we arrive at the way station and then what?"

"We keep in touch with the situation on Koda. Your great-grandfather set up a hyper-listening telescope which is perfect for monitoring Koda's airwaves," Mado said. "Depending on what's happening on Koda, we either load up everything and head back here immediately, or take some time to install the faster engines and field generators and load up the other equipment before we return."

"Why wouldn't we head back to Koda right away?"

"One way or the other, we'll return here, but how soon depends on lots of factors."

"I need more to go on," Yor said. "I'm not abandoning my planet when it needs me."

"Nobody said anything about abandoning Koda," Mado said, "but the decision regarding our return depends on the circumstances."

"That answer sounds vague to me," Yor said, sitting in the pilot's chair and looking out the window. "Maybe a hypothetical will make more sense."

Mado walked to Yor's side and joined him in observing the planet below and the stars filling out the view. "Reasonable enough."

"We arrive at A-1 and we listen in to Koda's situation. We're faced with three possible outcomes. First, the struggle between the Movement and the Global Assembly is still ongoing; second, the Movement is beaten; and third, the Movement wins, the Global Assembly concedes, and the Leader is ousted," Yor said. "In the first case, which is the most complex of the options, we'd have to assess the situation. In the last scenario, we'd obviously go back and organize a space program. As for the second, I'm not sure what we'd do."

"I agree on the last scenario—that's definitely the clearest case, and you're correct on the first—we'd have to evaluate how safely we could return and how we'd influence the situation at hand. If the Movement is beaten, that's a tough one, but I can see a high probability of the fight lingering for years along with the hard feelings over the brutal losses the Movement will incur under the Global Assembly's firepower. Possibly an underground war will continue for generations with Prevor Industries funding."

"Sounds like you've thought about that one."

"That's the scenario your great-grandfather thought most likely."

"He did think far ahead, didn't he?"

"As much as he could. After a century in space, he fully invested himself in the idea that patience, hard work, and endurance would win in the end," Mado said. "He did have a plan for that scenario, although I don't know if you'll like it. A few pieces of the plan are already laid out since they needed to be put into play if we happened to wind up out here instead of Shamba after Breeze Celebration and I couldn't return to the corporation."

"You dumbfound me, Mado."

"Sorry, I should have told you, but there was—"

"No, please. I'm thankful you're so far ahead of me. I'm not angry at all."

"Good to know, although you may feel differently when you hear the details," Mado said. "No offense, but the depths of it are more suited to your great-grandfather's disposition than yours. I didn't know him as a young man, but I imagine he was much like you, and the time he spent developing the SEEDER program and his years in space changed him into a much more patient and prudent man."

"You don't think I'm patient or prudent?"

"Far from it. You're impulsive. For instance, I wouldn't have gone to the library. I wouldn't have rattled that man's cage. Being more conciliatory toward him and less antagonistic might have stopped the slowdown of the parade he most likely instigated, which is why we're here," Mado said. "I'm not blaming you. That's simply who you are right now and maybe I should have considered its influence over the outcome of the plan."

"You're definitely right about the library, but I didn't feel like I had any other options in dealing with that man at the bungalow."

"That's your problem right there. In most circumstances, there are options," Mado said. "You need to alter your way of thinking in that respect. That change in your behavior will be necessary and will come in handy from this day forward."

"I'll do my best," Yor said.

"That's all I've ever asked of you and you've never failed me."

"I'd like to communicate with my mother before we leave orbit."

"Unfortunately, it'll be a one-way conversation. We can send a vid message via an operative on the planet. The Global Assembly will be expecting us to comm your mother, so a direct conversation would be easily intercepted and endanger her."

"I'd like to send a message to Mel and Insol, too."

"We can send it by the same messenger," Mado said. "Do you want to hear the plan if the Movement is defeated and the fight lingers?"

"I'd rather not mull over something for a hundred and thirty-four days that I may never need to make a decision about. Seems like energy misspent. I know my great-grandfather thought it likely, but there's always a chance he might've been wrong."

"He was hardly ever wrong. It was uncanny."

"I'd still like to wait until we arrive on A-1 and get a read on the situation before I tackle making a decision on whatever you and my great-grandfather cooked up."

"I respect what you're saying," Mado said, squeezing Yor's shoulder. "Let's get to work on those messages."

# Orn

Orn was fuming about Mar Jeps escaping his grasp as he sat in the Leader's waiting room. After he avoided the sonic grenade, Orn realized the cruiser hovering above the bungalow wasn't one of theirs and ordered the Global Guards to shoot it down, but the platoon's lieutenant countermanded his order, citing regulations against firing upward in the dome. The lieutenant and his regulations had kept Orn from knocking down the bungalow door in the first place, too. When the cruiser was out of range, Orn wrapped his hands around the lieutenant's throat, but before Orn could do any real damage, he was restrained by the lieutenant's men.

Orn also recognized the people impersonating Global Guards. They worked for Prevor Industries. Unfortunately, Orn's hands were tied when it came to Mado Prevor. Dealing with him was a tricky business. The Global Assembly and the Kodan people were indebted to him. Without him, the domes would never have been built, the environmental crisis would have wiped out Koda's human population, and Vidor Plemso wouldn't be the Leader.

Orn had long been suspicious of Mado Prevor's actions though. When the Vanderlord boy began interning at Prevor Industries and the restoration of the WAEF was approved, he warned the Leader and his top advisors about the dangers of a Vanderlord being reunited with the WAEF. Nobody would listen. They said, "A lack of confidence in our governance is showing in our internal polling and resurrecting the WAEF is an easy way back into the people's good graces. We know Mado Prevor will deliver, and the boy can't hurt us."

Orn thought, *That entire Vanderlord family is rotten. We should've disappeared them when the Great man landed back on Koda.*

Now, Orn was ushered into the office where the Leader stood staring out the window with his back to Orn. He said, "Please join me over here, Orn."

Black smoke from the fires in the Plaza reached the office windows even though they were fifty floors up. The Leader stood unmoving with his arms crossed over his chest. Orn stopped beside him. Below, Malrap vending stands were engulfed in flames, kegs exploding. Large weapons fire screeched through the air, then detonated. Global Assembly forces were attempting to dislodge well-positioned rioters who had built barricades out of kiosks and were throwing flaming Malrap containers at advancing soldiers.

The Leader said, "I'd love to be down there."

"I know you would, sir."

"So the Jeps woman got away from you?"

"Yes, sir," Orn said, "I tried—"

"Everyone is trying, but results have been lacking," the Leader said as an explosion below rattled the windows. He turned toward Orn. He looked tired and angry. "What's your evaluation of the global situation?"

"Manageable. We have a large enough percentage of the population still loyal to us and the rioters are clearly outgunned. It might take a handful of days, but it'll be under control soon. The bigger concern is a simmering underground revolt, especially with Vanderlord—"

"Yes, Vanderlord. Your obsession with that family is commendable," the Leader said, staring out the window again. "I should have listened to you and not my advisors or the suck-ups in my cabinet about that boy, but that's the past. We must look to the future. Wouldn't you agree?"

"I gave you advice, sir, but you have the wisdom of your position."

The Leader sighed and walked around his desk until it was between himself and Orn. "I expect the Powers-That-Be truth from you. I have too many lackeys around here who'll say what they think I want to hear. I expect you to speak your mind."

Orn reflexively snapped to attention, stiffening his body and clicking his heels together. "Yes, sir. I will do my best, sir."

"Have you seen Mado Prevor's vid?"

"Yes, I caught it on the way here."

"He's too important to the planet's current state of affairs and our future to have him siding with the Movement and threatening us. We need him working with us to forward our agenda whether he's on our side or not. That's why I withdrew our forces from his Complex. You understand me? I need to know his whereabouts."

"Absolutely, sir," Orn said. "Any clues to go on?"

"No. Our agents have interrogated a handful of his employees and they all tell the exact same story about him returning to the Prevor Industries Complex after Breeze

Celebration, which feels suspect," the Leader said. "The Jeps woman is at the Complex. I gave our boys clearance to take a shot at her when her cruiser landed, but the morons missed the mark. Must be her lucky day. Maybe you can have a talk with her and she can shed light on Prevor's whereabouts."

"Mar Jeps is not fond of me."

"I'm not asking you to take her out on a date, just do your job," the Leader said. "I'm aware you're not known for your charm, but muster whatever form of persuasion you can, outside of torture, and pry the information out of her. Prevor is the key to all our futures. Use her partner as leverage. I'm sure she wants to know whether he's alive or not."

"What about the Vanderlord boy?"

"You've probably heard the news of his untimely demise," the Leader said. He seated himself on a couch, waving Orn over to join him.

"I have," Orn said, moving out from behind the desk and seating himself on the couch across from the Leader. He put his hands on his knees. "I'm not sure that bit of fiction was wise. I believe it'll upset more citizens than it will hearten."

"I decided it was the best way to quell the rioters since their inspiration would be dead, and if news of his death does encourage others to act, then we can crush them now instead of later. It's a good first solution to ferret out the vermin before the purge."

"Where is the WAEF now?"

"Still in orbit. We're keeping an eye on it. He'll attempt reentry soon and that's when we'll take care of him."

"Dead or alive?"

"Alive would be best. I have questions about who he's been conspiring with and if he has information about his great-grandfather's discovery," the Leader said, standing up from the couch. Orn followed suit. "Now get me answers. Kel will have the global intelligence report for you at the reception desk on your way out."

"May I inject one more thought, sir?"

"Please do."

"The greater concern here is a prolonged war of attrition like the Separatist Revolts. I'm aware of our planetary surveillance capabilities, but there are citizens who have obviously been harboring discontent for decades, so who's to say this fake death of the Vanderlord boy won't turn him into a martyr for the Movement?" Orn said. "I understand this is a political conundrum for you, but it might be best to capture the boy and reprogram him to our side like we tried and failed to do with his father. I don't believe the boy is as strong as his father."

"I'll take that under advisement," the Leader said. "And by the way, I've arrested the lieutenant of that Global Guard platoon from the Jeps' bungalow. He's currently in a cell at the GSS. Do what you like with him."

"Thank you, sir. That's kind of you."

"Now you have your orders."

Orn saluted the Leader and on his way out of the office picked up the report from the receptionist. She wished him a "glorious day" as he left and he heard her words like one notices the bleating of a farm animal.

He rode a lift up to the roof where Global Guards

saluted him as he passed, and he returned the same. A cruiser awaited him and its engines began powering up at his approach. When Orn stepped into the passenger compartment, the pilot said, "Where to, sir?"

"Prevor Industries Complex, but do a pass around the Plaza and the Old Quarter first and activate the cruiser's cams and the viewing screen back here," Orn said, slamming the door shut as they lifted off. The screen descended from the ceiling showing five cam views—the nose, both sides, aft, and below. After the cruiser cleared the Global Assembly building, Orn selected the view from beneath the cruiser.

He pressed the screen to zoom in on the streets below. The military in riot gear was marching in formation, driving the remaining mob from the Plaza into the narrow streets of the Old Quarter toward awaiting contingents of Global Guards. Then the rabble split into small groups and ran in numerous directions, throwing flaming Malrap containers. Soldiers caught on fire in the explosions. The rioters fled into the surrounding buildings, using the black smoke of the smoldering Malrap bars as cover. Orn was concerned that their mobility against the unwieldy military foreshadowed a long-term conflict to come.

If the Leader had asked him, Orn would have advised against the WAEF-destruction propaganda. He considered it a mistake. He understood all too well the Leader valued his skills, and his place was in the shadows, but since the Vanderlord boy's speech had altered the delicate balance of power between the Global Assembly and the citizens, he was hoping going forward that the Leader might consult him before acting on rash strategy. Nevertheless, he had his job and he would carry it out as always.

When Orn was fifteen years old, a filthy, homeless, barefooted runaway living on the streets of Majinor, stealing food to survive, that's when it all started. Global Assembly soldiers had been occupying the coastal city in the Norian region, hunting the Separatist elements there. Although Orn had heard constant complaining about the occupation from the locals in the markets, he had grown fond of the soldiers who carried food packets in their satchels, handing them out to the homeless population for tips on Separatists' activities. Most took the food but gave false information to the occupiers and were eventually cut off. Orn was a willing informant. He hadn't eaten so well since he ran away from home, and he figured a worry-free life awaited him if he could get into the Global Assembly forces' good graces on a permanent basis.

Then one day, from an abandoned building's second-floor fire escape, Orn spied a Norian Separatist leader running down an alley and sliding through an open sewer grate to escape a platoon chasing him. Orn seized the opportunity. His plan entailed jumping on the man's back before he could fully emerge from his hiding place, beating him into submission with a brick, and handing him over to the Global Assembly soldiers patrolling the streets. This would be a big prize for them and they'd be grateful.

He climbed down the fire escape and grabbed a brick from a nearby lot where a building had collapsed in a Global Assembly bombardment. When the Separatist emerged, Orn dashed toward him, but tripped on a busted-up sidewalk.

The Separatist turned to Orn and said, "What're you doing, you little shit? What's that in your hand?"

Orn stared down at his hand gripping the brick. At first, he was shaking, but when he thought about his reasoning for what he was about to do and how it wasn't much different from what he did on his family farm, the quaking stopped and he felt reassured.

Orn said, "I'm going to beat you with this brick and get a reward from the soldiers."

"Go crawl back under your rock, you little shit," the Separatist said, patting away the dirt on his shabby clothes. Then he flipped his hand at Orn and walked away, dismissing him as some lesser being, just like his father always did after beating him.

Orn yelled, "Where do you think you're going?"

The Separatist continued moving away, flipping his hand at Orn again as if he were shooing a stray dog. Rage filled Orn. He charged the Separatist, leaping high on his back, and knocking him to the ground. The Separatist's head bounced off the pavement. Orn placed his knees on the Separatist's shoulders and screamed as he beat him in the head with the brick over and over again until the Separatist's skull was caved in and he wasn't moving. Orn's arm was covered in blood and hair up to his elbow. He was panting, out of breath, as people encircled the scene. Others who had witnessed Orn's deed from their apartment windows murmured and gasped in disbelief. One person asked Orn to climb off the dead man's back, but Orn snarled and swiped at him with the bloody brick.

Finally, the circle parted for four Global Assembly soldiers. One of them grabbed Orn by the shirt collar and pulled him upright. Orn still clutched the brick and swung it at the soldier.

"Whoa there, boy. Stand down," the soldier said. "You're not gonna hit me with that brick, are you?"

Orn didn't answer. He stared at the brick, reliving what he'd just done.

"Look what we have here," another soldier said, identifying the victim. "This young man is a hero." He told the crowd to disperse and the other two men in the unit lifted the body by the arms and legs.

"You're coming with us," the first soldier said, gripping Orn's collar.

Orn did what he was told, still staring at the bloody brick. As they passed through the marketplace, the crowd gawked at the horrific parade of soldiers escorting the dead body with its mutilated head and the bloodied boy. Women and small children shrieked.

A homeless boy who regularly joined Orn to rob street vendors called out, "Go get 'em, Orn."

Orn held up the brick in a victory salute to his friend and the entire crowd gasped and took a step back in fear.

Night had descended by the time they reached the Global Assembly encampment on the outskirts of the city and soldiers exited their brightly lit tents one by one to applaud the parade. Arriving at a larger tent than the others, the two soldiers dropped the corpse to the ground.

One of them talked to the sentry outside the tent, then the sentry entered the tent and exited a few moments later, holding open the tent flap and waving the soldier still gripping Orn's collar to come inside.

Orn didn't know what to think of his current situation as the adrenaline subsided and he came out of his daze. He was still hoping to be rewarded for his actions, but he was beginning to feel more like a prisoner when the soldier holding his collar shoved him inside the tent. He flew forward, landing face first in the dirt with the brick tumbling out of his hand.

"Get up, young man," a commanding voice said to Orn. "I hear we have a few things to talk about." Then the voice said to the soldier, "You're relieved, Lieutenant Suron."

"Good luck with this one sir," Lieutenant Suron said and exited the tent.

Orn got to his knees. Sitting at one end of a long table covered in a bountiful amount of food was a young officer in pristine battle fatigues. "Stand up," the officer said. "Come sit. I was about to eat dinner with my officers, but you've taken center stage and you look like you could use a bite yourself." Orn leapt up and plunked himself down in the chair beside the officer, who was already filling a plate with food. He placed the plate in front of Orn, who grabbed at the meats with his hands, taking ravenous bites, devouring every last morsel. When he was done, Orn panted as if he'd put off breathing to eat the food as quickly as possible.

"That was impressive and explains a great deal," the officer said, rising from his chair and picking up the brick from the floor. "This is impressive, too." The officer returned to the table, dropped the hair- and blood-caked brick onto Orn's empty plate, and sat back down. "Now, what made you do such a thing?"

Orn pointed with both hands at the food.

"Whoa!" the officer said, reacting to the deep scars on the backs of Orn's hands. Orn put them in his lap. "Just food, huh? You could use a bath, too, I can tell you that."

Orn looked down at the brick on the plate. He didn't know the man he'd killed and he didn't care. His actions had gotten him here. He pointed at the food again.

"I see you want more and I can make that happen, but I want to know what you were thinking when you bashed in the brains of my best intelligence asset," the officer said, his tone becoming angrier.

Orn was confused. He didn't understand why the officer was upset. He had done him a favor. Orn lifted his arm from his lap and jabbed his finger in the direction of the food.

"Yes," the officer said. "The food, the food, but you need to speak and explain yourself first."

"I was hungry," Orn said. "I thought you'd be grateful."

"Why would I be grateful?"

"He's your enemy…or was your enemy. If you eliminate your enemies, then you're victorious and that's what you want."

"That is a basic tenet of war," the officer said, "but who told you to do it?"

"I don't understand," Orn said, noticing the officer was examining his hand and placing it under the table again.

"Did the person who told you to do it hurt your hands like that?"

"No."

"That's 'No, sir,'" the officer yelled at Orn. "Lay your hands on the table palms down."

Orn thought about this request. The last time somebody made it, they hurt him although the officer was nothing like the person who had abused him. The clean-shaven officer was in his late twenties and well groomed. He smelled of bath salts sold in the market. He appeared kind and although he sounded annoyed by Orn's responses, he didn't have the look of rage that preceded acts of violence. Orn knew that look well. He still didn't trust the officer, but he'd come this far and there was all that food, so he laid his hands on the table palms down. It was worth the risk.

"You don't need to be scared," the officer said. "Unless you did something wrong. Who did that to you?"

"My father."

"Did he tell you to kill the man?"

"Nobody told me to kill that man."

"Then explain what compelled you to do it."

"I saw your soldiers chasing this man through the streets. I saw him escape them. Your soldiers give food to people like me in return for information. I thought if I did their jobs for them they'd be even more generous."

The officer laughed. "You think you can do their jobs better than them?"

"Yes. I watch them all the time. I see how they're outwitted by the Separatists."

"That's 'Yes, sir.'"

"Yes, sir. I see it every day."

"You do?"

"Yes, sir."

"Do you feel like the Separatists are a good thing for Nor?"

"No, sir, I think they've caused hardships, although some people still support them. Life was fine here before the Separatists began their campaign. People supported them at first because they wanted to pay less taxes, but not now, not for the price of this suffering."

"I like your insight," the officer said. "But that man whose head you bashed in was feeding us information."

"I don't think so. A few days ago, he directed an attack against your forces and he mocked your efforts to his people, bragging about how he duped you."

"What?" the officer said, banging his hand on the table, knocking over glasses and rattling the plates full of meats. Orn prepared to grab the brick and defend himself. "How do you know for sure?"

"I observed all of it," Orn said. "I watch the streets from the fire escapes of abandoned buildings, and nobody pays attention to someone like me unless they're afraid I'll steal from them."

"Interesting," the officer said. "I'll have to point that out to the Security Service. In the meantime, how would you like to work for me?"

Orn pointed at the food.

"Yes, we'll feed you, but you can't get too fat. That'll give you away to the enemy, and we can't clothe you any differently, but I promise that when this action is done, I will personally guarantee you a position in the military. You'll have to go through training, but I think you can handle it. You've already survived worse. Would you like that?"

"Can I keep the brick, sir?"

The officer laughed. "Yes, by all means, son. What's your name? I'm Major Vidor Plemso."

Now, Orn could see the Prevor Industries Complex in the distance and formulated a plan on how to approach Mar Jeps.

# MAR

After showering, Mar couldn't sleep. She lay down in her new bed and peered at the walls and ceiling with her mind racing. She worried about Yor and Rajer. She relived the scene at her bungalow and the artillery attack she'd survived and thought about how close she came to dying. She kept checking the clock, and time seemed to pass slower than normal.

Eventually, she commed Gols and told him that she was ready to see her office. Gols stammered he'd meet her at the lift in a few moments. She dressed and gathered her viewer and the two envelopes then stood by the lift, expecting to hear the car coming up. Instead, there was the sound of a door opening and closing inside the car, already at her floor, and the lift doors parted to reveal Gols on the other side.

"Ready?" Gols said.

"I'm exhausted," Mar said, "Let's run through the basics and we can work on the details tomorrow. Any word on my partner Rajer?"

"Unfortunately not, but the Leader is sending a representative to talk with you. Maybe you can get some answers then. Follow me," Gols said. "Would you like me to carry your things?"

"Yes, please," Mar said, handing the viewer and envelopes to Gols.

Mar stepped into the lift with Gols, who pressed a button to close the doors then turned around and stuck his finger into a hole in the wall. There were a few dozen of these holes which were a nondescript interior design element common in recently constructed industrial buildings. They appeared in a random pattern around the entire car. Mar had barely noticed them earlier on the way up, especially in her frazzled state of mind. When Gols removed his finger, the wall slid away to reveal a corridor-like office. He waved her inside, then the entrance closed behind them so one of her office's walls was a hidden doorway.

The office's polished metal walls displayed framed commercial fotos of Prevor Industries products. Facing into the room at the far end was a desk, a large half-circle of metal with a viewing screen mounted in a track running along the outer edge of the semicircle so the screen could be moved from one end of the desk to the other. An intercom box sat at the far-left corner. If one were sitting behind the desk, there was a door to the left and a couch, the blue of the company logo, to the right along the wall. The desk chair looked like the pilot's chair on the WAEF, and two visitors' chairs stood in front of the desk.

Gols said, "I have to show you something, but your son is safe."

Gols reached under the right corner of the desk and appeared to press a button. Behind the desk, a large framed image of the corporate logo faded to reveal a viewing screen showing current news. The sound was off and the headline across the bottom of the screen read "WHEN ALL ELSE FAILS Shot Down." Mar's legs betrayed her, and she took a few steps back and fell onto the couch. Gols deactivated the viewing screen and hurried to her side.

"Sorry," Gols said, "I couldn't think of a better way to reveal the news. This is all a sham. Your son is fine."

Mar said, "How do you know?"

"Because one of my jobs is tracking the WAEF, and it still exists in orbit."

"In orbit?"

"Yes."

"Is there any way to communicate with my son?"

"I actually just received a one-way transmission from him and Mado," Gols said. "If you sit at the desk, I'll play it for you."

Mar rose from the couch and made her way over to the desk chair and sat down. Gols removed a memory wafer from his pocket and inserted it into the side of the viewer mounted on the desk. A static image of Mado appeared.

Gols said, "You can start it whenever you like. I'll be over here if you need me." Gols sat down on the couch, leaned back, and stared up at the ceiling.

Mar pressed the start button on the screen.

"Hello, Mar," Mado said. "I hope you're doing well considering the upheaval in your life. I'm currently in the living chamber of the WAEF with Yor and we're orbiting Koda. I know you want to hear from your son, but there are a few details that need to be worked out between us first. I'm sorry this can't be a conversation, but this is our status right now.

"First off, the Global Assembly doesn't believe I'm in orbit on the WAEF. They believe I'm on Koda and that my message was broadcast from the planet's surface. Their techs have no idea where the broadcast originated, because the signal was bounced around the globe. You need to keep them in the dark regarding my location. That's an advantage for us. They'll want to find me. Not that you won't be an authority figure as the CEO of Prevor Industries, but my tech is installed in the domes, so the idea that I'm on planet and can harm them before they can stop me is an effective deterrent. We were supposed to be in Shamba so I could slip back into Capitol City sooner than later and deal with the Global Assembly and the Leader, but right now, I can't say when we'll return to Koda.

"The Leader will want to discuss reenergizing the domes' power generators. In our agreement, Prevor Industries has the legal rights to maintain the generators, and the government believes the reenergizing process entails detailed knowledge of the tech. You need to keep that myth alive. I've planted it in their minds and it puts us in control when it comes to making demands. In sixty-five days, the generators will need reenergizing," Mado said, making air quotes with his fingers as he pronounced the word reenergizing. "If the date were closer, my threat would be more intimidating, but Yor's premature actions at the Royal Library pushed up the scheduling of our Breeze Celebration maneuver and that's how everything is falling into place. In reality, when the day comes to reenergize the generators, Gols will explain how to do it.

"We also need to publicly keep up one more charade—the shooting down of the WAEF. We can work it to our advantage too. The Leader thinks he pulled a fast one, but this may backfire on him and put more people on our side for many reasons too lengthy to discuss here.

"One last thing—I know you've taken on the burden of running Prevor Industries out of love for your son and your planet. I know you'd rather be doing something else, so I'd like to apologize for putting you in this position and, strangely enough, I have a message from Yorlik himself. Knowing he wouldn't be around for this part of the plan, he wanted me to remind you of the day you and I first met at the estate and you two went outside to the back patio. You attempted to compel him to reveal his plan and he refused for your safety and Yor's. He told you that you'd understand in the future. He instructed me to tell you when this day arrived, 'Mar, welcome to the foreseeable future…'"

Mar laughed when Mado paused, and when he made one of his awkward smiles, she laughed some more.

Mado continued, "Yorlik hoped reminding you and relaying his message from the past would bring some levity. There's so much more for you to understand about your new position and the plan, but I can't tell you everything on this transmission so rely on Gols."

Mar peered over the screen to where Gols was sitting in the same exact position as before. She noted his eyes were closed.

"Gols knows the smallest details of Prevor Industries and can help you in any way you can imagine. Use your best judgment. I trust you. Oh—and please listen to Commander Warver. He's an acquired taste and can be pushy, but where your safety is concerned, he's the best. And now, there's someone here who wants to talk to you, so I'll sign off. Good luck, Mar. Be safe and may the Powers-That-Be give you strength on your path."

Mado stood up and disappeared from the vid. The viewer cam showed the back support of a recliner in the living chamber. Mar could hear Mado talking to Yor off-screen but couldn't make out what they were saying, then Yor sat down in front of the cam. She was heartened to see him. He looked tired and he rubbed his eyes with his fingers, then smoothed out his clothes and ran his hand through his hair. He turned to Mado, who was still off-screen, and said, "I'm ready…This is on? I didn't know…" Then he turned to the cam and said, "Hello, Mother. Sorry about that. I didn't know this was recording.

"I'm not sure where to start. Quite the show at Breeze Celebration, huh? I hope you're doing well with the changes that have happened in your life. We don't have much more broadcast time before we burn the person who is receiving this transmission down on Koda, so I'll cut to the points I need to cover.

"I know you're probably a raw nerve after everything you've experienced, but I didn't die in the crash of the WAEF so that's good, although we have no confirmation whether Rajer is dead or alive. We've reached out to our contacts and the GSS is keeping Rajer's status a closely guarded secret. Maybe no news is good news in this case. Mado is thinking if Rajer were dead, we'd know about it, and if not, the Leader will use his incarceration and possibly torture as a bargaining chip against Prevor Industries and Mado. I know that's not good news but there's hope, and Mado is quite good at this probability stuff."

Yor looked offscreen and said, "Okay, okay…Mado is telling me that I need to wrap it up. I want you to know I love you, and I'm proud to be your son."

Tears welled up in Mar's eyes, then began running down her cheeks.

"Mado and I are going on a little journey, but I'm hoping we'll return to Koda soon. I don't have time to explain why or where we're going, and we could be gone for over three hundred days, but we'll attempt to send transmissions. Gols knows how to reach us if there's an emergency. Mado has stated he's positive Prevor Industries will prosper in your capable hands, and I couldn't agree more. Did I say, I love you and I'm proud to be your son? Stay safe. Goodbye for now."

Then the screen went to the start-up image of Mado. Mar removed the memory wafer and the screen went black, then gave the wafer to Gols who was now standing by her side.

"Well, that was something," Mar said, wiping the tears from her cheeks. "Please keep that wafer nearby. I may want to watch it again."

"I can show you a safe place to stash it once we go through the envelopes," Gols said. "That shouldn't take long—I just need to explain the documents before you sign them."

Mar took a deep breath and slowly exhaled.

"Are you sure you want to continue, Mar?"

"Yes," she said, "It's funny. I'm so tired, it all feels like a dream. It reminds me of being on duty at the clinic during the DOME riots. Never-ending days. Catching a little sleep in the break rooms and then heading back into the mayhem."

"If you prefer, we can tell the government rep to meet us tomorrow and you can deal with the paperwork then instead. That's easily arranged."

"No, I'd rather get it all out of the way now so I can start fresh tomorrow."

The desk chair was on wheels, so Mar slid back from the desk as Gols removed the papers from the envelopes and conscientiously laid them out side by side on the desk in three piles.

Gols said, "I've put the signature page on top of all these documents to expedite the process unless you want to read them all now."

"I trust Mado. Just tell me what I'm signing. With everything being digitized, I don't think I've physically signed a document since I was a young woman."

"Yes, Mado Prevor prefers this old custom. He says Yorlik Vanderlord taught him this way." Gols handed Mar a pen, then pointed at the pile furthest to the right. "This was in the envelope you found in your bungalow. Mado Prevor left it there in case you were captured so they'd release you since you're named CEO here. They're already binding. Signing them is more ceremonial."

Mar moved closer to the desk and signed.

"Congratulations," Gols said, then pointed to the middle pile. "This one transfers all of Mado Prevor's shares—a controlling interest in the corporation—to you, to be held in trust for him until he returns. If he doesn't return by a predetermined time, the shares become yours."

Mar signed the document.

"This final document is your employment agreement with the corporation and stipulates your salary, which is to be transferred every eighteen days into an account of your choosing."

Mar quickly looked over the document, curious about her pay, and noticed she'd be earning 1,000 times the units she collected for her med work. "This can't be correct. This is too generous."

"This is the compensation Mado Prevor stipulated."

"But I'll never spend that many units," Mar said, signing the document.

"You can put some away for the future. However long that might be."

Mar was taken aback by Gols' statement at first. People didn't say such things out loud to a stranger. It was treasonous to insinuate the domes were only a flawed stopgap to temporarily preserve life on Koda, but this was Mado's assistant so she shouldn't be surprised. "Do many employees here feel that way?"

"I'd be discreet around the employees, but the vast majority do."

"Good to know," Mar said. "Is that it?"

"Yes," Gols said, gathering all the papers and placing them in a large folder. "Let me show you the office safe."

Mar followed Gols halfway back to the hidden doorway and they stopped at a framed commercial ad for the Holographic Gaming Device. At the bottom of the HGD ad was a person wearing the device with small circles the same color as the Prevor Industries logo emanating upward from the headset, ending at a cloud containing a realistic image of a person on a sailboat, riding rough waves and grinning. A slogan across the top read, "HGD… Giving you the life you deserve." Gols swung the picture frame open on its hinges, revealing a hi-tech safe behind it.

A cylinder jutted out from the center of the safe's door and to the right of it, between the cylinder and the outer edge of the door, was a lens.

"Mado Prevor installed this for you. Put your hand on the cylinder and your eye over the lens. DNA and retinal scanners."

Mar recalled Yor coming home and asking her to test a pair of Prevor Industries experimental HGD glasses that blinded her for a moment when Yor turned it on. He made the excuse that it must be broken. That's probably when her retinal image was imprinted. Her DNA would've been easy to obtain. Mar shook her head and laughed.

Gols said, "Something wrong?"

"Nothing," Mar said, grabbing the cylinder and looking into the lens, then there was the sound of a lock disengaging.

"May I?" Gols said, pulling open the safe door and laying the folder inside. In the back of the safe, there was a silver metal box with orange ribbon on the lid.

"What's that?"

"That," Gols said, "is something Mado Prevor requested you not open until the right time."

"When is the right time?"

"There may come a time in the future when you need the contents of the box, but that time isn't now so there's no need to open it. That's the best explanation I can offer."

"All right," Mar said. "I'm too tired to think about what that means or worry about it. Again, I'll trust Mado, but there'll be no more secrets around here if I'm running things." Mar yawned.

"That's wise." Gols placed the wafer containing the transmission on top of the folder, closed the safe door until the lock clicked shut, then swung the frame back in place. "Would you still like to talk to the government rep or are you too tired? As I said before, I can reschedule him."

"No. Give me a few moments to collect myself, then send him in. Can you bring me a glass of water?"

"Not a problem," Gols said, exiting through the side door.

Mar picked her viewer up off the couch where Gols had left it and placed it on the desk, moving the desk's viewer to the right on its semicircular track so it wouldn't obscure her view of her visitor, then sat down in the chair and pushed herself closer to the desk.

There was a knock at the side door and Gols stepped in. "You ready for your appointment?"

Mar sat up in the chair and smoothed her clothes. She felt fuzzy, but she'd get through it. "Send them in," Mar said.

Then the man with the scars on the back of his hands walked through the door. Her heart raced. Her first impulse was to yell at him to get out of her sight, but she gathered herself.

"Hello," Mar said. "Please have a seat. Your name is…?"

"I prefer to stand," the man said, "and my name…"

"Let me guess. Your name isn't important to this conversation," Mar said. "Well, you're in my office and I'm the acting CEO of Prevor Industries, and if you wish this meeting to commence, then you'll sit down and tell me your name."

The man stood with his arms crossed over his chest, staring at Mar.

She smiled at him. "If not, then you can leave."

In her new position as CEO of the most powerful corporate entity on the planet, showing strength in her interaction with this man, who was obviously representing the Leader, was the best way to establish their relationship. Although she wanted to know about Rajer right away, she was in control now and had to stay that way.

The man kept standing there glaring at her.

"Gols," Mar called on the intercom and Gols entered the office. "Please show this gentleman the exit."

Gols looked confused, but Mar nodded at him. "This way, sir," Gols said.

Awkward silence ensued. The man stood his ground, then raised his hand toward Gols. "I'm good. Is this where you'd like me to sit?" the man said to Mar, putting his hand on one of the seats.

"That'll be fine," Mar said. "Thank you, Gols."

"Let me know if you need anything else," Gols said and exited the room.

The man sat down with a huff. He already looked flustered, hands gripping the chair's armrests.

"You could have those scars surgically removed."

"So I've heard, but they're useful in my line of work and a reminder of how I got here."

"That sounds like an intro to an intriguing line of conversation, but I imagine you're not here for that," Mar said. "What was your name again?"

"If I give you an answer, do you think you'll have one over on me?" the man said. Mar could hear him attempting to contain his anger and regain control.

"I'm not sure what you're talking about. I'm sorry you think my knowing your name gives me an advantage over you, but my only desire is for us to have a professional and congenial discussion. Nothing more, nothing less. I feel knowing the name of the person sitting in front of me facilitates the discussion by putting each person on equal ground. Do you agree? Or would you rather we not be on equal ground?"

Mar thought she observed the man squirm in his chair and grip the arms of the chair more tightly. He appeared to be in a quandary about what he should do. That's when it dawned on her this circumstance was highly unusual for him. He was used to bullying his way into getting answers or hurting someone to retrieve them. She bet the Leader had ordered him to be diplomatic which wasn't his strong suit, so he wasn't sure how to respond to Mar's ultimatum.

"I'm not surprised you're good at this sort of thing," the man said.

"What sort of thing?"

"Coercion."

"Coercion? I'm not sure what you're talking about since the conversation hasn't even begun yet. I still don't know your name." Mar said. *He sees withholding his name as emblematic of his power. His refusal to relinquish it is uncanny.*

"You're not prepared to let that go?" the man said. Mar saw it was killing him to control the hostility he usually let loose as he pleased.

"I don't think I will." Mar pushed back her chair, stood, and pointed toward the door. "Shall I call my assistant again to show you out?"

The man closed his eyes, exhaled, and shook his head, continuing to clutch the arms of the chair. Mar waited. She was relishing this little gambit more than she'd expected. Maybe the Great man had seen something in her that she wasn't aware of herself. She waited. He'd have to relinquish control or return to the Leader and tell him that he had failed his mission. When the Leader inevitably asked, "Why did that happen?" the man would be forced to reply, "I refused to tell her my name." Mar didn't think that would sit well with the Leader, who was known to be quick to anger and probably more short-tempered than usual with the Plaza burning.

Mar sat back down and pushed in her chair. "Well? You awake?"

The man opened his eyes and glared at her as if he'd kill her on the spot were that action within the boundaries of his orders. She already knew he was a person who liked to get his way, but the look he gave her was chilling nonetheless.

Mar said, "I'm waiting."

The man cleared his throat and said, "My name is Orn. Orn Shiv."

"How would you like me to address you? Orn Shiv? Orn?"

"Orn is fine."

"See, we're making progress. Now, what can I do for the Global Assembly, Orn?" She sang his name like he did hers at the bungalow.

Orn recognized what she was doing and let out a nervous laugh. He loosened his grip on the arms of the chair, leaning back and surveying the room in his peripheral vision, moving his head slightly left then right.

*He'll attempt to get back in control now*, Mar thought.

"I was surprised when they told me you were acting CEO and that I'd be speaking with you."

"I'm not sure if I ought to be insulted by that comment," Mar said, thinking she should keep him on the defensive.

Orn smiled. Her gambit amused him. "You know that's not what I meant. I asked for Mado Prevor when I arrived."

"I really don't know you well enough to know what you mean."

"Oh, come on, Mar. We've known each other on and

off for twenty-four years. Well, I know you at least," Orn said in a condescending tone.

He appeared to be enjoying himself again. Mar could see the mischievousness reemerging as he worked to regain control of the conversation.

"You said you were surprised to find me here. Well, after today's events, maybe you don't know me, my family, or my son as well as you thought," Mar said, seeing anger return to Orn's eyes as he clutched the arms of the chair again. "What can I do for you?"

"The Leader would like to speak with Mado Prevor."

"Mado is unavailable."

"When will he be available?"

"He's off-site."

"Maybe the Leader can meet with him there."

Mar could see the man seeking a clue to Mado's location. "I'll inform Mado the Leader is asking for him."

"The Global Assembly has pending contracts with Prevor Industries and there could be dire consequences if Mado Prevor isn't prompt in getting back to the Leader."

"Dire consequences for whom?" Mar said.

"You know what I'm saying," Orn said. His frustration was showing. "That vid he broadcast to the Global Assembly could easily be seen as a hostile act and we both know where that might lead."

"Orn, Orn, Orn, are you threatening this corporation?"

"No. I'm simply attempting to make a point. The Leader has no idea where Mado Prevor stands in relation to the government. Is he with the citizens in support of law and order, or is he part of the Movement in favor of dismantling the status quo, causing chaos, and allowing criminals to control the domes?"

"I think you know the answer to that question. Mado Prevor is a man of the people. I believe his record of tech innovation that directly ensures the survival of the Kodan people speaks for itself," Mar said. "That being said, I will pass along your message from the Leader and consider this line of questioning at an end. Can I help you with anything else?"

"One more thing. I'm baffled by how well you're taking the news about your son."

"What?"

"Your son."

Mar saw through what Orn was doing and she knew exactly how to play it. "What about him?"

"Didn't you see the news?"

"What news? What's happening with my son?" Mar said, raising her voice and standing.

"You don't know? I figured someone would have told you by now."

He appeared to be buying Mar's act of bewilderment and concern. "My bungalow was destroyed. I was airlifted here, and shot at, and I've been inundated with information regarding my new position," Mar said. "So no. I don't know. What's happened?"

"I find it hard to believe nobody has told you," the man said, a smile forming on his face. "You know how I hate to be the bearer of bad news, but the WAEF was shot down over the Mlimoan mountains."

Anger rose in Mar as she saw Orn's enjoyment in

delivering this news to her. "Get out!" Mar screamed. "Get out of this office now!" She pointed at the door.

Gols entered the office, looking frightened.

Orn rose from his chair. He didn't know how to deal with Mar's outburst. He was caught between his own harsh tactic, from which he'd been deriving pleasure, his worry about angering the Leader by making relations more difficult between Prevor Industries and the Global Assembly, and—worst of all—of disappointing the Leader.

"Gols, please escort this man from my office."

"This way, sir," Gols said, waving Orn toward the door.

Orn stood there, thinking of something to say.

"This way, sir."

Orn said, "We'll talk again soon."

"Get out!"

Orn exited with Gols following him and the door closed behind them.

Mar sat back down and basked in the silence. She was pleased by how she'd manipulated the entire scenario, but while it felt liberating to yell at that man and get away with it, she'd probably overplayed her hand. She also needed to come up with a better scenario for Mado's absence next time, but for now she had contained the problem. Then it dawned on her that she had discovered nothing about Rajer before sending Orn out of the room.

Gols returned with a glass of water. "Can I do anything else for you, Mar?"

"Tell Warver to relay a message to the man who just left."

# VIDOR

**V**idor's intercom buzzed and his receptionist said, "Davik Atmar is here, sir." Vidor ignored it.

The sun was setting outside the Capitol City dome. In the streets below, the explosions were less frequent and many of the troop carriers were leaving. The skirmish with the rioters was nearing an end, but the Malrap vending stands still burned out of control with the black smoke snaking upward to the ceiling of the dome. The first and second floors of the Plaza's administrative buildings smoldered in ruins. Firefighters and troops contained the flames, hosing them down with fire-retardant since water couldn't be wasted. It was Koda's most valuable resource.

Vidor recalled how the Vanderlord boy had embarrassed him in front of the entire planet by showing the vid of the Great man's return to Koda. Years ago, he banned that vid by executive decree from being shown publicly, labeling it as "terrorist propaganda." Before he left the stage, Vidor leaned toward the boy and whispered in his ear, "Don't think you'll get away with this. Your father, your grandfather, and your great-grandfather certainly didn't." To which, the boy replied, "Catch me if you can."

*You good-for-nothing smartass*, Vidor had thought.

Later, behind the stage, Vidor regained consciousness from the sonic cannon blast and his security detail rushed him out of the Arena through the underground tunnels below the Plaza to the Global Assembly building. In his office, a handful of his most trusted civilian advisors awaited him and told him what had happened while he was unconscious. They described the vid in which Yorlik the Great lectured the citizenry on how they'd been duped by the Global Assembly, and about the scene from Yorlik's discovered planet. His military advisors apprised him of disturbances breaking out at six of the nine Breeze Celebrations, and detailed how the WAEF had evaded the Global Assembly air-battle cruisers and traveled into orbit.

"He thinks he's out of my reach," Vidor yelled. "He'll never get away with it." Vidor called for a purge of all the Movement agitators currently on the list compiled by the GSS. His civilian advisors scoffed at the idea, so Vidor asked them how they'd proceed instead as he paced back and forth, full of fury.

Head of Planetary Relations Armic Rect suggested they produce a viewing-channel campaign to discredit the entire Vanderlord presentation and manufacture a story about the WAEF being shot down. Once a strapping military officer in Vidor's battalion, Armic Rect had grown fat working for a corporate entity before being tapped for his current position.

Armic Rect said, "Land two or three out-of-service air-battle cruisers in the Mlimoan mountains—should be quick and easy enough with the base nearby—then blow them up, vid the smoldering wreckage, and say it's the WAEF. When those traitors learn they don't have a leader anymore, it'll demoralize their movement and possibly provoke the outraged into making a violent push in the name of their leader. Then we can flush them out and arrest them, much like your purge idea."

"I am the Leader, you fat bastard!" Vidor said, grabbing Armic Rect by his suit jacket, yanking him close and yelling in his face. "I am the Leader!"

"Of course, sir," Armic Rect said. "Of course. You're the only Leader."

"Don't you forget it," Vidor said, releasing his hold on Armic and patting him on the cheek with his hand.

"Never, sir."

"I like it, Armic. In particular, I like how it works into the purge. If enough of the agitators act out, then we can break out the list. Get on that disinformation campaign and let's crush the life out of them before this goes any further."

"Are you sure that's a wise course of action?" said Chief of Affairs Davik Atmar. He was Vidor's right-hand man who had started as a foot soldier under his command. Davik had lost a great deal of his hair and his face had bloated, but he still looked like he could put on the Global Assembly uniform and charge the field. "You may create a martyr and what happens if he physically returns? How do we explain it?"

"That piss-boy a martyr? Never," Vidor said. "If he returns. there'll be nothing to explain. We'll just nab him before people find out he's alive. I want everyone to think he's dead! I'm the Leader. Don't you forget that, Armic."

"Never, sir," Armic said, instinctually snapping to attention.

"You have my full authority, Armic. Make this happen."

Later, after the cruisers had been destroyed and the viewing channels were spreading the news, Orn arrived at his office and told him that fabricating the WAEF's demise might not have been the best strategy after all. That's when Vidor commed his receptionist to call Davik back to his office immediately.

Again, his intercom buzzed. "Davik Atmar is still waiting, sir. Should I tell him you're busy and send him away?"

"No. Send him in."

Davik entered, appearing harried. The top button of his shirt was undone, his jacket wasn't buttoned at all, and his pants were creased.

Vidor said, "Davik, you look like you just fell out of bed."

Davik peered down at his clothing. He hurriedly buttoned his shirt and jacket. "I'm sorry, sir," Davik said. "I'd just arrived home when I received your comm demanding I return here."

"Demanding?" Vidor said, becoming upset. "Demanding? When I call, it's a request from your sovereign and you should be pleased I want you in my presence."

"Yes, sir," Davik said, clicking his heels and standing at attention. "Sorry, sir. It's just been a long day and I was looking forward to seeing my family."

"Don't you think I'd like to see my family?" Vidor said, throwing the framed digi-foto of his partner and sons across the room. Davik ducked and the foto smashed against the wall behind him, leaving a mark in the paint. "But you're here to serve the Kodan people, which means serving me."

"Yes, sir. Sorry, sir."

"Maybe you need to have a conversation with Orn."

"No, sir. My sincerest apologies. What can I do for you, sir?"

"Why didn't you advise me better on Armic's idea?"

"I told you what I thought," Davik said. "I told you the idea might turn Vanderlord into a martyr."

"You're my Chief of Affairs, aren't you?"

"Yes, sir."

"Then you need to advise me better."

"I'll do better next time, sir."

"I want it on the record that you're to blame for any fallout from this decision. Do you understand?"

"Yes, sir."

"Now get out of my sight, Davik. Go back to your family," Vidor said. "Send Rata my regards."

"I will, sir. She'll be pleased about that."

"And how is she doing at that lobbying job I arranged for her? That lucrative paycheck is an enormous help on top of your salary, isn't it? What if she lost her job or something happened to you? It'd be a shame if you couldn't afford that new extension on your home or the tuition at Capitol City Military Academy for your boys. That would be tragic, wouldn't it?"

"Yes, sir."

"Now, go home and kiss your partner and hug your children and think about what I just said. You're dismissed."

Davik turned and marched out of the room. When the door closed behind him, Vidor went to the other side of the room and picked up the shattered digi-foto. The framed image was blank now and he tossed it to the floor. He wouldn't spend time with his family today and probably wouldn't tomorrow, either, but such was the burden of his position.

Vidor understood the importance of family. He thought of his father and everything he gave him. *I wouldn't be here without him.* He thought of his partner Flomina and his children and how his plans for the future were built around them. He thought about the events of the day and the When All Else Fails flying off, and about the Vanderlords. That family was obsessed with defying him, starting with the Great man.

After Yorlik had landed and embarrassed Vidor in front of the entire planet, Vidor was told about Yorlik's discovery. He convened his advisors and they all agreed this news couldn't get out. They'd invested too much time and too many units into the DOME project and Vidor's supporters would be unhappy if he cut off their "research and development" funds. Orn suggested they simply wipe the Vanderlords from the face of the planet. Take them out to an uninhabited area—the Great man, Tetrick, Mar pregnant with Yor—and end the family line once and for all. Vidor's advisors scoffed at this tactic. They were concerned about the media, which wasn't under their control yet, and the citizens' reaction when Yorlik the Great disappeared so soon after his return. Suspicion would point to the President, especially after the Great man showed him up at the landing. They advised a softer approach. Vidor recalled Orn saying, "You'll regret it.

Mark my words," before he stormed out of the meeting. That's when they decided to reason with the Great man, and Vidor chose to handle it himself.

Vidor flew with Davik to the military base where Yorlik the Great was being quarantined. They found him alone at a table in the base cafeteria with a viewer in front of him. He stood when he heard them come in, walking the length of the cafeteria to greet them. His beard had grown longer and fuller and his grey hair flowed down past his shoulders. He'd obviously felt no need to trim his beard or do any maintenance on his hair while he was detained on the base by himself for seventy-nine days.

"Good to see you, President Plemso," Yorlik said, approaching them. "I'm honored you've come all this way to see me. And Davik—good to see you again, too. No offense, but it's nice to see anybody other than the soldiers around here."

Vidor said, "Is there a place we can talk?"

"Here is fine," Yorlik said. "I like it here. None of the rooms in the WAEF are this spacious, so for me, this is kind of like being outdoors."

"Shall we sit, then?" Vidor said.

"Please, this way to my office," said Yorlik, chuckling as he headed back toward the table where his viewer lay open.

"How have you been passing the time?" Davik said, walking beside Yorlik.

"Catching up. I've been gone quite a while, as you know," Yorlik said, chuckling again and slapping Davik on the back.

"Anything in particular catch your eye?" Davik said.

"Lots of general and intellectual history. Overall, there's a sense of doom and gloom in the writings, but look at what's happened since I've been gone."

"It's easy to be critical when you've been flying around the universe for a hundred years," Vidor said, walking ahead of Davik and Yorlik. Vidor promised himself that he'd contain his temper, but his patience was already slipping.

Davik increased his pace and appeared to Vidor's right. Shielding his face from Yorlik with his hand, he mouthed the word "No" a few times in Vidor's direction, shaking his head.

Yorlik appeared to Vidor's left. "I'm sorry, President Plemso. I know we got off to a bad start on the day I landed, and I apologize for what I said then and what I said now. After a century by myself, you have to understand that my mouth runs without thinking about the nuances of human interaction. Please let's start fresh."

"I'd like that," Vidor said.

"Then we've agreed on something and that's a good beginning," Yorlik said. He quickened his pace, reaching the table ahead of Davik and Vidor, and hurriedly closed his viewer in a way that made Vidor suspicious.

*What is he looking at?* Vidor thought. *I bet there's something on there he doesn't want us to see.* Vidor sat down. Yorlik and Davik followed suit.

Yorlik said, "I'd offer you some Malrap, but they're all out here."

"Yes, that's been banned from military bases for decades," Davik said.

"I ran out of it years ago on the WAEF."

"I think we can sneak in a bottle for our esteemed guest," Vidor said. "Don't you agree, Davik?"

"Absolutely, sir," Davik said, removing a digi-tablet from his jacket and making a note.

"So, I've been wondering why I'm still here," Yorlik said. "I believe everything is fine physically, and to be honest, one of the meds left me alone in an examination room and I read my chart on his viewer. I'm sure you're aware I have med training."

"Yes, we're all aware of your vast achievements," Vidor said, feeling like the Great man was always trying to demonstrate his superiority. "What shall we call you? Colonel? Yorlik the Great?"

"Yorlik is fine."

"Yes, you've been cleared by the med staff," Davik said. "And the planet is clamoring for you to be released."

"That's good to hear," Yorlik said, slapping Davik on the back again.

Vidor was irritated at Davik. He'd already given up their bargaining position. "I won't insult your intelligence if you don't insult mine," Vidor said. "You know why we're here."

"Of course," Yorlik said. "I imagine this has something to do with the look of concern on Davik's face when I told him about my discovery during my debriefing. To tell you the truth, I was expecting a little more enthusiasm and maybe a small jump for joy, but I guess you can't please everyone."

"No, but you have to please me," Vidor said. "So, let's get down to business. I have a planet to oversee."

"And you're doing a bang-up job," Yorlik said, dropping the congenial façade and taking on a sarcastic tone.

"Yorlik, what the President is trying to say—"

"I can say what I mean, Davik. You're here to observe and take notes. I don't need you to speak for me," Vidor said. "And I've done an unbelievable job as President."

"I'll give you that," Yorlik said. "From what I've observed from studying historical records, the job you've done is unbelievable. I certainly can't believe it."

"I won't sit here and be insulted. I can leave you here to rot if that suits you," Vidor said, knocking over his chair as he stood. Davik stood and righted Vidor's chair.

"That's all very dramatic," Yorlik said, glaring up at Vidor, "but as Davik said, the planet is 'clamoring for my release.'"

"That might be true," Vidor said. "But I would have no problem terminating your entire family, telling the Kodan people you died along with them, and leaving you in a dark cell to rot until you die of old age. I can live with the personal and political ramifications of my actions. Can you?"

"I'm pretty sure you can live with the personal ramifications, especially given what I've read about you, but you wouldn't be here if you thought you could survive the political ramifications. You need to create a compromise. Isn't that true?"

Davik said, "Well, that's—"

Vidor shot a disdainful look at Davik, then said to Yorlik, "You're the one who'll be compromising. Not me. You're in no position to dictate terms."

Yorlik sighed. "Tell me your terms, then."

"Davik?" Vidor said, sitting down. "Do your job?"

Davik seated himself, picked up his digi-tablet from the table, and pressed a few buttons. "The terms are as follows: the Global Assembly will return the entire financial value of your estate at the time of your launch, taking into account inflation of units. The deed to the Vanderlord home, which is currently a museum, will be put back in your name, and the household items and belongings in the museum will be returned to your possession. In exchange for this compensation, you will not mention your discovery in public and the WAEF database and star charts will become the possessions of the Global Assembly."

"I want the WAEF, too," Yorlik said. "It's mine."

"No, it's not." Vidor slammed his fist on the table and Yorlik's viewer flew into the air and fell towards the floor. Davik caught the viewer in the hand not occupied by his digi-tablet, then placed it back on the table. The entire time, Yorlik didn't budge. He wasn't disturbed by Vidor's outburst.

Vidor said, "The WAEF is the property of the government. When you landed, your mission ended and the governing body which launched the WAEF took control of it. There will be no more discussion on this topic."

"I guess I can live with that logic," Yorlik said. "As for the other points, the star charts were destroyed in a magnetic storm on the return voyage, and I want all the data in the ship's devices erased in my presence. If you won't tell the Kodan people about my discovery, then all knowledge of my journey needs to be destroyed."

"No. That data is the government's, too."

"Without my help, you won't be able to decrypt the files. In fact, there's nobody on the planet who can decrypt that data."

"We'll see about that," Vidor said.

"I guess we shall. Well, if those are your terms, then you might as well take my journal. You can lock it up in the SEEDER journal section of the Royal Library, but I'll give it to you sometime before my death," Yorlik said. "Davik—you can put that in the agreement, too. Also, I'd like to donate my spacesuit to the Royal Museum. I know it's owned by the government, but it'll be nice for something of my journey other than the journal to be kept for posterity. I'd like that in the agreement, too."

"I think we can do that for you," Davik said, "can't we, President Plemso?"

"That would be fine," Vidor said. *He is being awfully amenable. I don't trust him*, Vidor thought. "But let me make myself perfectly clear. You will not tell anybody in the general public about your discovery. We already know you've told your family, but if you or your family tell anybody else, then there will be dire consequences. Do I need to spell that out for you? And I will gladly ride out the political ramifications, if there are any."

"I'm assuming that last part won't be in the agreement," Yorlik said, smiling at Vidor.

"No—" Davik said.

"Shut up, Davik! Powers-That-Be, you're a moron sometimes."

"Did anyone ever tell you that you lack a sense of humor?" Yorlik said to Vidor. "But seriously, what if one of your lackeys who knows about the discovery leaks it and I'm blamed? No offense, Davik."

"None taken."

"Will you shut your mouth," Vidor said, glaring at Davik, who looked down at his digi-tablet rather than challenge Vidor's gaze. "I will know where the leak came from, and my people, especially Davik here, know the consequences of a treasonous act for themselves and their extended family."

"One more thing," Yorlik said. "I need access to the WAEF to remove my personal possessions."

Davik continued taking notes on his digi-tablet and didn't look up when Yorlik stopped speaking.

"Davik can arrange that for you," Vidor said, standing up with Davik following suit. Yorlik remained seated. "On the date of your release, you will be flown to Capitol City for a media conference with me. Good day, Yorlik."

Years after Yorlik died, Mado Prevor had suggested to a Global Assembly rep that the WAEF should be restored. Vidor hadn't thought about the WAEF in years, but the idea of using it as a public relations boost for himself at a Breeze Celebration sounded like a brilliant one. He would bask in the glory of Yorlik the Great's achievement and he relished the thought of how it would have galled the old man that Vidor used the WAEF to his advantage as his approval ratings skyrocketed.

*And then somehow it all blew up in my face.*

Vidor walked over to his desk and activated his intercom. "Kel? I want the name of the Global Assembly rep to whom Mado Prevor suggested the idea of restoring the WAEF, and I want him here tomorrow."

The smoke from the fires below had reached the top of the dome and was being sucked toward the air circulators. Vidor expected a report from his military advisors soon and he wondered about Orn's meeting at Prevor Industries. He felt lonely up here in the tower by himself, but such was his lot in life. He had chosen to lead his Kodan brethren through the crisis, and he was convinced he was performing an unbelievable job, no matter what the haters in the citizenry thought of him.

# ORN

Orn was pushing open the door to exit the building on the Prevor Industries Complex when he heard, "Lieutenant Shiv, can I have a moment of your time?"

Orn stopped in his tracks and let the door close so he was still standing in the building. Nobody had addressed him that way in years. He turned to see Wel Warver headed toward him.

Orn said, "Warver, look at you. You're a glorified security guard now."

"Always a delight," Warver said. "Still kissing Vidor's ass?"

"That's the Leader to you," Orn said. "And watch your mouth or I'll have you dragged into the Detention Facility."

"I'm shaking in my boots."

"I know it was you and Suron who rescued Mar Jeps. You're lucky I couldn't take a shot at you."

"You never had much skill as a military man."

"I don't have time for small talk," Orn said. "To what do I owe the displeasure of this conversation?"

"Vidor keeping you on a short leash these days?"

"The Leader," Orn said, thinking about the box in his pocket. Using its contents on Warver would give him great pleasure, especially after the dissatisfying conversation with Mar Jeps, but he thought better of it right now.

     *Howard Libes*

"What do you want?"

"I have a message from Mar Jeps for Vidor regarding Mado Prevor," Warver said. "She'd be happy to meet with Vidor regarding Prevor Industries business, but she doesn't want him sending you or any other assistant."

"The Leader won't like that message."

"I'm just the messenger," Warver said. "Not that I don't take pleasure in delivering it."

Orn let out a groan of frustration. Maybe it was due to the tiring day or his conversation with Mar Jeps, but the moment the sound left his body he regretted it as a smile spread across Wel Warver's face. Orn said, "I should have dealt with you when I had the chance."

"Say hello to Vidor for me," Warver said, still smiling.

"I'll let the Leader know about your insubordination."

Orn turned on his heels and exited the building. The sun had gone down. Orn felt the heat of the cruiser's engines as he approached. He climbed in and told the pilot to head back to the Global Assembly building, securing the door behind him as they lifted off. At cruising altitude, he could see the smoke being pulled into the circulators at the edges of the dome. The cruiser's compartment reeked of the burning rubble from the Plaza's fires.

The smell transported Orn back to his teens in Nor where buildings burned down daily, leaving the air stinking of soot. The ideal place to do his spying for Major Plemso was by the docks where the clean air came directly off the ocean. That was a treat. More often, he spent his days in the putrid aroma of the city, around rotting corpses or a broken sewer main. It was much like the life he'd lived before he met Major Plemso, but now he was compensated with regular meals.

Once while eating evening meal with his officers, Major Plemso said he'd rejoice when this campaign was over so he could put Majinor's stench behind him. He asked Orn how he felt about the scent of the city. Orn told him it smelled like home. All the officers around the table burst out laughing. Orn was offended, because they were laughing at him, the street urchin at their table by Major Plemso's side, not his statement, and Orn thought he deserved more respect from them. His espionage had enabled the Global Assembly forces to wipe out a majority of the Separatists in Nor, including their leadership, and the operation here appeared to be coming to a close.

Before that happened, Orn had an idea to take advantage of his position. He told Major Plemso about a cabin outside of the city limits where a valued target was hiding. The cabin was situated in one of the last forested areas in Nor at the base of the coastal mountain range.

The morning of the operation, aerial recon spotted the person of interest outside splitting wood. Later, when the loaded troop carriers arrived at the location, a cruiser circled overhead for tactical support. Thermal imaging showed the target inside the cabin and the fireplace was active. There was a chill in the crisp, clean air.

"You sure this is the place?" Warver asked Orn, spying the cabin with binoculars.

"I'm positive. Why?"

"Look around," Warver said. "This isn't exactly the

standard operating territory for the people we've been hunting. They're city dwellers who recruit from the urban population, not country folk living in serene locations like this one."

"You have the major's orders," Orn said with annoyance.

"Yes, I do, but something is off here," Warver said. "I'm going to comm the major."

Orn kicked at the dirt and stormed into the woods. *How dare he?* Orn thought. *This is my op, not his. My call, not his.* Orn sat on a fallen tree trunk and observed the house from behind the flora at the edge of the forest. On these ops, Orn was dressed in his beggar's rags to keep his cover in case somebody saw him lurking around. He didn't have a sidearm. The soldiers were now in camouflaged positions all around him and atop a ridge surrounding the back of the cabin, awaiting the signal to move in and take down the cabin's occupant. Orn snuck back to the vehicle convoy and removed a blasting weapon from a rack in a troop carrier. There were a few soldiers standing guard, but they all knew him and nodded to him as he climbed into the carrier and walked away with the weapon under his coat.

Orn crept from tree to tree until he reached a clearing to the side of the cabin. He couldn't get any closer without being spotted by the troops and, at any moment, Warver could be alerted to his position by the cruiser circling overhead, noting his thermal signature.

So he took aim at the window by the front door and fired twice. The first blast exploded the window and the second detonated inside the cabin. Orn waited to see if there was any sign of life, then the cabin's occupant peered out of the damaged window and their eyes met. The man didn't hesitate. He shot his weapon at Orn.

Orn dashed back toward the roadway as the troops opened fire. The flurry of shooting continued as Orn replaced the weapon where he'd found it, and as he exited the carrier, he heard the distinct sound of a handheld rocket launcher being fired followed by an explosion. He ran up to the lead vehicle in the convoy where Warver stood stunned at what was happening. He called over his comm for a cease-fire and ordered the troops to move with caution toward the cabin now engulfed in flames.

Orn heard a soldier yell, "He's going back into the woods," followed by an exchange of weapons' fire and silence.

"Hostile down," came over Warver's comm.

Warver replied, "Secure the area. Intelligence, scan the debris for any relevant data. Lieutenant Suron, I want a report on what just happened. I want to know who took the first shot without my order."

Warver looked at Orn suspiciously and stomped off toward the rear of the cabin. Orn hurried to an old stump and removed an ax stuck in it. He felt its familiar weight, swinging it around and chopping it back into the stump, then trotted toward the gaping hole where the front door used to be. Soldiers were suppressing flames and almost had them extinguished so the intelligence officers could take charge. Orn strode past them into the cabin. He grabbed an arm-long wood limb mounted above the mantel shelf and broke it over his calf, then tossed the halves into the fireplace and watched them burst into flame. He examined the area which served as a living room and kitchen. It was in shambles from the blast, furniture blown into pieces.

"You looking for something?" Warver said.

Orn was startled.

"You're looking around like you know the place," Warver said. "You want to tell me what this is all about?"

"That's none of your business."

Warver yelled, "None of my business?" A vein popped out on his left temple. "This is my business. This is my command. My soldiers risked their lives to come here. Right now, we have no idea who took the first shot, but if I were a betting man, I'd say it was you."

"That's absurd."

"I believe my men and my officers, and I also believe the cam in the cruiser recording this op, but I don't believe you." Warver grabbed Orn by his wrist and yanked him out of the house. Orn pulled back, but Warver was an adult—bigger, stronger—and was winning the battle. So as they passed the porch, Orn collapsed into the dirt.

Warver held on and said, "You can get on your feet or I'll drag you like the unruly animal you are. Plemso's pet. Did you know that's what we call you?"

Orn was aware that's what the officers and even some of the enlisted men called him, and he'd spent hours stewing on this nickname in private. His anger rose in him and he jumped to his feet, taking a swing at Warver with his free arm. Warver swatted Orn's fist away, then grabbed his other wrist.

"I'll have you restrained if you don't calm down."

"Sure, if that makes you feel safe."

Warver released Orn's wrists and used his leg to sweep Orn's feet out from under him. Orn landed with his face in the dirt, then Warver stepped onto Orn's back and cuffed his wrists behind him.

"You must get a lot of practice doing this with your whores," Orn said as Warver grabbed him by his forearm, lifted him up on his feet, and led him toward the field behind the cabin. Orn thought about tugging in the opposite direction, but he was outmatched, and he wanted to see what Warver was about to show him.

Intelligence officers were sweeping the field behind the cabin with scanners, searching for an underground bunker or buried evidence that might help in their cause against the Separatists. Two soldiers and a med chatted around a male corpse while an intelligence officer captured fotos of it with his cam.

Warver said to the men, "Please give me a few moments alone with the body." The soldiers, med, and officer saluted and Warver saluted back. They shot dirty looks at Orn and mumbled profanities at him as they walked away.

At Orn's feet, the corpse was damaged by blast fire. Chunks had been blown out of the arms, legs, and torso, and the hands and face were covered in burns. The clothes were charred and filthy. He'd obviously attempted to roll out the flames but died from his wounds.

Warver said, "This is not the man we came here to detain. Who is he?"

Orn couldn't contain himself and burst out laughing until he became hysterical. This had the effect of confusing Warver who loosened his grip on Orn's arm, and Orn broke free, kicking the corpse as hard as possible over and over again. The soldiers grabbed Orn's arms, lifting him up and pulling him back while he kicked at the air. Warver bent down and gave the corpse a closer look.

"Powers-That-Be," Warver said. "This is your father, isn't it? He looks exactly like you."

"Yes. Yes, it is. What're you gonna do about it?"

"I believe you've done all that can be done."

Traveling back to the encampment, Warver placed Orn under guard in a carrier. Two armed soldiers were seated on either side of Orn on a bench, and two others across from him, his legs shackled and secured to the floor of the vehicle where the corpse lay in a body bag.

Orn closed his eyes and thought about what he'd done. He would always have the scars on his hands to remember his father by, but now the scars were a badge of honor. He had risen above the cruelties perpetrated on him and persevered. His father may have won the battles, but Orn had won the war. He could have stayed away. In his position with the Global Assembly forces, he didn't need to fear his father ever again, but every day when he looked down at his hands, he reimagined the painful sting of the switch cutting into his skin and his father telling him this punishment was for his own good. When he was trusted enough by Major Plemso and saw the opportunity, Orn decided to do what was right for his father's good.

Orn was ecstatic at his accomplishment as he felt the scars on the back of his hand with his fingertips. He began giggling, then one of the soldiers told him to shut up and cold-cocked him with the butt end of his weapon. Orn opened his eyes for a moment to memorize the soldier's face and closed them again.

When the vehicle turned off a bumpy unpaved road onto a smooth paved one, Orn knew they were closer to the city. He began to worry about how he would explain his actions to Major Plemso, who would see this as a betrayal of his trust. He concentrated on the hum of the road under the vehicle's tires with his eyes still closed and concluded he would tell Major Plemso the truth. That was the only way to maintain trust between them. If the major decided to punish him, then Orn would take it in stride. He was at peace with his actions, which had ended an old chapter of his life, and he was now beginning a new one.

The convoy moved slowly through city traffic until the vehicle lurched to a halt at the encampment. The soldiers unshackled Orn's legs and led him through camp, two in front and two behind. Orn's head pounded from where the soldier had struck him and he stared back at the soldiers who gawked at him as he passed.

"Looks like Plemso's pet has been a bad boy," a soldier along the route yelled out and the soldiers around him laughed.

Orn didn't care what they thought. The only opinion that mattered now was the major's. When they arrived at the major's tent, Warver was already outside the entrance waiting for them.

"Looks like somebody left their mark," Warver said, poking at the bruise where Orn was cold-cocked. The pain was excruciating and filled Orn's head, but he didn't wince. He didn't want to give Warver the satisfaction.

"You four wait here," Warver said to the soldiers, grabbing Orn by the arm and leading him into the tent. Major Plemso was on his comm, wearing his clean battle fatigues with polished boots. His hair was perfectly coiffed. He put up his finger for them to wait.

"Yes, sir," Major Plemso said into the comm. "Yes, sir. It's an honor, sir. I will do my best to uphold your faith in me. Yes, sir. Thank you, sir. Good day." Then he put the comm down and said, "What's going on here, Warver?"

"Sorry, sir. I attempted to comm ahead, but seems you were on an important call."

"Yes, I was. Do you know who that was?" Major Plemso said.

"I have no idea, sir."

"That was a rhetorical question. Of course you don't know. Why would you? That was the President of the Global Assembly calling to commend the amazing job I'm doing here to end the Separatist uprising…"

Orn could tell Warver wasn't pleased when Plemso said "the amazing job I'm doing here." Warver was a team player.

"…And you know what he said? Rhetorical question again. I'm being promoted to colonel and I'm leaving for Capitol City in ten days for reassignment. You're being promoted to major and this is now your command."

"Thank you, sir."

"I was asked who could best fill my position and you were the obvious choice. You're a credit to my command and my victories," Colonel Plemso said, surveying the bruise on Orn's forehead and pointing to it. "What's the meaning of this?"

Warver told Colonel Plemso about his entire day from pulling up to the cabin to finding the corpse, including how he'd reviewed the recon cruiser's vidcam footage on the way back to camp, from which it was clear that Orn had fired the first unwarranted shot. During the entire telling of the story, Colonel Plemso paced around the tent with his head down listening until Warver finished by stating they'd positively identified the victim as Orn's father.

"What were you thinking, Orn?" Colonel Plemso said, then pointed at Orn's forehead. "Have you seen what this looks like? You should have a med check it out. You may have a concussion, too." Colonel Plemso walked over to a table next to his bunk and retrieved a hand-mirror, holding it up so Orn could see himself.

In the reflection, Orn observed that the left side of his forehead up near his hairline was swollen into a black-and-blue bump the size of a large fist with a bloody gash in the middle of it.

"Do you know who did this?"

Orn nodded.

Colonel Plemso took away the mirror and said, "So what happened out there? How did you get your hands on a weapon?"

"There's not much to tell that Captain—I mean Major Warver hasn't already told you, sir. I directed the troops there. I knew it was my father's cabin. I panicked when Major Warver questioned the operation, so I went into one of the vehicles and borrowed a weapon. I knew if I fired at my father, he'd respond with the loaded weapon he kept by the front door, and the subofficer would command the troops to return fire since the shots were headed in their direction. That part was pretty easy."

"Pretty easy?" Warver said. "Pretty easy?"

"That's what I said." Orn smirked at Warver.

"I won't stand for insubordination, Orn," Colonel Plemso said.

"Yes, sir. Sorry, sir."

"Major Warver is your superior. If we're to succeed in our mission, the chain of command must be followed."

"Exactly," Warver said. "His behavior requires disciplinary action as rank insubordination."

Colonel Plemso stood there for a moment, tapping the mirror against his thigh. When he stopped, the tent filled with the sounds from outside: vehicles passing, the voices of the soldiers at the tent's entrance, music in the distance from a soldier's audplayer. Colonel Plemso appeared in deep thought and Warver was visibly annoyed. To Warver, the course of action was clear and anything else was a mockery of his command.

Colonel Plemso said, "Yes, something must be done, but if you don't mind, since I brought Orn into my command, I'd like to deal with any disciplinary action personally."

"What'll you do?" Warver said.

"Not sure at the moment, but Orn has been an unbelievable contributor to our cause."

"I agree, sir. I'm sure whatever you decide will be just, although I want to request Orn no longer be assigned to me."

"I'll see what I can do about that. You're dismissed."

Warver shot an angry look at Orn, who was sure whatever Colonel Plemso had planned was nowhere near the harsh punishment Warver had in mind and Warver knew it too.

"Dismiss your soldiers at the entrance too," Colonel Plemso said, then pointed at Orn's wound. "And I want a word with the one who did this."

Warver saluted Plemso, then turned on his heels and exited the tent.

"Now, let's take care of these cuffs, shall we?" Colonel Plemso said, removing them. Orn rubbed his wrists where the restraints had cut into his skin. He'd attempted to pry them off the entire time he'd been bound, even though he knew it was a losing cause. The pain kept him focused.

"Now, sit down and talk to me about what happened," Colonel Plemso said, and removed two metal cups and a Malrap bottle from a shelf. "Aside from this little incident, we have celebrating to do." He poured Malrap into the cups. "Sit, sit, I insist." Colonel Plemso sat in his customary seat at the head of the table. He placed one cup in front of himself and the other on the table in front of the chair nearest to him.

Orn sat where the colonel indicated and said, "I've never had Malrap."

"I'm glad to afford you the opportunity then," Colonel Plemso said, laughing and lifting his cup. "A toast. Raise your cup. To the bright future ahead for the both of us. Now drink. That's an order."

The cup was full and Orn drank some of the liquid, feeling the warm sting as it went down his throat. His eyes watered.

"I remember my first time," Colonel Plemso said. "The sting will diminish the more you drink it. Now finish it."

Orn drank the remaining Malrap and Colonel Plemso reached over with the bottle in hand and filled the cup to the top again. "Now drink the entire cup. One gulp. Like a real Kodan."

Orn wanted to protest, but he was in a weak position to complain. If Colonel Plemso wanted to celebrate with him, then maybe the punishment would be lenient, so he swallowed the contents of the cup without question, and this time it did go down smoother. A warmth washed over him, and he felt like his spirit was separating from his body like when he had a fever, but instead of aching, he felt euphoric.

Colonel Plemso leaned forward, peering into Orn's eyes. Orn chuckled and he wasn't sure why. Colonel Plemso smiled. "Looks like the Malrap is doing its job. So, now tell me honestly why you'd take the chance of being sent back to the streets with this stunt of yours. I've gone out of my way to make an unbelievable life for you and you repay me by violating my trust and the trust of my officers," Major Plemso said, tapping the edge of his cup on the table. "I expect loyalty from you. Do you understand that we're tied together? I vouched for you."

"I know, sir. Sorry, sir," Orn said, although he wasn't sorry about what he'd done to his father.

"If Warver was dealing with you, you'd be stinging from the lash right now, locked up and staked down for days in the hotbox. So, tell me truthfully, why did you do it? Tell me everything from the beginning. There's no other way if we're going to move forward together to bigger and better things." Colonel Plemso poured Orn another cupful and said, "Go on. I'm waiting."

Orn peered at the contents of his cup, then tossed it back.

Colonel Plemso laughed. "I meant with the story, not the drink."

Orn didn't know where to start. He'd never told another soul about that part of his life. He contemplated remaining silent, taking Warver's punishment, and going back to the streets and surviving like he'd done before, but the potential of his position here appeared limitless. Colonel Plemso understood Orn, scars and all, and the colonel not only appreciated Orn's more gruesome characteristics but also allowed him to exercise them. Under the colonel's command, Orn could truly be himself.

"It's an ugly story. I'll tell you that," Orn said, slurring his words.

"Look around you," Colonel Plemso said. "So much of life is ugly, but I have plans, Orn. Big, majestic plans. You can be part of them, but we have to move past this bump in the road. Now, I don't have all day to sit around here with you so start talking."

"The only other person who knew the truth is dead and gone, and good riddance to him," Orn said. "I think I might be sick." He dry-heaved a few times and began sweating.

"Just take a few deep breaths and begin. I'm waiting."

Orn followed the colonel's advice and felt the sickness subside. "To start," Orn said, "my father did this to me." Orn held out the backs of both hands toward Plemso.

"I figured," Colonel Plemso said. "You obviously hated the man."

"He wasn't a man. He was a drunken lout, a beast. I did to him what I did to all the other beasts on our property that he loved more than me. I slaughtered them. I mutilated them, because he cared for them more than me."

"You tortured farm animals to get back at your father. Is that what you're saying?"

"Damn right, sir." Orn felt as if he was losing control. He didn't like it. "Sorry, sir. He had it coming."

"So how did all this start?"

"Where to begin?" Orn said. "It all started with my mother. I was her first pregnancy and it happened late in her life. After my birth, she fell into a depression and deluded herself into believing the only way to be attractive to my father was by staying young, to stop herself from aging. So she found a black market Rejuv Serum peddler to inject her with expired serum, and she contracted Rejuvium.

"Of course, her delusion was far from the truth. My father loved her. He was devoted to her. After she contracted Rejuvium, he spent his days attempting to discover a workable treatment for her, but if you know anything about the disease, there's no cure and it can last for years.

"I watched her day after day, year after year, as she writhed in agony from the pain until she didn't know who I was anymore and lost control of basic functions. We couldn't afford med care, so my father and I looked after her. From a young age, I emptied bedpans. I injected her with painkillers which lost their effectiveness over the years as the pain increased. I fed her. Helped bathe her. You get the idea.

"I took care of her from the early morning until I went to school. The moment I returned home from school, my priority was tending to my mother while my father worked the farm. He was worthless in the evening, drinking Malrap until he was in a stupor, so the entire burden of nursing my mother fell on me. My father never uttered more than, 'Go…take care of her…your mother needs you…' to me.

"She passed when I was twelve. After she was gone, my father fell into a depression. I cleaned the house and cooked all the meals, but I might as well have been a ghost. My father hardly said a word to me. I tried to talk to him. I tried to get him help. My aunts wanted to take me into their homes and become my guardians. They showed him my high grades and said there was a chance I could attend University with the proper environment. My father spat on them and chased them out of the house. He argued he provided for me. I always had food on my plate. I had a roof over my head and what else did I need?

"When he banished my aunts, that's when it really started to get bad. His Malrap drinking got worse and I felt condemned to live with this drunken lout. He ignored me unless he was verbally abusing me, calling me a 'waste' and saying he was 'sorry that I'd ever been born otherwise my partner would still be alive.' My anger and resentment toward him grew and I observed how he loved that farm more than me and showed the animals more compassion than he'd ever shown me.

"So one day, I had an idea—I slit the throat of a grazing animal. When he found it, he was furious and stormed into the house and asked if I knew anything about it. I confessed. That was the first time he beat me and the scars on my hands began. That was the most attention I'd received from my father in years and although the pain was awful, I'd finally found a way to receive affirmation that he cared. So I kept killing the animals, and I had to quit school because my hands were so mauled by the beatings.

"After a while, my father seemed to lose passion for punishing me. He began talking to my aunts about taking me, but when he told them what I'd been doing to the animals, they had second thoughts.

"So I found a way to end those conversations by torturing the animals instead of just killing them. I'd tie them up and slice their hides while they bleated in pain. I extracted their teeth and cut out their tongues. I removed their legs, creating my own tourniquets so they wouldn't bleed out and sewed the wounds shut so my father would find them mutilated. My father's fury returned and he beat me again with greater force than ever." Orn stood, removing his shirt and turning around to show Colonel Plemso the deep marks in his back.

"Powers-That-Be," Colonel Plemso said. "Why would you bring this on yourself?"

"I know it's hard to understand, but my father was demonstrating that he cared. I was relishing what I was doing to the animals because of the attention I was receiving from him in return. This back and forth went on for a few years. I didn't do it every day, but randomly so my father was kept unaware when I'd strike next. I became skilled in my vivisections, and through experimentation, I created my own poison so my father would have to watch the animals bleating in agony for hours or kill them himself. He carved a permanent switch and hung it over the fireplace. He pleaded with me to stop as he beat me, but I wouldn't.

"As time passed, when I was running out of new ways to engage my father, I had an idea. My father had a canine pet that followed him around all day. His name was Wulfee. My father loved that pet. Every night, Wulfee would curl up next to him on the couch and place his head in my father's lap, and my father would pet him. I was fond of Wulfee, too. He was a good boy who came to my room to comfort me after my father beat me.

"So one day when my father was out at the market, I fed Wulfee a treat laced with a drug so he was semi-conscious. I extracted his teeth, cut off half of his right front leg and half of his left back leg, then administered a diluted version of my poison so my father would discover Wulfee still alive, but slowly dying.

"As I waited for my father to come home, I remember cradling Wulfee's head in my lap, petting him, running my hand through his fur, scratching him below his ears where he liked it," Orn said, tearing up and choking on his words. "He looked up at me with those big brown eyes, whimpering every so often, licking my hand, loving me even after I did those things to him. I felt no remorse, though. I could only think about my satisfaction in my father's rage at what I'd done. When my father walked in on this scene, he said it was time to end it. He came at me with his hunting weapon and I ran away."

Orn put his shirt back on and sat down and looked down at his empty cup. "Can I have some more?"

"You've had enough Malrap," Colonel Plemso said. "So, let me get this straight. You goaded your father into becoming abusive to make him show he cared, then when he wanted to end it, you upped the ante by torturing his animals and the family pet. Then to get you to stop or just get himself to stop, he chased you out of the house with a weapon and you ran away. So why bother killing him with Global Assembly forces? You were already out of your father's reach."

"I began to think about my father's suffering, and how he would never be truly happy," Orn said. "He was a beast who could only show he cared by beating his son. He compelled me to do horrible things to those animals, to Wulfee, so he could continue to show he cared. I felt compassion for those animals as I tortured them just as he did when he tortured me. In that way, he made me into his own image. Today, after I blew those holes in his home, our eyes met and I knew he understood I had come to express my love for him and put him out of his misery for his own good."

"That's interesting logic. Perverse, but interesting," Colonel Plemso said. "Do you feel like you've accomplished what you set out to do? Do you feel satisfied with the final outcome?"

"Yes, sir. This is my family now. You're my family."

Colonel Plemso sat there silently staring at Orn who knew this look after spending so much time time in his presence. Colonel Plemso was assessing how to deal with him. Orn had been expecting more of a reaction, more questions about what he'd done, about his relationship with his father. Then Colonel Plemso said, "You'd be surprised. I can relate. But if you ever disobey my orders again or break chain of command, then I'll personally shoot you. Do you understand?"

"Yes, sir."

"I'm going to take you with me to Capitol City and make sure you acquire the proper military training. You'll work for me from now on."

"Yes, sir. I would like that, sir."

"And to show that I care, I have a task for you," Colonel Plemso said, marching out of the tent. He returned with the soldier who had struck Orn. He ordered the soldier to stand at attention in the middle of the tent and removed the soldier's weapon from where it hung on his shoulder.

Colonel Plemso said to the soldier, "Sergeant Davik Atmar, I'm disappointed to find it's you who perpetrated this abuse on Orn. You're one of my best in the field, highly dedicated and decorated. I was planning on promoting you and taking you with me to Capitol City to become my adjunct officer."

Davik said, "Sir, I—"

"Not a word," Colonel Plemso said, putting up the palm of his hand. "Now, Orn. Stand up and show this soldier that you care."

Orn was wobbly on his legs from the Malrap and used the table as leverage to assist him in reaching a standing position. His head pounded, but he rather enjoyed it. Colonel Plemso handed him Davik's weapon.

"What would you like me to do, sir?"

"What's happening, sir?" Davik said.

"I said not a word, Davik. You'll stand there and take whatever punishment this young man chooses to inflict upon you. If you move, if you flinch, I will have you shot for insubordination," Colonel Plemso said. "Orn, it's your move. Just don't kill him."

Davik was shaking. He reminded Orn of the farm animals.

"Don't close your eyes, Davik," Orn said as he lifted the butt end of the weapon and smashed it into Davik's nose, breaking it. Davik screamed, but he didn't move. His face scrunched up as blood flowed from his nose over his lips and down his chin, dripping on the floor. He didn't cry, and he kept his arms by his sides. Orn ran the fingers of his right hand down Davik's cheek, then used the same fingers to wipe the sweat from Davik's brow and licked them. "Just right," Orn said in a hushed tone.

Then he jammed the butt of the weapon into Davik's right side. Something cracked and Davik groaned in pain. Orn had broken a few ribs. Davik still stood at attention. "Good boy," Orn said, patting Davik's cheek. "You're doing awfully well."

Then Orn swung the weapon from the muzzle end, striking Davik's kneecap. Davik collapsed backward onto the floor, moaning in pain, then struggled up to standing with only one leg to support him, flinching as he reflexively attempted to put weight on the leg with the pulverized knee. A low moan emanated from his clenched lips.

Orn ran his fingers through Davik's hair on the side of his head and around his ear. "There, there, you did so well. Believe me, it was my pleasure," Orn said, handing the weapon back to Colonel Plemso.

"Orn," Colonel Plemso said, "you'll escort the sergeant to the camp's med, then report to Major Warver. You will tell him that I've sentenced you to forty lashes for insubordination, after which you'll be staked down naked in the solitary hotbox for four days as punishment for breaking chain of command. Afterward, you and the sergeant will pack your gear and personal items and accompany me to Capitol City."

Almost thirty years later, Orn was still working with Vidor Plemso who had given him a life he could never have imagined as a homeless youth in the streets of Majinor. He was in a cruiser flying over Capitol City.

The fires down in the Plaza had diminished, but he could see the intermittent flash of weapons discharging in the Old Quarter.

Orn remained confused and unsettled by his meeting with Mar Jeps as the cruiser descended to the landing pad on the top of the Global Assembly building. He was concerned how the Leader would react to the message relayed by Warver, but however the Leader responded, Orn was glad to be of service to him, and in due course, he would gladly take the backlash.

# VIDOR

Vidor plopped down on the couch in his office. He was ready to go home. Although the executive med had given him pills to ward off the aftereffects of the sonic restraint, his head was aching again and he was feeling woozy. He was anxious to hear Orn's findings, but he didn't know how much longer he could wait for Orn to return. Then the intercom buzzed. He rose from the couch, almost lost his balance, then steadied himself and walked to his desk.

"Yes, Kel," Vidor said, "I was just about to ask you to summon my cruiser."

"Yes, sir. I can do that right now and it'll be ready by the time you're done talking to Orn Shiv. He's here to see you."

"Perfect," Vidor said. "Send him in."

When the door opened, Vidor knew immediately that Orn wasn't bringing good news. Orn hated to disappoint Vidor and his face bore a look of dejectedness.

Vidor sat down behind his desk and instructed Orn to place himself in the seat across from him.

"So, nothing good to tell me?" Vidor said.

"Is it that obvious?" Orn said, wiggling uncomfortably on the wooden chair. "That woman has always been a handful, but now Prevor has given her power. This doesn't bode well for the future."

"Prevor will return soon enough and I'll deal with him."

"I don't know. I get the sense his absence is long-term," Orn said. "Do you want the blow-by-blow or just a general summary of what happened?"

"From start to finish."

Orn told him the entire story from the moment he'd left Vidor's office to leaving Mar Jeps. "She is formidable. I could tell she already knew what's been reported about her son on the viewing channels, but she decided to give me the entire dramatic counterpoint as if I was the bearer of the bad news. Tears and wailing. She was quite convincing, but I noticed a slight hesitancy. This is all new to her, but she'll get better at it. Prevor put her in charge, which leaves me wondering what he's up to. I don't buy her story about his whereabouts. Off-site? What does that mean?"

"How would you suggest proceeding?"

"I'd have GSS agents on alert in every region ready to comm me if they catch a whiff of Prevor, but he was last seen boarding the WAEF at the parade launch point and he might be in orbit now."

"I doubt he's on the WAEF—that makes no sense for someone with his corporate responsibilities, and our analysts have been over the recording—the time code is after the WAEF left orbit and the vid was filmed at the Complex."

"I know you've invested a lot in Prevor, sir, but there are strong signs he's working for the other side. Who else could have pulled off the Active Glass in the dome?"

"Taking into consideration the project he started for us, that makes little sense," Vidor said. "My first thought is that his close relationship with the Vanderlord boy and the Jeps' is the basis for his actions. We do know he's nonviolent, considering his invention of the sonic restraint."

"So do we call his bluff? If he's so nonviolent, would he let the power go off? If there's no power going to med clinics or running the air circulators, that could take lives in the domes around the planet."

"I don't think we call his bluff, but we may want to hold off on his demands," Vidor said. "Make him sweat. Maybe he'll raise his head as we get closer to the deadline. In the meantime, we have to deal with Mar Jeps."

"I failed to mention my run-in with an old colleague of ours. He relayed a request from the Jeps woman."

"When I say start to finish, I mean it," Vidor said. "Old colleague? Relayed a request? I'm exhausted, Orn. Get to the damn point."

"Commander Warver met me as I exited the Prevor Industries building. Did you know he was working there?"

"Prevor actually asked me if I was all right with Warver working there and I approved it. You have a problem with that?"

"No, sir. Other than I don't like the man."

"He can be a pain in the ass, and considering he's head of security over there, you might want to keep an eye on him," Vidor said. "But what did he have to say?"

Orn relayed Jeps' message to Vidor, then said, "I'm not sure it's a good idea to give in to this request. She's the mother of the man who attempted to sabotage your government."

"Who's going to know? We'll induce a news blackout and deny the story to the few digi-media outlets we don't control. We'll simply call any report false news." Vidor stood up and looked out the window at the fires still burning in the streets. "I'll have her over to my home. I'll show her that I'm a family man doing the best for my children and Koda's future."

"You know she'll ask about Rajer Jeps."

"There's no reason to keep her in the dark, and that'll give me the opportunity to use her partner as leverage to get what I want like I told you to do when you confronted her."

"Yes, sir. I should have used it. It was a good idea."

Vidor heard Orn rise from the chair and walk to his side. "Of course it was. How could you be outwitted by her? That's just pathetic. Are you going soft on me?"

"No, sir," Orn said, standing at attention and clicking his heels together. "I'll do better, sir."

"I need you, Orn," Vidor said, clutching Orn's arm and pulling Orn toward him. "I need you now more than ever. Even if we squash today's uprising, I have a bad feeling your hunch is correct. Vanderlord's speech and this crash debacle may open the floodgates for the population to become more vocal in stating views that run counter to our policies. You'll need to be vigilant in dealing with them."

"I understand, sir," Orn said, clicking his heels again and saluting with his free arm. "I'm always at your service."

"I expect your actions to be as ruthless as those you implemented during the DOME riots. Crack down on anything that appears treasonous. Do you understand? I don't want anyone to think that it's all right to question our authority. Those are your orders, and let me know if you hear anything about Prevor."

"Yes, sir," Orn said. "Do you want me to inform Mar Jeps that you'll contact her?"

"No, I'll handle it," Vidor said. "You're dismissed." Vidor released his hold on Orn's arm, and Orn marched out of the office.

The intercom buzzed. Vidor's cruiser was ready and his security team awaited him outside his office. He grabbed his viewer then opened the desk drawer where the smashed digi-foto of his family lay and put it on top of the desk. He realized he was still wearing his suit from the Arena, too. Vanderlord had made a mess of things, but Vidor didn't get this far without persevering through adversity.

Vidor gazed out the window in the direction of the Prevor Industries Complex. He wasn't clueless. It was clear Mado Prevor was involved in what happened at Breeze Celebration—how else was the Active Glass pane behind the Complex rigged for the WAEF's escape?—but Mado Prevor's cooperation with the Global Assembly's future plans was paramount.

If Prevor had become loyal to the Movement, then Mar Jeps as CEO of Prevor Industries could be Vidor's only option to accomplish his future plans, and holding Rajer Jeps in custody would be helpful in overcoming any setbacks. Vidor thought about the last time he met Mar Jeps at Yorlik the Great's landing. His bachelor days were over, but he could still turn on the old charm. Orn got nowhere, but Vidor thought a subtler approach might work to lure Mar Jeps into his fold. Taking on the role of easygoing, sensitive family man might do the trick.

Vidor pressed the intercom button and said, "Kel, I'll be right out. Can you get the digi-foto on my desk repaired? Also, comm the Detention Facility and arrange a meeting with Rajer Jeps tomorrow after my appointment with Roneh Rayush, and set up a dinner at my estate with the CEO of Prevor Industries."

# YOR

**"**...and this is not a lush rainforest or Yorlik the Great. That's an actor in a mock-up of a SEEDER spacesuit with the Great man's head edited onto it, and the actor is standing in front of a green screen where hi-tech animation of a rainforest is inserted. Looks real if you don't have the expertise to recognize a fake," said the vid expert to a viewing-channel news personality. The expert was a professor who was an acquaintance of Yor's at the University. Across the bottom of the screen, a headline read "ATROCITY AT THE ARENA." A supposed live shot of the WAEF burning in a crater played in a loop at the corner of the screen.

"There you have it," the viewing-channel news personality said. "A poorly executed piece of trickery foisted on the Kodan people, on a sacred day of celebration. Further coverage of the Atrocity at—"

Yor pressed a button on the armrest of the living-chamber recliner, cutting off the viewing-channel feed. He was appalled by what he'd just witnessed. Mado had warned him that he wouldn't like it, but Yor had to see for himself.

He was well aware that the Global Assembly would go out of its way to debunk his speech and the presentation. These viewing-channel broadcasts were powerful propaganda, and this was how most citizens informed



*Howard Libes*

themselves, but there was nothing Yor could do about it. He had lit the flame and it was in the Movement's hands now to propagate the truth. Word of mouth was something the Global Assembly couldn't completely suppress and Yor was confident the Movement's operatives would spread the truth that the WAEF was still flying and Yor was alive, and what was shown at the Breeze Celebration was real.

In the engine room, Yor found Mado standing in front of a junction panel, holding a spanner. Each engine had a panel containing a motherboard full of circuitry to regulate the power converter. Mado had been moving from engine to engine, running down a checklist for each one, ensuring they were ready for the voyage. He left each engine's panel open to keep track of his progress. He had one more to go.

"How's it coming?" Yor said.

"Almost there," Mado said. "The output level on engine number three is a little off. I have an idea what the problem is."

"Can I help?"

"I'm good. Once I'm done with the diagnostics, I'll synch the engines."

"So, I was watching the viewing-channel broadcasts."

"How was that?" Mado said, giving Yor his undivided attention.

"Frustrating."

"Maybe you should stay down here, give me a hand and tell me what you're thinking."

"I don't know. I guess in the back of my mind, I was hoping what we did at the Celebration would cause a spontaneous realization among the planetary population about the government's lies," Yor said. "Now, saying it out loud, that sounds naïve."

"You shouldn't blame yourself for being hopeful. I understand how you're feeling. I was once young and idealistic like you, but it's going to take the will of the Kodan people to create change…and time." With the spanner, Mado attempted to tighten a bolt on engine three's limiter, but his efforts only budged the bolt slightly. "Automated tools would have made this easier. There's plenty where we were going in Shamba, but I should've remembered to pack them in the ship. See, I don't think of everything." Mado grunted as he turned the bolt further.

"You said finding out the effect of what we did would take time. Any idea on how long?"

"I know you're probably sick of me bringing your great-grandfather into every conversation," Mado said, handing Yor the spanner before walking over to the next junction panel and pointing at the screws on the cover. Yor placed the spanner down in a pile of tools on a tarp, picked up the required screwdriver, and gave it to Mado, who began removing the screws.

"I actually enjoy hearing the stories. Adds to my life's work."

"I've mentioned before that he was all about the long game. First of all, he would have been giddy with pride at what you pulled off at the Celebration, but he understood that was one action in a chain of necessary events," Mado said. "He was cognizant that once the Breeze Celebration event happened, it might take decades, after a string of actions and reactions, for the right number of Kodans to understand that unless they rose in mass to force change, they'd become extinct." Mado handed the screwdriver and screws to Yor, removed the panel cover, and began tinkering inside the compartment.

Yor said, "So, in simpler terms, you're telling me that I need to be thinking further into the future?"

"Correct. You need to understand that your presentation blowing the lid off the Global Assembly's lies was just one of many actions required to secure the future for your people," Mado said, walking over to the engine control console and synching up the engine outputs. "Any action needs to take into consideration all the possible reactions, which allows further actions to be devised in response to all those possible reactions, and so on, steering your way to the desired results. With that way of thinking, you'll never get caught unprepared."

"Sounds exhausting," Yor said. "So, this trip to the way station was always part of the plan?"

"Yes, but it occurred sooner because our timing backfired at the Celebration. The virus Harmin released was an action, and due to outside factors, the reaction was that the virus wouldn't cover our tracks to Shamba. With that possibility in mind, I also planned for flying through the Active Glass pane in the dome and coming out here. That's why we're here safely and headed to the station."

"I'm getting a dizzy just listening to you talk about it," Yor said. "Glad you're here to do it."

Mado pressed a series of buttons on the control console and the engines began to hum as power from the core coursed through the conduits into the power converters, signifying the engines were back online.

"You'll get used to it and it'll become second nature to you," Mado said, turning to Yor. "Head on up to the control room and take us out of orbit. Plan a course away from Koda into open space toward the way station. I'll come up there once I assess the state of the engines down here."

"I've never done that for real, only in your simulations."

"Well, now it's time to see if you learned anything. Run along."

Back in the control room, Yor operated the holo-device, charted a course, and programmed it into the navigation hub, then intercommed Mado from the pilot's chair that he was set to go.

"I need to check one more thing," Mado said. "Make sure you secure the chair's harness."

Yor had forgotten. He was fighting his nerves, keenly aware that the vacuum of space was just outside the hull and that his life and Mado's depended on him keeping the ship undamaged. He'd waited his entire life to fly the WAEF in space. He recalled his great-grandfather telling him stories of his test flights where he broke all previous speed and distance records including his own a few times.

Years ago, sitting next to his great-grandfather on the couch in the estate's library, Yor had asked, "Were you scared?"

"Me, scared?" the old man said, giving Yor a playful shove. "You bet. I was scared out of my mind. The only thing that kept me from jittering out of my seat was the harness. I put up a brave front for the viewing-channel cams and Kodan

Space Control, but every time I had to fire up those engines and pushed them to maximum capacity, I was frightened the outcome might not be favorable to the continuation of my existence."

"So how did you do it, then?"

"I thought about your great-grandmother and your grandfather and your great-aunt and all the Kodans who were counting on me to find a better life for them. Courage doesn't exist without fear. You have to push through to the purpose of your actions and let that take hold."

Yor peered up at his great-grandfather smiling in the foto. "I won't let you down," Yor said to the foto as he secured the harness.

Mado said, "Everything's ready here."

"Harness in place."

"Start out slow," Mado said. "If it feels right, then let her go to full speed."

"Feels right?"

"You'll know what I mean soon enough," Mado said. "And if anything bad happens down here, I'll let you know."

Yor engaged the navigation hub, then kept one eye on the control console for warning lights as he throttled up the engines. The WAEF swung out of orbit and the window filled with stars. He pushed the throttle up further and further and the ship responded, moving faster and faster through space. At that moment, if someone asked Yor about his feelings, he might say that he was having an out-of-body experience.

Then Yor heard an explosion and the entire ship shuddered.

# Roneh

Roneh Rayush was nervous and sweating as she sat in the waiting area of the Leader's office. Meeting the Leader was beyond her wildest expectations. She was eager to ask the receptionist what it was like to be around the Leader day after day, but she didn't want to come off as nosy.

Suddenly an intercom buzzed, and the receptionist told her the Leader was ready for her. Roneh stood as a door slid open and looked over at the receptionist, unsure what to do next. "Just go in," the receptionist said. "He won't bite."

Roneh paused to compose herself, then marched into the office. The door slid closed behind her. The Leader was standing in the middle of the room; Davik Atmar, the Leader's closest advisor, stood behind him to his right.

"Please come in," the Leader said, waving her further into the room.

As Roneh approached him, it was like a dream come true. She admired the Leader more than any other and here he was beckoning her before him. She thought he exuded a sort of ruggedness. She stopped in front of him and put out her hand. Her palms were sweating, and she didn't want to wipe them off on her pants in front of the Leader, so she put her hand down.

"I'm sorry. I…" Roneh said, at a loss for words.

"Please speak freely, Roneh Rayush," the Leader said.

Roneh said, "I just wanted to say it's an honor and a blessing to meet you, sir."

"The honor is all ours," the Leader said. "Isn't it, Davik?"

"Yes, sir. It is, sir."

"You're a hero to all Kodans," the Leader said. "We're both in awe of your bravery yesterday in attempting to apprehend the terrorist Yor Vanderlord. Aren't we, Davik?"

"Absolutely, sir," Davik said.

"Now, please have a seat on the couch and let's talk," the Leader said, pointing to her left.

Roneh looked over at the couches. She was so transfixed by the Leader that she hadn't even noticed them. "Where should I sit?" Roneh said.

"Well, there are two, so you choose."

Roneh sat down on the couch closest to the door. The Leader placed himself on the couch across from her. Davik Atmar stood behind the couch to the right of the Leader.

The Leader said, "We have so much to talk about."

"We do?"

The Leader chuckled. He turned around to Davik Atmar who stood at attention until the Leader was looking at him, then he chuckled, too.

Roneh needed to shake herself out of her daze. She was in shock at being here, but she wanted to live up to the honor.

"I'm sorry," Roneh said. "I'm a little overwhelmed. I've worked my entire life for the good of the Global Assembly and here I am sitting across from you."

"No need to apologize," the Leader said. "I've seen your reaction to the trappings of this office before. Haven't we, Davik?"

"Yes, sir. We have, sir."

The Leader continued, "Now, just relax and tell us how you evaded the sonic device that knocked everyone else unconscious."

"I'm not sure. Sheer luck? I may have been standing outside of the sonic-blast perimeter or by the time I took action the device stopped firing. I'm not sure."

"That sounds plausible. Luck plays a definite part in our lives, but the smart people are in the right place at the right time to take advantage of that luck," the Leader said. "Seems like your timing was perfect. Just too bad you couldn't have captured Yor Vanderlord."

"I regret giving him too much warning. I should've fired right away," Roneh said, anguished at telling the Leader of her weakness. "I've never fired a stun weapon before. Maybe that's why I hesitated. I don't know. I don't know what happened. It all happened so fast."

"Don't be so hard on yourself," the Leader said. "You're probably right. Inexperience with a weapon could cause somebody to freeze. I assume you've never shot anybody before?"

"No. Never."

"Well, you see. There it is. Don't be so hard on yourself," the Leader said. "We shot him down so it all worked out in the end."

"For the good of the globe."

"Yes, for the good of the globe," the Leader said, leaning back in the couch cushions, studying Roneh and nodding. "The initiative you displayed at Breeze Celebration, that's what I'm interested in. That's what the Global Assembly needs nowadays, especially with the terrorists stirred up by Vanderlord's lies. Initiative. That's what Koda needs. Young people like yourself are invaluable in helping to keep the peace in these troubled times."

The Leader waited for Roneh to say something, but she was stupefied by his praise. The Leader peered over his shoulder at Davik Atmar who shrugged. "How do you feel about what I just said, Roneh?"

"Of course, you're absolutely correct, sir."

"That's what I like to hear," the Leader said, chuckling and looking at Atmar again who began laughing himself. "I want you to be the face of a new initiative. I want you to speak at Kodan schools and tell the planet's young people how the Global Assembly intends to bring them a glorious future by overcoming the environmental crisis. I want you to recruit them into being vigilant, keeping an eye out for sedition against the Global Assembly and reporting it. I want you to appear on all the viewing channels and debunk the lies spewed by Yor Vanderlord. I want you to tell Kodans your story about being the daughter of a Separatist Revolt veteran who was crippled preserving the Global Assembly and how you acted on the day of Breeze Celebration to do the same. How do you feel about that?"

Roneh wasn't surprised the Leader was aware of her family history. "I'm not sure if I'm worthy of the honor, sir."

"After what you did out there in front of the entire planet?" the Leader said. "How do you feel about Yor Vanderlord?"

"He was a traitor to the good of the Global Assembly. His words and vids were the sign of a mentally ill person who will say and do anything to hurt the noble efforts of the Global Assembly to protect and preserve the Kodan people," Roneh said. "He personifies the sedition and evil on our planet that must be snuffed out if we're to survive as a united people under the domes until the planet heals around us."

The Leader smiled and looked up at Davik Atmar. "Let's put more money into those Allegiance Camps. They certainly work wonders," the Leader said. "I think we've found our girl—don't you, Davik?"

"Yes, I do, sir," Davik said.

"We'll provide you with a makeover and clothing for all your appearances, and we'll give you talking points to memorize. You'll be tremendous in your new role as spokesperson for the Global Assembly."

"I'm honored to represent the Global Assembly, sir."

"As well you should be," the Leader said. "It's an incredible honor. You'll be representing myself as well, so I expect great things of you."

"I'm doubly honored, sir," Roneh said, feeling herself blushing.

"Fantastic to have you onboard," the Leader said, standing up. Roneh stood as well. "On your way out, my receptionist will give you Davik's direct comm line in case you have any questions, and you'll be contacted by our

PR people tomorrow to prepare for the viewing-channel interviews which will begin in a few days."

"Thank you, sir," Roneh said, wondering whether she should shake the Leader's hand or salute. "I'll make you proud, sir."

"I know you will," the Leader said. "I chose you personally and I'm the best at judging people. Aren't I, Davik?"

"Yes, sir. You are, sir."

"And Davik should know—he's been by my side for over thirty years."

Davik said, "It's been an honor and a privilege to serve you, sir."

"He was just a lowly soldier, a scrawny maggot crawling around in the mud, directionless, and look where he is now," the Leader said, turning to Davik Atmar and patting his cheek. "He'll show you out."

Roneh said, "Can I ask you a question, sir?"

"Of course."

"Will I be giving up my duties at the Department of Education and Well Being?"

"Yes, you're receiving a promotion. You're of utmost importance for the good of the globe now."

Roneh snapped to attention and clicked her heels together. "For the good of the globe!"

"For the good of the globe," the Leader said. "You're dismissed."

# Rajer

Rajer stood at the back of the detention cell splashing water from the sink onto his face simply for the sensation. He was sick of feeling numb, and the same thoughts and images ran through his mind. Had Mar returned to the bungalow or was she in custody herself? And what happened to Yor? He recalled hearing the roar of the WAEF's engines and rolling onto his back to catch a glimpse of the spaceship rocketing above the Arena. Then that woman was standing over him, glaring at him. A Global Guard appeared beside her with his weapon drawn, saying, "You get a good look?" before stunning him unconscious.

He awoke naked on the bottom bunk in this all-white cell—no wider than two average-sized men standing side by side, four meters in length, no windows. A neatly folded white prisoner coverall and cloth shoes lay on the floor next to the bed.

With the exception of the guards bringing him a few meals consisting of a protein bar and a bowl of lukewarm, tasteless soup, he had no visitors. The guards wouldn't speak to him when he asked whether legal counsel would be provided or if he would be speaking to anyone of higher authority. He heard no voices from the cells adjacent to him and the Active Glass wall in front of the cell's entrance kept out all sound from the corridor.

 *Howard Libes*

He spent his time lying on the metal, mattress-less, pillow-less bunk bed with his eyes closed. He clutched at himself to stay warm. He guessed the temperature was no more than 7 degrees Celsius. He attempted to sleep, but his mind was preoccupied with concern for his family. He did ponder his own future, but the outcome was clear-cut. He had acted in support of sedition against the Global Assembly and he'd signed and spoken the Loyalty Oath which stated any such activity would mean the termination of his life.

Now, as he was drying his face with his coverall sleeve, Rajer heard a knock. Lek Valsted stood on the other side of the Active Glass wall, wearing his work attire and his security ID badge, staring at Rajer like a zoo animal. He waved Rajer over to him and pressed a few buttons on what Rajer assumed was the control panel beside the doorway. A slit opened in the Active Glass around the height of Lek's head.

"Come over here, Rajer," Lek said. "I don't have much time."

Rajer hurried to the door, crouching slightly because the ceiling was only about two meters in height. "You're a sight for sore eyes. How long have I been here?"

"A little over a day," Lek said. "And before you ask, Mar is fine."

"What about Yor?"

"Officially, the WAEF was shot down over the Mli-moan mountains. No survivors," Lek said, turning his head to the side. "Unofficially, not sure. I've been around here long enough to know when something doesn't smell right. The only people who know the truth are above me."

"Does Mar know?"

"All she knows is what every Kodan knows—that the traitor Yor Vanderlord is dead."

"Can you get word to her about Yor and that I'm alive?" Rajer saw a look of annoyance come over Lek's face.

"Really, Raj?" Lek said "You should be glad I'm here telling you what I know. I could get put to death for aiding the enemy."

"Sorry, Lek," Rajer said. "You know I appreciate it. I'm just concerned about her."

"Yes, I know, but at this moment, I'd be more concerned about yourself. I'm sure you know what your impulsiveness means for you."

"Do they have the execution scheduled?"

"Oh, no. You're not that lucky. They've got plans for you."

"What sort of plans?"

"They'll want to know what you know and I'm certain they're going to use you as leverage."

"Leverage over what?"

"No—leverage over whom," Lek said. "That's right, you haven't heard—Mar is now CEO of Prevor Industries."

"What?"

"Are you sure you didn't know?"

"Is this a friendly visit or an interrogation?"

"Just seems like something you might have known," Lek said. "And you're a terrible liar."

"Why would I lie to you?"

"Look where you're standing and look where I'm standing," Lek said and laughed.

Rajer laughed along with him. He knew his situation was dismal, but it felt good and that's why Lek was doing it. "True," Rajer said. "In this case, you'll have to believe me."

"I don't know if I do, but I'll have to, won't I?" Lek said, chuckling again.

"Yes, you will," Rajer said. "I'm glad you find this all so amusing."

"You're an idiot," Lek said.

"In my current state, you could reach that conclusion. I could argue otherwise."

"You're an idiot, because you placed yourself in a position where even I can't get you out of it."

"Yes, I've certainly put you in a jam. Sorry about that," Rajer said. He couldn't help but laugh again. "Can you do anything about the food in here, at least?"

"Sorry, I don't have any pull in the kitchen," Lek said. "I should probably get going. In the meantime, stay out of trouble."

"Very funny," Rajer said. "I'll do my best. Send my regards to the family."

"Will do. See you on the other side," Lek said before pressing a button on the control panel and closing the slit. He smiled, waved goodbye, and disappeared down the corridor.

Rajer felt bad lying to Lek, his oldest and dearest friend, but he could only trust him so far in this setting. Lek was a loyal servant of the Global Assembly and the odds were high that his superiors had sent him down here to squeeze information out of their prisoner.

Rajer didn't know much, anyway. Mado and Yor swore him to secrecy, and had told him only that he and Mar would be taking on roles at Prevor Industries post-Breeze Celebration. They'd refused to give him any additional information and Rajer didn't fault them for not being more forthcoming. He'd already violated their trust by blabbing to that woman who almost shot Yor.

Rajer sat down on the edge of the bed and thought about Mar and the news regarding Yor. In his heart, Rajer wanted to believe Yor was alive, but he feared the Global Assembly had erased him from existence. He imagined Mar's grief at the news and could do nothing to console her. He hoped she understood that his actions were the product of his love for Yor rather than a bruised ego from being manipulated by that woman.

Then Rajer heard a knock. A large, tall GSS guard with arms as big as Rajer's thighs stood on the other side of the Active Glass wall. He waved for Rajer to come toward him, then pressed buttons on the control panel until the thin red line running across the middle of the Active Glass wall disappeared, which meant the wall was down.

"Put your hands behind your head and turn around," the guard said in a baritone voice.

Rajer did as he was told, and the guard grabbed his arms and cuffed his wrists behind his back.

"Don't make any trouble," the guard said. "You'll regret it." He took hold of Rajer's right forearm and steered him down the all-white corridor past more detention cells on the same side of the hallway as Rajer's. They were occupied by inmates dressed in the same coveralls. One was doing push-ups. A few were standing directly behind the Active Glass, angrily saying something that couldn't be heard. Others were lying in their beds.

When they reached the end of the hallway, the guard used a security ID to open the door and they entered an identical hallway except for the real doors lining it on both sides. They stopped about halfway down the corridor; the guard opened a door to their left with his ID and said, "Get in there," shoving Rajer inside and closing the door behind him.

Rajer immediately recognized the Leader standing beside an interrogation table in the middle of the room. He was staring down at his comm and wore a suit and tie with a Global Assembly lapel pin. He'd only seen the Leader in gatherings, speaking from a distance, and he was taller in person than Rajer had imagined.

The Leader looked up and barked, "Sit!" He pulled back a chair from the table with both hands. "We've got a few things to talk about."

Rajer noticed the whooshing sound filling the room. He could feel himself becoming unnerved and anxious, or maybe that was just the Leader's presence. Back in the old days, before Mar and Yor, he would've considered it an honor to meet Vidor Plemso. Now all he could feel on top of his other emotions was fear. Vidor Plemso's history as a ruthless interrogator was well documented.

"Sit!" the Leader said, lifting the chair and slamming it against the table. "Don't dawdle. Move!" His voice was booming in the small room.

"Sorry," Rajer said. "First time out of my cell. Feeling disoriented."

"I don't care. Sit!"

As soon as Rajer sat, the cold metal chair began to chill him through the thin coveralls, and he noticed he was directly under an air-cooling vent in the ceiling. He couldn't clutch at himself with his wrists cuffed so he shivered.

The Leader leaned forward so his mouth was close to Rajer's ear and whispered in a sarcastic tone, "Are you comfy now?"

"I'm fine."

"Good. I wouldn't want to put you out," the Leader said, circling the table to stand in front of Rajer. "You're sure you're fine?"

"Yes."

"Excellent. Now, let's talk about your predicament, which is pretty bleak. Defending a seditious act. Breaking your loyalty oath. You've put yourself in quite a fix."

"What do you want me to say? I'm sorry?"

"Sarcasm. The last vestige of a man without hope," the Leader said, pulling out the chair across from Rajer and sitting down. "Yor Vanderlord is dead. I had the WAEF shot down. How do you feel about your actions now? They were meaningless."

"I'd do it again if I had the chance."

"You realize your death is imminent?" the Leader said matter-of-factly, as if telling Rajer that his shoelaces were untied.

"Yes, and it beats having to eat the food here."

"I don't like your attitude," the Leader said, raising his voice and leaning toward Rajer. "I don't like what you did." He slammed his open palm on the table. "I take it as an affront to myself and the Kodan people and I'd like to slit your throat right now."

"Then why don't you?"

"We don't always get what we want," the Leader said, sitting back in his chair.

"You seem to be doing all right in that regard."

The Leader sighed. "You know I could've sent one of my subordinates to deal with you, but I wanted to meet you and have a civil conversation. I thought we could come to an arrangement that works well for both of us."

"I don't see how that's possible."

"You're not making it easy."

"I've been told I have a short attention span."

The Leader punched Rajer in the nose with two successive blows. "Do I have your attention now?"

Rajer's heart was racing. He was disoriented, and he could smell blood.

"Drop the attitude," the Leader said, taking hold of Rajer's chin. "Are you with me?"

Rajer nodded, getting his bearings. His nose throbbed.

The Leader stood, walked to the door, opened it, and said, "Get in here." The guard entered, closing the door behind him.

"Remove his cuffs," the Leader said. The guard unlocked Rajer's cuffs and attached them to his belt. "You can leave now. I'll be all right." The guard hesitated for a moment until the Leader gave him a dirty look, then he exited the room.

Rajer rubbed at his wrists and noticed blood dripping onto the table from his nose. The Leader handed him a handkerchief and Rajer applied it to his nose.

"You can keep the handkerchief," the Leader said. "I apologize for striking you, but I need you to pay attention and drop the sarcasm so we can get down to business."

"Is that what this is?"

The Leader shook his head in disgust. "I'll consider a pardon if you do something for me and the Global Assembly," the Leader said. "Your partner is now CEO of Prevor Industries."

Rajer made sure he looked surprised. "When did that happen?"

"Right after Breeze Celebration."

"First I've heard of it."

"You're not a good liar," the Leader said. "And now Mado Prevor is missing. Do you know where he is?"

"How would I know?"

The Leader bent down and spoke into Rajer's ear. "Do you know where he is?" Rajer could feel the Leader's hot breath on his cheek. Rajer wasn't sure if it was a cologne, but the Leader had a fruity scent.

"I don't know where he is."

The Leader was still bending down when he grabbed Rajer by the back of the head and slammed it into the table, then the Leader turned Rajer's head so they were face-to-face. "Where is he?"

"I have no idea."

The Leader remained face-to-face with Rajer, examining him for the truth. "Where is he?"

"I don't know."

The Leader released his hold on Rajer's head, stood up straight, and walked around the table. He clutched the back of the vacant chair. "I need Prevor Industries on the side of the Global Assembly," the Leader said. "I need your partner as CEO of Prevor Industries on my side, ensuring that Prevor Industries–Global Assembly joint projects move forward as planned."

"So how does this involve me and a pardon?"

"You must have some idea where this is going."

"I do. I just want to hear you say it."

The Leader shoved the vacant chair into the interrogation table, causing the table to slide forward and smash into Rajer, knocking the wind out of him. "Enough of that," the Leader said, pulling the chair back. "Or would you like another?"

Rajer shook his head as he attempted to catch his breath.

"Good. I'll spell it out for you. If you can convince your partner to normalize relations between the Global Assembly and Prevor Industries, especially keeping the power activated in the domes and allowing the status quo to proceed between the two entities, then I'll consider staying your execution and giving you a pardon."

"How could you pardon me? How would that look?"

"I can make the news what I want it to be. You shouldn't worry yourself on that account."

Rajer didn't believe the Leader would ever pardon him, but maybe he could finesse some concessions. "I'll agree, but when I meet with my partner, I want to meet her in a way of my choosing."

"You're brazen for a man on the verge of execution."

"I have nothing to lose, and you're asking for a favor."

The Leader hesitated, then leaned forward and struck the top of the table with the palms of his hands. "You might be smarter than you look," the Leader said. "Whatever you're planning must meet my approval."

"Of course, that goes without saying."

"You have a message you want relayed to your partner in the meantime," the Leader said. "I'm sure she doesn't know you're alive."

"Please tell her that I'm alive and well."

"Look at that, we're working together already. This will be an unbelievable relationship, you'll see. I wouldn't be here otherwise," the Leader said, slapping the table with the palm of his right hand twice and patting Rajer's cheek as he walked by.

Rajer said, "And if it's not too much of an imposition, tell her I love her."

"You can tell her when you see her."

The Leader exited the room, then the guard walked up behind Rajer and cuffed him.

# LEK

When Lek returned from visiting Rajer, he switched his office's Active Glass to opaque. He decided to drop his professional façade for a few moments, unplug the vidcam in the upper-right-hand corner of his office ceiling, and succumb to his sad and frustrated mood.

He ended up answering a handful of calls on his comm, then opened his viewer. On the screen, a vid was paused of Rajer tackling the woman at Breeze Celebration. Before visiting Rajer, Lek had watched the vid a few times. He understood Rajer's intention when he performed this act in front of the entire planet and even respected him for it, but his friend's execution was a foregone conclusion. He could do some small things for Rajer without pushing the boundaries and endangering himself and his family. For instance, during Lek's visit to Rajer, he turned away from the vidcams when he told Rajer about Yor and Mar, ensuring that the movement of his lips wouldn't be recorded.

There was a knock at his door, then somebody attempted to open it. Director Ret Thuta, Lek's superior, said through the door, "Lek, you have a visitor. Why is your door locked?"

Lek had no idea he'd locked it, but he closed the vid, shut his viewer, reconnected the vidcam, and unlocked the door. When he opened it, there stood Director Thuta with the Leader flanked by guards. Behind them, all of Lek's coworkers were standing at attention in their cubicles.

Lek stepped aside. Thuta and the Leader entered his office with a guard who closed the door and told Lek to move further into the room. The Leader sat behind Lek's desk, adjusting the seat and pushing himself in. He examined the objects on the desktop and activated the framed twenty-second digi-vid of Lek's baby daughter in her high chair, singing the nursery rhyme "When All Else Fails." The Leader forced a smile. "They're so innocent at that age," he said, pausing the digi-vid, then he looked up at Lek. "The Director said you had a discussion with Rajer Jeps."

"Yes, sir. I haven't had time to write a report."

"Tend to the bureaucracy later, soldier, and tell me what he said."

Lek glanced over at Director Thuta, a towering and imposing man who rose through the ranks of the military to Special Tactics Officer with the Global Guard. It wasn't normal procedure to discuss an interrogation before a debriefing and a report. Thuta usually did things by the letter.

"Don't stand on ceremony, Valsted," Thuta said. "This is special circumstances. The Leader asked you a question."

"He told me nothing of significance."

"I talked to him and he seems unrepentant," the Leader said. "Wouldn't you agree?"

"Yes, sir."

Thuta looked concerned at Lek's responses and said, "As I told you earlier, Valsted is an old friend of Rajer Jeps, sir. With that in mind, I thought he might have luck getting Jeps to speak without utilizing more vigorous means. If Valsted's sympathies are getting in the way, then I'll take him off the case."

"That's right. You said something about their relationship over the comm."

"Yes, sir," Thuta said. "But you're a busy man. It's understandable you forgot."

"I didn't forget. I have an unbelievable memory. I simply thought you'd handle it," the Leader said. "Do I need to find someone else to do your job, Thuta?"

Thuta snapped to attention, clicking his heels together. "Sorry, sir. I didn't mean—"

"Doesn't matter, Thuta," the Leader said. "Jeps is the kind of man who'd spill more information with a lighter touch. Since Valsted's his old friend, he might have a chance at getting Jeps to open up."

"Brilliant idea, sir," Thuta said.

"I didn't just get this job for being good-looking," the Leader said and laughed. Thuta forced a laugh and looked over at Lek who laughed as well. "Do you think you can get him to reveal any of Vanderlord's deeper connections in the Movement, Valsted?"

"If Director Thuta will allow me, I'll take another crack at him."

"I think that's best," the Leader said, "so of course we'll allow it. Won't we, Thuta?"

"Absolutely, sir."

"We're all in agreement, then," the Leader said, standing up and patting Thuta's shoulder as he passed him.

"Keep up the good work, the both of you. I'll check back soon."

Thuta exited the office behind the Leader and his guard. Lek sat down and readjusted his chair. He picked up the digi-vid of his daughter, taken years ago. There was a more current foto on the desk of himself, his partner Linara, and their six-year-old daughter Ara on an outing in Myla Park. He kept the vid and the foto on his desk to remind him why he performed this job even though over the past few years, he'd developed reservations about GSS tactics.

There was a knock at the door. Director Thuta entered, closed the door firmly behind him, and marched up to Lek's desk.

"So, that was exciting," Thuta said. "We've never had a visit from the Leader before."

"I thought you were friends."

"Friends? More like acquaintances. We travel in different circles. I see him at departmental meetings and functions sometimes."

Lek recalled how Thuta constantly bragged about knowing the Leader personally. "Seems like he's taken an interest in this case."

"Can you blame him?" Thuta said, then peered over his shoulder at the vidcam in the upper-right-hand corner of the ceiling. He walked over to the cam and unplugged it. "Between you and me, Yor Vanderlord made a fool out of the Leader in front of the entire planet. He's got a long way to go to save face, although I don't think he really cares—he just wants to figure out this conspiracy."

"Conspiracy?"

"Yes, that's what he said to me before he left—'Let's find out who else is behind this conspiracy,'" Thuta said. "So you need to work on Jeps before he's passed to another department. This could be a big win for us and lead to an increase in our budget."

"We're analysts, not interrogators."

"I know. This is new territory, but I'm counting on you to break Jeps. I have faith in you. It could even mean a promotion for both of us. I know you're friends with Jeps, but for the good of the globe, right?"

"Yes, sir. For the good of the globe."

Director Thuta plugged in the vidcam and exited the office, then ducked back inside. "Clear your windows, Valsted. You don't want your subordinates to think you're hiding something."

"Will do, sir," Lek said and Thuta exited again.

Lek placed the digi-vid back in its place on his desk and contemplated his next interrogation of Rajer. He doubted Rajer knew anything at all about Yor's seditious activities. Yor cared about his mother and Rajer and was too smart to implicate them in his plot. When Lek inevitably got nothing, Rajer would be passed on to interrogators who would use severe tactics, which would still amount to no new intelligence. Lek needed to figure out how to slow this potential chain of events. He and Rajer had always been there for one another.

They met as lower classmen in the dorms at Royal University, then moved into an apartment together as roommates the next year. The apartment was dank, dark, and moldy and had its issues with vermin and insects, but it was their place to bring back women and throw parties while they labored through their studies. Rajer was a city dweller. He grew up in the small city of Aven about 140 kilometers from Capitol City.

Lek was from the small town of Rapid Springs which was thousands of kilometers away. His parents were ranchers and Global Assembly loyalists. Even as the environmental crisis accelerated and the value of the ranch declined, and the farming subsidies dried up as government funds were funneled toward research and development for the DOME project, his parents remained steadfast in their fealty. They attempted to instill the same allegiance into Lek, although they encouraged him to pursue his education and focus on a different kind of career as they saw the future of their ranch in jeopardy.

During his time at University, Rajer's parents perished in a high-mortality weather incident brought on by the crisis, which pummeled Aven with 300 km/h winds, destroying their home with no warning. After the funeral, before they returned to University, Lek had the idea for a trip to help Rajer over his grief.

So they hit the road to Lek's parents' ranch. They drove in Lek's two-seat vehicle through the afternoon, the evening, and into the next day, alternating driving while the other slept. The only real hazard was the heat. They had to pass through the Zambar Plains which was experiencing a record-setting heat wave. Lek was unnerved. He worried his vehicle would overheat and rest stops with water only occurred every 150 kilometers on the plains.

To avoid a breakdown, Lek turned off his vehicle's cooling system and rolled down the windows, exposing them to a blast-furnace-like breeze for the majority of the trip.

Rajer had never experienced the wide-open spaces where there was no sign of civilization for hundreds of kilometers at a time except for the occasional rusted mining rig dotting the landscape. He had never seen the spectacular Fell mountain range and its beautiful vistas at the highest altitudes along the road. As the kilometers passed, Rajer's dark, morose mood gave way to his characteristic funny, inquisitive persona.

When they arrived at Lek's parents' house, Lek's mother was aware of Rajer's loss and wanted to do everything she could to lift his spirits. She set up a cot for Rajer in Lek's childhood bedroom. Rajer kidded Lek about the When All Else Fails wallpaper and the posters of his favorite childhood bands tacked up around the room. Lek took it in stride since he was happy that Rajer was reverting to his old self.

Lek's father welcomed Rajer to his home, but didn't say another word to him after that. He didn't understand why his son would spend precious units and drive all the way home to make his friend feel better. He thought Rajer should get over his loss like a man and move on with his life.

During the visit, Lek drove Rajer to a few of his favorite childhood haunts around town. They hiked to a peak where he and his secondary school friends had built a herder monument with rocks, and he and Rajer added a few stones of their own. They went to a Malrap pub where Lek first got drunk with his pals. A few childhood friends who still lived in town met them there. Lek was delighted to see Rajer connecting with his friends and loosening up on Malrap, but he noticed the locals giving Rajer dirty looks. Most of the regulars had lost their ranching jobs, or had been laid off when the local resources were exhausted and the global mining consortiums moved on. Lek was at the bar, buying another round when he was confronted by one of them.

"Who's your friend?" an old acquaintance of Lek's father asked. He stank of Malrap and body odor. He was a veteran of the Separatist Revolts and a miner who hadn't been employed in a long time.

Lek said, "A friend from University."

"We don't appreciate his kind here," the man said and turned to the other people at the bar. "Do we, fellas?" The men at the bar didn't look up from their drinks.

"He's no threat to you," Lek said. "Why don't I buy you a Malrap?"

"I'll take you up on it, Lek, but you should know better than to bring his kind around here."

"Whatever you say," Lek said.

He bought the man a shot of Malrap and was carry-ing a full tray of drinks to his table when the man called out to him, "Don't think because you're at that fancy University that you know better than your elders." Then the man tossed back his shot and added, "I thought your parents taught you better, but those big-city folks must've tainted your morals."

"You have a good day, too," Lek said and returned to Rajer and his friends.

Lek decided to stay sober and didn't drink anymore. Afterward, he and Rajer drove up to a cliff overlooking the town. They sat at the edge in silence as the blood-red sun descended into the horizon. The landscape below was soon shrouded in inky-black darkness, except for the smattering of lights on the horizon from the drilling rigs still operating and the few streetlamps lit as the town attempted to conserve energy. The temperature dropped, coming close to tolerable.

Rajer said, "You know I appreciate this, Lek."

"No problem. I know you'd do the same for me."

"Yeah, probably," Rajer said and laughed.

Lek laughed, too, and said, "Just do one thing for me. I know you grew it in mourning for your parents but shave off that ridiculous beard when we get back to University."

Rajer stroked his beard a few times, then pulled on the hairs coming out of his chin. "You don't think it's sexy? You don't see the ladies flocking to its charms?"

At one point in Koda's history, beards were considered attractive, but in the past fifty years they'd become associated with the worst elements of Kodan society, especially the overgrown kind like Rajer's.

"If you actually trimmed it, but knowing you, I don't see that happening," Lek said. "Maybe when we get back, you can find another way to keep your parents in mind."

"Maybe you're right. You're always looking out for me," Rajer said. "You're a good friend."

As the visit was coming to an end, Lek found it difficult to ignore his father's annoying behavior. He scowled at Lek in passing and mumbled incoherently under his breath in response to questions. His father wasn't much for communication, but this was bizarre even for him. When Lek asked his mother what was bothering his father, and why he'd been scarce around the house during his visit, she said, "Your father has his hands full with the ranch right now."

"It feels like more than that," Lek said.

"If you want to know what's on his mind, then ask him. You're so much like him sometimes," Lek's mother said. "You may get an answer. You might not. You might get an answer you don't want to hear."

Lek waited until his mother said good night and Rajer was asleep. He found his father sitting on the porch in a wooden chair, puffing on his pipe, gazing off into the darkness. He was listening for any disturbance of the livestock by predators. The porch reeked of burned tobacco mixed with his father's scent of rich soil, manure, and sweat.

Lek sat down in the wooden chair next to him and said, "So?"

His father removed his pipe from his mouth, blew out smoke, then banged the pipe's ash out on the chair's armrest and swept it away with the back of his hand. "Hmmm…" his father said, packing the pipe from a pouch on his lap.

"Well, I guess that's as good a place to start as any."

"I guess."

A liquid-fuel lamp burning on the table beside his father didn't give off much light, but Lek could see how tired his father appeared and how he was becoming an old man. Lek hadn't noticed the years showing on him this much before. His father had deep creases in his face and grey hair shooting out from his wide-brimmed, sweat-stained hat.

Lek said, "We haven't spoken much since I've been home."

"I don't have time to play around like you."

"I'm on vacation."

"Vacation?" Lek's father said. "You know how many times I've had a vacation in the past twenty years?"

"None except for the time we drove to Capitol City for my orientation at the University."

"Exactly."

"I did come here to visit you and Mother, so I wouldn't call it a vacation."

"Call it what you like," Lek's father said, "but you haven't been working here."

"You haven't asked."

"Do I have to ask my only son to help out on the ranch that feeds his father and mother?"

"I'm sorry. You're right. I hadn't thought about it that way."

"See, that's the problem," Lek's father said, turning and pointing at him with his pipe. "For an intelligent young man who is doing so well at University and aims to make the Global Assembly proud with his service, you don't think too clearly sometimes."

"I simply thought—"

"No, like I said, you weren't thinking," Lek's father said, standing up and leaning over Lek, still pointing at him with the pipe. He raised his voice, saying, "You come and visit here like some dignitary with your mother waiting on you hand and foot. You know damn well I need help around here. Back in the day, after school when you lived here, you seemed to want to help, but now that you've gone off to the city and your mind is being filled with highfalutin ideas, shoveling shit is beneath you."

Lek's father stood there silent, breathing heavy. Lek smelled the Malrap on his breath. His father was never much of a drinker. He wobbled on his feet, then sat back down.

"I'm sorry, Pops."

"Sorry," Lek's father said and sighed. "Everyone's sorry. Your mother. The Global Assembly who cut off subsidies. The banks who don't want to lend me units."

"I didn't know about that."

"And why would you? Your mother doesn't know." Lek's father sighed again. "And then to top it off, you bring that Shamban scum here with you."

"Shamban scum?"

"Yes, your buddy. I thought I raised you better than that."

"Rajer isn't Shamban. Maybe a distant ancestor was Shamban. Are you referring to his beard?"

"The beard. The pallor of his skin. I don't want that kind in my house. This is a small town. You think I haven't heard about you parading your Shamban buddy around? That reflects on me!"

"Whoa! I always knew you were a globalist, but I've never seen this racist side of you."

"So disrespectful. Call me whatever you like," Lek's father said, raising his voice and pointing his pipe at Lek again. "All I know from what I've been watching on the viewing channels is that the economic problems stem from the impact of the Separatist Revolts and the Shamban terrorists who are still causing problems."

Lek laughed.

His father was not amused and gave Lek a stern look. "You think that's funny?"

"The economic problems and the fact your ranch is barely functional are caused by the environmental crisis spiraling out of control. What do the predators coming down from the mountains and slaughtering your livestock or the fact there's no more grazing land have to do with Shamba?"

"The predator and grazing problems are just part of the natural environmental cycle, and I can't get loans to keep this place running because the Global Assembly has spent so many units on those damn revolts and containing Shamban terrorism."

"You must be watching some crazy viewing channel. The reason you can't get a loan is because this ranch is a lousy investment and your lifestyle will be erased in the next five to ten years by the environmental crisis. The Global Assembly is investing their funds in the DOME project, not doomed agricultural ventures."

"You're being brainwashed by your Shamban pal."

"No, I'm stating fact, not propaganda."

Lek's father jumped up from this chair and began yelling at Lek. "I want that Shamban out of my house at dawn! Do you hear me? I won't have him in my house no more."

"Then I'll leave as well."

"So be it," Lek's father said. "If you're going to side with that Shamban scum over your family then you're no son of mine. You shouldn't come back here or communicate with us anymore."

"What're you saying?"

"You heard me. Now get out of my sight! Get going! Get!"

Lek stood and entered the house. On the other side of the doorway, his mother was waiting. She embraced him.

That was the last time he saw his parents in person, although he and his mother continued comming each other without his father knowing. When the domes were sealed, his parents were left on the outside and he never heard from them again.

Lek opened his viewer and rewatched the scene of Rajer running down the ramp toward the woman. He watched it in slow motion so he could observe the determined look pasted on his friend's face as he lunged at the woman and tackled her off the ramp. "You idiot," Lek said. "You beautiful idiot."

Lek closed the vid and shut his viewer, then thought of something he might be able to do for his friend.

# MAR

Mar was lying on the couch in the morning, reading up on the corporation's cryo-project when she stopped for a moment to look around. Mado had done an incredible job making sure she was comfortable here.

In her first days living in the apartment, whenever Mar woke up after a night's sleep, it took her a few moments to realize she wasn't in her bungalow, although the lag time between feeling she was home and the reality of her current housing situation faded over time. She continued to miss Rajer, who might be dead, and her son, who was somewhere in outer space. She was no longer a practicing med, but CEO of a corporation which challenged her intellect daily when it came to tackling the details of the research projects. On top of it all, she had to take an active part in the planet's political intrigue and was in constant danger. Basically, her life had been rewritten. She was confident she could rise to the occasion, but for now, she felt lonely and out of place.

The doorbell buzzed.

This morning, Gols had scheduled time to inform her about the most important Prevor Industries project. He thought it best to save it for the days leading up to her meeting with the Leader.

Mar said, "Come in, Gols."

Mar could tell from the regimented footsteps coming toward her that it wasn't Gols, but Warver. She had requested they meet at her office later today.

Mar said, "I wasn't expecting you now."

Warver stood beside the couch. "I was nearby. I have a tactical meeting with my men about the memorial you'll be attending at the University tomorrow. I assume you'd want an update on your partner. I know that's important to you, so I thought I'd drop by."

"That's considerate of you," Mar said, feeling a surge of excitement to hear about Rajer. She assumed he was still alive otherwise his death would be all over the viewing channels. "Did your operative contact Rajer's friend Lek Valsted?"

"Unfortunately, she hasn't heard anything."

"Can you follow up or find someone else to make contact?"

"No answer is an answer unto itself," Warver said. "It's not wise to push—that wouldn't be safe for any of the parties involved or their families. Sorry."

Disappointment and sadness swept over Mar. "I guess that's understandable. Thanks for trying."

"Anything else?"

There was a knock at the front door and Mar could distinguish Gols' small strides as he approached.

Mar said, "No, but thanks again for trying."

Gols stopped beside Warver and said, "Commander."

"Gols," Warver said. "I'll take my leave of you two now. Let me know if you need anything else." Then Warver made an about-face and exited.

Gols stood there smiling. "Did you sleep well, Mar Jeps?" Gols always asked that question in the morning. Mar tried to give him a different answer each time to make the ritual less monotonous, and Gols was an easy target when it came to amusing him.

Mar said, "You know how it is. Better than some nights, not as good as others."

Gols giggled with his hand over his mouth. His laugh was like the cooing winged creature called the Kuchekesha. Mar found it endearing. Gols told her how he liked to laugh and how Mado went out of his way to insert humor into their day, so Mar thought it would be a nice thing to do the same. Gols was her closest friend in this new and sometimes unsettling existence. He looked after her needs and appeared to care about her.

Gols said, "Are you ready for the day, Mar? We have a busy one ahead of us."

"Nothing new. When don't we?"

"Well, I can recall—"

"Rhetorical question, Gols."

Gols giggled.

"I'll be ready in a moment." Mar rose from the couch and entered her bedroom where she removed her sleeping apparel and dressed. Her work attire was comfortable clothing from her med-clinic office hours. Mado's employees were all rather casual and appeared happy. That was the atmosphere Mado had cultivated at the Complex, and Gols never told her she needed to wear anything different.

When she was ready and exited the bedroom, Gols

was standing in the exact same spot where she'd left him with his head bowed and his eyes closed.

"You powered down?" Mar said.

Gols giggled. "No," he replied, with emphasis as if Mar was serious. "I was thinking about how to approach the subject we need to tackle today."

"Is it outside of my scientific knowledge?"

"No," Gols said. "Now that the WAEF is finished, it's probably Mado's most secretive project, and he usually takes care of this kind of presentation himself. I've acquainted myself with the details, so I can answer any of your questions."

"I'm sure you'll do fine."

"I appreciate your confidence in me," Gols said. "In this case, you'll hear from Mado, too."

Mar was excited. She'd had no contact with the WAEF since the transmission after Breeze Celebration. That was eleven days ago. "I had no idea we were going to speak with them."

"No, I'm sorry," Gols said. "This is a vid Mado recorded long before they left."

"Oh," Mar said, surprised by her tone of disappointment.

"I'm so sorry, Mar. I should have spoken with more specificity. I know you're looking forward to hearing from your son."

"Please, Gols. No need to apologize. I projected onto what you said. Let's get to work."

In the office, Gols asked Mar to sit in her desk chair. He had obviously been prepping for the presentation:

his open briefcase lay on the couch and three deactivated digi-tablets had been set up on the desk. Gols checked that all the digi-tablets were spaced the same distance from one another and lined up straight. He smiled at Mar as he noticed her observing him. He was being extra compulsive about whatever he'd been tasked to reveal, which made Mar curious.

Mar said, "So this is something extraordinarily important to the corporation, huh?"

"Not only the corporation," Gols said. "But…you'll see…Can I have your attention on this viewing screen?" Then he inserted a memory wafer into the desktop viewer and a blue start-up screen appeared. He clicked play and seconds later, a recording began of Mado sitting in this office at the desk.

"Hello, Mar," Mado said. "I imagine Gols is nervous about this presentation, which is understandable. All will be made clear soon, but consider these two projects as one. If our efforts are successful, our project will mean the survival of the remaining population of Koda. The Global Assembly's blundering has decreased the global population, sadly, but that has made our job easier. I haven't told Yor about the project yet. I need him focused on the WAEF.

"The Leader's project is about the survival of his family, his loyal followers and benefactors. He sees himself as the founder of a ruling dynasty. In Malrap-sodden moments, he revealed his obsession with passing Kodan leadership on to his sons. You can use this project to your advantage over him. The public would be shocked to learn about it.

Just don't push the Leader too hard. He is a vengeful man and violence comes easily to him. You've seen his wrath in the past with Tetrick's father and Tetrick so tread lightly. A man with his ego and power lashes out with impunity. I have faith in you, Mar. Do what you think is best."

The vid returned to the blue start-up screen and Gols removed the wafer. "Any questions?"

"From this buildup, I'm positive I'll have plenty once it's explained, but none at the moment.'

Gols reached down and activated the digi-tablet on the far left of the desk. "Please turn around."

The digi-tablet interfaced with the large viewing screen behind the desk, which lit up and revealed an aerial foto of a mountainous region. A slide show commenced with each foto zooming closer to a dozen massive warehouse structures in the valley of a remote mountain range. There was nothing around the facility except for the roads leading in and out. A fence surrounded the entire facility. Then slides displayed a series of images: a vehicle entering through a security gate flanked by armed guards; flatbed trucks the size of large bungalows laden with machinery moving about the compound and entering the buildings. As the slideshow stopped, Gols stepped in front of the screen.

Gols said, "This compound resides in the most remote area of the Mauan mountain range and is a high-security project in coordination with the Global Assembly."

"But what is this project about?"

"Spaceships." Gols activated the middle digi-tablet and as a vid scrolled through mechanical drawings, Mar could tell these ships were based on the design of the WAEF. The dimensions written on the drawings of the exterior noted these ships were about ten times larger than the WAEF. The mechanical images dissolved to a banner reading "Control Room," then cut to an animation of a hi-tech control room with people manning their stations and windows looking into outer space. The animation moved through the room to a lift at the rear which transported the viewer down to another level and followed a hallway into a cavernous cafeteria where people were eating, then turned back down the hallway and into another lift. On the next level, the animation explored quarters for two crew members with enough room for two beds and two desks, then exited that room and went further down the hall into larger quarters with living area, office, and bedroom, possibly for an officer. The image dissolved to a banner reading "Engine Room," then cut to an animation of a enormous space filled with engine conduits, much larger than and different in design from the WAEF, and people at control consoles around the edges of the room. The image dissolved again into a chamber of metallic tubes, ten floors of them, hundreds lining each floor, then the animation zoomed toward the tubes and zipped by displays of EKG readouts and people's names, ages, and ID#s, then panned up to a realistic drawing of a person's frozen face inside the tube.

Mar was startled. The animation ended. "I was just reading up on the cryo-project this morning. So this is its application?"

"Part of it. That's why I gave you that prospectus of the cryo-project a few days ago," Gols said. "These are the spaceships the Global Assembly is building for the wealthiest and most loyal, so they can leave the masses behind while the planet dies of the crisis."

"I don't understand," Mar said. "Why would Mado facilitate a project that backstabs the Kodan people? That doesn't make sense."

"First of all, Mado told you in his introduction that this project gave him immense power over the Leader, and that it was one of two projects," Gols said, sounding a little annoyed that Mar would question Mado. "Let me show you what's happening in Shamba and you'll understand everything better, I hope."

Gols was correct. Mar was confused, but she had a feeling Mado wouldn't let her down.

Gols activated the final digi-tablet on the desk and said, "Here we go."

The screen presented a silent vid of a cam traveling across a desolate landscape in a vehicle, heading toward a high-peaked mountain range in the distance. Mar could tell this was Shamba from the abandoned boarded up farms passing by. With each cut in the vid, the vehicle moved closer and closer to the mountains, then turned off road until the foot of the mountains was merely a few hundred meters away where it stopped and the picture went black. The vid started again, with the cam now handheld, entering a cave, proceeding down a passageway surrounded by people in brown Shamban military uniforms with their faces hidden by scarves and carrying stun weapons. Then the vid cut to snaking through a work area filled with machinery, forklifts, and people in coveralls and construction helmets, to a railing where the cam focused on a gigantic underground cavern. In the distance were a half-dozen colossal spaceships which were clearly different in design from the ones she'd seen in the previous presentation. The ships on the vid were in various stages of construction, ranging from bare-bones to mid-completion, so Mar couldn't tell what the completed ships would look like. Netting stretched above the entire area where the ships resided, possibly to keep any rock fall from damaging the work. Then the vid stopped.

"Is that a natural cavern or man-made?" Mar said.

"A little of both," Gols said. "The WAEF was supposed to arrive in Shamba and that's where Yor would have become aware of this project and been informed of the Global Assembly project. They are sister projects, if you will." Gols put his fist up to his mouth and cleared his throat. "When it was revealed to the Leader in a high-security report that the dome collapses were the result of flawed design, the Leader approached Mado, saying he'd found a way of funding space travel and he'd like Mado to lead the project. Of course, Mado took him up on it. He told the Leader he'd always wanted a crack at space travel and he'd learned quite a bit from Yorlik the Great.

The Leader told Mado he only wanted to build a few spaceships so Mado decided to run his own parallel project to save the rest of the planet's population. He charged the Global Assembly nine times what it actually cost Prevor Industries to build the facility in a remote location like the Mauan mountains. He made sure the books weren't audited. Then he used the profits to build his own secret facility in Shamba. When the government facility was complete, Mado began overcharging for ship construction, parts, and tech support to continue funding the Shamban ships.

"As we all know, the Global Assembly considers Shamba their greatest adversary. The Leader decided long ago that instead of pouring military resources into suppressing the region, he'd just cut them off from any global trade once their dome, which was smaller than all the rest, was sealed. That would effectively deal with the Global Assembly's perceived problem because the majority of the Shamban population would die off from the crisis.

"So Mado saved the Shamban people by creating a safe, thriving environment in the caverns under their largest mountain range, which contains a vast underground water source known only to the locals. As long as the Shambans didn't make trouble, then the Global Assembly was happy to leave them alone, and Mado was provided with a vast workforce to build ships."

"That's brilliant," Mar said. "But will there be enough ships?"

"Mado likes to say he has a wait-and-see attitude on that. His plan is to keep building until the time comes to leave, then see how many can be saved. Each ship being built in Shamba carries approximately 85,000 people."

"How many ships have been built to completion?"

"None on the Global Assembly side. False malfunctions in new tech have served to further finance the

Shamban project," Gols said. "In Shamba, there are five completed and ten in various phases of completion."

"A cunning move on Mado's part."

"He is a genius," Gols said. "Before you meet with the Leader, I'll brief you on exactly what he knows about his project and what new information you'll be able to tell him."

"Perfect," Mar said. "Do these projects have names?"

"The Global Assembly project is designated XAF-758," Gols said, "Mado's Shamba project is called Project FoFu, which stands for—"

"Foreseeable Future." Mar shook her head and laughed. "By the way, you said something about the dome collapses occurring because of flawed design, and that the Leader knows about it."

"Yes,"

"So the arrests of those terrorists for the collapses and their executions was a way of tricking the Kodan people?"

"Yes," Gols said, "I have the report on the flawed design here somewhere. When you're interested, I'll get that for you."

"Another thing to hold over the Leader?"

"That might infuriate him. From what Mado has said, the Leader is sensitive about the failure of the domes. Bringing up the report would be like rubbing his face in it and knowing about the spaceships kind of implies you know about the domes."

# ORN

Orn struck the door with his fist as hard as possible to startle and frighten the person inside. As he hammered away, he examined the hi-tech Prevor Industries security system installed on this Royal University building door. He'd seen the tech before but noted that no normal academic could afford it apart from the one with a personal connection to the Prevor Industries CEO.

He continued knocking until the door swung open to reveal an indignant Mellick Zonor saying, "What is it?" When Mellick caught a glimpse of Orn and the outrage on his face dissolved to fear, Orn couldn't have wished for a better response.

"I think you probably have a good idea why I'm here," Orn said, stepping past Mellick into the office. "You can close the door now."

"I don't have time for this. I'm prepping for something and I'm in a rush."

Orn observed that Mellick was wearing a black suit with a black tie. He walked over to the windows on the other side of the room and gazed out onto the campus green. "Quite the view. This is an upgrade from that glorified closet you used to call an office."

"Really, I need you to leave."

"Brave yet selfish words. Have you forgotten about your family?"

 *Howard Libes*

"Look," Mellick said, approaching Orn, "I'm not going to be held hostage by you anymore. I love my family, but they wouldn't want me to stop being myself. They said whatever was necessary to save themselves in that vid, and why would I believe you'd stick to any bargain?" Mellick lifted his viewer and held it out toward Orn. "You have something to show me?"

Orn cackled and walked past Mellick to the middle of the room, then turned around to face him. "Seems like this big office may have caused your balls to drop, and I have nothing to show you."

"So why are you here?'

"So rude to an old friend."

Mellick blew out air from his nose in exasperation. "I have a memorial service to attend."

"I'm aware you're going to an event to memorialize a Kodan traitor on a campus subsidized by the Global Assembly. I should arrest everyone in attendance," Orn said making sure he was standing between Mellick and the door.

"Do what you will," Mellick said, heading toward the door. He attempted to get around Orn who blocked his path, shoving Mellick back.

"You're not going anywhere until I get answers to a few questions."

"And if I don't answer, then what?"

"I'll arrest you and you'll definitely miss this travesty you call a memorial."

"You'll arrest me on what grounds?" Mellick said. "Consorting with a man you shot out of the sky?"

"I wouldn't put it so dramatically," Orn said. "I'd call it consorting with a known enemy of Koda and conspiring to hack Global-Assembly servers. Although you did benefit from your friend's death so maybe I should let you go about your business, then put the word out that you're working with us. Vanderlord's Shamban whore wouldn't like that one bit."

"Nobody would believe you, and this appointment as chair of the department could be temporary. I was given the position based on Yor's recommendation and the Dean still needs to make it official," Mellick said. "So, let's cut the crap and tell me what you want. Arrest me if you like. It'd be better than standing here listening to you."

"I doubt that," Orn said. "I'm actually thinking if the Dean leaves you in this office, you'll be in a position to lead me to more members of your Movement cell since the chatter among you seems to be increasing again." Orn was pleased when he saw concern spreading across Mellick's face.

Mellick removed his comm from his pocket. "I'm on the clock here so get to the point."

"All right," Orn said. "Was Mado Prevor on the WAEF with Yor Vanderlord when it took off from the Arena?"

"How would I know?" Mellick said, making a quick move around Orn toward door.

Orn put out one arm and blocked Mel, then pressed his other hand against the door to hold it closed.

Mellick said, "I already told you I'm running late."

"Mado Prevor was last seen boarding the WAEF. Did Prevor leave the Arena with Vanderlord?" Orn said, putting his back up against the door.

"So Mado Prevor is missing?"

"I didn't say that."

"Then why don't you question him?"

"I'm asking you."

"I have no idea," Mellick said. "So now that we have that settled, I'd like you to leave. Good day."

Orn found Mellick Zonor's new attitude toward him galling. All of a sudden, this spineless academic had grown a backbone. Orn's first impulse was to break one of Mellick's limbs to teach him who was boss, but he had another idea. He grabbed Mellick by the throat and threw him up against the door, then applied pressure until Mellick was choking.

"You've already told me Mado Prevor was on the WAEF—it was all over your face. And while we're being so honest with one another, I should probably tell you that your sister is dead after some special treatment by a platoon of soldiers and your mother was so distressed when she heard the news, she hanged herself."

Orn enjoyed watching the look on Mellick Zonor's face change from fear at being out of air to distress at giving up Prevor and grief over his sister and mother. "Now!" Orn said. "Good day!" He released his hold on Mellick who collapsed to the floor, then Orn stepped over Mellick and exited the room, closing the door behind him. He leaned his back up against the door and closed his eyes, basking in the memory of Mellick gasping for air and weeping at the same time. He felt a rush of satisfaction at the effectiveness of his tactics.

"Are you going to arrest that criminal?" Orn opened his eyes to Harmin Leeno standing in his office doorway, pointing toward Mellick Zonor's office.

Orn laughed. "He's more useful to me where he is."

Harmin yelled, "In possession of my job?" His face was red with anger.

"Lower your voice," Orn said, striding down the hall toward Harmin, who backpedaled into his office. When Orn arrived at the doorway, he shoved Harmin who fell over a pile of books. Orn closed the door behind him. The office was the exact same size as Mellick Zonor's old office. Cabinets lined the walls, overflowing two-to-three deep with books on each shelf and yet more books stacked in front of them. The office had no window and reeked of mold.

Harmin struggled to his feet, clutching at himself. Orn's actions had created the results he was looking to achieve. Fear was tattooed on the man's face.

"I didn't mean anything by it. No disrespect," Harmin stammered, his voice quaking.

"Don't ever raise your voice to me," Orn said, raising his own voice and poking Harmin in the chest after each word. Harmin began shaking with fright. Orn was enjoying himself but decided it might be time to back off. "Relax, Harmin. Go sit down at your desk." Orn was concerned the man might pee himself and wanted him as far away as possible.

Harmin scurried around the desk, dropping into his chair.

Orn said, "They really did a number on you."

"I don't know what you're talking about."

"Come on, Harmin. It's nothing to be embarrassed about. I read the report on your interrogation. The GSS boys were a little tough on you, but you made it through like a man. I would've stopped them, but you're my informant and I didn't want anyone to know. It's terrible what Yor Vanderlord and your colleagues have done to you."

"Yes."

"Mellick Zonor is your boss because of it. It's a disgrace. It really is," Orn said, watching Harmin getting upset at what he was saying.

"Can you have someone put in a word for me?" Harmin said. "A Global Assembly rep or the Leader even?"

"The Leader won't get involved. This is far below his station and it isn't my jurisdiction, either, but I'll see if I can find someone to help you." Orn didn't intend on doing anything. "Just take some deep breaths and remember you're a valuable asset to the Global Assembly."

"But I—"

"I know you feel like you've been forgotten. I mean, look at this office," Orn said and chuckled. "But have a little patience. It's taken some time, but we've pretty much eliminated all your competition, so sooner or later you'll be in that big office down the hall."

"I've been waiting decades already."

"Has it been that long? Well, that's not all our fault. Turns out you're not the easiest man to get along with and Mado Prevor blocked your plans," Orn said. "By the way, have you heard anything about Mado Prevor lately?"

"Like what?"

"Has he communicated with Mellick Zonor or Vanderlord's Shamban whore?"

Harmin laughed. "I haven't heard anything. Has something happened to Mado Prevor?"

"Nothing for you to concern yourself about."

"I'd like to be in the loop."

"You'll be in the loop when I say you're in the loop," Orn said, raising his voice and stepping toward Harmin, who leaned back in his chair and caught himself before he fell over backward.

"All right. I understand."

"You'll comm me if you hear anything, correct?"

"Of course."

"Because if I hear you've been holding out on me, you're not going to like the consequences. Those interrogators who worked you over were child's play compared to what I'd do to you." Orn couldn't help himself. Harmin Leeno was such an easy mark. "Do I make myself clear?"

"Yes," Harmin said, his voice shaking again. "For the good of the globe."

"Right," Orn said, opening the office door as the smell of urine wafted from Harmin's direction. He looked up and down the hall to see if anyone was coming. "Now, pull yourself together, clean yourself up, and get to that memorial. You don't want to be late. You're not beloved like Ador Wint, and I bet more than half the people around here blame you for his death like they do for Tetrick Vanderlord's." Then Orn stepped out of the office and slammed the door shut. He couldn't stop the smile spreading across his face. He loved his job. Now he headed to Ador Wint's memorial to spy on the crowd and delight in the results of his work.

# MAR

The memorial service took place in a lecture hall which had served for decades as Ador Wint's classroom. Mar sat at the back. She didn't want her security contingent being the center of attention.

Onstage was a foto of Ador, enlarged so even the people in the back row of the packed 700-seat hall could see it clearly. The foto was from around thirty years ago when Mar met Tetrick. Ador possessed a curly head of dark hair, wire-rim glasses, and a beard. He always had the look of a person with an astounding thought in the back of his mind, but what usually emerged would make you fall down laughing.

Colleague after colleague took the stage, regaling the audience with personal stories of Ador's generosity, intelligence, compassion, and sense of humor. They talked about how he perceived the tragedy of the Kodan existence like no other citizen on the planet. He seemed to have been supportive of everyone he ever knew and went out of his way to create connections between people who might never have met otherwise. That was surely the case when it came to Mar's experience. Ador was key in introducing her to Rajer. He shepherded the teen Yor through his first years at the University when Yor had few friends due to his age. He attempted to shield Yor from the truth of his father's treatment at the hands of the

    *Howard Libes*

Global Assembly while others in the Movement wanted Yor to know right away. When Ador saw he would lose that battle, he thought it best to break the news to Yor himself before others did.

Mellick Zonor took the stage, looking haggard like he'd been crying, which made sense at this event. His voice sounded raspier than usual. He wore a green scarf which didn't fit with his black attire. His speech told the story of Yor introducing him to Ador when he first arrived on campus from his teaching position in Nor.

"Of course, I knew of him already. I'd respected his academic writings for years, and I have to admit some hero worship on my part. Just meeting him was overwhelming. I told him I made my mark as a SEEDER-program scholar at a small college where I was a big man on a rather insignificant campus. Now I was here in this prestigious place of learning, the center for intellectual discussion on Koda, and I was anxious about being an insignificant man on a major campus. He stood there listening and then laughed. I wasn't sure how to take it. I'd poured my heart out about my deepest fear to this man I admired, and he was laughing at me. Then he said in that sincere, cutting to the heart of the matter way Ador possessed, 'First of all, we know you're a bumpkin…'"

Everyone in the lecture hall laughed.

"'…but that's a good thing. Embrace who you truly are. There's nothing to fear. Now that you're here, you have room to aspire to greater things.' The meaning wasn't lost on me: remain true to yourself and you'll overcome your fears. I carry it with me to this very day. In losing

Ador, Koda is now missing a rare commodity: a person filled with magnanimity who can tell the truth with humility and humor. I will miss him, but I'm delighted we're renaming this classroom the Wint Lecture Hall. In a way, he will always be with us. Thanks for listening." Mel walked offstage to applause.

A few other people spoke, but Mar hardly heard them. She was thinking how Mel had not only lost Ador, but also believed Yor had been killed and Insol was still in a coma. Although Mar considered it unwise, she still wanted to tell him Yor was alive.

When the service ended, Ador's partner Shika was surrounded by people. There hadn't been a funeral service since Ador was cremated, so this was the only opportunity for people to express their condolences. Mar hurried out of the building and stood near the doorway. She thought this might be a better place to meet Shika. She wanted to remain inconspicuous but couldn't escape the fact that she was the mother of an infamous traitor or hero, depending on your point of view. Warver was doing his best to keep his men out of sight, too, but the contingent of ex-military personnel forming a perimeter around her stood out on campus. Warver himself stood a few meters away from Mar, talking to his team via audio implant.

People leaving the memorial service streamed past her and gathered in front of the building, chatting with each other. Mar saw Harmin exit the hall and he approached her even though he was aware she disliked him.

"Mar! Fancy seeing you here."

"Harmin, what can I do for you?" Mar said.

Warver took note of the interaction.

Harmin was wearing an overcoat and gave off a rank odor. "I just wanted to say I'm sorry about Yor. He was a fine young man. So tragic losing him and Ador in such a short span of time. And then the incident with Rajer— you must be beside yourself."

"I'm holding it together running a quadrillion-unit corporation," Mar said. "You must be excited?"

"Why would I be excited at such tragic circumstances?"

"You're the obvious candidate for the department chair."

"Oh, who can think of such things in times like these?"

"You could. Knowing you."

"I don't know what to say, Mar. You think so little of me."

"That's about right."

"Well, good day," Harmin said, walking off in a huff. Mar could've sworn she saw a smile forming on his face as he turned away.

Warver took a few steps toward her. "That looked unpleasant."

"Just an old acquaintance I'm not fond of, but I'm fine."

That's when Mar saw Lek heading away from the building. She did her best to catch up with him, winding her way through the crowd. This was the last place she would've expected to see him. Lek and Rajer had met the older Ador when they were lower classmen and Ador was working on his advanced degree. Lek was once close to Ador, but the GSS wouldn't sanction Lek consorting with a principal member of the anti-DOME movement.

According to Rajer, Lek always regretted cutting ties with Ador.

He finally slowed his pace and Mar chased him down, grabbing his shoulder.

"Mar," Lek said. "Great to see you, and I see you brought your protection with you."

Warver was standing a few meters away again. "Yes, that's my lot in life now," Mar said. "I'm surprised to see you. Won't your supervisors have a problem with you being here and then talking to me?"

"I was given clearance to attend under the guise of monitoring the crowd. There's just some paperwork to fill out when I get back to the office. And Ador isn't a threat anymore."

"Your people have seen to that."

"Come now, Mar," Lek said, looking uncomfortable. "That's not fair."

"I believe it is," Mar said, "although it's not your fault directly and I don't mean to take it out on you. Just been a tough time recently with Yor and Rajer."

"Yes, Yor and Rajer," Lek said, embracing Mar, then whispering in her ear. "Rajer is alive and well. I'm doing my best to make sure he stays that way."

Mar hugged him back with such enthusiasm, she heard Lek groan as she whispered, "Thank you, Lek. Now I understand why you risked coming here. I won't forget it."

"I appreciate it—but please don't tell anyone and you didn't hear it from me," Lek whispered. "Tell your man I heard from his operative, too, and not to try it again, it's not safe."

Mar let go of Lek and held his forearms. "You don't know how I've…" Mar started crying.

Lek put his forefinger to his lips. Mar stopped speaking and wiped away her tears.

Lek said, "Looks like there's somebody else who wants to talk to you." He gestured with his head to Mar's right.

Mar turned and noticed Mel standing beside her. He stepped forward and hugged her. When they separated, Mar said, "Great to see you, Mel. Have you met…?" She turned to where Lek had been standing but he was gone.

"Who was that?" Mel said.

"An old friend of Rajer's, but I guess he had to run," Mar said, looking around the crowd and not seeing Lek anywhere. "How are you faring?"

"With Yor and Ador gone and Insol a long way from recovery, it's been quiet around the department except for today." Mel pointed straight ahead of him. In the distance, Orn Shiv was leaning against a tree observing the people leaving the lecture hall. His hands were deep in his pockets, and he had a wide smile on his face.

"What's he doing here?" Mar said.

"Plying his trade. He made a visit to the department, wanting to know about Mado Prevor." Mel pulled aside his green scarf for a moment. His throat was black and blue.

"You should have that examined." Mar reached out to get a better look under the scarf, but Mel grabbed her hand, which caused Warver to take a few steps toward them.

"I'm fine and we don't want to make a scene at Ador's memorial," Mel said, letting go of her hand.

"You're right. You should still have it examined, though. That man is a monster."

"That's putting it kindly."

"And now, after all the changes, you're left with Harmin. That can't be much of a consolation prize. He's probably aiming for Yor's job."

"Maybe a person in your new position can apply their influence?" Mel said. "A contribution would help."

"I understand. Leave it to me," Mar said. "Sorry I haven't commed you lately. You must be hurting."

"I'm working through it. Sometimes bad news isn't what it seems," Mel said, taking Mar's hand and squeezing it, then winking at her.

*Does he know Yor is alive?* Mar thought. "I need to visit Insol. Have you seen her lately?"

"Yes, she's been out of the induced coma for a while, but she's got a long recovery ahead of her."

"The whole thing is a shame," Mar said. "A damn shame."

"None of us had any delusions about coming out of this unscathed."

"I just hope Yor's actions weren't in vain."

"Me, too," Mel said. "There's other things in the works, though."

"Such as?"

"I'll let you know," Mel said. "We'll keep in touch. I've got to run—I have a class to teach." Mel gave Mar a parting hug and headed off.

Mar watched him leave. She told Warver about Lek's message, then pointed at Orn who noticed and waved at them.

"Yes, I spotted him earlier," Warver said. "Do you want me to go over and speak with him? I'd be glad to put Orn in his place."

"You two on a first-name basis?"

"Unfortunately, we go way back."

"I'd like to hear about that sometime."

"I don't know, it's not pretty."

"I can't imagine anything involving that man being pretty. Leave him. Let him think he's being useful," Mar said as she looked around for Shika but couldn't find her. "We don't have time to wait around. I'll stop by Shika's house in a few days. I'm sure she's overwhelmed right now. I have to prepare for my meeting with the Leader this evening."

Mar ignored Orn Shiv as she passed him with her security contingent surrounding her, but she observed Warver slowing to salute him.

# ORN

Orn watched as Mar Jeps, Wel Warver, and the Prevor Industries security personnel walked away from the building where Ador Wint's memorial had taken place. He relished the sadness he'd caused, how one simple action had created so much pleasure for himself. Looking around at the crowd, Orn found no real surprises among the attendees. He even predicted Lek Valsted would be here and his contact with Mar Jeps interested Orn the most. Valsted was a loyal GSS man and although his connections to suspicious elements had always been part of his file, that didn't deter his superiors from constantly promoting him. Orn would need to take a closer look.

As Mar Jeps' group passed by, Warver took up the rear. He stopped, turned around to stare at Orn and smiled, then he put his hand up to salute Orn and held it there. His smile widened, then Warver completed the salute, turned on his heels, and walked off. Orn knew exactly what Warver meant by his actions and he was furious.

The last time Orn wore a military uniform, he was a lieutenant leading a Global Assembly company protecting an outpost in an unpopulated region of Mlimoa bordering Shamba. His orders were to hold the outpost and comm his superior officer if there was any activity around the garrison. He was told not to leave the post without a direct order or make a show of force unless fired upon.

    *Howard Libes*

Standard operating procedure for that sort of post, but the specific orders were given for Orn's benefit. As Commander Plemso moved higher in the military command structure, Orn no longer reported to him directly. Orn became infamous for running his men counter to procedure, considering his superiors buffoons unworthy of their positions of authority. Commander Plemso regularly bailed Orn out of any disciplinary action, and before Orn was reposted somewhere else, Commander Plemso made sure Orn's record was wiped of any charges.

Commander Plemso had come to the end of his rope, though. He warned Orn that this new posting was a final chance for him to fit into the military command structure. Orn's superior officer would be none other than Colonel Warver. Orn had alienated all the other officers and nobody else wanted Orn under their command. Colonel Warver owed Plemso for his most recent commission and took on Orn as a favor. Their dislike for one another had never waned so Warver placed Orn in the least desirable post under his command, far from his sight. Orn had no other choice but to take the position. Disappointing Commander Plemso was the last thing he wanted to do.

On the Shamban-Mlimoan border, the post was in a treeless, shadeless high-desert landscape which was searing hot during the days. The temperature hardly dropped at night and the darkness never lasted long enough. Nothing lived in this terrain except for sparse desert flora and the creatures that stayed underground during the day and hunted for morsels above ground at night. Situated on a ridge, the view from the outpost was about 20 kilometers in all directions. Anything larger than desert vermin would be picked up by sentries with binoculars, thermal imaging, and vidcams.

Orn chastised his men for complaining about the posting. He told them they were doing the bidding of the Global Assembly and they should do it with pride, but after a month of this duty, Orn was in a foul mood.

One day, two large trucks were spotted in Shamban territory moving parallel to their position. Orn commed command regarding the situation and was told to stand by for orders. Most of Orn's men were restless and had no desire to wait around while the potential insurgents got away, but Orn preached patience. Then the trucks changed direction and headed toward the border about twelve kilometers north of them where there was no official border crossing. Orn commed command once again to apprise them of their new observations. He was told once again to hold position and await orders.

Colonel Warver's order not to make a move without instructions was clear, but Orn couldn't sit around and wait as this potential threat approached the border under his supervision. Orn directed the bulk of his troops to suit up and his comm man to relay any messages from command while leaving a small force to guard the outpost. He gathered his forces before they jumped into their two troop carriers and two armored vehicles and spoke to them about being vigilant for any suspicious behavior, but they weren't to take any offensive action unless given the order by him.

As their convoy approached the Shamban trucks, Orn decided he would simply detain the vehicles and their drivers and wait on his prescribed actions from command. That seemed like the best way to proceed. They easily stopped the trucks which were loaded down with weapons and explosives. The drivers, who looked Shamban and were dressed in civilian clothing, possessed no travel papers or manifests for the cargo. They pled innocence and said they were hired for the job with no idea what the trucks contained. Orn's men cuffed the drivers and placed them in the back of one of their own vehicles.

Hours passed with no orders from command. Orn felt like his men were vulnerable in their current position. The solution seemed simple. Bring the trucks and drivers back to the outpost and await word from command. So he ordered two of his men to drive the seized trucks back to the outpost.

As his convoy drove back, they received a comm from the outpost saying two more trucks were following the same trajectory across the landscape as the others. Orn ordered the troop carrier with the two drivers back to the outpost with an armored vehicle as escort for the two seized trucks, then Orn headed back to intercept the two newly spotted trucks with half his original deployment. He told his comm man to inform military command of their current status and ask for instructions on how to proceed.

Orn sat in the passenger seat of a troop carrier with the incoming vehicles in sight and thought nothing felt right about this situation. This was too sporadic for any sort of invasion and it didn't resemble a clandestine maneuver, either. Orn couldn't wrap his head around it.

Command finally responded to hold off engaging any of the trucks until more men and air support were brought in, but before Orn could tell his driver to turn around and comm the accompanying vehicle, both of the incoming trucks stopped short of where Orn's men had detained the first two. Two men wearing brown Shamban Separatist uniforms jumped out of each truck and shot rockets at his vehicles.

His driver tried his best to avoid the rocket as it zipped past the cab and struck the rear of their vehicle. The explosion blew them into the air and landed them on their side on fire. Above Orn, the unconscious driver was still strapped into his seat and the comm was shattered to pieces. He could hear the screams of his men in the back of the vehicle being cooked to death by the flames. Orn realized his arm was broken and he probably had a concussion. Through the shattered windshield, he saw the enemy trucks pull up closer and more men wearing Shamban uniforms leapt from the vehicles firing their weapons. Then Orn passed out.

When Orn regained consciousness, the pain in his arm was excruciating and his head was throbbing. He unbuckled himself and bit down on his lip as his body weight fell onto his broken arm, then repositioned himself. He could smell the burned bodies of his men in the smoldering wreckage of the vehicle. It was night outside and he waited for a short time to see if any lights appeared or he heard any sounds. When he was sure the enemy had dispersed, he bit down on his lip again, painfully shifted his weight, then moved his legs so he could kick at what remained of the windshield over and over again until it broke free of its frame and dropped away.

Orn took a deep breath and bit down on his lip once more as he lifted himself onto the dashboard, crouched to squeeze through the windshield space, and then fell to the ground. Shooting pain and waves of nausea washed over him. He breathed in the clean air of the high desert until the nausea passed, then struggled to his feet and made his way over to one of his slain soldiers. He took the soldier's weapon and ammo. He drank down the contents of the soldier's canteen and found another to quench his thirst. Once he was hydrated and feeling clearheaded, he took in the scene before him. The dead soldiers' bodies closest to their vehicles were burned and shot. Orn surmised they escaped the flames only to be gunned down by the Shambans. The dead soldiers furthest from their vehicles appeared to have put up a fight, firing on the enemy. He spotted dead Shambans in the distance.

Orn suspended his broken arm with a weapon sling, removed a canteen and binoculars from another of his dead soldiers, then took a portable light from their vehicle and began the trek on foot back to the outpost. From the position of the stars, he estimated he'd make it to the outpost before dawn. On the walk, every other step pained him from an injury to his right side. He thought about the scene behind him and the deaths of his men. He second-guessed his strategy in approaching both groups of trucks and wondered whether he should have stuck to his orders after all. He went over his decisions again and again to keep his mind off the heat until he saw the lights of the outpost in the distance and spied it with his binoculars.

The four Shamban trucks were parked in the compound, and there was a pile of corpses, some of his soldiers, at the far end of the outpost. Shamban rebels guarded the entrance to the biggest tent in the compound which was used as the outpost's mess tent. Orn assumed the rest of his men were being held there.

This appeared to be the Shambans' plan all along. Lure them out, thin their numbers, and take the compound. The rebels were now fully armed with their own munitions. He wasn't sure how to proceed. He estimated the Shambans at over two dozen and he was armed with one weapon. He had no way to comm his higher-ups and the edges of the horizon were brightening as dawn approached.

At that moment, two air-battle cruisers flew overhead and strafed the outpost. The Shambans fired back with their weapons and handheld rockets. The cruisers turned around for another pass and the mess tent exploded. There would be no prisoners. The cruisers returned at a higher altitude and Orn knew exactly why. He threw himself down on the ground as a series of deafening explosions rocked the landscape. Orn lay there and didn't get up for quite some time. He didn't want to look. Those soldiers in the tent were his responsibility and he had failed them.

Then he heard footsteps coming toward him and before he could look up, a boot kicked him in the ribs. He tumbled over onto his injured side and broken arm and screamed in pain. Orn heard someone say, "He's one of ours, Colonel."

"On your feet, soldier," a familiar voice said.

Orn used his good arm and his legs to reach a standing position. In front of him stood Colonel Warver surrounded by a handful of armed soldiers.

"Looky what we have here," Warver said. "Look closely, boys. Seems like the sole survivor is the commanding officer of this grand shitshow."

Orn snapped to attention, clicked his heels together, and reflexively attempted to salute with his broken arm, groaning in pain, then snapped a salute with his other arm. In the midst of this disaster, Warver was the last person Orn wanted to see. "Colonel Warver, sir," Orn said.

"Lieutenant Shiv." Warver saluted in return.

Weapons fire rang out from the direction of the garrison. Orn, Warver, and his soldiers took cover and readied their weapons. Orn observed the scene. The outpost buildings, tents, and lookout towers had been vaporized by what Orn assumed were incendo-pulse bombs dropped from the cruisers. There was only an empty pit where they once stood and the Shamban trucks were just burning frames.

When the weapons fire ceased, there was silence for a moment, then the whoop of victory from Warver's soldiers who had been fighting in the outpost. Chatter came over comms confirming that the Shambans who had survived the bombing had been neutralized.

"Those Shambans are tough to stomp out," Warver said. "Aren't they, Shiv?"

"Yes, sir, they are, sir."

"Looks like they put one over on you, didn't they?"

"I wouldn't say that, sir."

"Then what would you say happened here, soldier?"

Orn stood there in silence. His first response was reflex, in defense of himself. Warver's statement about the Shamban victory was true and he was aware Orn had no answer, so he let the silence go on and on until it became awkward. Then Warver said, "That's what I thought." He shook his head in disgust and turned to the soldier closest to him. "Take the lieutenant to the med. Lieutenant Shiv, we'll talk at HQ. Me and my men have mopping up to do."

"You might want to check the vehicles—"

"You mean the ones about eight kilometers from here? My men are on it. We saw them on our flyover," Warver said. "You're dismissed for now, Lieutenant Shiv."

Orn saluted Warver who held his salute in return and observed Orn with derision. "You've made quite a mess here, Shiv. You'll need to look into another line of work," Warver said, then finished his salute.

Warver was correct. A board of inquiry found Orn guilty of disobeying orders and causing the deaths of his men. The prosecution called for a court-martial and a lengthy prison sentence, but Commander Plemso stepped in, pulling political strings. Prison and court-martial were taken off the table in return for an honorable discharge if he resigned his military commission.

As a civilian, Orn was hard on himself. He had failed the only person who ever put faith in him. He had no direction. He began going to Malrap bars, getting drunk and provoking fights with the patrons. He picked weaker opponents. He liked it that way, because he could choose how to damage them. He broke their noses and limbs before knocking them unconscious. He even gouged out one opponent's eye with a broken glass. He maimed them without murdering them, then got arrested and spent days upon days in local law enforcement lockups. He started fights there, too. When he was freed, it didn't take him long to become a prisoner again. He lost track of time.

Then one day, upon release from yet another stretch in jail, a field commander's vehicle awaited him outside. A driver held open the back door and inside, Orn seated himself across from Commander Plemso who said, "Orn. You smell like crap. You look awful, too. Is that vomit and blood on your clothes?"

Orn said, "It's not my blood, sir."

Commander Plemso laughed.

Orn felt the vehicle pull away from the curb. "Where are we going, sir?"

"That depends on you."

Orn noticed that the commander smelled of expensive cologne and hairspray. His hair had been recently cut, probably only hours before. He wore an overcoat with the buttons undone over his dress uniform. "Shall I assume you haven't heard the news?"

"No, they had me in solitary so I wouldn't hurt the other prisoners."

Commander Plemso laughed again. "Same old Orn," he said. "The Separatist Revolts are coming to an end."

"We've beaten the Shambans?"

"We have control of the region and in the peace treaty, we've convinced the other regions to isolate them, so they won't be a problem going forward."

"Sorry I wasn't there to help. I failed you, sir."

"Yes, you did," Commander Plemso said. "Yes, you did. Now look at you. You're pathetic. Weak and pathetic. You should be ashamed of yourself. You've sunk to the bottom of the barrel."

"I know. I failed you, sir," Orn said, a wave of sadness washing over him like he hadn't felt since his mother died. "Just drop me off at the nearest Malrap bar."

"If that's what you want, but I've got plans, and I want you to be a part of them. You'd obviously have to clean yourself up first."

"I'm sorry, sir. The military's not for me."

"You're right about that. You're an awful fit for the military," Commander Plemso said. "But I have plans. I'm not going to be in the military forever. Politics is the next step, and I'm setting the stage for it with the formation of the Global Guard—a special military group for me to wield when I take power. I've received permission from the Global Assembly to form the first unit and they'll need an interrogator, which is the perfect place for you."

"I don't know what to say."

"I'll assume you're interested. You'll have free rein to do your job. Hone those skills you learned as a boy, and you'll be answerable only to me. How does that sound?"

"When do I start?"

Commander Plemso pressed a button on the interior wall and said, "Driver, please stop here." The vehicle slowed and a few moments later the door opened. "Get out. You start right away. The info for your assignment will be sent to you this evening. And clean yourself up, for Powers-That-Be sake."

When Warver saluted Orn on the Royal University campus and walked off, he was reminding Orn of his failure in the past and how Warver still outranked him and that making a hasty move on Mar Jeps might be just as costly for Orn's current career. Deep down, Orn detested Warver, and he knew exactly what he needed to do.

Orn removed a large pillbox from his pocket and took out a ring, which he put on his forefinger. The ring was smooth brown metal with nothing written on it and the palm-side was larger than the top. He returned the pillbox to his pocket and dashed down the campus path. He was out of breath when he reached the cruiser pad where Mar Jeps and the Prevor Industries security personnel were about to board the cruiser.

Kush Suron noticed Orn approaching and yelled, "Incoming."

One of the security men, who Orn recognized from the Majinor days, grabbed Mar Jeps by the shoulders and guided her toward the cruiser door. The rest of the guards surrounded Mar Jeps in a half-circle as she boarded.

Suron stopped in front of Orn and said, "Been a while."

"Not long enough, Kush."

"A charmer as usual."

Warver stepped between Suron and Orn. Now face-to-face with Orn, he said, "What can I do for you, Orn?

Do you have another message from Vidor?"

The cruiser engines began to power up and the rest of the guards climbed aboard.

Orn said, "No, I don't have a message from the Leader. I just wanted to say hello to Mar Jeps." Orn pressed the side of the ring with his thumb on the same hand.

Warver said, "Call Mar Jeps' assistant and make an appointment."

"That's a pity, but if you say so." Orn reached out to pat Warver's arm. Warver attempted to swat away Orn's hand, but he was too late. Orn made contact and Warver flinched.

"Oh, sorry, my ring does that sometimes," Orn said. "Always a sincere displeasure to see you two." Then Orn turned around and marched off, pressing the side of the ring to retract the needle that had carried the poison into Warver's arm.

# VIDOR

Vidor ignited his lighter and put the flame to the end of a Norian cigar, puffed until it was lit, and took a long pull. He delighted in the rich, fruity flavor of the smoke. Since the port city of Ynor was destroyed in the environmental crisis, there weren't but a dozen boxes of Norian cigars, containing eighteen each, left on the planet. Vidor had already smoked half of the box on his desk and the humidor in his Malrap cellar held another. Vidor exhaled, blowing the thick smoke toward the ceiling and taking another pull on the cigar.

Tonight, Vidor was meeting Mar Jeps. He wanted to coordinate the evening himself to ensure everything went impeccably, so he decided to spend the day working from his study at home. After all the overtime he'd put in during the twelve days since the Yor Vanderlord incident, being home all day long was a luxury. He was able to eat morning meal with his partner at his side while his two boys told him about their school day ahead.

Vidor loved his home, which had been modeled to his specifications by an architect renowned for creating lavish spaces for Koda's wealthiest citizens, but his study was his sanctum. When Yorlik Vanderlord died and his estate was auctioned off, Vidor spent hundreds of thousands of units to purchase the estate's library—ceiling, flooring, walls, bookshelves, books. Owning a part of the Vanderlord estate gave him great personal satisfaction. Vidor leaned back in his chair and blew smoke toward the lofty ceiling, relishing the thought of how much the Great man would've hated Vidor possessing his library. This room was Vidor's trophy. He'd beaten the Great man. His son and grandson couldn't beat him, and neither would his great-grandson. Vidor was still Leader of Koda and nothing could stop his future plans if his dinner with Mar Jeps went well.

He flicked his lighter a few times to create sparks, then placed it in the box with the cigars. It was a silver-metal lighter given to him by his father, Gruger Plemso, when he graduated first in his class with high honors from the Royal Military College. His father had engraved on it: *To Vidor, ALWAYS strive to be the best and you'll be the BEST.* That was the mantra his father harangued him with his entire life up until he passed away a few years after Vidor had risen to the Presidency. Gruger Plemso never saw him become Leader, but Vidor liked to think his father would be proud of him, even though the man never expressed that particular sentiment to him in his lifetime. Vidor's father had other ways of showing his approval.

Vidor took another drag on the cigar and blew the smoke into the corner of the room, studying the portrait of his father through the dissipating cloud. This was the man Vidor remembered as a child. The right breast of his military dress uniform was covered with service ribbons, and each ribbon had a story of bravery and courage. When his father visited from postings around the planet, Vidor sat in his lap and pointed at a ribbon, and his father would tell him the tale behind it. Sometimes when he asked about a specific ribbon, Vidor's mother Minta, who painted the portrait, would say to his father, "Do you really need to tell him about that one?" and his father would say, "How else is he going to become a man?" His mother would reply, "There's more to becoming a man than war," and his father would say, "Go away, woman. What would you know about it?" Then Vidor's mother would sigh and walk off.

When Vidor was nine years old, his mother died and Commander Gruger Plemso transitioned out of military life so he could be home to raise his son. He was employed as a military weapons consultant for the most prominent weapons manufacturer on Koda and rose through the corporate ranks to become CEO of Capitol Weapons Dynamics.

Vidor was sent to Leen Academy, the best military academy on Koda, when he was fourteen years old. His mother never would have consented to such a move. She never wanted a military life for her son, but his father was in charge now. In the military, Gruger Plemso was known as a tough disciplinarian and a stickler for the rules, expecting his men to lead by example by being the best in the military. He applied that same mind-set to raising his son. If Vidor received anything less than perfect marks in school, he wouldn't be permitted to do anything but stay home and study. Gruger hired a retired sergeant from his brigade to keep an eye on Vidor and guarantee the work was done. When his father returned from a long day at the office, he personally went over Vidor's assignments to confirm they were finished in a manner befitting his idea of perfection.

One time, when he was sixteen and his father and the sergeant weren't home, Vidor snuck out of the mansion so he could meet his schoolmates and watch a popular vid at one of their houses. He planned on making it back to the mansion before anyone returned, but Vidor lost track of time. In the midst of the vid, his father showed up, pounding on the front door, and shouting for Vidor to come out. Vidor and his schoolmates cowered in fear. When the front door wasn't opened, his father lost his patience and broke it down with a handheld battering ram he kept in the trunk of his vehicle for emergencies. The rage in his father's eyes was horrifying as he entered the room. Vidor had never seen him like that before.

With the battering ram in hand, he pointed to Vidor's schoolmates and said, "If you truly were my son's friends, you wouldn't be keeping him from his studies. From this day forward, you're not his friends anymore. You will not contact him outside of school grounds." Then he marched over to Vidor and grabbed him by the arm. Vidor resisted, and he could tell his father was baffled by Vidor's strength. In his rage, he had forgotten that Vidor was a muscular teenager in the Military Activities Club at school where he ran for miles, performed calisthenics, lifted weights, and held the record time for the school obstacle course.

Vidor's resistance only increased his father's rage and he struck Vidor in the ribs with the battering ram, knocking him to the ground. Vidor writhed in pain.

"Get up," his father said. "Get up and come home with

me now if you don't want more of the same."

Vidor glanced around at his friends' faces. Some were shocked, and others looked embarrassed for Vidor. They'd never see him the same way again. He stared down at the ground and walked out of the house, then climbed into his father's vehicle and they drove home in silence. Every once in a while, he peered over at this father who had a stern look on his face. Gruger caught Vidor observing him and said, "I've always given you everything you ever wanted when you performed admirably, and this is what I get in return. I'm trying to make a man out of you. A man above all others."

Years before, when Vidor came in second place at a school foot race, Vidor heard his father express the same sentiment to his mother. Gruger had trained him personally and couldn't understand why Vidor failed. At the time, they were living in a small home on his father's military stipend, so Vidor could hear his parents arguing downstairs from his upstairs bedroom even with the door closed.

"He's a child," Vidor's mother said.

"He's a child who will be a man before you know it and no son of mine is going to come in second place," his father said, then there was a loud smack. Vidor's father wasn't hitting his mother. Vidor knew it was the meter stick. "He has to finish in first place now, otherwise he will never live up to his potential."

"Maybe if you didn't push him so hard, he might enjoy what he's doing. He'd want to excel instead of feeling pressured to finish first."

"Maybe I'm not pushing him hard enough," his father said, followed by another smack from the meter stick.

"Why don't you put that thing down and have a conversation with the boy?"

"This worked for my father on me and I can't see any reason why it isn't good enough for my son. Let go, woman."

Then Vidor heard his father's regimented footsteps coming up the stairs and he knew exactly what was coming.

So, in the vehicle driving home from his friend's house, Vidor knew all too well what to expect, but this time his father was more enraged by Vidor than he'd ever seen him before. Vidor was scared. When they arrived at the mansion, his father said, "You know the drill," and turned off the engine. Vidor followed his father into the mansion, past the sergeant who was standing by the front door with his suitcase packed and wearing his coat.

Vidor's father stopped in front of the sergeant and said, "You're a disappointment. You're fired. Comm me your new address and I'll send your final pay. Proceed, Vidor."

They marched silently past the bannister leading upstairs, through the living room and the dining room and into the kitchen. His father dismissed the head cook who was working on dinner and removed a wooden meter stick from a utility closet. The numbers on the stick had faded with time although the stick had hardly been used for measuring: it was the same stick his grandfather had used on his father, and which his father had applied to Vidor after the foot race and many other times.

"Drop them," his father said. "Now!"

Vidor stood there, mortified by the intensity of his father's rage.

"Drop them," his father said. "Or I will drop them for you."

Vidor dropped his pants and his underwear.

"Assume the position," his father said.

Vidor leaned against the food-prep table, bent over, and braced himself.

"Remember, this is for your own good, because I care about you."

Gruger swung the stick and struck Vidor's bare bottom with all his strength. He struck his thighs. He struck him over and over again. The stick whizzed through the air as Vidor's father took bigger and harder swings. Vidor had a high threshold for pain and refused to react out loud to the beating to spite his father.

His father said, "Not good enough, huh?"

"I think you're losing your edge," Vidor said, regretting his words immediately.

Vidor's father began hitting Vidor harder in the same places. When Vidor's mother was alive, she screamed and clawed at his father until he stopped. With his mother gone, Vidor's father felt no restraint. The barrage continued, his father swinging with wild abandon over and over. Eventually, Vidor felt his bowels loosening and attempted to hold on, but failed and shat himself. As the excrement oozed down his leg, the smell infused the air, stinking up the kitchen. Vidor was ashamed.

"You're pathetic. Weak and pathetic," his father said,

grabbing Vidor by his collar, focusing all his energy into each swing. Vidor winced and hollered in pain. Finally, he heard the stick break with one half skittering across the floor. His father threw the other half across the kitchen.

"Now get dressed and clean yourself up," Vidor's father said, "and we'll see how you feel about disobeying me in the morning."

When Vidor awoke the next day, he couldn't move without excruciating pain. He didn't go back to school for thirty-six days. One of the maids who had been with them since Vidor was a child looked after him. His father's office assistant brought him his school assignments every day, and in all that time, Gruger never spoke to him, not even when they passed each other in the halls of the mansion. At first, Vidor hated his father and swore when he was well enough, he'd run away from home and never return. But as time passed and Vidor felt better, and he received his completed assignments back from his teachers with perfect marks, he began to see that his father was actually teaching him a lesson about how great he could be if he put his mind to it.

When Vidor was dressing for his first day back at school, there was a knock at the door and his father entered. He was dressed in his work suit and the smell of his cologne wafted into the room with him.

"Are you ready?" his father said.

"Yes, sir."

"You've already had your morning meal?"

"Yes, sir."

"Come, then, I'll drive you to school. Hurry up now."

His father drove him in silence to school in a brand-new vehicle. The car of a younger person: a vehicle bought more for its streamlined looks and ability to accelerate to a high rate of speed than to display wealth like somebody of his father's place in society would usually drive. They pulled up at Vidor's school and his father said, "I see you're feeling better. I hope you've learned a lesson from your travails. I only want the best for you. If you always strive to be the best, you'll be the best. If you keep to that doctrine, you just might make something of yourself." Then his father handed him the automatic locking and ignition device for the vehicle and said, "Enjoy the car, it's yours."

As his father exited the vehicle, his usual vehicle pulled up with his assistant driving. He climbed into the passenger seat and closed the door. Vidor rolled down his vehicle's window and called out to his father to thank him, but his father looked straight ahead, ignoring him. Gruger's assistant noticed Vidor and said something to his father, who pointed straight ahead and didn't so much as glance at Vidor as the vehicle drove off.

Now, Vidor was the Leader of the Global Assembly, the Leader of the planet Koda. He hadn't inherited a healthy planet, but he was planning on making the best of a bad situation and he required Mado Prevor's presence and for Mar Jeps to fall in line. He took a big drag of the cigar and gently snuffed it out, half-smoked, to preserve it for next time, then blew smoke rings one after the other. He'd learned this party trick from his father. It was an effective icebreaker in social settings.

Vidor pressed a button on his desk console and a viewing screen rose from the floor in front of him. He had added modern touches to his study when he decided to turn his home into the Presidential mansion. If a situation emerged where a face-to-face with one of his staff or a government official was necessary, he could communicate via this screen. More often, he simply watched the latest viewing-channel news.

Using the same console, he flipped through the channels. Roneh Rayush was appearing soon and he didn't want to miss her. He'd been keeping track of her tour through the viewing-channel talk-show circuit, but tonight would be the most important so far. She was appearing on *The Lure*, the most influential and highest-rated news talk show on the planet.

After Vidor was done watching Roneh Rayush's interview, he'd see about the preparations for his dinner and meeting with Mar Jeps to ensure that it all worked out for the best.

# RONEH

Roneh paced around the waiting room to calm herself. *The Lure* was the most respected news show on Koda, airing for over forty years, so this might be her most significant appearance to date. On the walls of the room were fotos of past guests on *The Lure*'s simple set, which consisted of a table for drinks between two chairs and a backdrop featuring a fishing line hooking an old school media journal. Physical journals were outlawed decades ago, but the backdrop had never changed with the times. There was a foto of *The Lure*'s host Paresh Taren interviewing the Leader when he declared his candidacy for President. There was a foto of Yorlik the Great, probably the year he landed, and a foto of Ruler Tamin at an advanced age. Tamin was the last member of the Royal family to lead the Global Monarchy. This was probably the oldest foto on the wall, and Paresh Taren appeared to be in his twenties.

Roneh sat down in front of the waiting-room mirror. Earlier, the makeup person had done her job and left. When Roneh began making appearances, she hated being plastered in makeup. It wasn't her style, but she was getting used to it as part of her new job. She hardly recognized herself as she peered in the mirror and began rehearsing for the show. She sounded shocked and appalled as she spoke about Yor Vanderlord's defiling of Breeze Celebration with his blasphemous speech. She channeled her devout belief in the Global Assembly when she explained her motivation for attempting to apprehend Yor Vanderlord.

Roneh wanted the Leader to be proud of her, but she found it difficult getting her on-air appearances right. The Leader had sent critiques of Roneh's performances to his public relations staff, and an acting coach was dispatched to Roneh's apartment. She was coached on how to look sincere and how best to use body language to express herself. That's when she was told to practice in front of a mirror, and this had become her obsession, but right now she was beginning to sweat and ruin her makeup.

There was a knock on the door.

"Come in," Roneh said, then cleared her dry throat.

A man in his mid-twenties wearing a headset and carrying a digi-tablet ducked into the room and said, "Roneh Rayush, we're ready for you." He was dressed in slacks and a white button-down shirt. He pulled a bottle of water from a holster on his belt and held it out to Roneh saying, "You sound like you need this." Roneh grabbed the bottle and drank down the contents in one gulp, much to the young man's surprise. "There'll be more water on the table next to your seat on the stage. I'll send the makeup person to touch you up. Please follow me."

They exited the waiting room and Roneh kept pace with the man as he strode down the hallway. They passed through an open door into the backstage area and through a curtain so they were now standing beside the set. The man said, "I'll get makeup. Have a fun show."

Roneh's other viewing-channel appearances had been on shows with audiences. The crowds were enthusiastic about her loyalism and supportive of her remarks, applauding after she made statements whether she stumbled nervously over her words or not. They gave her unconditional love. This one would be different. Here there was no audience in attendance. Just her, Paresh Taren, the vidcam crew, and one of the largest viewing audiences on the planet watching from their homes.

Sweat ran down Roneh's forehead to the tip of her nose. The studio felt hotter than the waiting room. She reached up to wipe off the sweat and heard a voice say, "Please don't do that. You'll just make it worse." The makeup person approached, carrying a small pink zippered pouch. She was in her mid-twenties, too. "Please take your seat on the set and I'll fix you up."

Roneh did as requested. She knew where to sit—she'd watched this show her entire childhood with her mother, who thought Paresh Taren was the most insightful man on the planet.

"Now, just stay still and let me do my job," the makeup person said as she touched up Roneh's runny cosmetics. "Relax. Breathe in, breathe out, and close your eyes."

Roneh shut her eyes and recalled the cramped two-bedroom shack where she grew up on the edge of town, in the midst of Capitol City's industrial district. Her parents rented from the corporation that owned the factory across the street where her father worked.

Her father was a welder at the factory. When the DOME project began, the factory started constructing the pane frames for the domes and her father became a quality inspector there. Roneh's mother was on disability from the military, having lost both her legs in the Separatist Revolts as a platoon sergeant. She'd been offered prosthetics incorporating the newest tech, but she could never hold down a job, so she declined them. According to her disability file, she was labeled "Not bearing the temperament to work with others," so she was a stay-at-home mom.

Roneh's mother was a strict woman, but she was caring. She aspired for Roneh to attend university and she was diligent in guiding Roneh through rough patches at school. Roneh's mother was in her first year at Royal University on a full academic scholarship when she volunteered for the military. She reenlisted three times when the revolts spread from region to region and lost her legs in her seventh year of service. She had frequent nightmares, screaming in terror and waking the household. She rarely left the house unless there was a gathering of her fellow soldiers at a nearby Malrap bar or she had a med appointment.

Even scraping by on her mother's meager disability payments and her father working double shifts, Roneh's parents were Global Assembly loyalists. Roneh remembered as a child watching *The Lure* with Tetrick Vanderlord as the guest and her mother being outraged at his claims. She screamed at the viewing screen, her face turning red, "We should send you up in a rocket all by yourself with a limited supply of oxygen…How can you say that without any evidence?…Oh, you've done some research…Why would anyone believe you?…It's people like you who encourage the terrorists…You're a terrorist…The environment will heal itself once we're inside the domes…You tell him, Paresh. Don't let him get away with it."

Now, years later, Roneh was the guest on *The Lure*.

The makeup person said, "You can open your eyes now. Want to see what you look like?" She offered Roneh a handheld mirror.

Roneh took the mirror and peered into it. Makeup for her appearances usually made her look like a painted corpse, but this person had gone for a more natural appearance. "Looks great," Roneh said. "Sorry I was so quiet before in the waiting room. I'm just nervous. This entire experience is like a bizarre dream."

"I saw you on the *Cela* show," the makeup person said. "Paresh isn't going to ask you if you have a boyfriend or what kind of music you like. He's all about the news and the people who make the news. I can see you're a no-nonsense woman. You probably never watch those other shows, do you?"

"I've never even heard of them."

"You've seen *The Lure* before?"

"Been watching it my entire life."

A familiar voice said, "Always great to have a regular viewer on the show. Saves me explaining what we do here."

Roneh lowered the mirror to find Paresh Taren standing beside the makeup person. Physically, he appeared to be the same man Roneh had watched as a child. He was an athletic-looking figure in his suits. His face had lines here and there, although his makeup probably concealed most of his aging. His dark-brown hair was stylized with a grey streak running through it. She'd recognize him anywhere. Roneh jumped up to shake his hand, almost knocking over the makeup person.

"We've got a live one here, Tarla," Paresh Taren said to the makeup person, laughing and taking Roneh's hand. "She has strong grip, too." He met her strong grip with his own. Roneh wouldn't expect anything less from him.

Roneh said, "My mother never missed a show. She always made me watch it with her."

"Sounds like a woman with impeccable taste," Paresh Taren said. "Can I have my hand back now?"

Roneh released her grip. "I'm so sorry."

"I'm just kidding," Paresh Taren said, laughing. Tarla laughed with him.

"I do apologize, though."

"A nervous one, too," Paresh Taren said to the makeup person. "Are we all set, Tarla? We need to prep before the show, then sound check."

"All done here," Tarla said, then turned to Roneh. "You'll be fine. He's the best in the business."

"Definitely the most experienced. Does that make me the best?" Paresh Taren said.

Tarla giggled and blushed. Roneh realized she was smitten by him. "Have a great show," Tarla said and left the set.

"Please sit," Paresh Taren said, taking his usual seat as Roneh sat down across from him.

Roneh picked up the full glass of water on the table between them and drank the contents. She was thirstier than she realized.

"Roneh will need more water," Paresh Taren called out, then lowered his voice to ask, "Is it okay if I call you Roneh?"

Roneh leaned toward him, saying, "Yes, of course."

"Don't ever lean. Just sit up straight in your chair. I'll raise my voice at showtime."

Roneh sat up against her seat back. A stagehand appeared and filled her glass.

"That's better. Relax," Paresh Taren said. "Now, let's have a conversation before the show. A sort of getting to know one another, a warm-up before we're on air."

"That'd be helpful."

"Wonderful," Paresh Taren said, smoothing out the wrinkles in his blue suit jacket and making sure his red tie was straight. "It's always best to sort out our positions in advance."

"How would you like to start?"

"Tell me what you'd like to achieve by being here."

"I'm just here to tell my story." The public relations person had directed Roneh to make this statement if asked her objective by the interviewer.

Paresh Taren covered his mouth, coughed, and smiled, then said, "Your story?"

The PR person hadn't provided contingencies for when the interviewer began quizzing her more closely so Roneh outlined her talking points. "I want to tell people about what happened on Breeze Celebration. I want to explain my reaction to Yor Vanderlord's presentation, which was a hoax being foisted on the Kodan people, and how the Global Assembly and particularly the Leader have the citizens' best interests in mind."

"Sounds more like a political statement than a story."

Roneh was at a loss for more words. She searched for a response.

Paresh Taren cleared his throat. "This isn't the *Cela* show where you can say whatever you like and the audience will go wild because Fretopin has been pumped into the studio and they're trained to cheer when the applause light comes on," Paresh Taren said. "This is my show. Don't expect me to sit here and not challenge what you say."

"I wasn't expecting that. I—"

"Maybe not, but you were expecting me to lead you down the path so you could shill for the Global Assembly."

"I would never presume—"

"Oh, sure you would," Paresh Taren said. "I've been reading up on you, young lady. I've done my research. You've had it in for Yor Vanderlord for years and you've been a lackey for the Global Assembly your entire life, but especially since graduation from University."

"Why wouldn't I have anything but contempt for Yor Vanderlord? The man was a disloyal fool who meant to harm our Leader," Roneh said, raising her voice.

"Good," Paresh Taren said. "Good. Let's be honest with one another. That's what I want to do here. I know about your mother. You were raised in the dogma of the Global Assembly, but that house of worship doesn't convene here. I'll let you say whatever you want to say, but you won't get affirmation from me. You'll get skepticism and probing questions."

"I wouldn't expect anything less," Roneh said, shifting around uncomfortably in her seat.

"I know what Vidor wants, but he and I have an arrangement that allows me to keep my integrity while he gets his message out even if I utterly disagree with his policies," Paresh Taren said. "You look surprised."

"I am."

"That's the kind of mindlessness I expect from his followers and I'll take it as a compliment since it demonstrates my talents. On the other hand, it's sad that I've made a career toeing the line, but I'm hoping that'll change one day."

Roneh was shocked. "What you're saying is sedition."

"Is it now? Are you going to snitch on me? I wouldn't waste your breath. As I said, your beloved Leader and I have an arrangement. So don't worry yourself—I'll make sure by the time this broadcast is over that you're the darling of the Global Assembly."

"Why are you telling me all this?"

"I want you to understand your place here. I want you to understand when this goes well and the Leader praises you up and down, he knows I made it happen, not you, and you know it, too," Paresh Taren said. "I don't want you to think the light of the Global Assembly shone down on your brilliance and this show revealed it. You're nothing special. You're just another cog in Vidor Plemso's machine and eventually you'll be replaced when you've run your course."

"That's all I want."

Paresh Taren laughed and coughed. He didn't entirely cover his mouth this time and Roneh smelled Malrap.

"I seriously doubt that or you're more brainwashed than I thought," Paresh Taren said. "Keep in mind I've been doing this for over forty years. I've spoken to them all, from the monarchs to the Global Assembly Presidents to your Leader himself, and they all had one message they thought was more important than anybody else's, and they all thought being on this show would guarantee that the Kodan people would see the truth of their message. And that's why the Global Assembly booked you here."

The studio lights flashed six times.

Paresh Taren said, "That means we're getting close to starting. We still have to do sound check. You have any more questions?"

"No."

"Maybe you should think about asking more questions instead of being led around by your nose," Paresh Taren said, taking a swig from a mug on the table with *The Lure* logo on it, then he exhaled with his breath reeking of Malrap and cleared his throat.

"Do you drink Malrap before every show?"

"So you do have another question." Paresh Taren drank again from the mug, then held it aloft for Roneh. "Yes, young lady. This makes it all easier."

# MAR

Mar leaned on the terrace's railing and gazed off at the Capitol City skyline. She was starting to love this view. Right now, the sun was setting. The entire dome was turning different shades of red as the sunlight dimmed and the city lights began to illuminate the interior of the dome.

She felt anxious and wasn't looking forward to this evening. By the end of it, the results of her actions could dictate the future of the Kodan people. The thought occurred to her that a shot of Malrap might help, then she chuckled at herself.

"Are you ready to depart?" Warver stood in the doorway wearing a black formal dinner suit with a white shirt. Mar thought the yellow bow tie was a bold choice.

"If I'm not out of line, you look rather dapper," Mar said, walking toward him. "You're a bit flushed—are you coming down with something?"

"I'm feeling a little under the weather, but well enough to do my duty," Warver said, stepping aside to allow Mar to pass into the apartment where Gols was standing beside the couch.

Gols said, "You look fantastic in that dress, like a million units, Mar."

"The dress almost cost as much, but that fashion consultant you hired knew her stuff."

Gols said, "Is there anything you need from me before you leave?"

"No, I'm all set, I think."

Checking his comm, Warver said, "The cruiser is ready and we should probably get going. Vidor hates when people are late."

Mar noted Warver was sweating through his collar and rashes were present on his neck. "Looking at you closer, maybe you shouldn't go. There'll be children there," Mar said. "I'm sure Suron can take your place."

"Suron would do an excellent job, but I'm fine."

"All right, but when we get back, you should have the Complex's med check you out."

"Will do," Warver said, holding out the dark-red Ashtecki coat the consultant recommended for Mar. The jacket cost more than the dress, but Mar had always wanted one and on her current salary, she could afford it and she needed to look her part. She slipped her arms into the coat and buttoned it up, then ran the back of her right hand over the plush fabric.

She and Warver rode the lift down to ground level, exited the building, and climbed into the passenger section of the sleek red Prevor Industries corporate cruiser. Its engines were already powered up.

Warver secured the door, then patted the pilot's shoulder to get her attention and gave her the thumbs-up.

The sound of the engines increased in volume and the vessel lifted off, reaching cruising altitude in no time. The wealthy used this kind of personal cruiser to avoid riding the rail cars across the city with the masses. Although it possessed a weapon-proof body and windows, this chassis was lightweight, and the engines topped out at 450 km/h. It carried half as many people and was twice as fast as the military cruiser that rescued Mar from her bungalow, and the engines quieted as it accelerated. Mar was knowledgeable about all these facts because Prevor Industries was contemplating developing a new cruiser.

The Complex was behind them in a matter of seconds, and Mar observed the city rushing by below them for a while. "I could get used to traveling this way."

"I think you will," Warver said, checking his comm. "Looks like we'll be right on time."

"I was going to ask you if you had some insight to share on the Leader."

"Maybe more than you'd like to know right now," Warver said, staring out the front window of the cruiser. "As you know, I was an officer directly under his command for six years during the Separatist Revolts and in those kinds of situations, you get to know the other person about as well as if you were partnered with them."

"So what can you tell me of value before we land? Something I can use to my advantage or be wary of."

Warver turned to Mar and said, "His need for approval is bottomless. That's a major flaw in his personality. Maybe something you can use to your advantage."

"Anything else?"

"Don't underestimate his ruthlessness, especially if he feels slighted, whether it's justified or not."

"You're the second person to point that out," Mar said. "From your interaction on campus, seems you know that monster Orn Shiv, too."

"All too well," Warver said. Mar could hear the disgust in his voice.

"He's quite the prize."

"He's Vidor's attack animal. His go-to man. Orn carried out the Shamban massacre that I refused to take part in," Warver said, growing visibly upset. "Anyway, you get the picture."

"Disturbingly so," Mar said.

"We're coming up on the estate, starboard side," Warver said, pointing to the right. "This was his father's mansion and Vidor built onto it."

The entire planet was knowledgeable about the Plemso estate. The building itself didn't have much character from the air. It was a big square box with rectangular boxes coming off it where Plemso had expanded the estate over the years. It was famously painted Global-Assembly blue when then-President Plesmo decided to live here instead of the Presidential mansion. Vidor Plemso wanted to signify to the citizens that his home was the home of the Kodan people.

The park surrounding the estate distinguished the landmark more than the building itself, featuring trees not seen anywhere anymore on Koda outside of an arboretum, and the horticulture was maintained by utilizing invaluable water resources. Plemso argued for his water usage, saying the President's house should stand as a symbol of what Koda was and will be again, and these plants were being preserved for Koda in the post-dome era. A majority of Kodans approved of this reasoning so Plemso got his way even though there were arboretums funded in every dome to preserve local plant species.

The cruiser circled the entire grounds a few times and Mar heard Plemso's security over the comm's speaker giving them clearance to land on a pad at the far end of the estate. The cruiser slowed, then descended.

Mar thought about the first time she'd been introduced to Kodan political intrigue on the day of the Great man's landing. *Funny how all the roads in this future seem to lead back to him.* She began to feel anxious again about the weight of responsibility thrust upon her as the cruiser settled on the landing pad.

Warver patted the pilot's shoulder and said to her, "I'll let you know when we're ready to leave."

"Copy that," the pilot said while flipping switches, and the engines powered down.

Warver said to Mar, "You ready?"

"As I'll ever be," Mar said, taking a deep breath and exhaling through her mouth to calm her nerves.

"You'll do just fine," Warver said. "If you don't mind one last piece of advice since you already asked?"

"No, please," Mar said, unbuckling herself.

"Before you enter a room with Vidor, tell yourself you're in control and keep that thought in your mind until you climb back in this cruiser to leave. The moment you give him a millimeter, he will expect you to fold to all his demands," Warver said. "If you do give in to anything, make sure it's on your terms and not his."

"I'll keep that in mind," Mar said. "Now, we don't want to keep people waiting." Mar pointed out the cruiser's window at Davik Atmar standing at military attention with a serious look on his face although he was wearing a formal suit much like Warver's.

Warver peered out the window and laughed, then slid the cruiser door open and exited. Mar followed.

Davik Atmar was a head shorter than Warver. He began to chuckle as Warver approached him, then said, "It's been a long time."

"At ease, Atmar," Warver said, patting Davik's shoulder and gripping it for a moment. "I have to admit, it's good to see you. How's the family?"

"The girls are graduating from University and the boys are attending the Capitol City Military Academy."

"You and your twins. They're all grown up. Makes me feel old."

"Because you are old," Davik Atmar said, patting Warver's shoulder.

Mar said, "I guess you two know one another."

"Yes, we served together," Warver said and stepped aside. "I'm being unprofessional. I apologize. Mar Jeps, this is Davik Atmar, the Leader's Chief of Affairs."

Of course, Mar recognized Davik Atmar. Tetrick referred to him as the Leader's lackey back in the old days. He'd been Vidor Plemso's Chief of Affairs since he was first elected President. "Pleasure to meet you," Mar said.

"Pleasure to meet you as well," Davik Atmar said, bowing to her.

Warver returned to the cruiser, closed the door, and waved to the pilot, then trotted back to Mar and Davik Atmar

Mar asked Warver, "So when did you two serve together?"

"Under Vidor's command when he was Major Plemso," Warver said. "It was many years ago, but we're not here to reminisce and we don't want to keep Vidor waiting."

"Yes, we can catch up some other time," Davik Atmar said. "And please call him Leader when you're in his presence."

"Right," Warver said. "I know how sensitive Vidor is about his rank."

"All right, let's go, then. The Leader will take it out on me if we dawdle. Follow me," Davik Atmar said, chuckling nervously, then headed toward a mechanized cart for transporting two people.

Warver said to Mar, "Nothing much has changed there."

"I heard that, Warver," Davik Atmar said, climbing into the driver's seat of the cart and starting the engine. "Mar Jeps, you might recognize this contraption, although we've cleaned it up and painted it."

"Me?" Mar said and glanced over at Warver who shrugged and climbed onto the back. She examined the cart, then it dawned on her this looked exactly like the cart at the Vanderlord estate, except it was painted Global-Assembly blue. "This can't be…is this?"

"Yes," Davik Atmar said. "The Leader purchased it from the Vanderlord estate auction, among other things. He thought a great deal of the Great man."

*I bet he did*, Mar thought. She climbed into the passenger seat and Davik Atmar drove down a paved path beneath a canopy of healthy green leaf trees. Winged creatures chirped overhead and small forest creatures scattered out of the cart's path, fleeing into the flora beneath the trees. Mar was in awe.

Mar said, "This is incredible. How do you keep the winged creatures and animals from leaving the grounds?"

"You probably know about the energy field Mado Prevor gifted to the Leader. It envelops the property, and when we open a window in the field so cruisers can land, the winged creatures are too frightened to fly out."

Mar hadn't seen such lush landscape since she was a young girl four decades ago. This was the Leader's private sanctuary and from the way it was maintained, he obviously cared about it a great deal. Mar was now aware of another reason why the Leader didn't want the power going out.

Then the cart began ascending a slight rise in the terrain, exiting the forest canopy to find a green lawn spread out around them, and Mar caught the smell of freshly cut grass. The cart continued climbing and the three-story estate emerged from the green landscape with multicolored blossoms surrounding its entire foundation. As they approached the estate, the scent from the abundance of flowers was overwhelming and Mar spotted the Leader waving to them from a second-story terrace.

The cart slowed and stopped a few meters from a staircase to the right which climbed to the terrace. Davik Atmar said, "We've arrived. The Leader awaits you." Mar wondered whether this was something Davik Atmar was ordered to say because it made Vidor Plemso sound like a ruler.

She took a moment to breathe in the scent of the blossoms. She didn't know when she'd get the chance to experience such an extravagance again, and it took her back to the childhood flower garden cultivated by her parents.

Mar hadn't spoken to her parents in years. She believed they still lived in the Mlimoan dome, or at least that's what she last heard from childhood friends in touch with them. Her parents were decent people loyal to the Global Assembly, so it wasn't shocking when Tetrick's anti-DOME agenda didn't sit well with them, and they disowned Mar for partnering with him. Mar was reminded that even people like her parents who were loyal to the Leader and the Global Assembly were good people. They were committed to their points of view whether Mar agreed with them or not and they were worth saving as much as people in the Movement.

Warver said, "Everything all right, Mar Jeps?"

"Oh, fine," Mar said, inhaling deeply and indulging in the blossoms' fragrance as she exited the cart. "Just taking a moment to absorb the beauty here. It reminds me of my childhood, and it's not something you encounter every day, unless you're the Leader, his family, or you work here."

"The First Lady does invite Capitol City schoolchildren and tour groups from the other domes to visit," Davik Atmar said. "To remind them what Koda will be once again."

Prompting herself to be diplomatic, Mar said, "A wonderful gesture. Now, I don't want the Leader to think me rude by keeping him waiting."

"No, of course not," Davik Atmar said. "This way." Davik Atmar exited the cart and began climbing the stairs.

Mar glanced at Warver who said, "I'll be right behind you."

Mar climbed the stairs. When Davik Atmar reached the top, he stepped to the left and waited for Mar to arrive, then said, "May I present Mar Jeps."

The Leader stood a few meters away, a cigar sticking out of the corner of his mouth. The end burned red, then he removed the cigar from his mouth and blew smoke rings. *He does have a flair for theatrics*, Mar thought. *Something to keep in mind.*

The Leader said, "Here we are finally." He looked tired with dark rings under his eyes. "Welcome to my home, Mar Jeps."

The Leader wore a formal suit like Warver's, but Mar could tell at first glance that his suit wasn't bought off the rack but had been tailored to fit him. He wore a Global-Assembly-blue tie. When his eyes landed on Wel Warver, there was a moment of disdain, then his eyes widened and a smile spread across his face. Mar thought in a perverse way he was actually happy to see Warver.

"Commander Warver," the Leader said, "I heard you were working for Prevor Industries, but I never expected to see you this evening."

"I'm head of security at Prevor Industries," Warver said as if he was talking to a stranger. "Protecting Mar Jeps is my primary responsibility, so I took it upon myself to provide security for this meeting. And I haven't gone by commander for years, not since I left the service."

"So formal. Well, I guess it is the occasion," the Leader said, pulling on the lapels of his suit jacket. "She won't need security here, though." Then he pointed to Davik Atmar with his cigar. "Did you see Warver here, Davik?"

"Yes, sir. We met at the landing pad."

"It was a rhetorical question," the Leader said. "This guy hasn't gotten any sharper since the old days, Warver. Now, Davik, go inside and see where the First Lady is keeping herself and inform her the guest of honor has arrived. Tell the kitchen we'll begin dinner shortly."

Then the Leader turned to Warver and said, "Warver, I don't mean to be rude, but you're not looking well."

Mar thought Warver appeared noticeably worse since they'd left the Complex. He was definitely more flushed.

"I'm just fine." Warver removed his tie and unbuttoned the collar of his shirt. There seemed to be more rashes on his neck. "A little warm, perhaps, but thanks for your concern."

"Would you like a Norian cigar? I always have a backup nearby at gatherings like these."

"I'm on duty, but if you're offering, I'll take one for later. It's been years."

"Can't pick these up on raids anymore, can we?" the Leader said and chuckled. "This is my second of the evening. There are a finite number left, but I can't help myself. I'd say their cost is well out of your price range these days unless Prevor Industries is overpaying you."

"We pay him well," Mar said. "And he is well worth the units."

The Leader was smirking at Warver. He was pleased with his dig about Warver's station in life compared to his own, but Warver was unflinching and annoyance spread over the Leader's face when Warver didn't respond.

Then the Leader turned to Davik Atmar and said, "Why are you still here? Didn't I give you an order? Do your job!"

Davik Atmar darted off into the building.

Then the Leader snapped his fingers. A waiter wearing a black pullover and black pants stepped forward with a tray of drinks. "Can I interest you in a glass of Malrap or a tumbler of Eglew juice?" the waiter said to Mar, then handed a cigar to Warver.

"I'll take an Eglew juice," Mar said.

"Very good," the waiter said, handing Mar a tumbler of purple liquid.

The fragrance of Eglew juice was unmistakable. Once a popular Kodan drink sold over the counter at corner stores, the region where the fruit was cultivated in Maua had been devastated by both the Separatist Revolts and the crisis. Only boutique companies grew the fruit now and only the wealthiest could afford the juice. The boutique version of Eglew juice was said to have a kick closer to Malrap than the original, which brought on a mild euphoria. Gols had warned Mar that Eglew juice might be offered along with Malrap and that she should be wary of indulging too much.

The waiter said to Warver, "Would you like me to light your cigar and may I bring you a drink, sir?"

"Nothing for me, thanks," Warver said and placed the cigar in his jacket pocket.

The Leader picked up a glass of Malrap from a round table covered with a white cloth and said, "A toast. To a glorious dinner, friends new and old, and a meeting of the minds."

Mar raised her glass as well and said, "I'll toast to those sentiments and the best possible future for the Kodan people."

"Yes, I concur," the Leader said, "I'll drink to that."

Mar sipped her juice and the taste triggered a memory of hiking the hillsides around Calem Falls with her father and mother as a teenager. The ecology around the Falls had already started to show the impact of the crisis. The thick canopy of trees had always made the hike pleasant in the heat of the day, but now the canopy was torn open in more and more places by falling trees, exposing the trail to the harsh sunlight. She recalled one day they stopped at a fallen tree to drink some water and after they hydrated, her father returned the bottles to his pack and removed a bottle of Eglew juice. The price of the product had already started to skyrocket and corner stores no longer carried it, but somehow her father had discovered it at an affordable price and purchased it, knowing this was her favorite.

Mar said, "Father, you shouldn't have. This must've been expensive."

"Nothing is too good for my little girl," he replied, wiping the sweat off his brow with the back of his hand.

"I'm not so little. Remember, I'm going off to University next year."

"So how much longer will we be able to spoil you?" Mar's father said, holding out the bottle to her. "Take it."

Mar took the bottle and cracked it open. She recalled sipping the juice and her mouth exploding with the sweet tangy flavor. That might've been the last time she'd drunk the juice until now.

Mar said to the Leader, "It's been years since I last tasted this. It's a treat. Thank you."

"You're welcome, and to be completely honest, I had my secretary comm your parents and ask them what your favorite beverage was," the Leader said, pleased with himself. "Funny story is they didn't believe it was my secretary comming them, so I got on the viewing screen. They were excited to meet me. I hope I wasn't too out of bounds. I just want you to have the best experience possible here."

"I'm sure they were overjoyed to speak with you." Mar said. "We haven't talked in a while."

"Sorry to hear that. They seem like fine people, but that happens sometimes."

"Yes, Koda can be a complicated place."

"And that's exactly why we're here," the Leader said, clearing his throat. "The First Lady appears to be running late. Probably tending to the boys."

"I'd love to meet your children."

"Maybe later. They've eaten already. They're supposed to be doing their homework now."

An awkward silence ensued. Mar glanced over at Warver who smiled at her. He was putting up a good front, but he looked miserable. The Leader stared through the doors into the house as if he did it long enough and hard enough his partner would appear, then he tried to smoke the cigar, but it had gone out.

Mar thought, *He hasn't scripted much small talk, hoping his partner would fill up the time.* She walked to the railing of the terrace and gazed out over the estate grounds. The green lawn stretched to the forest, and once again she caught the scent of the abundant flowers below.

"The landscaping is remarkable," Mar said and sipped at the juice.

"Yes," the Leader said, removing a metallic lighter from his suit jacket pocket. He ignited the end of the cigar, puffed on it, and blew out a stream of smoke. "I take great pride in the appearance of the Plemso estate. I want it to be a symbol of what the Kodan people can achieve when the domes are no longer necessary." He flicked the lighter, creating sparks as he spoke.

His answer about the landscaping was well rehearsed. Mar had seen him discuss the topic on a viewing-channel program created to reveal the Leader's personal life. Probably arranged so the Kodan people could feel closer to him. As Warver said, Vidor Plemso was obsessed with approval. Mar had steered the conversation onto this topic for a reason: it would play to his ego until the First Lady appeared.

"Where did you find such an abundance of healthy trees and blossoms?"

"That's an interesting question," the Leader said. "The original planting of the forest was started by my father, who purchased the neglected trees at the Royal Palace before the Global Assembly transformed it into a museum. I transported many of the trees from other domes' arboretums and transplanted the trees that would have been lost in the excavation of Myla Park during the construction of the foundation for the Capitol City dome."

"How about the flowers? I've only seen many of them in books."

"They're from Myla Park, the Palace, and various arboretums. My most prized specimens were grown here in the property's greenhouse using seeds and grafts from the arboretum in the Mauan dome. After an exhausting day in the office, I like to walk around these grounds and reconnect with my purpose in life. Remind myself why I do what I do. Of course, the boys remind me of that every day, too."

Mar felt like applauding the Leader's performance, but just smiled at him and said, "Yes, it's remarkable." Mar could tell he wanted more praise from her as he stared at her in silence and nodded.

"Is he going on about the landscaping again?" a female voice behind them said. "That's one of his favorite subjects. I find it a bore."

Mar turned and there stood the First Lady of Koda. She wore a strapless purple dress that hugged the curves of her body down to her thighs. The fashion consultant had shown Mar this dress, but she felt too old for such a garment. The dress was made from a rare Klish-insect webbing which became a second skin on top of your own. One needed the figure to pull it off properly. The First Lady was seventeen years younger than the Leader and she hadn't lost her figure as she aged and had children.

The Leader said, "Mar Jeps, this is the love of my life and mother of my children, Flomina."

First Lady Flomina Folt was a renowned beauty as a Mauan teenager who modeled for the best-known Kodan fashion designers. The Folts were one of the wealthiest families on Koda, and Flomina was far wealthier than her partner. Her father Nomeer Folt had won the contract to lay the foundations for all the domes. He spent decades accruing billions of units in research and development funds, perfecting the formula for the mixture of materials to produce the strongest dome foundation, then his company was awarded the hundred-trillion-unit contract to pour the foundations for all nine domes. Flomina's global popularity as an heiress celebrity model and her lavish wedding to Vidor Plemso, shown on every viewing channel, undoubtedly helped Vidor to win his second Presidential term.

Flomina walked up to Mar and began petting her coat. "I love love love Ashtecki. I can't get enough of it. I have this exact coat," Flomina said, stepping back from Mar. "I'm sorry. That was inappropriate of me. Vidor is constantly chastising me about my behavior."

The Leader said, "I wouldn't call it chastising. I'd say pointing out when you cross the line of diplomacy, dear."

"She doesn't look too offended," Flomina said.

"I'm fine," Mar said.

"Always so serious, Vidor."

"I am Leader of the planet, dear." The Leader walked over to Flomina and leaned in for a kiss, but Flomina moved her face away. Mar thought perhaps she didn't want her makeup mussed, but when the Leader attempted to take her hand, she swatted at it. He noticed Mar observing this interaction and forced a smile.

"I love your dress as well," Flomina said. Mar felt like she was being genuine. "You have great taste. When we're done with dinner, I'd love to show you my wardrobe. It's magnificent."

"And expensive," the Leader said.

"What do you care? I bought most of it with my own units."

The Leader shot a stern glance at Flomina, who smiled back at him and planted a peck on his cheek as if they were on their first date.

"You can never take a joke, dear," Flomina said, then pointed toward Warver. "And who is this tall drink of a man? Your partner?"

Warver said in a monotone, "Security detail, First Lady."

Flomina laughed. "Well, that's awkward. I apologize. I guess I crossed that line, Vidor."

"Charming as ever, my dear," the Leader said and leaned in to kiss Flomina's cheek, which she allowed this time.

Flomina said, petting Mar's coat again, "It's exciting to meet a woman in a position of power on Koda. The last CEO of Prevor Industries was an odd one, but he and Vidor seemed to get along and he was good to us."

"Mado is certainly quirky."

"Yes, quirky," Flomina said. "That's a good word to describe him. Let's head to dinner, shall we? The chef gets testy if his food doesn't hit the plate when he wants it to and I'm famished. Please take your drink with you. Vidor, put out that nasty cigar before we get to the table.

You know I don't like it stinking up my home."

When Flomina said "my home," the Leader closed his eyes, shook his head, and sighed, then he placed the cigar in an ashtray on the table beside him. "Waiter," the Leader said, "put that ashtray with the cigar beside the armchairs in my study."

"Yes, sir," the waiter said.

"Shall we?" Flomina said and linked arms with Mar.

"Flomina and I need to talk for a second," the Leader said to Mar. "Please excuse us for a moment."

Flomina unlinked arms with Mar and said, "What is it now, Vidor?"

The Leader said in a commanding tone, "Over here." He gently took hold of Flomina's forearm and whispered something in her ear.

Flomina made a face like she had something sour in her mouth, then she and the Leader walked together to the other side of the terrace.

Mar took a few steps back to stand beside Warver, bent toward him, and whispered, "You all right?" She could feel the heat coming off him.

"Hanging in there," Warver said, then leaned toward Mar and whispered back, "Looks like marital bliss."

At first, the Leader and Flomina spoke to each other in hushed tones, then the conversation ignited into wild gestures toward each other, although they still kept their voices down. Mar thought this had happened before in front of guests and they were practiced at this kind of turmoil. The Leader leaned into Flomina's tirade as if she were a gale-force wind. Mar tried to hear what they were saying without acting as if she was listening in. They were speaking to one another in Mauan. Mar took several years of the Mauan language at University and had picked up a few Mauan words and phrases in the Leader and Flomina's conversation. "Disrespectful… charlatan…don't speak to me that way…guests…no idea…waiting."

On the last word, the Leader turned toward Mar. He caught her listening but had no idea Mar understood. She smiled at him. She thought she could take advantage of this rift between the couple, but when she assessed what she was thinking, she was disgusted with herself. *Is this the person I'm going to become?* Mar thought. *I need to check myself when I start thinking this way, but this angle could come in handy.*

The Leader pointed at Mar, leaned toward Flomina again, and said to her clearly in Mauan, "Behave yourself. You're ruining everything. Think of our children." Then the Leader said something to her at a quieter volume which Mar couldn't hear, and they hugged and walked together back to Mar.

Flomina said, "Sorry about the interruption. We had something urgent to discuss." She linked her arm with Mar's again and said, "Let's go eat."

As they headed toward the house, the Leader walked on the other side of Mar and said, "Partnering isn't always easy."

"Yes, I know a thing or two about that," Mar said.

"I didn't mean…" the Leader said.

"That's fine," Mar said, chalking one up over the

Leader. After his fight with Flomina, he was off his game. Mar knew he'd attempt to rebound so she decided to ignore him and began talking to Flomina about her dress.

On entering the house, they walked down a hallway carpeted Global-Assembly blue with the symbol on it, then took an escalator down to the first floor. They stepped off the escalator onto a marble floor, and the blue ceiling, maybe fifteen meters above them, was higher than any other building she'd been in besides the library at the Royal University or the main hall at the Royal Palace. Mar presumed this was an intentional reflection of those historic structures. The air was perfumed to smell like the blossoms outside. The scent was pleasing to the senses and mildly euphoric, but it didn't feel as if it was meant to take over a person's mood like Fretopin. Mar enjoyed it and didn't believe she'd ever experienced anything like it.

Flomina smiled at Mar.

"What is that scent?" Mar said. "I love it."

"Me, too," Flomina said. "I don't know how I could live without it."

"She says that about everything in here," the Leader said.

"Not about you, my dear," Flomina said, chuckling and shoving him playfully.

"Funny," the Leader said. "But seriously, that scent and the decorating are all Flomina's doing. Coming home from the Global Assembly building is something I dream about, especially after a tough day. Flomina is a planetary treasure."

The Leader smiled at Flomina and she smiled back, which looked genuine, then Flomina stuck her tongue out at the Leader and they both laughed. The tension between them appeared to have dissipated. Maybe it was the comfort of entering their home or the perfume, but there was a new dynamic between them, one of mutual admiration. They obviously had a complex relationship.

Further into the room, tables along the walls displayed vases painted with intricate landscapes and blossoms. Mar recognized a few of the paintings on the white walls as historical masterpieces depicting the great battles of Global Unification: there were the bloody faces of warriors suited in metallic armor, wielding blades and maces, portraying the agony of defeat and the joy of impending victory.

Mar said, "Are those…?"

"Yes," the Leader said. "I borrowed them from the Royal Palace when we remodeled to make this the Presidential mansion. It only seemed right."

"Vidor loves them," Flomina said, smiling at Mar. "Not my style, but this is his home, too, and I understand he needs to project his manliness as well as his statesmanship." She stuck her tongue out at the Leader again. He didn't laugh this time.

# Vidor

After dinner, Vidor lounged in an armchair in his study. He picked up the cigar that the waiter had brought from the terrace, lit it, puffed until the end glowed, and blew smoke up toward ceiling.

Flomina had taken Mar Jeps to see her wardrobe, then introduce her to the boys who hadn't attended dinner. Vidor had told Mar Jeps the boys were absent so they could focus on their studies, but that was a half-truth. Vidor originally considered using them as props to endear himself to Mar Jeps but had second thoughts. They were harder to control than their mother. *Who knows what they might have said around Mar Jeps?* They were generally well behaved at Global Assembly events but in less formal environments, they tended to act in a less diplomatic way. They had already asked him about the man who tackled the woman off the ramp at Breeze Celebration and told him the lift-off of the WAEF was "one of the most incredible things they'd ever seen." Vidor controlled himself rather than taking it personally and losing his temper. They were children and were curious. Politics was a dirty, nasty business which a child wide-eyed with wonder couldn't be expected to master.

Overall, the dinner went well. Mar Jeps complimented the chef who came out of the kitchen for a bow, and most of the dinner conversation was dominated by Flomina. She talked about Mar Jeps' dress and how she was acquainted with the designer from her days as a model. She gave her opinion about the new fashions. She told some inappropriate stories about partying with male models on the islands off the coast of Nor, which were now underwater because of the crisis.

Mar Jeps gave her undivided attention to Flomina as she went on and on, although Vidor could tell Mar Jeps was being polite. *What does a med living in a bungalow care about high fashion?* Vidor had thought. He listened half the time and when Flomina asked, "Don't you think so, Vidor?" he nodded, saying, "Yes, dear." The only time the conversation got out of line was when Flomina gave Mar Jeps condolences for the death of her son. Flomina had a good heart and she was being sincere when she said, "I would be devastated if anything happened to my boys. Such a terrible way for a young life to end. Don't you think so, Vidor?" He had a glass of Malrap to his lips about to drink when she uttered these words and Vidor froze in position staring at Flomina, hoping she'd realize the error of her ways in asking the man who killed Mar Jeps' son this question. Maybe she'd change the subject before the silence at the table became more awkward and he'd need to say something. Instead, Mar Jeps said, "My son was fully aware of the consequences of his actions, and the loss of a child at any time is a tragedy, even worse at a young age. Potential gone forever." While Mar Jeps was speaking, Vidor could see it was dawning on Flomina that her mouth had run ahead of her brain. She said, "Yes. Again, my condolences. I can't wait for you to meet my boys." Then she began talking about the boys and their differences and how she was proud of them. Vidor thought about Mar Jeps' cold and calculated response regarding her son and began to understand why Orn called her "formidable."

In his study, Vidor puffed on the cigar and blew the smoke up toward ceiling again. This part of the study was set up with four armchairs, two across from each other, forming a square with a low table in the middle. The armchairs were from his father's old study. Vidor ran his hand along the Rexok leather on the armrests. His father and his military buddies and later his corporate colleagues would sit in these chairs for hours, smoking cigars, discussing current events and the global markets, and they plotted how they'd influence them for their future gain. Business empires and political intrigue were hatched by the men sitting in these chairs.

When he was nearing graduation from college, Vidor was summoned into one of those meetings and told that he would rise through the military ranks, and when the Separatists were defeated, he'd become President of the Global Assembly. Vidor sat and listened. His father never asked him whether he liked the idea or not, but Vidor knew better than to contradict him. He never saw himself as a politician and at first, he thought this was a lofty and ridiculous idea. His father told Vidor that he'd graduate first in his class, then Gruger Plemso would persuade the military to grant Vidor a higher rank than they'd usually give someone with his lack of field experience. When Vidor was commissioned a major out of college, he learned firsthand the influence his father could wield, and as he rose in rank, he found he thoroughly enjoyed his position of power over people, so he made attaining the Presidency a priority. He was aware of the hard work required to achieve this long-term goal, and he was more than willing to commit himself each and every day to become and stay the best on the planet.

Over the years, Vidor had grown confident he could triumph over any problems thrown in front of him. The DOME riots were difficult, and when discretion failed, he unleashed the military. He manipulated the lever of politics to construct the domes and save the Kodan people from a planetary crisis. He bested Yorlik the Great, one of the greatest minds in Kodan history, by outsmarting him. The Breeze Celebration riots were suppressed, and he was in the process of delegitimizing Yor Vanderlord's presentation in the minds of Kodans.

Now, the stakes couldn't be higher. In order to put his future plans back on track, he was required to work with the mother of the person he supposedly killed. Dealing with Mar Jeps required sensitivity and that was not his strong suit. By bringing her to his home, Vidor hoped to demonstrate they weren't so different. He was Leader of Koda, but he was also a family man who cared about his children. She understood what it was like to be a parent, and she was a practicing med who pledged to look after the well-being of all Kodans. Most importantly, she said earlier in the evening that she wanted a better future for the Kodan people. This was common ground on which the foundations of their new relationship could be built.

Vidor took another drag on his cigar, blowing the smoke toward the ceiling. He ran his hand along the armrest again. The leather was cracked in places from age and discolored by the hand sweat of the chair's occupants over the decades. All the chairs had those imperfections. At the start of their partnership, Flomina insisted on reupholstering or buying new armchairs and it became a bone of contention between them. She called the chairs "an abomination." Vidor fought her, and she eventually gave up when Vidor told her, "This is our home, but I'd appreciate it if you left the chairs the way they are. That would mean a lot to me." He made it seem like she won and was the more gracious person by letting him have his way. They never discussed it again. Maybe that was the way to deal with Mar Jeps, too.

Vidor had thought about forgoing diplomacy altogether though. There was no doubt he'd prevail with the full military might of the Global Assembly behind him, or he could poison Mar Jeps now, but if he used force, it might set back his plans far longer than the time he possessed. Prevor Industries held a strong negotiating position. Vidor flicked at the lighter with his thumb, producing sparks, then stared into them and thought, *Well, at least I have options.*

"You don't want to wear that out." Mar Jeps stood in the doorway of his study with Warver behind her.

"Not likely," Vidor said, putting the lighter down by the ashtray on the low table. "I could always replace the flint."

"Might be difficult to replace the flint in an antique like that."

"You'd be surprised what you can fix with the correct motivation."

Mar Jeps laughed and stepped into the study. "Are we still talking about the lighter?"

Vidor left the cigar in the ashtray and stood up. "Please come in and close the door behind you," Vidor said. "I'd like to have a private conversation. No need for Warver here."

Mar Jeps glanced over at Warver and nodded, then Warver stepped back out of the room, closing the door.

"You and Warver have quite the history," Mar Jeps said, walking further into the room and observing her surroundings.

"Yes, but that's the past. I prefer to look toward the future. Please have a seat," Vidor said, gesturing toward the armchairs. "I have some Malrap here." Vidor pointed to the table between the armchairs where there was a full carafe of Malrap with a filled goblet and an empty one beside it.

"No, thank you."

"Or I can comm the waiter for something else."

"I've had my fill this evening. The hospitality has been first rate." Mar Jeps walked over to the armchairs and sat down in the one across from where Vidor had been seated.

"We aim to please at the Plemso estate," Vidor said, sitting back down. The cigar was still smoldering and he started to extinguish it.

Mar Jeps said, "Please don't put that out on my account. I enjoy the aroma. Reminds me of one of my favorite uncles. Always had a cigar in the corner of his mouth."

"Good man?" Vidor said, picking up the lighter.

"He had his moments," Mar Jeps said. "I haven't seen him in years. I heard he didn't make it inside the domes."

Vidor thought Mar Jeps might be baiting him, but he wasn't going for it. He placed the cigar in his mouth and went to light it, then just sparked the lighter a few times. "Are you positive you're okay with this?"

"If we're going to have a business relationship or whatever this is, you can be certain I'll always say what I mean," Mar Jeps said, scrutinizing the study. "I was aware people purchased parts of the Vanderlord estate, but I thought that meant the furniture and paintings and knickknacks. I had no idea someone literally bought the library. Sitting here brings back memories. This was like a living appendage of the Vanderlords. I always loved this room, but it feels out of place here. It feels like you've attached somebody's nose to somebody else's face and it doesn't fit. No offense."

Vidor was offended. He always saw a distinct similarity between himself and the Great man. They were both men of vision, so why wouldn't the intellectual center of the Great man's home fit here? "I disagree," Vidor said. He relit the cigar, took a big pull, and blew the smoke up at the ceiling. "But that's a conversation for another time, perhaps."

"Yes, you're right," Mar Jeps said. "It's getting late. By the way, your children are adorable and charming. I can see you and your partner in them."

"They get the adorableness from their mother," Vidor said and laughed.

"So where do we start this conversation?"

"Wherever you like."

"The best way to start is to say I have no intention of shutting down power on the Kodan people. Mado was obviously concerned about the repercussions of Yor's actions, but that seems to have passed. Am I right?"

Vidor was surprised by this opening statement. He'd expected more of a hard-line approach, but he decided this was a ploy to keep him off guard, especially after saying she'd be up front about her true sentiments. He'd have to keep on his toes around her. She might be more savvy than he originally surmised, but he knew how to get the upper hand.

"You're correct. And there's no need to speculate about your partner," Vidor said. "He's alive and well." He saw joy spread over Mar Jeps' face. A tear ran down her cheek and Vidor surmised this was a genuine tear of joy. *If this is fake, then she is formidable.* One thing for sure, he'd be able to leverage her relationship with Rajer Jeps to his full advantage. He'd been correct on that count from the start. "You can see him anytime. When I spoke with him, he asked about meeting with you and I was waiting for this evening to tell you."

Tears streamed down Mar Jeps' face and she wiped her cheeks with the back of her hand. "Sorry," she said, "this isn't very professional of me." She sniffled, then wiped her eyes with her forefingers.

"No need to apologize. I completely understand."

"You know, maybe I will take some Malrap."

Vidor was surprised again and reached for the carafe,

pouring a healthy amount into the empty goblet and handing it to Mar Jeps.

"Whoa!" Mar Jeps said. "That's a lot."

"Just drink what you want," Vidor said. "Better to have your fill in front of you than less than you desire. My mother always said that."

Mar Jeps smiled and took a big swig. "That's smooth Malrap."

"Vintage," Vidor said, "from Yorlik the Great's Malrap cellar."

Mar Jeps chuckled, then peered into the goblet. "He did love his Malrap."

"No surprise it's vintage. The Great man was pretty vintage himself."

"Yes, that's true," Mar Jeps said, taking another swig. "When he returned, he could relate to vintage items better than anybody else on the planet. His obsession with the WAEF is proof of that."

"Indeed. He went to great lengths to possess it."

"Yes, and you were willing to accommodate him," Mar Jeps said, then smiled and took another drink of Malrap. She'd already consumed more than half the goblet. "That didn't turn out well for you."

Vidor was shocked by this clear insult. The Malrap was noticeably affecting her—he could see it in her eyes, and there was a bravado in the tone of her voice that wasn't there before. Vintage Malrap was stronger than the vendor variety. Offering it to her might have been a bad idea—she was clearly a lightweight when it came to drinking it. That wasn't in her file, but he would make an addendum.

Vidor quipped, "If one were paranoid, one might think the Great man was planning what happened at Breeze Celebration all along."

Mar Jeps chuckled a little more exuberantly. Vidor figured it was the Malrap. "Preposterous, but one might," Mar Jeps said, then she began stroking at the sleeve of her jacket in a steady rhythm as if she was stroking a house pet. Vidor thought she was uncomfortable and that this was an involuntary move to calm herself. Then she retrieved her comm from the pocket of her jacket, stared at it, and said, "We should probably finish up. It's getting late."

"What else is on your mind?"

Mar Jeps drained the last of her Malrap and placed the empty goblet on the low table between them. "One thing I want to make clear," Mar Jeps said, her voice suddenly filled with authority, "if I perceive a surge in unwarranted arrests of Kodans who are not doing anything wrong other than talking contrary to the Global Assembly agenda in public, then Mado's threat will be back on the table."

Vidor cleared his throat and sat up straight. "So you're saying that my administration is under your scrutiny. How am I supposed to know what you consider beyond your tolerance when it comes to arrests against the anti-government terrorists? Am I supposed to gauge policies based on your judgment? That seems rather arbitrary. Am I supposed to contact you before I make a decision? Are we talking about your son's cronies at the University?"

"Those are all good questions. I'd say if I hear about citizens being rounded up and locked away because they spoke against Global Assembly policy, then I will alert you of my displeasure and we can take it from there. I understand that if violence occurs against citizens or the Global Assembly, then you need to act."

"I'll take that under advisement," Vidor said. Mar Jeps had set him back on his heels, and he didn't like it. "Anything else?"

Mar Jeps picked up the goblet from the table. Vidor understood from the look on her face that she hadn't realized she'd finished the entire thing.

Mar Jeps said, "Now is not the time to get into details, but I've been informed of the secret project constructing interstellar craft. It can also be stopped at any time if your actions become intolerable, but right now, I'm behind it one hundred percent."

"Mado told you about that," Vidor said with shock in his voice. Now he understood that Mado really had put her in complete control of Prevor Industries—this wasn't a temporary maneuver. "So Mado isn't returning anytime soon, then?"

"No. Unfortunately, you'll have to deal with me," Mar Jeps said. "After what happened with Yor, Mado is distraught and he has no desire to run his corporation. He needs to reevaluate his priorities. That'll take an indeterminate amount of time so I'm now in charge. Is that a problem for you? I know everything he knows, and I'll tell him about this conversation."

"It'd be beneficial to hear from him."

Mar Jeps said, "You don't trust me."

"Trust? Our history hasn't exactly fostered trust. It would've been nice to hear from Mado, but I see you're in command, I mean in charge," Vidor said. "I know Mado was close to your son, so I understand how he may feel about his death. I appreciate you understanding my actions when it came to your son. That means a lot to me. We both want a better planet to live on."

Mar Jeps sighed. "As I said before, my son understood his actions had consequences."

"I'm glad we're on the same page, then."

"But putting business aside," Mar Jeps said, then stood up from the armchair. She was unsteady on her legs but regained her balance and pointed at Vidor. "You murdered my partner Tetrick. That's something I will never forgive. Did murdering him make the planet a better place to live? I don't think so. As far as my son is concerned, you can send that Roneh Rayush woman and these vid experts out to spin your lies, but we both know my son revealed the truth." Mar Jeps was shouting by now.

Vidor sat there and remained calm. Her loss of control put him in command. He let silence seep in before he said anything. Mar Jeps was so upset, she was shaking. Obviously his Flomina gambit hadn't worked and he'd touched a nerve, probably due to the Malrap unmasking any diplomatic façade.

Vidor stood and called, "Warver, we're done here." Vidor attempted to take a puff of the cigar, but it had gone out. He smashed it into the ashtray, breaking it apart.

The door to the study slid open and Vidor said to Warver, "I think Mar Jeps is ready to go."

"Sorry about that…I…the Malrap."

"No need to apologize. You said what you meant. I appreciate it."

"I didn't mean…" Mar Jeps said. "I had a wonderful time this evening, and I didn't mean to be rude."

"Don't worry yourself. I have a thicker skin than you might think," Vidor said. "If we're being honest with one another, I know your son revealed the truth, but when the truth is simply outside the best interests of the governing body, well-crafted lies are necessary."

Mar Jeps was stunned by Vidor's words.

"Of course, that's between us. I'll deny saying it," Vidor said. "On that note, good night, and my office will reach out to arrange the meeting with your partner. We'll definitely talk soon."

Mar Jeps exited the room with Warver. Vidor followed them to the door and closed it behind them.

He picked up the cigar and placed it in his mouth, forgetting what he'd done, and when he noticed its condition, he tossed it across the room. *This situation cannot stand*, Vidor thought.

**AFTER DAVIK ATMAR INFORMED HIM THAT MAR** Jeps' cruiser had gone, Vidor told Davik to relay a message to Flomina that he'd be working late. He wouldn't be upstairs to say goodnight to the children and she shouldn't wait up for him. This had occurred more than a few times since Breeze Celebration, but he was usually at the Global Assembly building monitoring troop movements against the rioters in each dome or meeting with his staff who were strategizing ways to extinguish the doubts stoked by Yor Vanderlord's performance.

The dilemma ignited this evening was far more personal and enraging. Vidor didn't believe he could ever trust Mar Jeps like he had Mado Prevor. It took Malrap to reveal her true feelings, and her attitude toward him was appalling. There was too much history between them to establish a working relationship. She'd never be loyal to him, and what Prevor Industries was undertaking was far too important for him to sit back and let her dictate terms to him. Fortunately, Vidor had leverage over her.

In the meantime, Vidor would put Orn on the job. Orn had already been sent on a survey of planetary security, but Vidor commed and ordered him to make it his priority, beyond what they discussed earlier, to marshal all GSS resources to track down Mado Prevor. Vidor would craft a digi-mail to the GSS Division Directors to give Orn whatever he required to accomplish this goal. He told Orn to operate with the utmost discretion so it wouldn't get back to Mar Jeps. She was the one person on Koda who could defy him and place his future plans in jeopardy, and the most important task on Koda now was locating Mado Prevor.

Vidor recalled the first time he met Mado Prevor. He was in a tight race for his third six-year Presidential term and was attending a campaign fundraiser organized by the DOME project think tank, Domes Over Koda (DOK). The members of DOK consisted of corporations who lobbied for their businesses' inclusion in the DOME project and proposed legislation for the research and development funding.

Vidor was running against four contenders, and polls showed this election wouldn't be a landslide like his first or a solid victory like his second, but rather a closely fought battle. Possibly a squeaker. The biggest issue against Vidor was the DOME project. The citizenry was doubtful the domes would happen as Kodans were dying at a higher rate than ever due to the crisis: Intense weather—heat, mega-storms—and rising sea levels were wiping communities off the map; populous regions were becoming uninhabitable as resources ran thin and starvation was widespread. Tetrick Vanderlord's anti-DOME movement was gaining fervor and accusations were rampant about how the DOME project was a fraudulent scheme to make the rich richer and the poor poorer. Vidor's opponents used this issue against him at every turn and his lead in the polls had begun to slip. His speech at the fundraiser was meant to put him firmly on top and clinch his reelection as the major viewing channels were on hand to broadcast it.

Vidor stood at the podium, looking out at the tables filled with his campaign contributors, the wealthiest Kodans, and said, "Today, I announce at this prestigious event that the Global Assembly budget in the coming session will forgo the sum allotted for research and development of the DOME project, which has dominated the budget for decades, and we will begin funding the first phase of the project. This will include subsidizing the building and outfitting of factories in every region for processing raw materials necessary for the dome foundations and for manufacturing the dome panes, frames, and air circulators. No longer will this crisis hang over us. No longer will the Kodan people wake up each day and wonder about their children's future. We must move forward with haste. Not only will the DOME project in its completion bring safety and security to the Kodan people, but the vastness of the project will afford employment for all able-bodied Kodans and guarantee no Kodan will go to sleep hungry. The project will unite us like no other event in Kodan history, putting all Kodans to work for the future of our families, the future of our neighbors, the future of our species, and the future of our planet."

The people at the fundraiser rose from their seats and applauded, and Vidor raised his arms upward in victory for the Kodan people and his campaign. Afterward, Vidor was greeted by the crowd who stood in line to promise their support. One of those people was Joro Camtur. Vidor had been introduced to Joro at a fundraiser by one of his largest benefactors years ago, then Joro threw a dinner party for Vidor at his mansion and in a private moment pledged to throw his considerable wealth behind Vidor's second election. At this DOK fundraiser, standing beside Joro was Mado Prevor.

At a glance, Mado Prevor fit the bill for someone in his profession. He was average height and build and at the age where he had begun to lose his hair. He appeared awkward in this social setting, looking more at his feet than the people around him. Everyone in the room recognized Mado Prevor. Since the release of HGD, his face could be seen on countless media outlets and his invention had made him one of the wealthiest men on the planet. Joro introduced him to Vidor.

"An honor to meet you, Mister President," Mado Prevor said.

"Pleasure meeting you, too," Vidor said. "Of course, Joro didn't have to introduce you. You're maybe the only toymaker in the room."

"Toymaker?" Mado Prevor said and laughed.

Vidor thought it an odd laugh, like a high-pitched squeal, but Mado Prevor was known to be eccentric.

"Toymaker?" Joro said. "The President has quite the sense of humor. Mado's HGD is a hi-tech masterpiece, the likes of which Koda has never seen."

"Yes, it's rather hi-techy," Vidor said. "But Kodans use it to escape reality. It's hi-tech escapism for play and therefore it's a toy."

Mado Prevor laughed again. "The President has a rather limited take on my accomplishment," Mado said. "That won't deter me from making a sizable contribution to his reelection campaign. A sizable one for a mere toymaker."

"Well, we don't want to take up any more of your time, President Plemso," Joro said. "People are waiting. Wonderful speech and—"

"I'm curious," Vidor said to Mado Prevor. "Why would somebody so close to the Vanderlords contribute to my campaign?"

"I had the utmost respect for the Great man. He was a mentor and one of my closest friends. He schooled me in the ways of Kodan business and introduced me to investors like Joro who made the HGD possible, but I don't see space travel as a viable solution to this looming crisis. The DOME project is the best path toward salvaging the future for the Kodan people even if there are problems in successfully constructing them."

Joro said, "Mado, I don't think this—"

"Problems can be overcome," Vidor said. "And we will overcome them."

"I have no doubt," Mado Prevor said. "And I think you're the man to do it."

"I appreciate your confidence in me, your contribution, and your vote, but I should get back to working the room."

Mado Prevor said, "Just so you know, I'm developing a fully renewable power source that's just right for the domes."

"Really? Interesting, but I believe we've got it covered."

"That's not what I've heard."

Vidor wanted to move on from these two, but he wouldn't allow himself to be challenged by Yorlik the Great's pupil. "What have you heard?"

Joro said, "This isn't the time or the place for this conversation, Mado."

"No, please, Joro," Vidor said. "I'd like to hear what the toymaker has to say about why, after a decades-long, trillion-unit investment, the power source for the domes won't work, and how his tinkering with toys has given him this insight."

Joro said, "He didn't—"

"I've lived a long time, Joro," Mado Prevor said. "I can speak for myself."

"Yes, please, Joro. Let the toymaker speak for himself," Vidor said, raising his voice so the people surrounding them stopped to listen. He wanted to humiliate and put this toymaker, who was in league with the Vanderlords, in his place once and for all. "We all want to hear what the toymaker has to say about how he's going to save the Kodan people from the crisis with his toys. Please tell us, Mado Prevor. We're all listening. We're all ears. Come, now—everybody wants to hear."

Vidor looked around. Most of the room was staring at Mado Prevor, waiting for him to speak. Vidor was satisfied he'd set him up to be humiliated in front of the wealthiest and most powerful people on the planet.

Mado Prevor peered around at the crowd and forced a peculiar smile. Vidor surmised the smile was a product of the awkward situation. Then Mado Prevor said, "Excuse me," to Vidor, pulled out a chair from one of the banquet tables, and stood on it.

"Hello, everyone, can you all see me and hear me? Rather than going into the tech minutiae of my proposal, I'll break down my power source to its basic concept." Mado addressed the room as if he were pitching to a board of directors. "With all due respect to Voila Komrit, whose corporation has been working on this problem for decades, in a year or so, I will release a product called the Atmospheric Ionic Device, or AID. The device will provide every household on Koda with permanent access to energy for their homes without the interminable interruptions due to the failing Global Net." Almost on cue, the lights in the banquet hall turned off, flickered, then lit the room once again.

"The power failures and outages have become a part of daily life on Koda. We've put up with them as an annoyance that won't go away. Well, with AID, this problem will never occur again for a price that every Kodan can afford. AID will cost less than a yearly Global Net bill and one purchase will last a lifetime. My corporation will provide financing for any citizen who needs it. No longer will citizens have to rely on the Global Net grid, which is approaching complete failure. Again, without going into the details of the tech, AID utilizes a small reaction within its core, absorbing all the energy surrounding us in our daily lives—kinetic, solar, wind, electrostatic…et cetera—to create power. The greater the power required, the greater the power drawn from the surroundings.

"Again, with all due respect to Voila Komrit who I'm sure is here…" An elderly woman wearing a glittery gown and a priceless necklace of multicolored jewels held up her hand. "Yes, there she is. With my power source, there is no fear of the domes ever running out of energy. My power source will supply the energy required by each dome to run all the households, all the businesses, all the factories, all the air circulators, all the public rail cars by drawing on the sheer life-force within the domes without the need for dozens of power plants and transformer stations.

"This tech will be brought to market soon by Prevor Industries. However, in decades of research and development funding, Voila's power source has never met the standards necessary to power one dome of the nine proposed by the DOME project. Thank you for listening." Mado Prevor stepped down from the chair and the banquet hall was silent for a moment, then exploded in applause equal to the intensity after Vidor's speech.

Vidor was appalled at being upstaged. When the applause ended, the crowd around them dispersed with individuals one by one patting Mado Prevor on the back and saying they looked forward to seeing this power source first hand. A few gave Mado their business card and offered to invest. That weird smile was pasted on Mado's face and Vidor wanted to punch the self-satisfaction off it. Joro leaned over to Mado and whispered in his ear. Mado Prevor's smile disappeared and he put his hands on Vidor's shoulders. Mado Prevor's grip was stronger than Vidor ever imagined.

"I can't wait to show you," Mado Prevor said. "I believe it'll be the answer to the DOME project's power needs and will push the project forward to construction and completion." Mado Prevor stared at Vidor with sincerity and Vidor was filled with confidence in this man. His animosity toward Mado Prevor was washed away and forgotten.

Mado Prevor removed his hands from Vidor's shoulders.

Vidor said, "I look forward to hearing more about AID, but now I should mingle with my guests."

"Again, an honor to meet you," Mado Prevor said with that smile on his face once more, but now Vidor found it endearing.

Vidor was reelected, and a year passed. In that time, Vidor's view of Mado Prevor shifted back to suspicion as his corporation's influence grew in the Global marketplace and Prevor's pitch to the Global Assembly military for a sonic weapon to reduce civilian casualties was endorsed wholeheartedly by the public. Vidor couldn't help but authorize funding for the weapon, especially while the monumental civilian losses in the Separatist Revolts still persisted in the memory of the Kodan population. Mado Prevor's popularity on Koda soared. He was seen as a wealthy tech entrepreneur who had the people's concerns at heart. Vidor wondered at Prevor's true intentions. Would he run against Vidor in the next election? Was he attempting to position himself to undermine Vidor's authority?

Vidor ordered Orn to place Mado Prevor under surveillance and interrogate Prevor Industries' employees, but Orn found nothing suspicious. Mado Prevor continued development of the power source and labored long hours on his projects. Vidor always returned to the fact that Mado Prevor was close to Yorlik the Great, so how could he ever trust him? Vidor had to assume Yorlik told Mado Prevor about his discovery, too.

Vidor was finally compelled to summon a meeting of the CEOs from all the corporations receiving DOME project funding. The death toll from the crisis was increasing exponentially. Polling on the DOME project had sunk to an all-time low, which said something since the project spanned close to a century, and Vidor's own approval ratings were dropping as well. Vidor planned on running for another term, so he saw this as a call to action.

In the meeting, he told the CEOs in no uncertain terms that the project needed to break ground in the coming year. One by one, each corporate head agreed they were ready to move forward with the exception of Lia Komrit, who ran Komrit Energy for her mother Voila. She told Vidor her corporation required more time to work out the kinks in their power source. At the end of the meeting, Vidor asked Lia to stay, directing her to take a seat across from him at the table.

Lia was the same age as Vidor. They'd grown up in the same social circles and had even dated when they were teenagers. Lia was an only child groomed from an early age by her mother to take charge of the family business. She wore typical women's business attire consisting of a one-piece red-violet dress. Nothing fancy, but functional. Vidor still found her attractive. She was a dark-haired and curvaceous beauty. She wore no jewelry except for her partnering ring, which cost more than four years' salary for an average Kodan.

Vidor said, "Lia, Lia, Lia. How long have we known one another?"

"You know how long, Vidor," Lia said. "Don't patronize. Simply tell me how we can make this right."

"Always so 'let's get to the point' even when we dated."

"Well, you were younger and better looking back then."

"Ouch. I deserved that," Vidor said. "I'm actually sorry for what I said, that was unprofessional of me, but in all honesty, I'm angry and frustrated by this news that you're not ready to roll out the power source. Your family has been sucking the Global Assembly's tit for decades upon decades and you still can't make it work, after all these years, after trillions of units have been dumped into your family's lap. You aren't ready. The other corporations at this table are ready and they received far fewer units than you. I don't understand. Why aren't you ready? Make me understand."

"I can send you a memo, Vidor, but there are problems and we need more time."

Vidor slammed his fist on the table. Lia jumped in her chair. A few of the water glasses on the table fell over, then there was the sound of liquid draining from the table onto the floor. "I don't care. I don't," Vidor said, raising his voice. "If you don't come up with a solution that can produce tangible results that my engineers can confirm, then your funding will be cut off. You have a hundred and eighty days, and don't you dare call me for an extension. My decision is final."

"Who else can do our job?" Lia said, as if she had the advantage on Vidor.

"I'll find somebody," Vidor said. "Don't disappoint me, Lia. You've known me a long time. Have you ever known me to make idle threats?"

"No, Vidor. I just—"

"No justs. No buts. You heard my deadline. Now, why are you sitting there gawking at me and wasting time?"

"I don't think you—"

Then Vidor snapped and yelled, "Go! Get out of my sight! Now!"

Lia bolted out of her seat, collected her viewer and

briefcase, and strode out of the room as if it were on fire. Vidor hoped his insistence and his ultimatum would motivate Lia to get the job done.

On the 114nd day after the meeting, Lia called Vidor on his private comm. It was far past regular office hours. Vidor didn't take the call, but he listened to the message in which Lia pleaded for more time and before the message ended, he threw the comm across the room where it shattered against the wall. He had checked his internal approval polling which arrived at the end of every day and a downward trend still persisted.

Vidor wanted some good news, so he opened his viewer and realized his favorite news show, *The Lure*, was coming on the air. He was comforted when the introductory music began and the name of the show filled his viewer's screen. Then the announcer said the name of the guest, Mado Prevor. Vidor brought his hand up to close his viewer but decided to hear what Prevor had to say. Vidor figured he couldn't be any more frustrated, and maybe this was the real reason Lia wanted to talk to him.

The interview opened with Paresh asking Mado Prevor how he felt about the quick rise of his corporation in the markets and how Kodan society had embraced his corporation like no other in recent memory.

Paresh said, "…and the HGD takes Kodans from their troubles to places on Koda that don't exist anymore, places that make them ecstatic. The sonic cannon is considered the most ethical piece of military gear in Kodan history. Kodans love Prevor Industries."

"Well," Mado Prevor said, "that's heartening. I obviously think Kodans are a brilliant species. I'm here talking to you, right?"

Paresh gave one of his signature guffaws. Vidor couldn't help but laugh along.

Mado Prevor continued, "If we learned anything from the SEEDER program, Kodans are a rare marvel in the universe. Yorlik the Great, by far the greatest space explorer in Kodan history, was gone for more than a century, searching for a planet similar to the one we live on so the species could survive. He obviously thought the Kodan people were worthwhile, too."

Paresh chuckled again and said, "Yes, the Great man was a persistent fellow and if it wasn't for him, we might not have you on the scene brightening our lives. He must've seen something in you."

"I'm grateful to Yorlik. I was fond of him. He definitely saw something in me that others could not," Mado Prevor said and laughed.

"Why is that funny?" Paresh said. "What did he see?"

"Kind of an inside joke between us," Mado Prevor said. "Obviously, he understood me for the man I truly am."

"That must've been uplifting," Paresh said. "Why do you think that bond existed?"

"We spent a great deal of time together. There was mutual respect and we both valued life in the same way, in a sacred way. That aspect of our personalities drew us closer and I think that has truly been the priority in my work here to this day."

"Yes, that's commendable," Paresh said, clearing his

throat and taking a sip from his mug. "You're here to discuss this new and exciting project you're working on."

"Of all the Prevor Industries projects to date, I'm most proud of this one for the good it will do the Kodan people."

"I'm excited as well. Please tell us about it."

Mado Prevor stood and brought from behind his chair a silver cube-shaped box and placed it in front of his chair, then seated himself again. Vidor surmised the cube was a little over a half a meter on all sides. Mado patted it with the palm of his hand and said, "This is AID." Then he launched into a speech that was similar to the one at the banquet a few years ago, but this was more polished and to the point.

Paresh gaped with wonder and when Mado Prevor finished his explanation of his invention, Paresh leapt from his chair and said, "May I?" holding his hands out.

Mado Prevor said, "Please."

Paresh picked up AID, then raised and lowered it, feeling its weight. "This right here is going to do all you've said? It's so light."

"Yes, Paresh."

"How is that possible?"

"Corporate secret, Paresh. A wonder of Prevor."

Paresh pretended to sneak off the set with the cube. The crew behind the cameras laughed along with Mado Prevor, then Paresh returned with the cube, sat down and placed it on the stage in front of himself.

"So, I believe you have a demonstration of this little wonder for us," Paresh said. "Let's see it."

The viewing channel feed cut from *The Lure* set to a vid of Mado Prevor standing outdoors illuminated by stage lighting. It was nighttime and darkness surrounded him. He was in front of a four-story building with all the windows lit, and a sign across the front reading *Prevor Industries* was lit, too. The cube was at Mado Prevor's feet and a man in blue coveralls stood beside him. Mado Prevor said, "Here we are in front of the Prevor Industries building. This is Gols and he will assist in the demonstration." Gols waved, then a handheld cam with a light followed him as he walked with small strides, tracing the path of a cable to a power box on the side of the building. He reached up and grabbed the lever on the power box and pulled it down, then the vid cut to the other cam showing Mado Prevor standing outside the building where behind him all the windows and the sign went dark.

Mado Prevor said, "Gols has disconnected the building from the Global Net by flipping off the power box. Now AID will provide enough power not only for this entire building's lights, but for all the viewers and viewing screens, lab equipment and security features inside."

Mado Prevor reached down and pressed the flashing button on top of AID. The cube's edges glowed blue until they were fully lit. A moment later, all the windows of the building were lit again along with the sign.

"Now come with me," Mado Prevor said, and the handheld cam followed him to the front door of the building. He activated the palm scanner beside the door and the bolts clicked open. "This is one of our offices," he said as he entered the building and walked through a large open room full of desks and cubicles. The cam followed his direction as he pointed around the room. All the screens on the walls were displaying viewing-channel shows and the viewers on the desks were powered up, too. Mado Prevor reached another door with a small window at about eye level. He used another palm scanner and opened the door to a science lab. He only walked a few meters inside, but he pointed around the room again where all the equipment was running and whirring. "We can't go any further without giving up corporate secrets, but I hope you can see the power of AID in this demonstration. Back to you, Paresh."

The vid feed cut to Paresh and Mado Prevor. Paresh said, "This small box lit that entire building and powered everything in it?"

"Yes," Mado Prevor said. "What you've seen on the vid isn't a trick. This version of AID has the capacity to light up a four-story building of about four hundred square meters a floor and supply all its power needs."

"If this is true, then this is a game changer. A turning point in Kodan history."

"Let's not get ahead of ourselves, Paresh, although I love your enthusiasm."

"Seriously, with the Global Net going down, this is huge. Latest figures are seventy-five percent of the Kodan population is without power for more than half their day and the outages can happen at any time. And you said this device is easily affordable for every Kodan. That's incredible," Paresh said. "I've also heard from many sources that this could energize the domes. Is that true?"

"Again, let's not get ahead of ourselves. Prevor Industries will release AID later this year and then we'll see if President Plemso is interested. I'm fully aware Komrit Energy has the DOME project power contract, and until the President contacts me, I'll conclude he isn't interested."

"Well, we all know the President is a wise man who will do the right thing. I also know the President watches my show regularly," Paresh said, then turned and looked directly into the cam. "So, President Plemso, here you are. Take this into consideration."

"I support the President in whatever he decides."

"We all do," Paresh said. "Mado Prevor, thank you for coming here and giving us a glimpse of this miraculous device. Always a pleasure having you here, come back anytime, and I wish you the best of luck getting AID to every Kodan."

"Thanks, Paresh. I appreciate you having me and allowing me to demonstrate AID."

Vidor closed the viewer and thought about what he'd witnessed. Paresh would've done his homework before allowing this story to air. Still, Vidor was skeptical. He didn't trust Mado Prevor. He couldn't see past the issue of placing one of the most important aspects of the DOME project in the hands of someone who lauded Yorlik the Great.

Vidor's office comm buzzed. It was Lia Komrit. She must've tried his busted private comm, then commed here. He let it buzz a few more times before he decided to activate the connection.

Lia said, "So, were you watching *The Lure?*"

"Yes, were you?"

"Yes, my public relations person alerted me to it."

"I assume that's why you called me earlier—doing damage control?"

"Yes, I figured you'd be watching. What did you think?"

"I'm on your side, Lia, but unless you can present a functional power source, ready for installation into each dome, then I have to consider alternatives. I gave you a deadline and I expect you to meet it."

"You're being impossible, Vidor."

"Impossible?"

"Yes. What will people say about your administration, about the Global Assembly paying my corporation trillions of units all these years, and getting nothing out of it? How will that reflect on you?"

"Are you threatening me, Lia? It doesn't suit you."

"It's not a threat. Just a dose of reality."

Vidor laughed. "Reality? What would you know about reality? While I was off fighting and watching good men getting blown to pieces, you were out at the most exclusive clubs in Capitol City, drinking and carousing and finding a new bed to sleep in every night in your quest for the perfect wealthy partner to bring home to your mother. Reality? Your corporation took trillions with no results. I think the Kodan people will be interested in how you bilked them," Vidor said. "You don't want to test my mettle."

"I thought we were friends."

"I thought we were, too, but this power source is about something much bigger than our friendship. This is about the survival of the Kodan people."

"No, this is about the survival of your Presidency, and your place in history."

"Believe what you will, Lia. That doesn't change the fact the clock is ticking. You should be busting your engineers' balls," Vidor said. "I hope you figure something out. I don't want to go anywhere else for the power source, but you're leaving me no choice. I told you last time we spoke that my decision is final. Believe me, I want you to succeed, because if you succeed, we all succeed."

"I'll see what I can do, Vidor," Lia said and disconnected the comm.

Vidor was sincere in what he said. The DOME project would not succeed if Komrit Energy failed to provide their vital contribution. He might have an alternative, but he was reluctant to put his faith in Mado Prevor.

So Vidor waited for Lia Komrit to comm him with good news. In the meantime, he dispatched his top military engineer to investigate the problems with the Komrit power source. The engineer returned to report Komrit Energy's power source was highly flawed in its concept. The project was based on the theory of perpetual motion, which had never been used in a practical way and none of the personnel at Komrit had the genius to transform the theory into a power source. Vidor kept sending his own experts, but one after the other, they returned with reports of incompetence to buffoonery in the Komrit workforce. He even called the DOME project research-and-development inspectors, who let this sham continue for decades, into his office and jailed them for treason.

The deadline passed and Vidor digi-mailed Lia to tell her that he hadn't lost faith in her. In the meantime, AID hit the stores and was a resounding success. Prevor Industries stock skyrocketed in the Global Markets. One couldn't turn on a viewing channel or read a digi-media outlet without discovering a story about AID, Prevor Industries, or Mado Prevor himself. He was hailed as the inventor with the most profound impact on Koda since Yorlik the Great. Sales went so well that Mado released a statement saying he was halving the price so more Kodans could access AID and giving the purchasers of the first run a rebate. AID's sales increased even more and Mado Prevor expanded his factories to meet the demand. A poll was released showing Mado Prevor to be the most popular and beloved person on Koda, while President Vidor Plemso's popularity was still plummeting.

Vidor was beside himself for days. No word from Lia Komrit, and he was aware what he needed to do for the Kodan people. He searched for the reasons not to work with Mado Prevor, but all he could come up with was his distrust of anyone connected to the Vanderlords and not wanting to give Mado Prevor's popularity any credence. His political advisors told him that he should get over his gripes for the good of Koda. They also suggested an association with Mado Prevor would prop up his approval polls, because people would acknowledge his wisdom in bringing Mado Prevor into the Global Assembly fold. Eventually, he decided to meet with Mado Prevor before putting his misgivings aside.

Vidor invited Mado Prevor to his estate when the Global Assembly was out of session. He wanted the get-together to appear more casual than official. He didn't want the digi-media getting the idea he was courting Prevor Industries and alarm Lia Komrit.

That day, Mado stopped in his tracks as he passed through the doorway of Vidor's study. "Well…well… well…" Mado Prevor said, observing his surroundings. "Joro told me you bought Yorlik's library, but I had to see it to believe it."

Sitting behind his desk, Vidor said, "I don't think it looks too bad here." He rose from his desk chair to greet Mado Prevor.

"No, it's a fine-looking library," Mado Prevor said, strolling around the room, removing a book and reshelving it, then continuing his rounds.

"I think so."

"Looks like you're doing lots of work around the estate. The landscaping is all torn up and the hallways are full of scaffolding and the smell of paint. Redecorating?"

"Yes, Flomina is on a rampage to get the estate the way she wants it before she gives birth to our first child," Vidor said. "You don't want a pregnant woman dealing with decorators, painters, and landscapers. She has them running around scared, but she's getting the job done and it's costing me a fortune. You probably don't know what I mean?"

"No. Never been partnered. I heard from Joro you're planning on having another child and paying the hefty fine for having more than one?"

"Yes, I've always wanted a few children. I was an only child who wished for a sibling and Flomina's keen to have another one. It's worth the fine."

"Family is a noble thing," Mado Prevor said, sitting down in one of the armchairs. "I've heard a rumor you'd like this place to be your permanent home as President rather than the Presidential mansion."

"Yes, I prefer my own home to that drafty building and I'd like to raise my children here instead of there, but it's a public relations nightmare."

"I may be able to help you with that problem," Mado said. "I have an idea that might sway the Global Assembly and the Kodan people."

"Please enlighten me," Vidor said, astonished Mado Prevor was sucking up to him already.

"Let's talk about the issues at hand before we get there."

"Yes, it's a pretty simple proposition. Do you think your corporation can take care of installing the power sources in all the domes?"

"If that's all you wanted to discuss, you could have asked me over the comm," Mado Prevor said. "I assume you have concerns which have prevented you from asking me before. I know Komrit is at an impasse with their power source."

Vidor chuckled and seated himself in an armchair across from Mado Prevor. He did like the fact that the man got straight to the point. That was one aspect of his job as a politician that he often found tiresome. As a military commander, you gave an order and that was the end of it, everything progressed from there. Politics required a dance and he didn't mind it most of the time, but there were instances when he would just like to give an order and move on. Mado Prevor reminded him how he was so caught up in the dance these days. It was nice to take a break from it.

"Well, all right then," Vidor said. "All right. Do you drink Malrap?"

"I haven't in a while, but considering the social setting, I wouldn't say no to a glass."

Vidor stood and opened the cabinet behind his desk, removed a carafe of Malrap and two glass goblets, then walked back to the armchairs and said, "Full or half-glass?"

"A full glass seems about right," Mado Prevor said. "Malrap can be both elevating and useful."

"Indeed. I agree." Vidor poured two full goblets, handing one to Mado, then sat down in the chair again across from him, setting the carafe on the table between them.

"Well, here's to getting to the matter at hand," Vidor said and held his glass up for a toast.

"I'll drink to that," Mado Prevor said and took a sip of the Malrap at the same time as Vidor. "I know this Malrap. This is the vintage Yorlik drank."

"You're a man who knows his Malrap. This is the Malrap from Yorlik the Great's cellar when he passed away. I bought the entire lot the same time as this room."

"You obviously have a refined palate."

"I appreciate the compliment. I'll take it."

"It's yours. No strings attached," Mado Prevor said, holding up his glass for a toast and Vidor joined him, draining his glass.

"That's my favorite type of compliment," Vidor said. "May I call you Mado?"

"Please do, President Plemso," Mado said, placing his goblet down on the table. "As I said, I haven't drunk Malrap in a while. I already feel it going to my head." He had consumed half of what Vidor initially poured.

"You won't mind if I do?" Vidor said, holding up his empty glass and the carafe.

"No, please go right ahead. Don't stand on ceremony for me."

"I won't," Vidor said, filling his glass. "Mado, you're correct. If this was just about the power source, I could have commed you and that would have been that. I asked you to my home because I feel like I need loyalty from the people who work with me and I don't have that from you. Maybe it's my military background or my upbringing, but I find you get the best results that way."

"I can certainly understand that sentiment in your current position," Mado said, leaning forward and placing his hands on his knees. "I'm not a man who believes in blind loyalty, though. Loyalty is grown out of experience, knowing you can trust the person and they can trust you. It's born out of respect."

"I couldn't have said it better myself," Vidor said.

"So, bottom line," Mado said, "you don't trust me. And if we're being completely honest, I'd say the same about you."

Vidor was taken aback for a moment. Nobody had spoken to him like this in quite some time. "Why would you say such a thing?"

"For the exact same reason I just explained. I don't know you as an individual. We've never had any dealings. I can't be expected to trust you just because you're President. And as I said, I don't believe in blind loyalty."

"So we're starting in the same place," Vidor said. "I'd consider that a good place to start."

"Agreed."

"Then let me ask you this—did the Great man tell you about his discovery?"

"Yes, he did," Mado said without hesitation.

"Did you tell anyone else?"

"No. Yorlik bound me to silence."

"Did he tell you the coordinates of the planet?"

"No."

"I suppose the Great man didn't think much of me, did he?"

Mado chuckled and drank down his remaining Malrap. "Sorry, what you said wasn't funny. I was just thinking what Yorlik would've said if he could see us sitting across from one another having this conversation in his library, in someone else's home, drinking his Malrap. That being said, can I have another splash?" Mado held out his empty goblet.

Vidor reached over with the carafe and filled Mado's glass a quarter of the way. "More?" Vidor said.

"No, but thank you. I'm going to nurse it. I'm enjoying the sensation, but I don't want it to overwhelm me."

"You never answered my question."

"Oh, about how Yorlik felt about you? Let's say you weren't his favorite Kodan. Not primarily because you wouldn't let him tell the Kodan people about his discovery—"

"What discovery?" Flomina said. Vidor turned to the entrance of the study. Flomina stood there leaning against the door frame. She was eight months pregnant and she appeared exhausted.

"Please, dear, I'm in the middle of a meeting. I told you about it," Vidor said, standing and walking over to her. He kissed her on the cheek. "Mado, this is my partner Flomina."

Mado rose from the chair to greet her.

"Don't get up on my account," Flomina said. "I was bored and decided to check up on the workers' progress around here. I didn't mean to interrupt. Nice to meet you."

"Nice meeting you as well," Mado said, seating himself in the chair again.

"You stay right here," Vidor said to Flomina.

Vidor yelled down the hallway outside of his study, "Davik, where are you? Davik! Davik!" He had explicitly asked Davik to keep watch over Flomina to ensure his meeting wasn't interrupted. Davik came scurrying down the hallway. He was chewing food with his mouth open.

Davik spoke through the food in his mouth. "Sorry, sir. I was just—"

"I can see what you're doing. You're disgusting. Have some dignity. Take Flomina back to her bedroom," Vidor said, then kissed Flomina on the cheek again.

Vidor said to Flomina, "You let Davik take you back to our bedroom. Get some rest and I'll be there shortly."

Flomina threw her arm over Davik's shoulder.

Vidor said to Davik, "We'll talk about this when I'm done with my meeting. You've got some explaining to do."

"Sorry, sir," Davik said, swallowing the food in his mouth.

"You will be," Vidor said and watched as Davik escorted Flomina down the hallway. Vidor took a deep breath through his nose and exhaled, composing himself, then turned back to Mado.

"She looks ready to pop," Mado said, picking up his goblet as Vidor made his way back to the armchair and sat down.

"Can't happen soon enough. She's not a woman who can lie around and do nothing and this bed rest is driving her crazy," Vidor said, taking a gulp of Malrap. "And me, too. Where were we?"

"I was saying, Yorlik was frustrated because you wouldn't let him tell the Kodan people about his discovery, but when you threatened him and his family, then he hated you. For him, you crossed a line. When you crossed that line, you became his enemy."

"I'm not going to apologize for my actions. Do you understand why I did it?"

Mado had been cradling his goblet the entire time and took a sip. Vidor assumed he was gathering his thoughts, because whatever he said next could make or break the most lucrative contract in his corporation's history.

"To be honest, I completely understood your stance as President of the Global Assembly. So much time and so many units had been invested in making the DOME project a reality, you had to protect its integrity. If you told the Kodan people about Yorlik's discovery and they demanded you ditch the DOME project for building spaceships and you capitulated, the move would have been catastrophic. How would you build enough spaceships in the time left before the environment became unlivable? The domes were the only answer for the survival of the Kodan people, so you had to stay the course and keep Yorlik's discovery under wraps. If the truth came out, the civil unrest would have been unimaginable."

"You understood my predicament, then," Vidor said. "But do you agree with how I dealt with Yorlik?"

Mado put his goblet on the low table beside him and sat up in the chair. "With all due respect, President Plemso, I don't agree with threatening the lives of a man's family to convince him to agree with your course of action. Now that you're about to become a father, when the safety of your family will become the most important thing in your life, you may think differently about how you dealt with Yorlik."

Now, sitting in his study after his meeting with Mar Jeps and sending off his digi-mail, Vidor thought of how Mado changed his mind about utilizing his power source with that one statement. He didn't agree with Mado: he would never waver from his decision to threaten Yorlik's family. If he had to make that decision again, he'd do the same thing, but Mado's statement helped Vidor reach the conclusion that he required Mado Prevor's genius to complete the domes and save his own family. He had to admit he had that one thing in common with the Great man. His family meant the most to him. And once again, Mado Prevor was the solution to their survival.

# Yor

"Liar!" Yor yelled and shut off the viewing screen in the living chamber.

The control-room door slid open and Mado entered. He had removed his prosthetic and Yor was amazed at the sight of him in his alien form as some sort of walking aquatic creature. His eyes appeared to protrude from their sockets with eyelids that seemed to hardly blink. He had no nose but two slits for nostrils. A mouth but no lips. His skin shimmered in the light.

"Is everything all right?" Mado said. "I heard you from the control room with the door closed."

"I forgot Prevorian hearing is so sensitive," Yor said. "I was watching a recording of Roneh Rayush on a viewing-channel show. I told myself I wasn't going to watch it, but I did anyway. I'm still infuriated by this campaign to discredit our work."

"We knew all along they wouldn't let the truth stand, but that's why we have people like Mel and Insol on Koda to keep the truth alive."

"I appreciate your optimism, but I can see this effort by the Global Assembly reestablishing their lie and winning over Kodans. They have all the viewing channels and most of the digi-media backing their story. How could it not overwhelm word-of-mouth efforts by Mel or anyone else in the Movement?"

"Unfortunately, that's out of our hands now and we have to trust the Movement to keep going," Mado said, walking over to the replicator. "I noticed you haven't eaten much lately."

"I've been focused on keeping the systems running at full capacity since the explosion. That was the task you gave me. Seems like more than a few things need fixing now. The breakdowns are never-ending."

"You must eat," Mado said, punching a food-request code into the replicator control panel.

"It's the life support systems that concern me the most. I'm worried about a cascading failure."

"I'll give them a once-over if you like," Mado said, waiting by the replicator as it whirred and clicked while it prepared his food. "The old girl wasn't fully prepared for space flight. We don't know the full extent of the damage from the explosion yet, although I think we'll make it to the way station all right. We can do a thorough rundown of all the systems there, perform major repairs and replace parts using the Industrial Parts Replication Device. If I might make an observation, you seem preoccupied beyond these concerns, though."

"I'm sure Prevorians in their advanced stage of evolution have the ability to compartmentalize emotions and thoughts and keep them from affecting daily life, but yes, you're right I'm preoccupied. I have no idea what's happening on Koda with my mother or Insol or Rajer or anybody I care about."

"That's rude, Yor. Prevorians are not insensitive. I know you're upset, but that's no excuse for taking it out on me." The replicator beeped signaling Mado's meal was ready.

Yor stood up from the recliner, walked over to the water dispenser, and filled a glass.

"I apologize, Mado," Yor said, sipping at the water. "I've just got a lot on my mind, and it feels like forever since we last communicated with Koda."

"It hasn't been that long. Twenty-seven days. But time is a little different out here—no sunrises or sunsets. You need to get used to it," Mado said, removing a steaming platter from the replicator. The food was Prevorian again and smelled like spoiled Kodan food.

Yor walked back to the other side of the room and sat down in a recliner, pinching off his nose. "Sorry, that smells awful."

"Something else you need to get used to," Mado said, placing his face over the food. Yor assumed Mado was smelling it. "Seriously, you need to deal with how time passes in space. I realize you've had no training out here, but you have to set up a routine that gets you from waking to sleeping step by step."

"I'll work on it," Yor said. "So, when can we communicate with Koda and actually have a conversation?"

"We need to wait awhile longer. Warver has a few Prevor Industries' specialists keeping an eye on the GSS surveillance search patterns for comms in general, and facial recognition searches on vid conversations have increased manyfold since we left. The specialists have confirmed they're concerned about you speaking to the Movement, and they're looking for me. We need them to think I'm still on planet," Mado said. "My techs are working to further encrypt our comms and vids so they can be two-way without the GSS watching or listening."

"That makes sense. Why didn't you tell me this before?"

"You didn't ask."

"If we're going to be cooped up in this ship together, then this has to be a partnership—you need to keep me updated and come clean about whatever else you've been concealing from me."

Mado nodded as Yor spoke. He attempted to smile, but without the prosthetic it was obvious how difficult it was for him as his cheek muscles strained and twitched. Mado picked up one of the Prevorian treats from the platter, popped it into his mouth, and chewed. After he'd swallowed, he picked up another treat and tapped it on the platter.

"I agree," Mado said. "That's what I had with your great-grandfather—a true partnership. You're right—it's about time we put ourselves on equal ground. Being open and honest is a matter of mutual respect. In regard to communicating with Koda, I will keep you updated on any developments."

"I appreciate that," Yor said. "So what else have you been withholding from me?"

"You mind if I come over there and sit down?"

"No. Please come over. I should attempt to get acquainted with the smell of your Prevorian meals or at least desensitize myself if we're going to travel together."

Mado carried the platter to the recliner nearest to Yor. He pressed a few buttons on the recliner's armrest panel and a table emerged from the floor and unfolded. When he was settled, he picked up one of the treats and held it out to Yor. "I ate Kodan food for twenty-four years. You could at least try one."

Yor gagged at the idea, but maybe the taste would be better than the smell. He figured he should give it a try, so he took the treat from Mado and bit into it without a second thought. The taste was repulsive. Before he could identify exactly why it was so bad, he'd spat it out and dashed to the sink where he vomited up the contents of his stomach. Then he drank down his glass of water, filled it again, and drank it all down.

Mado made a whooping sound. "I guess that means you didn't like it."

"Is that your scientific analysis?"

"Yes," Mado said. "I have to say, I'm impressed. All those years traveling with your great-grandfather, I made a valiant attempt at getting him to eat it, but he'd never do it."

"He was clearly smarter than me."

"Maybe he knew more than you, but he wasn't as brave," Mado said, laughing again. "Now, sit down and let's talk."

Yor filled another glass with water, cleaned the sink and the treat off the deck, and seated himself. Mado told him about his great-grandfather's idea to convince the Global Assembly to build their own spaceships, because it was clear the DOME project was a swindle to enrich the wealthy and create a ruling oligarchy in the guise of saving Kodans from the crisis, which had gone beyond ever reversing itself. He told Yor how the Leader had decided to secretly construct only two ships for a select portion of the population.

"I'm sure building ships for a select portion of the population wasn't what my great-grandfather had in mind."

"Not at all,' Mado said. "I devised a backup plan, though."

Mado explained how he'd funded ships for the populace by bilking the Global Assembly on his costs to construct their ships. The other ships were being built in a secret location in Shamba. If their plans hadn't changed, that's where they would've ended up after Breeze Celebration.

"Let's just say the Global Assembly project has experienced some setbacks and cost overruns," Mado said with a tone of self-satisfaction his voice. He popped a treat into his mouth and practically purred with pleasure.

"So, if I apply this new knowledge to our previous conversation," Yor said, "if the Movement wins, then we've got ships ready and can construct more. If the Movement takes longer to overcome the Global Assembly and ends up victorious, then more ships will be ready. If the Movement is crushed, then we just need to wait as the Global Assembly loses power due to its ineptitude and even more ships will be ready for launch."

"Correct, and as I've told you, the last scenario is the most likely and could take decades to play out," Mado said, popping the final treat into his mouth. "This is where you told me you wanted to pause before hearing any more about the plan. Do you want to know more now?"

"I guess I can wait to see how things go on Koda, and my first instinct about not wanting to know more until we reach the way station was probably correct."

Mado walked over to the kitchen and placed the platter in the dishwasher. "Good, because I'd rather wait until we reach A-1, too. Think of it as a planned meeting rather than me holding out on you," Mado said. "Now, let's get back to the repairs."

# Orn

When Orn entered the Leader's Global Assembly office, he was aware right away the Leader was furious. He looked haggard. His tie askew. His hair uncombed. This was the buttoned-up by-the-book military man. He sat with his palms down on the desk, striking it with his fingers in a constant rhythm, staring off into the corner of the room. He'd seen the Leader like this before over the years and his mood was always dark.

The Leader broke from his daydreaming when his eyes landed on Orn standing in the doorway. "Come on, Orn. Hurry up. I don't have all day."

Davik Atmar stood in the right-hand corner of the room, looking like a scolded pet.

"Davik, are you still here?" the Leader said. "Go attend to one of the matters we discussed."

"Which one?" Davik Atmar said, holding his digi-tablet up against himself with both hands as if he was ready to fend off whatever the Leader might throw at him.

"After all these years, you'd think he'd know better than to ask such an imbecilic question, wouldn't you, Orn?" the Leader said. "Sometimes, Davik, I wonder why I keep you around. Choose one and do it, then do the other things in whatever damn order you please. Just get them done, for Powers-That-Be sake. Now get out of my sight." Davik Atmar exited the side door. Orn couldn't help but be amused.

"Sit down, Orn," the Leader said. "You know you make me nervous when you hover."

"Yes, sir," Orn said and sat down in the chair across from the desk, gripping at the wood of the chair's arms.

"You just returned from the Norian dome. Is that correct?"

"Yes, sir. That's what I told you over the comm."

"Am I detecting attitude from you?"

"No, sir. Never, sir."

"Then give me your report on the state of planetary security."

Orn told him how he'd traveled to all nine domes and inspected their surveillance apparatus and personnel. He conducted interviews of the dome residents suspected of anti-government activity. A majority of the domes had captured Movement terrorists who were active in the Breeze Celebration riots and locked them up in their local GSS facility. He conducted in-depth interrogations of those prisoners, accumulating a list of newly active Movement collaborators at large. "Normally, I would have called for arrests, but considering the sensitive nature of the standoff with Prevor Industries, I thought I'd wait until I consulted you. If we don't use the names now, you can keep them for whenever you do your purge."

The entire time Orn was speaking, the Leader was pounding his fingers on the desk harder and harder. "I don't like this situation. I don't like it a single iota, especially after I had that dinner with Mar Jeps at my home."

"Yes, you told me when you commed to send me on the Mado Prevor assignment."

"Attitude, Orn."

"Sorry, sir," Orn said. "You didn't go into detail about it."

"The dinner was fine. Flomina took charge. You know how she is."

"Not really, sir."

"Oh, right, I forgot she doesn't like having you around. Probably for the best anyway."

Orn first met Flomina at a Global Guard event honoring the then-President before they moved in together. She took an immediate dislike to Orn, banning him from their social circle and home when their first child was born. Orn didn't like her, either, but he could see the political and societal advantage to partnering with her, and he had to admit she had good instincts when it came to people in the Leader's life, including him.

"What does she call me again?" Orn said, knowing full well, but he was aware it amused the Leader.

"'The vile cretin.'" The Leader stopped drumming his fingers and chuckled. "You have to hand it to her—she has a way about her. Anyhow, Flomina charmed Mar Jeps and they got along. Flomina genuinely liked her and afterward talked about inviting her over for charity events at the estate. The trouble started when I had my meeting with Mar Jeps in the study and she began dictating terms to me—to me—about my policies and that she was going to hold me accountable if I didn't follow her terms. Can you believe it?"

"No, sir, I cannot."

"I am the Leader, am I not?"

"Yes, you are, sir."

"She basically told me if I crossed a line she saw as unwarranted when it came to my political opponents, she'd call me on it and take action against me if need be."

"Unbelievable," Orn said. "What's happening with the dome power?"

"She conceded the reenergizing without firing a shot!" the Leader yelled and smacked his palm down on the desk. "Can you believe it? She didn't ask for anything—not even her partner's life. Now I don't have to release the little shit from prison. I informed her I'd let her visit him, but now I don't see why. She's not a great negotiator like me."

"You are the best, sir."

"I am."

"So, what's her leverage for holding you accountable?"

"Reenergizing the domes or the spaceships." The Leader smacked his palm down on the desk again, then sprang out of his chair. "That's why I'm in such a state right now. We had another setback on the engines and the cryo-units. It's going to put us behind schedule and nobody knows for how long."

"That's horrible news, sir."

"The top tech told me the spaceships development has been severely hampered by Mado Prevor's absence," Vidor said. "So what's your report on Mado Prevor? His disappearance has gone on long enough."

"You think Mar Jeps is to blame for these setbacks, sir?"

"In this case, she's in over her head," the Leader said,

turning to gaze out the window. "The dome looks beautiful this time of day. A magnificent achievement. I did one hell of a job getting the domes built. Didn't I?"

"Yes, you did, sir."

"Without Mado Prevor's solution on power, this could never have happened. I need the smartest man on the planet working on those ships."

"Yes, sir. I do have the report on him you requested after your meeting with Mar Jeps, twenty-three days ago."

The Leader turned from the window and smiled at Orn, then hurried to sit on the edge of the desk opposite him. "Yes, well, what did you find out?" He was acting like a child who was anxious to unwrap his gifts. "I can always count on you, Orn. Let me have it."

Orn decided to temper expectations beforehand. "It isn't exactly the results you wanted."

"Come on, Orn. Where is he?"

"I ran a facial recog scan on all the surveillance feeds in every dome and even the few outside the domes since Breeze Celebration. I performed a similar search on the cams at the Prevor Industries Space Facility, and I even visited the outlying military bases. Just to be thorough I did the same using GSS resources on planetwide vid conversations."

"And?"

"Absolutely no sign of him."

"How is that possible? Could he be in some remote area outside the domes or somehow be erasing his presence like you do?" The Leader stood up and sat down behind his desk. "Explain."

"First of all, even if he went to a remote area, the vid-cams would have caught him leaving one of the domes or the cruiserports. In this case, there is absolutely no sign of him. The last known image of him was during Breeze Celebration. That was on all the viewing channels and digi-media when he landed at the military park and boarded the WAEF for the parade," Orn said. "There is no sign of tampering on the feeds, although a man of his genius could probably have worked out how to get away with it. I double-checked and found nothing of note."

The Leader said, "Where is he, then?"

"There is a rational explanation, but you're not going to like it."

"Are you saying I'm irrational?" the Leader said, glaring at Orn.

"No, sir, I would never stoop to insubordination, sir."

"I read your report on your interrogation of Mellick Zonor. I know what you're going to say so I'll save you the trouble. You're going to say Mado Prevor is on the WAEF with Yor Vanderlord. That he escaped with the Vanderlord boy through the Active Glass pane behind the Prevor Industries Complex—which has finally been replaced with DOME glass, by the way," the Leader said, leaning back in his chair and crossing his arms. "But I have a hard time believing without concrete proof that he is somewhere in outer space with the Vanderlord boy right now. That makes no sense at all. You don't know him like I do. He was dedicated to his work which helped the people of this planet survive and he was proud of it. Now he's building the spaceships to save the last deserving Kodans before the domes collapse. Maybe he helped Vanderlord with the Breeze Celebration plot, shutting down all the government servers and building the Active Glass into the dome. All right, he did do those things, but he is the key to getting us off Koda before it's too late. Nobody else on this planet can complete those spaceships in the time we have left. I may not be around to see the new planet, but I'll be damned if my children are going to die here."

"So you don't think there's any chance he's on the WAEF with Vanderlord?"

"What about the vid he broadcast after Breeze Celebration? We've had our experts go over and over it and they agree there's been no trickery on the time stamp."

"You don't think a tech genius like Prevor could have altered it?"

"Why would he do such a thing? Why would he give up everything he built over decades for a shot at convincing the Kodan people of the Great man's achievement? He had to know it would never succeed."

"People tend to put hope over realism. I see it in my work all the time."

"Prevor isn't like those people. He's one of a kind."

"Doesn't that concern you, sir?"

"Why would it?"

"Since when do we tolerate individualism?"

"I see where you're going with this, Orn. Maybe his individualism caused him to be swayed by the Vanderlords over our policies," the Leader said. "I've begun to wonder if that vid of the Great man on the viable planet was something passed on to Prevor by the Great man and he gave it to the boy."

"Yes, sir. I was thinking the same thing."

The Leader rose from his desk and looked out the window again. "I don't want to revisit the past anymore, it's time to deal with the present and work toward the future," the Leader said and turned toward Orn. "Did the shooting down of the WAEF work as effective propaganda?"

"There's definitely a level of agitation among the citizenry that didn't exist before Vanderlord's presentation. The citizens are angrier and there's a certain degree of mistrust and doubtfulness about the Global Assembly. I've seen it in the recent arrests and interrogations. Like I predicted, the fake downing of the WAEF didn't help."

The Leader lapsed into silence. Orn was becoming uncomfortable as his hip injury from the ambush never healed properly and was acting up sitting in this chair. He began to squirm.

The Leader turned from the window and observed Orn. "You have somewhere to go. Am I boring you?"

"No, sir," Orn said. "Sitting too long in this chair. It's not comfortable."

"I'm fully aware it's uncomfortable. That's exactly why I placed it there. If you need to stand, go right ahead. You won't be here much longer," the Leader said. "By the way, I interrogated and locked up the Global Assembly rep who pushed for restoring the WAEF. Let's just say he won't be able to convince anybody of anything anymore without his tongue, and I sheared off a few fingers for good measure. Somebody needed to take responsibility."

"He had it coming."

"Yes," the Leader said. "How's the viewing-channel disinformation about the Great man's vid and Rayush's appearances faring in the minds of the citizens?"

"Of course, the skeptics believe the vid and the loyalists believe the viewing channels. The undecideds seem to be slowly leaning toward the skeptics, unfortunately, but those are the ones who are rather reticent about the political situation and don't pose a threat," Orn said and stood up. Not that he couldn't withstand muscle spasms, but it was difficult to talk while they were happening, and he wanted the Leader to understand his thoughts clearly. "The Rayush gambit is actually more effective than I would've predicted. There's a certain sex appeal that makes people listen to her—at least, that's what I've surmised."

"You don't have a thing for our poster girl, do you, Orn?" the Leader said and chuckled.

"No, sir. Not at all, sir. Why would I? I was talking from a singularly professional perspective, sir."

"All right, all right," the Leader said, still chuckling. He walked over to Orn and patted his shoulder. "It's fine if you do. I just need you sharp now. I have a sense that our control isn't what it was before Breeze Celebration. I'll have Kel notify our PR people, keep Rayush on her schedule, maybe add a few more appearances."

"You're always correct about these things, sir."

"Of course I am. Time will calm down dissent. Let's keep an eye on the Movement, especially Vanderlord's university mates. Or at least the ones still active," the

Leader said. "In the meantime, find Prevor. Get a fix on his location. If you fail, I have an idea on how to persuade Mar Jeps to hand him over or take control of Prevor Industries, but let's see how Rajer Jeps' interrogations pan out."

"You think Valsted is the best person to handle it?" Orn said.

"Now, now, Orn," the Leader said, grabbing Orn by the shoulders and shaking him. "I know you want a crack at Rajer Jeps but this is more of a finesse job. I've got a plan in play there. Our people are softening Jeps up before the Valsted interrogations and Valsted is an old friend of his."

"That's my concern, sir. Although Valsted's one of our best analysts, he's not an interrogator, and I don't believe the friendship is helpful."

"Are you questioning my methods?"

"No, sir."

"I saw him speaking with Mar Jeps at Ador Wint's memorial, too."

"Yes, I read your report on the memorial, and I plan on using their friendship to my advantage."

"How so?"

"You'll see. I also heard about Warver. Smart move. It'll give Mar Jeps second thoughts about challenging me in the future," the Leader said, taking a few steps back from Orn. "Anything else?"

"No, sir."

"Then go find Prevor. That's your primary mission now."

# Mado

Mado had been working on the WAEF's engines for days now. The explosion had knocked out one engine entirely, and he was still evaluating why he couldn't get the engine started even after he'd replaced the damaged parts with his meager supply of spares. He did figure out why the accident happened in the first place.

The strength of the metal in the newly manufactured engine parts wasn't up to the standards of a century ago when the WAEF was built. His employees told him the parts would never meet the original ship specs because of the lower quality of metal available. They joked, "Well, the WAEF isn't really going to fly anyway," so Mado told them to do their best. Originally, he figured their best would be good enough to get them to Shamba, and he calculated the probability of the WAEF being required to reach escape velocity, breaking free of Koda's gravitational pull at less than twenty percent. When Yor decided to visit the Royal Library early, that probability shot up, and with the WAEF restoration accelerated, Mado had no time to do the proper stress testing of the engines for leaving Koda.

The biggest hurdle facing them right now was making it safely around the red dwarf and landing at the way station. They'd need all the engines at full throttle for the maneuver, but Mado feared that one of the metallic engine parts shattering like glass in the explosion was a foreshadowing of what might happen again. Other than attempting to restart the damaged engine, he focused on stress testing the other engines one by one. Each time, he ended up shutting the engine down far short of full power when warning lights came on. He was upset about this quandary but determined to overcome it.

When Yor wasn't helping with the engines or performing his daily maintenance chores, he disappeared into the ship. Mado didn't pry into his whereabouts because Yor seemed in a better mood when he emerged after a long absence. Mado was aware young humanoids had a higher degree of moodiness along with hormonal outpourings and he assumed Yor missed Insol. Mado anticipated Yor would disclose his activities when he was ready.

Then one day, Mado grew concerned when Yor didn't show up at all for work on the engines. That wasn't like him so Mado searched the ship. He eventually found a door on a storage room slightly ajar with the lights turned on inside and slid the door open to find Yor sitting on a crate, slumped over asleep on the closed viewer in front of him. The viewer sat on top of a makeshift desk constructed of more crates.

On the wall above the desk, Yor was using lubricant for the landing gear and creating tally marks to count the days since they'd been gone from Koda. Traditionally on Koda, a complete set was five horizontal lines and one diagonal running across them so they totaled six. Yor's tally of their current journey was up to date. There were seven sets and since leaving Koda, they had been gone for forty-two days. Mado could see how counting the days would bring a sort of order to Yor's life.

Mado watched for a short time wondering if he should wake Yor who was snoring. Mado was aware Yor was having trouble sleeping since they'd left Koda, so even though Yor appeared to be sleeping in an uncomfortable position, Mado decided to leave him in slumber. He was sneaking out of the room when Yor yelled in his sleep and lurched backward, eyes wide, almost falling off the crate. He was unsure of his whereabouts. He stared at his viewer, then turned to see Mado standing there.

"Welcome back," Mado said. "Bad dream?"

"Sort of. I was dreaming I fell out of the WAEF while it was flying over Capitol City and I ended up falling into the Arena and it was packed with people like on the day of Breeze Celebration. I woke just before I hit the ground."

"Well, that could be interpreted many ways."

"I'd rather not dwell on it," Yor said, repositioning himself on the crate. "So you discovered my little hidey-hole?"

"I came looking for you when you didn't show up for work on the engines. I was a little worried considering your state of being since we left Koda."

"I guess you have reason to be, but since we had the conversation about maintaining a routine, I've been working down here in my spare time, keeping my mind active."

"Are you writing a journal?" Mado said, pointing at the viewer.

"No, nothing like that. I brought my personal viewer onboard with a few of my academic wafers when we did the engine tests before Breeze Celebration. I figured I could work on my new book in Shamba, and now with all the time it's going to take for us to reach the way station, I thought it might be a good distraction. It's helped me relax."

"I encourage it especially if it's helped you unwind enough to fall into a deep well of sleep, as we say on Prevor," Mado said. "You probably needed it, too."

"Can't deny that," Yor said. "But it's kind of fortuitous you showed up. I was reaching a point where I wanted to ask you a few questions about your plan with my great-grandfather and why you two decided to take the actions that led us here."

"Of course, whatever you need to know," Mado said, sitting on a crate beside Yor. "What are you working on, exactly?"

"Well, you know how the next book is going to be a biography of my great-grandfather?" Yor said. "Now, thanks to you, I've got info on his travels that nobody else on Koda possesses. Everyone knows about his life before he launched, but I've set up shop here to record the stories you told me about your travels together—"

"I think that it's best—"

"Yes, no need to remind me that it's best nobody knows about your true identity. This will never get out until the time is right and you approve," Yor said. "This exercise is more for my sanity at the moment than for publication."

"That makes sense," Mado said. "There's plenty to tell."

"Knowing you, once I get you going it'll all spill out."

"Storytelling is a finely honed tradition of the Prevorian people."

"Yes, I noticed," Yor said, chuckling as he stood up from his crate and stretched his legs, then raised his arms to the ceiling. "Let's finish the engine maintenance and maybe we can get a bite to eat and you can answer some questions afterward, which I'm sure you'll do in great depth."

When they began working on the engines, Yor appeared more engaged in the job than before. Mado presumed Yor was inspired, because when this job was finished, there was the prospect of Mado uncovering more of his great-grandfather's past. Yor's state of mind paid off when he spotted a defect in an irreplaceable part. The component was made malleable by the force of the engine when it was required to be inflexible. This caused a violent vibration in the engine as power increased past three-quarters capacity, requiring immediate engine shut-down before parts broke. So Yor had pinpointed why the engines couldn't be pushed past three-quarters power and possibly why the explosion occurred.

Yor was pleased by his discovery. Mado praised him. He was proud. Yor had picked up on the flaw before him, but they decided to leave fixing the problem for another day. They both concluded they were becoming bleary-eyed staring at the engines and nothing constructive was coming of it, so they took a break for a meal which they both ate ravenously and silently. When they finished eating, Yor suggested Mado join him in the storage compartment to help him with his project. Mado grabbed a few pillows for comfort and headed there.

Mado was wary about Yor typing up what he told him about his journey with Yorlik. That sort of behavior felt one step away from others learning Mado's true identity or his plan with Yorlik. He thought nothing good could come of it. On the other hand, they were in a ship hurtling through space far away from Koda. The probability of them interacting with anyone on Koda, who was not in their inner circle, for hundreds of days seemed unlikely and when the time approached for meeting with any of those Kodans, Mado would take the appropriate action.

Yor was already typing into his viewer when Mado arrived at the storage room.

"Would you like a pillow?" Mado said, holding one toward Yor who didn't look up from the screen. "That crate can't be comfortable on your hindquarters."

"I'm fine," Yor said, still not looking up.

"Suit yourself," Mado said, placing the pillows on top of a crate beside Yor. "You know, there's a synchronicity to you using this room as your office. This is where I hid when the WAEF landed and your great-grandfather was in quarantine at the military base."

"Really? It seems like an easy place to find somebody."

Mado walked over to the furthest corner of the room and felt around the wall with his fingertips for a springy section that housed a hidden latch. When he found the spot and pressed, the wall slid away, revealing a slim entrance. He and Yorlik fabricated this space by manufacturing a fake wall and using a small part of the storage compartment.

Yor peeked inside the space. "So this is how you arrived on Koda?"

"I was in the control room when we landed with the radiation shield down so nobody could see me, then I hid here. These walls are shielded, so any scans of the ship would appear normal while I hibernated with food and water until your great-grandfather found an excuse to return to the ship and sneak me off unseen.

"I ran out of rations after eighteen days and had one of the longest hibernations of my existence. Funny thing about hibernations, when my species closes our secondary eyelids more than three times in a row, we pass into a deep sleep called a hiber-dream where the line between dream and reality is erased and dreaming becomes more like waking consciousness.

"While I was waiting for your great-grandfather to return, I hiber-dreamed I was headed home in a pod I'd constructed. As I approached Prevor, I transmitted a distress call over and over again, but received no response. I achieved orbit with those stunning blue oceans below me and continued my barrage of distress calls as I passed over the planet's nightside and saw the lights of the sprawling cities beneath me. I couldn't reach the ground or oceans in the pod without burning up in the descent, so I continued sending messages. Days passed and my supplies ran out. Panic set in. I observed Prevorian spacecraft launched from the planet, but they passed by, ignoring my hails. I took apart and reassembled my transmission device to make sure it wasn't broken. Then the maneuvering capability of my pod malfunctioned and its orbit deteriorated.

I was out of choices, and in desperation, I decided to take the chance I wouldn't burn up and began reentry into the atmosphere. The pod shook and the metal groaned under the stress. I felt the intense heat charring my skin inside my spacesuit, the pain beyond anything I'd ever experienced in my lifetime. That's when I heard Prevorian mission control asking me to identify myself and whether I needed assistance. It was too late. I was doomed to die without ever seeing my people again.

"Then I heard your great-grandfather's voice and woke in the compartment. He'd been granted permission to remove personal items before the government confiscated the ship, which gave him the opportunity to retrieve me. He apologized and informed me that I'd been hibernating for eighty-five days and he feared I'd perished since there was no latch inside for me to escape. I was dehydrated and famished.

"I was happy to see your great-grandfather and glad I wasn't frying in the pod above Prevor. In my culture, hiber-dreams are considered premonitions of future events. While I hydrated, ate, put on the prosthetic devices which were stored on a shelf in the chamber, and dressed myself in a military uniform your great-grandfather stole from the base's barracks, I must've appeared frightened. Your great-grandfather kept asking me if I was all right.

"Years later, I was still haunted by the hiber-dream and I told your great-grandfather about it. He responded, 'Your consciousness was telling you through your dream that you were dying in the compartment…but just in case, when you return to Prevor inside the pod, you should approach the crisis differently than in the hiber-dream.'"

Yor backed away from the entrance and said, "Well, you won't have to worry about that anymore."

"For now," Mado said, reaching up and pressing the latch. The wall slid back into place.

"What does that mean?"

"I'll explain later," Mado said. "You know this is also the storage room where your great-grandfather built the first HGD?"

"I'll make note of that. Now, I was thinking that you once told me," Yor said, sitting down on the crate and reading aloud from his viewer, "that my future plans don't bear any connection to the government's misguided policies which are driven more by greed and ignorance than wisdom and fact."

"I told you that when we first met," Mado said. "Your eidetic memory is failing you, though. I said 'wisdom and scientific fact.'"

Yor stared at Mado, then shook his head as if he was rattling something loose in his brain. "You're absolutely correct."

"Of course I am."

"A Prevorian thing?"

"Yes, our memories are legendary," Mado said. "Now, what would you like to ask about that statement?"

"So, if that statement was true, how could you team up with the Global Assembly on the power source? Why not follow my father's lead and back the anti-DOME movement?" Yor said. "I know it's outside the scope of the biography, but it could help me understand the history of our current situation better."

"All right, I have an idea where to begin. Feel free to ask questions or stop me if you want to go forward or back in time."

"That sounds reasonable."

"When am I not?" Mado said and laughed.

"You're a funny…Prevorian," Yor said. His smile stretched out as if he was holding back a sneeze, then he made a snorting sound and laughed loudly.

"You're right," Mado said. "This process is good for you. Nice to see you laugh that way again."

"Definitely feeling more like myself," Yor said. "Please start where you think best."

"All right," Mado said. "After the WAEF was safely parked in the hangar at the estate and the erasure procedure implemented, your great-grandfather had a physical examination performed by a med who was a friend of the family. He went over the results with the med and your mother. A cellular analysis showed a rapid breakdown in the structure of his cells which was increasing his aging at a faster rate than normal. Your mother had always suspected this was happening which is why we did the test. The prognosis was that your great-grandfather had maybe a year to live, so whatever we hadn't set in motion or planned for the future had to be figured out as soon as possible.

"As I said, the WAEF was already parked awaiting its future restoration and HGD 2.0 was a smash hit with Prevor Industries riding high financially, so Yorlik and I discussed how to proceed. We laid out the probabilities of each scenario with or without President Plemso in power."

"Wait a moment—I just thought of something," Yor said. "How did my great-grandfather know you? I thought his memory of the expedition was erased? I figured the planning was done before that."

"No, only the discovery was erased. He could recall most everything up to a few years before the planet's discovery, then his memory continued about a year into the journey home."

"What about the foto?"

"After the procedure, I told him about the planet and how we took the foto so he was aware of its significance. I even showed him the vid of the planet we used at Breeze Celebration."

"But when I asked him about the foto, he said he couldn't discuss it because, 'I no longer have those memories. They were taken from me.'"

"I recall him relaying that conversation to me. He definitely couldn't tell you much about when the foto was taken, but he intentionally didn't inform you of the foto's significance and the discovery."

"Why?"

"First of all, his memory was erased and he wasn't supposed to know," Mado said. "Secondly, he didn't tell you because you were too young to understand the danger of telling anyone else…and he was aware how much it meant to you."

"So he lied to me?"

"He didn't exactly lie."

"Did he tell me the truth?"

"We discussed this before. Facts were withheld to keep you safe—"

"That seems to be the theme of my childhood."

"We made sure you worked it out eventually, which suited our future plans."

"How did lying suit your future plans?"

Yor was becoming agitated. Over the years of working together, as Yor labored to figure out the truth, Mado never told him the entire truth for his safety. Recently, he'd unburdened himself to Yor about hidden facts like the foto and the journal. Now, in a moment when he was thinking more about making Yor happy than the consequences of his words, Mado had spilled a truth about the past which he never meant to give away. He'd need to traverse these waters carefully.

"I'm afraid you might not like what I'm about to say."

"I can see that," Yor said. "Out with it."

"All right," Mado said. "There was a bond between you and your great-grandfather that brought more joy to him than I'd seen in all the years of our friendship. Maybe more than when he discovered the planet. I recall the day you were born—your great-grandfather was ecstatic. He noted your intelligence at a young age and paid for your tutors, and he reveled in your thirst for knowledge. Your great-grandfather saw how much his voyage meant to you. Then one day he came to me and posited whether it would be fair to make you part of our plan. We talked about the restoration of the WAEF and how it could be unveiled as a big event. He thought if a Vanderlord were involved, and that could never be your father, it would only make the resurrection of the WAEF all the more powerful.

"When we received the report on your great-grandfather's deteriorating health, we got together to discuss the future, and the subject of your involvement came up again. Your great-grandfather thought it might be necessary to push the process along and encourage your enthusiasm about his journey, and in that way guarantee your entanglement in the future plans we were laying out."

"Did you two manipulate me?"

"Who's to say?"

"That's not an answer. Yes or no?"

Mado plotted his words in his mind. He was keenly aware of the delicate nature of his current circumstance. "Before I go any further, I'd like to say it's not as diabolical as it sounds. However your great-grandfather acted, he did it out of love for you. Because of the family history—his, Naivim's, your father's—you carried with you the distinction of being a Vanderlord which you'd never be able to shake. You were an enemy of the Global Assembly. For instance, although we kept the knowledge from your father, we were told by a confidential source via Joro that your mother had been threatened that if you ever became aware of your father's torture at the hands of the government, then you'd be taken into Global Assembly custody and brainwashed into becoming a follower of their policies. They didn't want another Vanderlord making problems for them, coming after them with revenge in their hearts, and if you were brainwashed, they'd make you into their best propaganda tool. A Vanderlord supporting their lies."

"Yes. My mother told me that she lied about my father's torture to keep me safe, but I'm just hearing from you the extent of the punishment if I'd found out."

Mado cleared his throat. "So, your great-grandfather decided to inspire you to learn the true facts about the SEEDER program and his mission on your own. Your enthusiasm for his personal history and love for him mixed with a little bit of hero worship would put you firmly and safely in our camp and negate any future efforts by the government to take you from the family, because your path would be born of intellectual curiosity and not revenge. That's why he had you visit the estate for an extended stay before he passed. He wanted you to absorb your heritage, all the books in the library and the historical remnants of the SEEDER program around the estate. After he was gone, the estate and the library would no longer be in the family's possession."

Yor said, "That's what that visit was all about?"

"And spending quality time with you before he passed."

"I know he loved me, Mado. I loved him, too. I can remember as a child how much I couldn't wait to visit, to see him. As you've said, there was a special bond between us. And in a way, I did worship him," Yor said with emotion in his voice. "But this revelation makes me feel like just another piece in the plan the two of you put together. It was a calculated manipulation of a young and impressionable mind by a highly intelligent man using my love for him as bait. Now it's clear that when he told me, 'Lies can be just as powerful as the truth,' he was referring to our conversation in that moment about the foto and not some great mystery behind his voyage, correct?"

"Yes, but—"

"I just can't wrap my head around it. It's like my entire life has been a lie. On top of that, we discussed my visit to the estate before and you never corrected my misinterpretation of it. Why?"

Yor was worked up. Mado understood the reasoning behind his emotions. In this instance, Mado needed to be honest with Yor even if it might explode in his face.

"I actually argued with your great-grandfather about this kind of subterfuge before it occurred because I thought it wasn't fair to you, but he was truly concerned that the Global Assembly would take advantage of you, and if truth be told, we both saw the value in you being part of the plan.

"When he said, 'Lies can be just as powerful as the truth,' he noted right away that you took it as being connected to his voyage, and he saw no need to correct you because your interpretation was true as well…and look how it inspired you.

"So you interpreted what your great-grandfather said in a different way than he might have initially meant it. How much does this detail matter now? You were happy in your studies, in your endeavors. You built a life for yourself. You were more successful and achieved more at a younger age than any other person in your field. You became a professor. Wrote a global bestseller. Why does it matter?"

Yor stood up and yelled at Mado, "Because people have died and risked their lives defending me." Then he stormed out of the room.

# YOR

As he sat in the WAEF's pilot chair, Yor could see the dwarf star as a red dot in the distance. He had the rear cam pointed in the approximate location of Koda. Every day since their launch, he'd stared at the image, watching as Koda diminished into a point of light, making a conscious effort not to lose sight of home.

Yor wondered every day about his mother, Rajer, Insol, Mel, and Shika. He pondered how his mother was managing as head of one of the most powerful corporations on Koda and how she was navigating the political ramifications of her station. He worried about Rajer. If he was alive. If he was imprisoned or executed. The thought of his mother losing him saddened Yor. He understood that Rajer was his own man who had saved him out of love, and like Insol and Ador he was responsible for his own actions, but Yor still felt guilty for what happened to all of them.

And now there was this revelation from Mado about his great-grandfather. Yor recalled as a child running around the Vanderlord estate with the old man chasing him while he giggled uncontrollably. His great-grandfather would lift him up off his feet and above his head while Yor screeched in joy as the old man held him at arm's length, his grizzled aged face beaming with love as he scrutinized Yor before kissing him on the forehead.

    *Howard Libes*

Had his great-grandfather taken advantage of him? Had he used his love to manipulate him? Yor had to admit his life was of his own making. There had been plenty of time in the past sixteen years to change his life's path if he so desired. Here he was years later in the WAEF traveling through space and there was no turning back time. He couldn't blame the Great man for being concerned about his safety, and it wasn't fair to turn his guilt about what had happened back on Koda into anger about his great-grandfather's actions.

Yor had been sitting in the control room for a while and was astonished Mado hadn't shown up to smooth out the tension between them. Mado didn't like discontentment and would usually go out of his way to find a solution. At first, he listened for Mado's footsteps and the control-room door sliding open, but as time passed, Mado never appeared.

So Yor went to look for him. He assumed Mado had resumed repairing the engines, but Mado wasn't in the engine room and the tools were exactly where they'd left them earlier. Yor decided to check the last place they'd seen each other. In the storage room, Mado had pushed together two large crates, placed the pillows on top, and was lying on them on his back, asleep. He had removed his shirt. Yor had never seen Mado unconscious in his iridescent Prevorian form. The bluish-silver hue of Mado's scales lightened, darkened, and shimmered as Yor examined him from different angles. He was beautiful.

Then Yor noticed Mado didn't appear to be inhaling and exhaling. Yor's heart raced. Although this wouldn't be the first time they'd argued, Yor feared he might have caused Mado's death with his outburst. Mado was an alien creature. Yor didn't know any better.

Yor touched Mado's hand. His skin felt more like Kodan flesh than he'd imagined. Yor took hold of Mado's three fingers and thumb and squeezed. He tightened his grip further, but Mado still didn't respond. Yor felt cold. He shouldn't have talked to Mado the way he had. Mado was like a father to him. He was always there for him.

Holding Mado's hand, Yor placed his ear by Mado's chest to listen for a heartbeat. Yor didn't know if Mado's heart was in the same location as a Kodan's, but it was a good place to start. Then he heard a clicking sound and looked up to see Mado's eyelids had opened to reveal not his eyes but another set of eyelids, then those lids opened and Mado's eyes were looking out at him. Mado tightened his grip on Yor's hand.

"I'm fond of you, too," Mado said.

"What?"

"You're holding my hand. Isn't that a Kodan form of affection?"

"What?" Yor said. "I thought you were dead."

"Dead? Dead tired, maybe," Mado said. "After your tantrum, I was sitting in this room with the engines purring nearby and realized I hadn't hibernated since we left Koda. So I set up this makeshift bed and let the engines lull me to sleep. I didn't think you'd come back down here for at least another of your sleep cycles."

Yor laughed and could hardly stop, having to fight to control himself. He was a little hysterical. Through the laughter, he said, "Will you shut up?"

"I believe I stopped talking," Mado said. "What's so funny?"

Yor continued laughing as he released Mado's hand and seated himself in front of his viewer and opened it.

Mado sat up. "Are you all right?"

"As I said, I thought you were dead."

"And that's funny?" Mado said, standing up and stretching. Prevorians were more flexible than Kodans, as Mado demonstrated by bending backward and touching his heels with his palms.

"No, I'm relieved. I was scared is all. I thought I'd lost you," Yor said. "I'm truly sorry I yelled at you."

"Not a problem," Mado said. "If I was concerned about our relationship being damaged, then I would've found you instead of taking the opportunity to hibernate."

"If you're up to it, maybe we can start our conversation again from where we left off before we got into our tiff."

"I'd enjoy that," Mado said, sitting back down on the cushions and putting on his shirt.

Yor said, "I do want to say something regarding this new information about my great-grandfather's actions toward me, and then I don't want to discuss it again. I want to put it behind me."

"Of course—what is it?"

"I want you to know—and maybe I'm saying this out loud for myself as much as for you—I still love the man as much as I ever did, but what you've told me changes my perception of him. It lends a darker twist to our relationship, and I don't think I'll ever think about him in the same way again."

"Yes," Mado said with sadness in his voice. "It's unfortunate when we find out our idols are flawed."

"It is. I just wanted to get that off my chest. Now, let's move forward."

"I'm all for that."

Yor said, "So, after weighing all the pros and cons, how did you reach the point where you were building spaceships? I assume from my knowledge of Kodan history that the first step was convincing the Global Assembly to use your power source for the domes."

"Well, it started earlier than that," Mado said. "As you'd imagine, your great-grandfather wasn't a big supporter of Plemso. Before Yorlik's diagnosis, we were both hoping he wouldn't be reelected a second time, but his military background and his reputation as hero of the Separatist Revolts convinced Kodans he was the man to lead them safely into the future. Bullying his political opponents and using fear to demonize Shambans were effective campaigning techniques, too. He had the best political apparatus that money could buy since the wealthiest Kodans were backing him, and partnering with Flomina Folt didn't hurt, either.

"Later on, it was no surprise when he suspended Presidential elections and lobbied the Global Assembly, who were bought with the same money that had won him the elections, to pass legislation making him Leader. It's disappointing Kodans have fallen for his fearmongering, but it makes sense if you look at the majority of citizens chosen for the domes through the Residence Selection Process, which utilized the files compiled on them by the GSS.

"But I'm getting off the subject and ahead of myself. We had to deal with whoever was President. The domes were going to happen sooner than later as the crisis was accelerating. I hacked the systems of the corporations who were building the main dome components—the pane frames, the panes, the foundations, the power source.

"I could've used Prevorian tech to step in on any aspect of the DOME project as Prevor Industries became an economic force, but the weakest link in the project was the power source, and fortuitously that's an area where Prevor excels. Yorlik and I were aware that Komrit Energy's idea for the domes was theoretically sound, but the tech didn't exist yet on Koda to produce the reaction on a scale required for the power source to sustain itself. We were also aware that the Global Net was failing, so there was a window to help the Kodan people by giving them AID which uses the same power source we'd pitch for the domes.

"Unfortunately, your great-grandfather passed sooner than anyone anticipated. He left this existence satisfied we'd laid out the path for the WAEF restoration and building spacecraft in the future. I was skeptical with all the obstacles ahead, but I had faith in myself and I'd promised a friend that I'd make the future unfold with the survival of the Kodan people my primary concern..

"Joro was crucial to our plan. He was on point to discover the best time to approach President Plemso about our AID-based power source. He kept tabs on the people inside the government to ascertain Plemso's thinking and saw an opening to make a move when Plemso ran for his third term. The crisis was worsening and Kodans were incensed that ground hadn't been broken on the domes yet.

"To our advantage, Plemso cornered himself by being reelected on the promise to start the DOME project, and he couldn't begin without a power source. With the public relations rollout for AID viewed planetwide and sales taking off, the President had no choice but to call me into his office. Took him a little while to warm up to me. The biggest hurdle with Plemso was my relationship with your great-grandfather. He insisted on a vow of loyalty from me, but on Joro's advice, I didn't give it to him. Joro said Plemso would never trust me if I gave him my blind allegiance. He would only trust me if I gave him something tangible in return. Joro's insight was spot on. As my popularity increased with Kodans embracing AID and the possibility of Prevor Industries working on the dome power source leaking to the media, I let Plemso take credit for building our relationship and his approval numbers increased in the polls.

"Then he began to trust me. I was invited to formal dinners at the Presidential mansion and private parties at Plemso's home. They were boorish affairs with the wealthy in attendance bragging about their latest purchases of jewelry or clothing or homes or cruisers. Luckily, Joro accompanied me at these events and we kept our ears open for anything that might further ingratiate me to the President.

"One evening at the Plemso estate, Joro and I were asked to stay for late-night Malrap drinking in the President's study. After some small talk, the President launched into a drunken tirade about how he wanted his family, which now consisted of one child and another on the way, to live full time on his estate. He refused to be forced to live in the Presidential mansion the majority of the time and only return to his own home on weekends and vacation. The First Lady had been living at the estate more and more with their son while what Plemso called 'arcane tradition' compelled him to live in the Presidential mansion by himself and host state dinners there. He believed that after all his service to Koda as a military officer and President, he should be allowed to decide where he lived. He thought his home was far superior to the Presidential mansion and that minor interior and exterior redecoration would make the Plemso estate fit to represent the people of Koda. His advisors told him the move would be a public relations nightmare.

"A few nights later, I met with Plemso at the Presidential estate and told him about my idea of putting the energy field around the Plemso estate and making it a nature preserve for Kodan flora and fauna. I suggested he might change the color of the house to Global-Assembly blue and borrow antiquities from the Royal Museum, possibly paintings and a few artifacts. From my briefcase, I removed a physical blueprint of the Plemso estate showing the energy-field generators in place around the grounds. I could have just brought a digital copy, but I thought this would be more dramatic for the presentation. After unrolling it and spreading it out on a table in the office, we each held down two corners of the blueprint and I explained how the generators would be positioned to form a greenhouse of sorts with the energy field enclosing the mansion. The field would oscillate at a frequency that allowed air into the grounds but prevented winged creatures from escaping. The plan included a landing pad area; the generators could be deactivated to open a window for cruisers to land, then reactivated when they were safely inside the field.

"The President released his side of the blueprint, which rolled up into my hands, and said, 'Can you do this, Mado? Can you make this happen? Does this sort of tech even exist?' I told him I'd been tinkering with the idea for a long time and this project would be a way of making it a reality. He'd be doing me a favor by allowing me to create the energy field around his estate.

"The President said, 'And we can use that. We can tell the citizens that this tech will advance Kodan civilization.' I told him that was exactly what I was thinking, and it would truly be the Presidential mansion because it would be imbued with every aspect of Kodan civilization, past, present, and future. The President was so excited, he hurried around the meeting table and hugged me. I told him Prevor Industries would pay for the project since it was a test of new tech and the PR itself would make it all right with the corporate stockholders. One mention of public relations and the President launched into a litany detailing how he'd sell it to the Kodan people, which was basically a reiteration of what I'd just said in his own words.

"Everyone on Koda knows the result of this interaction. Our friendship was sealed as well as it could have been with the transformation of the Plemso estate into the Presidential residence. I was invited over regularly for family dinners after the energy field was up. For us, for the plan, it put Plemso in my pocket, and that's why all of Prevor Industries' demands were met in the contract for the domes' power source, including the installation and wiring of the system, the maintenance of dome power in perpetuity, the exclusive patent to the power source, and the land on the edge of the dome for the Complex. That's why it was so easy to get permission to install the panes in the dome behind the Complex myself, which gave me the opportunity to place the field generators in the dome pane behind the Complex for future use."

Yor said, "And placing the energy field at the Plemso estate was the beginning of Active Glass, too."

"What better advertisement for Active Glass planet-wide? It was a massive success."

"Where would Koda be without Prevorian tech?"

"True," Mado said. "With the domes completed and powered, Plemso's poll numbers were higher than ever before. I now had Plemso endeared to me—"

"I don't know how you worked with that man."

"What choice did I have? Plemso's popularity waned at times, but he never really had a worthy challenger. Koda required a hardline President who would make any resistance to the domes ineffectual. Their construction was necessary for the good of the Kodan species.

"I would have gladly supported a candidate against

Plemso in the next election, but then he declared himself Leader. He knew he couldn't run for election and win again after the riots, and there was nothing Joro or myself could do about it while the wealthiest Kodans—or at least the majority of them—kept on supporting him, and the Global Assembly reps were a complete sham.

"So I forged ahead after the domes were sealed and your safety and education became my primary concern, alongside convincing the Leader to let me restore the WAEF. I maintained my connection with Plemso while fighting back his suspicion of me. I understood he would never fully trust anyone associated with a Vanderlord, so I buried his suspicions with gifts and by flattering his ego. He let his mistrust slide and sometimes even forgot about it if my contributions were opportune or helpful to him."

Yor said, "Kind of like a tyrant."

# MAR

Two days after Mar's meeting with the Leader, Warver's illness worsened and he was admitted to the Complex's clinic. Mado had constructed a functional med facility with the most up-to-date tech and fifty beds for his employees and their families. While she was running the corporation, Mar worked with the clinic's meds on Warver's case. He'd been poisoned. The point of origin was an injection into his shoulder and Suron was convinced this was Orn Shiv's doing. The poison acted like a virus. None of the lab techs had ever seen this strain so they isolated the virus and began studying it to develop a cure.

In the meantime, they attempted treatments on Warver, but none worked. The rashes became pus-filled sores and spread over Warver's entire body. He weakened as the poison slowly broke down his internal organs and his vital signs began to deteriorate. Warver had visitors: the men who worked for him and his military colleagues. His siblings were no longer alive or not in the domes and he'd never been partnered or fathered any children.

One night, sixteen days after Warver's admittance to the clinic, Mar was woken by Gols. She was told Warver didn't have much time to live. When Mar arrived at his room, Kush Suron was standing by Warver's bedside talking to him. Warver asked Suron if he could be alone with Mar. Suron exited and closed the door behind him.

Warver said, "Sorry I have to resign my position so soon." His voice was weak.

"Me, too," Mar said, taking Warver's hand.

"I just wanted to say it's been an honor working for you."

"It's a pity we never got to know each other better."

"For years, my job has been assessing people and you're extraordinary, Mar Jeps. Don't let anyone tell you different. Just trust your instincts."

"I don't know what I'm going to do without you."

"Rely on Suron. In some ways, he's more capable than me," Warver said and groaned in agonizing pain.

"I wish I could do something about that."

"I'll be free of it soon."

"Would you like me to stay?"

"No, I'd like to do this by myself."

"Goodbye, then," Mar said.  She squeezed his hand, then let go of him.

Warver said, "I wish you good luck for Koda's sake."

Mar sat in the hallway outside Warver's room with Suron in silence. When Warver flatlined, the nurses and attending med raced into his room. Mar rose and watched them call the time of death, Suron by her side.

Mar turned to Suron. "I don't know why he'd want to die alone like that."

"He was always a solitary figure."

"You have family?"

"Yes, I'm partnered, and we have a twelve-year-old daughter."

"You and Warver go back?"

"Yes, he was always my senior officer as we came up through the ranks," Suron said, walking out into the hallway. Mar followed. "You'll need a new head of security."

"I'm looking at him."

"I'll do my best."

"I know you will. Let's talk soon."

When Mar returned to her apartment, she sat by herself in one of the antique chairs on her terrace and thought about her rescue from the bungalow, Warver's death, Rajer awaiting execution, Mellick's black-and-blue neck, Ador's death, and the assault on Insol. She wept. She still awoke every day doubting if she was the right person for this job, which was far more challenging than simply being CEO.

Mar recalled telling Warver about her meeting with the Leader. Warver said her biggest mistake was not going further in challenging the Leader's authority. She should've asked for the release of her partner in exchange for reenergizing the generators. Warver told her that Vidor would've respected that kind of move. Now he would inevitably attempt to reestablish his authority and test her to see how far he could push back. Her partner would be the target, a weakness to exploit until she flinched.

Warver said, "If I were a betting man, I'd say Vidor will hold out on calling you about meeting with your partner. If you do reenergize the generators before he allows you to see your partner, then he'll hold out longer on letting you see him and make further demands of you."

Mar understood she needed to learn how to negotiate. Her first mistake was drinking Malrap, and although she had enjoyed lashing out at the Leader about killing Tetrick, it clearly was unproductive and changed the tenor of the conversation. She did feel good about setting parameters for arresting members of the Movement and her ability to convince the Leader she thought Yor was dead, but overall, she'd failed. She'd given too much away and alienated the Leader before she could get Rajer released.

Although she had reservations, after her conversation with Warver, Mar decided to wait for the Leader's receptionist to comm her and tell her when she'd be able to visit Rajer. She had time before reenergizing the generators became an absolute necessity, and the longer she held out and didn't hear back from the Leader's office, the more she thought Warver was correct.

Mar continued the standoff after Warver's death. She was contacted a few times by each of the nine Dome Power Commissioners about keeping the generators activated. Each time, she assured them all would be well. She considered whether these comms were made on the Commissioners' own initiative, or if the Leader was ordering them to put pressure on her so she'd reenergize the domes without meeting Rajer.

Tetrick always told her she should carry around a reserve of paranoia in a society like the one the Global Assembly had built. He would say, "Paranoia is normal in a society where lies are the norm." Living with Tetrick for years had certainly acclimated her to being paranoid in her own right. This job brought it to the forefront.

As more days passed, Mar began second-guessing her strategy. Prevor Industries techs told her Mado's prediction of sixty-five days to deactivation after Breeze Celebration was completely accurate, and each day closer to the generators going off-line, Mar felt more anguish about holding out. Her actions affected more than just her and Rajer. Koda could be plunged into darkness. Lives were literally at stake and the citizens had no idea. Was she putting her selfish desires over the people's needs? Warver had told her to trust her instincts. When she asked Gols what he thought, he said to wait as long as she wanted. Each dome power station had a Prevor Industries tech on site at all times who could initiate the reenergizing process in a matter of moments if given the daily reactivation code.

Now, with four days left before the domes were without power, Mar was lounging on her couch after work reading *Power Over the Future*. She'd decided to reread it, thinking it might be wise to understand the politics the Great man maneuvered in. Maybe she'd gain some insight into her current position. While she was reading about how Yorlik took charge of the SEEDER program, her comm buzzed and it was a more nervous than usual Gols on the other end of the line. The Leader was requesting a viewer conversation. Mar was hardly dressed for such an encounter. She had stripped out of her work clothes and was wearing sweatpants and a T-shirt with her hair pulled back into a ponytail.

Mar said to Gols, "Does this have to happen now? We could talk early morning tomorrow? Wouldn't make much of a difference."

"He was insistent and rather rude when I suggested you might be indisposed," Gols said. His voice was shaky.

"He even made a vague threat about having me investigated for treason for my impertinence or something like that. He's a little drunk."

"I get it," Mar said. "I'll take it on my living-room screen. Send it through after a twelve count." Mar rose from the couch and straightened herself out the best she could and was still standing by the couch when the living-room screen turned on. In his nervousness, Gols counted a little fast. The Leader was sitting at the desk in his study at the estate. He was clutching half a glass of Malrap.

"Mar Jeps, are you there?" the Leader said. "I see a bungalow living room on this blasted thing. That nincompoop—did he connect me to the wrong screen?"

"I'm here," Mar called out and hurried into the screen's view.

"There you are," the Leader said. "Did I call at a bad time? You look like—"

"Do you know what time it is? It's past business hours. The only reason I took the call was because you made it sound urgent," Mar said. "I don't appreciate you berating my assistant. What can I do for you?"

The Leader released a long sigh and drank down the remaining Malrap in his glass. "This is urgent...and I could call Mado Prevor at any hour of the day and he was fine with it."

"I'm not Mado Prevor."

"No, you're not. He isn't there, is he?"

"No, he isn't. Sorry to disappoint. What can I do for you?" Mar was losing her patience. She didn't have much reserved for Malrap drunks anymore, and she could tell the Leader was displeased by her tone. He straightened up in his seat, poured himself a full glass of Malrap, drank a swig, and ran both his hands through his hair.

"I am the Leader," he said, as if Mar had to be reminded. Then he ran the tip of his finger through some Malrap he'd spilled on his desk and licked it before taking another swig from the glass.

To break the silence, Mar said, "Yes, you are."

"When I call, it's always urgent."

"Yes," Mar said. "What can I do for you?"

"Yes, what can you do for me?" the Leader said, and another awkward silence ensued. He had forgotten why he called.

"Do you have something to tell me?"

"Oh, yes, yes—the Power Commissioners are in a panic and the Minister of Energy has been haranguing me every day for the past I don't know how many days but enough to be annoying, blabbing on about how you haven't scheduled the reenergizing of the domes and we are now days from a power outage. Can you tell me why I'm being bothered by this problem when we already discussed it right here in my study? What's the holdup?"

"The visit to my partner hasn't been scheduled yet."

"That wasn't part of our deal."

"It was implied, but regardless, I believe that when you say you'll do something, it's just common courtesy you'll make it happen."

"Common courtesy?" the Leader said. "You know what would be common courtesy?"

"What would that be other than being a man of your

word?"

"Allowing me to speak with Mado Prevor."

"That's just not possible," Mar said. "And if that's what you want then we don't have anything else to talk about. Good night."

"No, wait," the Leader said releasing a groan of exasperation. "I'll have my receptionist set up the visitation and she'll contact your assistant. Will that work for you to keep the power on?"

"As soon as I have the time and place and proper passes for the visitation…and meet with Rajer."

"Is there something more I can do for you, madam CEO?" the Leader said, his words dripping with sarcasm. He was pained at relenting to her.

"Not that I can think of."

"Then good night." The Leader reached out and disconnected the comm.

The next day, Mar was skeptical the Leader would remember their conversation, but at midday, his office called with a time and date, relaying all the necessary digi-materials to make the visitation possible. It was set for tomorrow.

Mar wondered if the Leader ever intended to let her visit Rajer until she forced his hand or if she'd won the gambit and the Leader had gotten the message that she wouldn't be controlled by him. Then it dawned on her that she was actually going to see Rajer.

A few moments later, Gols entered her office. "Have you seen the info?"

"Yes, I have."

"You look different."

"How so?"

"Maybe relieved, maybe happy," Gols said and left the office.

Gols was correct. She hadn't felt this way in a while. Yor, Rajer and her med job had given her life purpose, a sense of personal gratification and now that part of her life seemed over. Today, she felt that satisfaction in successfully beating the Leader and getting to see Rajer. She'd been thinking if she was going to be working at Prevor Industries for an indefinite amount of time without her family or her previous vocation, then she'd require achieving that level of gratification in doing this job every day. She had to embrace her new place in life and how she was feeling now shouldn't be an anomaly. She had a few ideas. Gols would be able to guide her.

In the meantime, she perused the digi-materials further and alerted Gols she was taking tomorrow off. She didn't want to miss one moment of the twenty-four minutes she was allowed to spend with Rajer.

The rest of her workday dragged on and when it ended, she walked behind the reception desk and into Gols' office. She stood in the doorway, realizing she'd never seen his office before. He always brought her whatever she required, sometimes before she even asked for it.

If someone didn't know Gols, they'd have thought by looking at his office that he just began working at Prevor Industries. His desktop contained a viewer and an intercom and one digi-foto of an elderly woman who Mar assumed was Gols' mother. The rest of his desk was empty and the walls bare.

"Mar," Gols said. He shot up from his chair, losing balance for a moment. "What brings you here?"

"At ease," Mar said, trying not to laugh at Gols' over-reaction to her presence. "Everything's great—"

"Tomorrow, yes," Gols said. "I've communicated to Suron that you want to arrive at least sixty minutes early in case there are any bureaucratic problems, so you can maximize your time in your partner's company."

Mar laughed at Gols' performance.

"Did I say something wrong?" Gols said.

"That's not exactly why I came here, but I'm glad you're always a few steps ahead of me."

"That's my job. If I wasn't, then I wouldn't be performing at maximum efficiency."

"I appreciate it," Mar said. "When I come back to work, I'd like to see a general overview of the current med projects. I want to spend time working on one or two of them—I think I can make a difference in the cryotech division. It'd be good for me to get my hands dirty, so to speak."

"Will do, Mar," Gols said. "Anything else?"

"Let's finalize the details of the trip to Shamba we've been planning. It'll be helpful to see the project and speak to the people there."

"I'm on it," Gols said. "Anything else?"

"Just keep up the good work," Mar said, waving good-bye and exiting Gols' office. While walking back to her apartment, she noted an extra spring in her step.

# Rajer

When Mar entered the all-white visitation room, Rajer was smitten all over again. His heart raced like the first time he saw her. In his current situation with the future so uncertain, all that mattered was this moment.

Mar stood before him wearing a floral print dress with an Ashtecki jacket and open-toe cloth shoes.

Rajer said, "The shoes don't exactly match the outfit."

"I was going for sexy and comfortable," Mar said, closing the door behind her.

If an Active Glass wall wasn't between them, Rajer would've rushed to her and embraced her. Through the intercom, the sound of her voice made his heart race some more.

Rajer said, "Then you hit the mark."

A smile spread across Mar's face and she hurried toward Rajer, then slowed as a look of disappointment came over her when she observed the wall. "Active Glass?" Mar said. "That bastard Plemso."

"They're listening," Rajer said. "Please sit at the table."

When they were seated at the tables on either side of the wall, barely two meters separated them. They each had an HGD box and interface in front of them.

"What's this about?" Mar said, picking up the HGD interface.

"You'll see."

All Rajer could think about since the Leader gave his approval for the visitation was seeing Mar again. It kept him going through the never-ending day in his brightly lit, windowless, white-walled GSS cell, and through the interrogations filled with beatings because he had no answers for the questions they were asking. He was speechless staring at her.

Mar said, "I'm glad you're alive."

"I'm so happy to see you."

Mar laughed. "What were you thinking?"

"When?"

"You know when. When you went after that Roneh Rayush woman. When you tackled her."

"How do you know her name?"

"Everyone on Koda knows her name. She's a global hero."

"Figures," Rajer said, pushing in his chair. He wanted to be closer to Mar. "I was protecting our son. I was aware of the penalty, but I couldn't let that woman take his life or arrest him. I was so proud of him that day. His act was pure bravery and I wasn't going to let her ruin it."

Tears flowed down Mar's cheeks.

Rajer said, "I didn't mean to make you cry."

"Shut up, you idiot," Mar said. "I've never loved you more."

"If I'd known, I'd have done something like it sooner."

Mar chuckled and wiped the tears away with the side of her hand. "So what is all this?" she asked, examining the HGD box on the table and the interface in her hand.

"It's a surprise," Rajer said, "but first..." He picked

up a digi-tablet from his table and read aloud, "Do you agree to normalize relations between the Global Assembly and Prevor Industries, especially with regard to keeping the power activated in the domes? If so, the Leader will consider staying my execution and giving me a pardon."

"All that says is he'll consider pardoning you."

"He was extremely concerned about you doing something rash in your current CEO position. Congratulations, by the way."

"Thanks, it's been interesting. Definitely different from the clinic."

"I'm so happy to see you, I can't tell you," Rajer said. "Were you really threatening to turn off the power in the domes?"

Mar began laughing.

"Did I say something humorous?" Rajer said.

"Sort of. It started with Mado, but I came this close to shutting down the power in all the domes," Mar said, holding her thumb and forefinger an eyelash-width apart. "I'd promised to reenergize the generators during a meeting with the Leader, then when it seemed like he was withholding this visit, I decided to wait on it."

"I don't think shutting the power down would've been good for my health."

"Now I know why he was withholding the visit though—he thought he'd already got what he wanted when we met at his estate and he was holding out to use you for something else," Mar said, sounding annoyed. "Warver was right."

"Who is Warver?" Rajer said, seeing sadness come over her face.

"Oh," Mar said, "it's a long story…" Her voice trailed off.

"Well, we don't have much time here so let's get this show on the road," Rajer said, picking up his HGD interface, then said more loudly for the people listening, "Do you agree to the terms of that statement, Mar?"

"Yes. I agree."

A moment later, both HGD boxes lit up. "I told you they were listening."

"Are we supposed to wear this thing? Yor always wanted me to try it," Mar said, holding up the interface. "I've never done this before."

"That's the first time I've heard those words come out of your mouth when we were alone."

"Don't, Rajer," Mar said. "People are listening." She smiled and winked at him.

"Just put it on. You won't be sorry."

"That isn't the first time I've heard you say that, either."

"True," Rajer said. "Now put it on." He watched as she placed the interface on her head, smiled at him, then flipped the goggles over her eyes. Rajer followed suit.

The darkness inside the goggles dissolved into light which formed into pockets of primary color which transformed into multiple shades and shapes both large and small until a scene came into focus. He was standing on a beach, the sun warming his skin as he gazed at the Falls which spanned 400 meters across at its crest. Large quantities of water dropped from a height of fifty meters to crash into rocks and water below, producing a thunderous roar.

Mar said, "Calem Falls?"

Rajer turned to his right to find Mar standing there dressed in a bikini like she was wearing in the foto that once resided in their bungalow. She was examining herself, placing her hands on her hips, cupping her breasts, holding long strands of hair in front of her eyes. She was checking for grey hair, but Rajer hadn't turned back time. Her body was the current version of herself, but she was just as beautiful to him.

"Yes. Calem Falls. Around thirty-five years ago, before the river that fed it started drying up," Rajer held his right arm out toward the water falling about twenty-five meters away.

Mar peered along the shoreline of the lake. "It's so real. I can smell those blossoms over there and feel the breeze—and what's up with the bikini? You perv." Mar smiled at him.

"Gets lonely in prison," Rajer said, "although I couldn't persuade them to agree to a conjugal visit."

Mar laughed. "I love your bathing suit."

Rajer's trunks had blossoms on them like the ones Mar liked to bring home from the hydroponics store. "Thanks. I thought you'd want to see my scrawny number-cruncher body."

"I love this body. And it's not so scrawny," Mar said as she walked up to Rajer and pressed her body against his. He felt the warmth of her skin as she embraced him and gave him a long, passionate kiss. "No conjugal visit, huh?" She reached down to Rajer's crotch. "Whoa! You weren't kidding."

Although Rajer was aroused, the GSS authorities demanded that their bodies not be anatomically correct in the simulation so where Rajer's genitals would have resided was a blank spot. The GSS wasn't going to count on the honor system.

"Well, you can't win them all," Rajer said.

Mar wrapped her arms around Rajer, embracing him. He felt a sharp pain in his ribs where the interrogators had been working him over and flinched.

"Be gentle. I hurt myself doing sit-ups."

"You? Sit-ups?" Mar said, releasing her hold on him.

"Gets boring around here."

Mar wrapped her arms around him more gently.

They held each other and stayed that way for a long time, then Rajer said, "You know I could remain this way forever, but we have limited time. I want to do more of this, but we should eat first."

"Eat?"

They both stepped out of the embrace. Rajer kissed her, then took her hand and led her along the beach to where a blanket was laid out with a picnic basket. "Please sit," Rajer said.

Mar picked up the picnic basket and said, "That's got some heft to it." Then she set it on the sand and sat on the blanket next to it, facing the falls.

"Yes, there's lunch inside. We won't have time to eat most of it," Rajer said, sitting on the blanket beside Mar and moving up against her. They kissed and Mar entangled her left leg with Rajer's right.

When the kiss ended, Rajer said, "Hand me the basket, please?"

Mar passed the basket to Rajer who removed a bottle of Eglew juice and two long-stem glasses. He popped the bottle's cork, then poured full glasses and handed one to Mar.

She kissed him on the lips and said, "So lifelike," and did it again. They clinked glasses and sat in silence watching the sun setting and the sky turning red as the falls roared, misting their half-naked bodies in the heat of the day. Rajer reached down with his free hand and ran it through the sand beside the blanket while sipping at the juice.

"You have to admire the workmanship," Rajer said. "Your boys did a fantastic job."

"Did Prevor Industries make this simulation specifically for us?"

"For you. It's good to know the boss,' Rajer said. "When the Leader told me I could dictate the parameters of our visit if I convinced you to be nice, I came up with this idea. I read somewhere that a few high-value prisoners have requested it. The HGD already had Calem Falls in the database. We made a few modifications, thanks to Gols and a sympathetic tech."

"Gols, that old romantic. I wish he'd told me."

"I asked him not to," Rajer said. "I wanted it to be a surprise."

"I'm glad you're still here," Mar said, intertwining her leg tighter with Rajer's and passionately kissing him on the lips.

"Let's see what else we have in store for us in the basket," Rajer said. He untangled his leg from Mar's, then placed the basket between them on the sand and removed two paper pads and writing utensils from the basket.

"What's this all about?"

"I thought you'd appreciate this Ashtecki meat sandwich," Rajer said, putting his finger to his lips and handing Mar a pad and utensil. He wrote on his pad, holding it out for her to read, "This is a way for us to talk without anybody hearing us or ever reading what we've written," Rajer scribbled. "Out there in the room, they'll think we're eating and drinking." Then he ripped the paper he'd written on from the pad and put it in the basket.

"I love you," Mar wrote, and they kissed, then she ripped the paper from her pad, crumpled it up, and handed it to Rajer, who put in the basket.

"I love you, too," Rajer wrote on his pad. "First of all, I'm devastated to hear about Yor."

Mar wrote, "That was just another lie. He's alive in outer space with Mado."

Rajer said out loud, "Really!" Then he covered his mouth with his hand and laughed. He wrote, "That's fantastic news." He reached over and squeezed her arm, then wrote, "And I need you to understand what I'm about to write—it's of the utmost importance."

"Of course," Mar wrote.

Rajer tore the top sheet from his pad and stuck it in the basket, then placed the pad between them and wrote, "I don't think we have much time left here so I'll get right to the point. If the Leader lets me out because you kept the power on, then I'm overjoyed. But I don't trust him, either."

Rajer ripped off the page and handed it to Mar, who took it and wrote on the back, "The Leader didn't say anything to me about releasing you if I kept the power on."

Rajer wrote on his pad, "Again, we have no reason to trust him. Lek has hinted I'll be used as leverage and said the Leader is turning the planet upside down looking for Mado. He's obsessed with getting Mado back in charge of the corporation." He ripped the paper from the pad, then looked over at her.

Mar wrote on her pad, "That's not going to happen."

"Then you're the second most powerful person on Koda now. You must think about the good of the Kodan people otherwise Yor's sacrifice is in vain," Rajer wrote. "Lek hinted that the Leader is planning to purge anybody marked as an agitator. It's been in the works since before Breeze Celebration. The Leader can't allow Yor's actions to have any lasting impact so Lek predicts it's coming soon. You're the only one in his way. They'll use me to stop any retribution from you. Follow your conscience. Don't let them do it. Even if it costs my life."

Mar put her hand on Rajer's pad so he couldn't write any more, then wrote on hers, "I'm not the savior of the Kodan people. I won't sacrifice your life!!!"

Rajer underlined two sentences he had previously written: "Don't let them do it. Even if it costs my life."

Rajer looked over at Mar who was gazing at what he'd underlined. A tear flowed down her cheek, then she wrote on her pad, "I don't want this responsibility. I'm in constant danger. My head of security was murdered and now I'm afraid for you. I won't let you die."

Rajer kissed her on the lips, then ripped the paper from his pad and wrote, "I love you, but if it comes down to it, I won't let good, well-meaning Kodans die because of me. You need to stop the Leader when the time comes. I won't be his pawn. THAT IS MY WISH."

Rajer wiped away Mar's tears and gave her a long, heartfelt kiss.

Mar wrote, "I WON'T LET YOU DIE."

Rajer said out loud, "I trust in my heart you'll do what's right. You always have, and you always will. That's another reason why I love you. Have courage for the both of us."

They embraced. Rajer's ribs pained him, but he didn't care.

They were still in the embrace when the simulation ended. Rajer stared into the darkness of the interface goggles and could still feel Mar's body against him. Then he lifted the goggles to see Mar sitting across from him with the wall separating them. Her goggles were lifted, too, and she was staring at him, tears in her eyes.

Rajer thought, *She's looking at me as if this might be the last time she'll see me.* He felt like he was about to cry but held back the tears, feeling his face contort. *She might be right.*

Tears streamed down Mar's face, and she said with sadness in her voice, "You don't have to be brave for me."

So Rajer wept as if he'd been holding it back since he was arrested. He fought through his emotions and said,

"I'll always be brave for you." He stood up from his chair and walked to the Active Glass wall. Mar did the same. Rajer stepped forward until the toe of his cloth shoe struck the wall. Mar moved closer as well. Rajer stared at her face, memorizing its appearance in this moment, then cupped his hands around his mouth and whispered in a low volume so the recording devices couldn't pick him up, "But, my dear, you need to be brave for everyone on this planet. You have the opportunity to make a difference where others have failed."

Then the door slid open and a guard stepped in. "This visitation is over, Mar Jeps. Follow me."

"We'll see each other soon," Mar said, wiping away her tears with her hand. She took two steps back, then mouthed the words, "I love you."

# LEK

Lek sat in his office and watched on vid feed as Mar exited the visitation room on the fifty-fifth floor. He had observed her entire visit. It felt intrusive, but he was still working Rajer's case.

During the visit, Mar had confirmed her agreement with the Leader, and Lek was the person who remotely activated the HGDs. All went as planned for the Leader, and Lek hoped all went well for Mar and Rajer. The covert HGD features worked exactly as Rajer hoped. In his report about the visitation, Lek would describe how Mar and Rajer demonstrated what he assumed was affection for one another in the simulation. Unfortunately, he'd need to report Mar's words about the Leader. Others were watching and he didn't have clearance to erase the remarks from the recording of the visit.

Currently on the vid feed, Rajer sat down on the floor and put his face in his hands. His body was heaving and Lek could hear him weeping. It hurt Lek to see his friend this way, but he felt solace in the fact that he was now doing everything he could to help him. It started with meeting Mar at the memorial, then he got word to Prevor Industries about designing the clandestine features in the simulation. He facilitated the delivery of the HGD boxes to his office for installation in the visitation room. He bypassed surveillance to relay sensitive info to Rajer during their talks. Maybe Lek couldn't free his friend, but he hoped these treasonous actions made Rajer's incarceration more tolerable. Lek found them liberating and it was easier to get away with than he ever thought possible.

Rajer continued weeping. The Active Glass wall was deactivated, and a guard ordered Rajer to his feet, cuffed his hands, then began walking him out of the room. Rajer said to the guard, "An escort back to my cell. You guys are the best. This place has top-notch service." The guard didn't react and Lek turned off the feed.

Lek was constantly inspired by his old friend's sense of humor throughout his imprisonment. Rajer ribbed the guards whenever they interacted with him. He was light-hearted when Lek visited, although their meetings were mostly business. Even with the aggressive interrogators, Rajer told the same story about how Yor had excluded Rajer and Mar from his subversive activities and even joked through the beatings. When Lek asked him why he seemed so undaunted by his dire circumstances, Rajer said, "Because I know I did the right thing."

Rajer was a kindhearted soul who was imprisoned and facing execution for protecting his stepson from harm. What had Yor done? He had spoken and shown the truth. Lek reflected on all the other citizens housed in the GSS facilities here and around the planet for not living within the boundaries of the Global Assembly lies. A few times over the years, Lek had questioned his loyalty to the Global Assembly. This time was different.

Lek reflected on how he'd got here and recalled when he was about to graduate from Royal University with high honors. At the time, government workers were in demand to inspect, monitor, and audit the units flowing into all facets of the DOME project, because a scandal involving those units had incensed Kodans about the lack of oversight. As a means of motivating citizens to apply for these jobs, the Global Assembly was willing to circumvent the DOME Residence Selection Process to guarantee places in the domes for government employees.

Rajer was a business major with a concentration in accounting and he was a perfect candidate to examine Global Assembly finances. Lek majored in global history with a focus on politics, and his career path was far less clear. He wasn't fond of the Global Assembly's agenda and didn't see academia in his future like his friend Ador. Consequently, he had no clue what he wanted to do after University, but he had no intention of going back home and taking up ranching as a vocation.

After graduating, Rajer decided to travel around the planet before applying for his Global Assembly job. He used the money he inherited from his parents for the trip and wanted Lek to come along, but Lek couldn't afford it. He was living off savings from the units his mother sent him during his years at University, even though he'd told her that his scholarships covered all his costs, but that wouldn't last long.

Lek scoured Capitol City for employment. He reluctantly applied for entry-level jobs at the Global Assembly. They were mostly administrative assistant opportunities, but he couldn't think of anything more tedious than bringing some bloated bureaucrat his morning beverage and was relieved when he was never called into interviews. He searched through the Help Wanted ads on the most prominent digi-media sites, too. Most of the jobs available to him were low-paying unskilled labor and dishwashing or waitstaff jobs of the kind he'd worked on school breaks. They'd cover the rent and his lifestyle, but with all his education under his belt he wanted more. Days passed and desperation about running out of units set in. He rationalized that at least he'd be happier earning something as a dishwasher while he bided his time waiting for a preferable position to open up.

One day, Lek's life took an unexpected turn. He was sitting at a table in a Malrap bar by himself, observing the scene around him. Work shifts hadn't ended yet, so the patrons consisted of the unemployed or Separatist Revolt vets staring off into the distance, fingering the condensation on their glasses or clutching their drink with a prosthetic hand. One man on a barstool was slumped over, passed out face-first on the bar as the bartender wiped the counter around him. Malnourished, haggard older women missing teeth and wearing low-cut dresses slunk up to patrons, hoping their seductive body movements would garner them a drink or two. Lek finished his Malrap and headed home where he found an invite to a GSS recruitment orientation in his digi-mail.

Lek wasn't sure why the GSS reached out to him. He never applied for a position there. When he read the mail, his first thought was that his father would be proud if he took a job that demonstrated his faith in the government's actions. Lek had no interest in working there, but he decided to attend the orientation. It was better than spending the day in a Malrap bar, watching the other patrons living out his possible future.

The orientation took place in the warehouse district. Lek rode a public transportation bus to get there, which passed through an industrial district full of vacant buildings. Signs posted on every block hailed the forthcoming revival of the district and the retooling of old factories for building the Capitol City dome parts. The signs read *This is where the Future Begins*, *The Parts Built Here Will Protect You and Your Family*, and *Be a Part of the DOME Solution*. On the bottom-right-hand corner of each sign was "DOME project" and the Global-Assembly symbol.

These signs had begun to fade, though. The promise of dome construction had dragged on for decades, fueling the anti-DOME movement. In a few places the signs were defaced. On one sign, the word "Solution" was crossed out and a new word inserted by hand so the sign read *Be a Part of the DOME Debacle*. Another sign had "Protect" crossed out and read *The Parts Built Here Will Enslave You and Your Family*. Lek found the editing insightful and he was aware that thought would never go over well with a GSS recruiter, but he would still rather be on this bus ride than sitting in that Malrap bar filling himself with despair.

When the bus reached Lek's stop, the only other person onboard disembarked with him. He was older than Lek. His hair was long and unkempt and his clothes—a long-sleeve button-down shirt and slacks—were stained and frayed. When they reached the assigned building, the front door was locked. They knocked more than a few times but nobody answered. Finally, the other man said, "I don't need this," and walked off in the direction of downtown, leaving his rank body odor behind him.

Lek was perplexed and a little angry. Why would he receive a request from the GSS with a wrong address? He was positive the digi-mail was real, and he never received an update with a new location. Then Lek noticed the man had gone half a block and turned down an alley. He decided to follow him but keep his distance by waiting where the alley met the sidewalk. The alley was narrow, barely the width of a body, and the man was determined in his course. Lek saw no reason not to keep tailing him. When the man reached the far end of the alley, he turned left and disappeared from view, then Lek headed down the alley. He quickened his pace so the man wouldn't get away. He turned left at the end of the alley and another man was standing there waiting for him. A smile spread across the man's face and he said, "Lek Valsted?"

The man had short-cropped hair, a deep scar over his left eye, and a "GG" tattoo on his neck. The Global Guard was a relatively new military unit formed by then-Commander Vidor Plemso and considered a ruthless and efficient battalion. They were well known for being inserted into hostile territory and eliminating the stray leaders of long-standing revolts. A head taller than Lek, the man wore a tight-fitting light-green short-sleeve shirt and his broad shoulders and muscular arms exuded a sort of brute strength.

Lek said, "Yes. That's me."

"I'm Tas Jerrick of the GSS. I'm conducting your interview."

"Who was that other man?"

"Oh, just some homeless guy. I paid him to see if you'd track him here." Tas Jerrick headed toward a flight of stairs leading up to a warehouse loading dock, then turned back to Lek. "Come on. We don't have all day."

Lek didn't like being tricked. He stood in place wondering if he should leave.

Tas Jerrick said, "Let's get a move on, soldier."

*Soldier?* Lek thought. That made him uncomfortable, too.

The man stared at Lek, then took a few long strides toward him. "Is there something wrong?" Tas Jerrick said as he grasped Lek's forearm and began walking toward the warehouse stairs still holding on. Lek followed along, up the stairs to the loading dock and into the back of the abandoned warehouse which was empty except for a table further inside the room with two chairs next to it.

"You can let go of my arm now," Lek said.

"Oh, sorry. Old habits," Tas Jerrick said, releasing Lek's arm.

"What's this all about?"

"This is your interview."

"I thought this was a recruitment orientation where I'd be told about GSS employment opportunities, and that there'd be other potential recruits here," Lek said, raising his voice which echoed in the empty warehouse.

"Oh, I've seen this confusion before," Tas Jerrick said. "No, this is an interview to see if you're interested in joining the GSS. You were sent the digi-mail because we think you're a perfect fit for the job, and you passed the first test by following that man here."

"I never contacted the GSS about a job."

"We don't take applications. We find applicants."

"A little paranoid about the eager ones?"

"Something like that," Tas Jerrick said, then gestured toward the table and chairs. "Shall we proceed?"

"Sure, why not," Lek said. "I guess it couldn't hurt."

"Don't be so sure," Tas Jerrick said and laughed as he he walked toward the table with a distinct gait. Growing up, Lek had seen many vets walking the same way, and he could tell by the sound of each step that Tas Jerrick possessed a prosthetic leg.

Lek followed him to the table, which had a thick folder sitting in the middle of it. Tas Jerrick stopped at the table and placed his palm on top of the folder.

Tas Jerrick said, "We keep an eye on promising university graduates for analyst positions. You were a top-notch student and all of your professors speak highly of your intellectual abilities and your capacity to think outside the box."

"Looks like you've done your homework."

"You wouldn't have made it this far if our research didn't show promise, and we wouldn't have spent money printing this out."

"I want to make it clear that I'm interested in the process, but I'm skeptical of the job."

"Yes, we know you have daddy issues," Tas Jerrick said and opened the folder, removing a stack of paper clipped together with a foto on top, which he tossed on the table. The foto showed Lek exiting a Royal University dorm.

"That foto of me," Lek said. "When was it taken?"

Tas Jerrick picked up the stack and looked at the back of the foto. "The 182nd day of this year."

In the foto, Lek appeared disheveled but content. He recognized the dorm behind him. "This was taken about thirty days before graduation after a one-night stand," Lek said, holding his hand out for the stack of papers. "You've been watching me for a while, then?"

"From a distance, yes," Tas Jerrick said, not handing the stack of paper to Lek, "and compiling a file on you."

"A file?"

"I should explain," Tas Jerrick said. "Would you like to sit?"

"No."

"I will, then. I need to get off my leg." Tas Jerrick sat down and returned the stack of papers back to the folder. "What I'm about to tell you is confidential and highly sensitive information about new programs we're preparing to set in motion. You cannot tell anyone about it. If you do, and we find out, there will be dire consequences for you, your family, and your friends. Do I make myself perfectly clear?"

"Maybe I should leave."

"Maybe," Tas Jerrick said. "That's up to you. If you want to leave, now would be a good time."

Lek had been manipulated to get him this far and now he was being asked to sit down and become informed about secret GSS programs which could put his life and the lives of his loved ones at risk. *This must be the can-you-keep-a-secret part of the interview*, Lek thought. He wasn't sure he wanted to go any further. Tas Jerrick sat there smiling up at Lek.

"Well…?" Tas Jerrick said.

Lek reminded himself he didn't want the job in the first place. On the other hand, he was here out of desperation. His prospects had dried up. His money would run out soon. Plus he was already here, so he might as well hear what the GSS was doing and at least he'd leave informed as to why he was being spied on. And, bottom line, he could keep a secret.

"So…" Lek said.

"Sit down then we'll get started," Tas Jerrick said, patting the seat of the vacant chair. "You asked about your file."

"Yes, the file," Lek said, approaching the table and picking up the folder.

Tas Jerrick reached over and grabbed Lek's wrist. His grip was firm and Lek couldn't move his hand in any direction. "I'd rather you not look at the file until you tell me that you understand the conditions for revealing it, then I can explain it to you."

"Yes, I understand."

"You understand what?" Tas Jerrick said. "Please drop the file. I need you to make a full statement." Lek dropped the folder back on the table and Tas Jerrick released his hold on him, then poked behind his ear. Lek assumed he was activating an audio implant. "Go ahead. Start 'I, Lek Valsted…'"

"I, Lek Valsted, understand that if I divulge what I'm told today about GSS activities to anyone, there will be consequences for myself, my family, and my friends."

"You got that," Tas Jerrick said, looking down at the ground. "I know—'divulge,' that's a new one. University students, am I right?" Then he poked behind his ear again.

"Who was that?"

"Just some of the boys back at headquarters."

"So are we set?"

"Yes. We're now under the conditions of the agreement. I'd prefer you to sit down and I'll tell you about the file, the future of the GSS, and the job we see you filling."

Lek sat down and Tas Jerrick cleared his throat. He commenced to tell Lek about how in the past few years the GSS had begun assembling a file on every Kodan citizen. The files contained basic information about an individual—name, date, time and place of birth, education, occupation—and an in-depth study of the Kodan's life—significant events, their associations, their family and friends, their proclivities. This compilation would be used to determine a citizen's loyalty to the Global Assembly. Health would also be considered along with estimated life-span, then a rating would be given as to whether the citizen was worthy to live in the domes. Of course, all this information would be reviewed and updated when the government established a date to enact the Selection Process as the dome-sealings neared. Tas Jerrick had printed out Lek's file so he could see the bounty collected on him, but ordinarily the files were digitized.

"Is this legal?" Lek said. "I don't recall hearing about any of this and I'm sure the media would've been all over such an invasion of privacy."

"Legality is all in the definition," Tas Jerrick said. "This protocol and others were instituted by our President in the name of safety and security in our current state of emergency."

"Emergency?"

"Yes—if you recall, a few years back, President Plemso declared the environmental crisis a planetary emergency. Years before that, the Global Assembly amended the constitution asserting specific Presidential powers in case of a planetary emergency, one of which is unilateral executive orders to carry forward decisions and institute policy without the consent of the Global Assembly. In this way, the files for the Selection Process were guaranteed funding through a high-security executive order. A smart young man like yourself who studied planetary politics would know about the PEP Act, which is part of the Global Assembly constitution."

To the best of Lek's recollection, the Planetary Emergency Powers Act was written to manage catastrophic global incidents. Obviously, President Plemso had decided on an interpretation that gave him overarching power in dealing with the environmental crisis and secured a prominent place in Koda's future for the GSS, the government's police force. The proposed design of the GSS building in the Global Plaza now made complete sense.

"Anything else you want me to know?" Lek said.

Tas Jerrick told Lek the GSS files would be the foundation for the Identification Cards Act. Each Kodan citizen under the domes would receive a card with a unique ID number and positioning chip which would be required for a citizen to perform their daily activities, such as using public transportation, shopping, or entering an entertainment venue. Dome residents would be mandated to carry the card with them at all times under penalty of arrest, and the accumulated tracking information would be used to constantly update each individual's digitized file.

"Then there's the vidcams. You may have noticed the poles going up around the city," Tas Jerrick said. He explained how vidcams would be placed on every corner, blanketing the city so that an individual's movements could be pinpointed and visually tracked with facial recognition. All crimes and conspiracies would be caught on surveillance. "You're probably wondering why I need to tell you all this?"

"It did cross my mind."

"The GSS needs smart young individuals like yourself to analyze all the data flowing through it and decide whether a citizen is fundamentally loyal and necessary for a domed Koda. We'll also need vidcam footage reviewed to spot everything from petty misdemeanors to crimes against the government. Analysts will be the cornerstone of the GSS. If a citizen is accused of committing a crime against the state, whether it's robbery, murder, or a terrorist act, we'll need analysts to track the citizen's movements, gathering evidence about their crimes and uncovering any co-conspirators or known associates." Tas Jerrick tapped the folder on the table. "So, do you believe you might have the stuff to make a go of it?"

"I don't know. I'd have to think about it."

"Yes, we presumed you wouldn't jump onboard right

away—you're a thinker and that's what we like about you. We believe you might move quickly up the GSS career hierarchy."

"To be completely honest with you," Lek said, "I'm not comfortable with spying on citizens and deciding who lives or dies."

"It's definitely not for the faint of heart and there will be tests of your abilities and your loyalty to the Global Assembly."

"I don't—"

"Let me stop you right there. Think about what I've told you. Think about the future of Koda and how we'll need good men like you to make it through the chaos this crisis will wreak on the fabric of Kodan society. We'll move beyond these surveillance techniques one of these days, but in the meantime, Kodan society will be torn asunder unless we safeguard it against the forces both natural and human that mean to do us harm," Tas Jerrick said. "Sorry, I tend to go on." Then he laughed.

"I can see you're passionate, but—"

"Tell you what. You don't need to give me a yes-or-no answer now. Let's meet here in nine days at this exact same time. You think it over and maybe you'll be clearer on what you want. How does that sound?"

Lek forced a smile. This guy wasn't going to take no for an answer and Lek was feeling uncomfortable about this entire interview, so he stood up and said, "Thanks for having me here. It was informative, and I'll consider your offer."

Tas Jerrick stood and stepped toward Lek, placing a

hand on his shoulder and gripping it. "Please remember that we haven't even gotten into the salary and perks yet. The work is grueling, but the GSS will make it worth your while. Everybody has a job to do and it's not always easy. We're serious about wanting you onboard. You'd be a fine addition to the corps."

"I appreciate it."

Tas Jerrick released his hold on Lek's shoulder which throbbed from the intensity of the grip, then Tas Jerrick said in an overly sincere tone, "Great meeting you and hope to see you in nine days. I'll be waiting for you. See you then."

Lek exited the warehouse and passed through the alley to the street. He checked the bus schedule at the stop and there wouldn't be another bus for a while, so he decided to walk the bus route home, hoping to catch one on its way back toward his neighborhood.

He hiked through the warehouse district and hadn't gone far when he noticed makeshift shelters—tents, tarps on poles, large appliance boxes—across the street in an undeveloped field. He estimated five hundred people or more, homeless families milling about, doing chores—cleaning dishes, cooking meals over open flames—playing musical instruments, and sitting in circles chatting while children entertained themselves with a game of kick the can. Since many of the local industries had folded with the crisis, these fields had become a place for the evicted unemployed workers and their families to make their homes.

On Lek's side of the street, he approached families in tattered clothes waiting in line at what he assumed was an old warehouse. A hand-drawn sign in front of the warehouse read: *SHELTER - All Are Welcome.* Since Lek wasn't one of the homeless, his presence was noted. A few grubby-faced children ran up to him and asked for spare units. When he pulled out his pockets and showed them they were empty, they ran off. As he passed the warehouse, Lek smelled cooking and realized this was a food line. One of the people in line said to Lek, "No cutting. Get back in line where you belong."

*Is this my future?* Lek had thought. Maybe he'd end up living in that field and standing in this line. He was a little scared for himself. Obviously, jobs were hard to come by these days.

When he returned home, he began considering the GSS position and everything Tas Jerrick had told him. He didn't agree with the Global Assembly's plans for spying on the Kodan people. He saw it as a violation of a citizens' rights, but he began wondering if he could make a difference. Could he work from within the system and temper the usage of those surveillance tools? Could he ensure they weren't abused?

Now, Lek was sitting in his GSS office years later and there was a knock on the door. Director Thuta poked in his head and said, "Get anything from the Mar and Rajer Jeps meeting?"

"No, nothing unusual. She agreed to the Leader's terms."

"Continue pushing Jeps. Our other interrogators will keep softening him up for you," Thuta said, then he disappeared from the doorway.

# MAR

"So, this is definitely your office now?" Mar said, standing in Yor's old campus office. The light shone through windows which offered a view of the campus green below.

"Yes," Mel said. "Somebody made a sizable anonymous donation to the University and requested I head the department. Harmin is displeased."

"You don't say," Mar said and they both laughed.

"Not that it isn't great to see you, but I assume there's a reason for this visit," Mel said, retrieving a jamming device from one of the desk drawers and activating it.

"Although I think you already know, my visit is primarily to tell you Yor is alive."

"Yes. A few of us were notified," Mel said. "How did you find out?"

"Vid transmission from Mado and Yor."

"How did they look? I'm sure Yor is excited to be in outer space."

"They looked fine. They said I wouldn't hear from them again for a while."

"That's what I was told, too."

Mar seated herself in an armchair. "The other reason I'm here is to see if you have any extracurricular activities planned."

"Insol and I have been discussing the current political

climate around the planet, so to speak. We've been cooking something up." Mel activated his comm and said, "Yes, come over. There's someone here to see you."

"What's that all about?"

"It's a surprise."

"I've had enough surprises for today," Mar said. "I just visited Rajer."

"Oh, how is he?"

"It's one of the reasons I'm here. I thought we needed to catch up."

"You might want to wait for our guest of honor," Mel said. "So how goes the transition from med at Capitol City clinic to CEO of arguably the most powerful corporation on Koda?"

"Challenging. A learning process," Mar said. "Every time I think I've got a grasp on it, there's some new facet of the business for me to learn about. Let's just say there's a lot going on."

"I can imagine," Mel said. "It's probably constantly evolving."

"That's one way of putting it," Mar said. "How's your neck?"

"Healing."

"Any visits from that man lately?"

"No. How about you?"

"I'm almost certain he killed my head of security."

"Sorry to hear that." There was a knock on the door. "I believe our guest of honor has arrived."

Mel opened the door and heard Harmin say, "What's going on around here? There's a military or GSS-looking fellow standing at either end of the hallway."

Mar called out from where she sat, "That's my security."

"Mar Vanderlord Jeps, I shouldn't be surprised," Harmin said, stepping into the room. "Come to gloat over your victory?"

"What're you talking about?"

"You're not fooling anyone, Mar. I know you're the one who helped Mel become chair of the department."

"Don't be paranoid," Mar said, smiling at him. "Isn't that what you always said to Tetrick?"

Then Mar heard Insol say, "Out of my way, Professor Leeno." Then Harmin stepped aside and Insol rolled into the office in a mechanized wheelchair.

Mar jumped up from her seat and strode over to her. She embraced Insol and kissed her on the cheek, then stepped back and examined her. The meds had reset her broken nose and performed reconstructive surgery on her face. They'd done a commendable job. Mar could see some slight scarring, but otherwise the surgeon's work was flawless. One of Insol's eyes was dead and completely clouded over.

"You look better," Mar said.

"I love you, Mar," Insol said and began to cry. "You didn't say I looked fantastic or great. That's what I've been hearing ever since I left the clinic. I love you for being honest…and it's wonderful to see you."

"Sorry I've been so scarce."

"No, it's just…" Insol said and turned to Harmin. "Why are you still here? Nobody invited you. Goodbye."

"So rude." Harmin huffed and shook his head. "Mar, always a pleasure."

"Oh no," Mar said. "The pleasure is all mine."

Harmin said, "Mel, see you around," then exited the office.

"That was a little harsh," Mel said to Insol while he closed the door, then returned to his desk.

"I see no reason to stand on ceremony with that man," Insol said, rolling further into the room, following Mel. "Do we still need him for anything?"

"We do still work with him. He sits on the committee to decide your tenure. Being cordial couldn't hurt." Mel reached his desk and tinkered with the jamming device.

"You be cordial," Insol said as she stopped the wheelchair and Mel turned toward her. "I see no reason to give that loyalist any degree of respect."

"If that's how you feel," Mel said.

"I don't think you want to know how I really feel."

"All right. I get it," Mel said.

"I don't think you do," Insol said, spinning the wheelchair around and rolling toward Mar who was back in the armchair. Insol stopped beside Mar's chair and they held hands. Mel sat down across from the two of them.

Mar said, "How is the rehab going? Are you walking at all yet?"

"No," Insol said, "far from it, but let's talk about other things."

"Mar was about to catch us up. She just visited Rajer, I assume at the GSS."

"Where else would he be, Mel?" Insol said. "So glad to hear he's still alive."

Mar squeezed Insol's hand and observed her. The once joyous, beautiful young woman was now ground down to an angry, bitter person. Mar raised Insol's hand to her lips and kissed it, then said, "Yes, I met with Rajer at the GSS. He's as well as can be expected. Maybe better than expected. I believe they've done some harsh interrogation, but he didn't tell me. Probably scared how I'd react. He believes they're set on using him as leverage to keep me in line."

"How do you feel about that?" Mel said.

"What a stupid question," Insol said, sneering at Mel.

"Insol, please," Mar said. "Obviously, I'd rather have him home with me. This is a dangerous game for them to play with Rajer's life. He told me if push comes to shove, I should do the right thing and sacrifice his life."

Insol repositioned her chair and hugged Mar as well as she could. Mar moved forward in her chair so she could fully embrace her. Insol said, "When will these sacrifices for the truth stop?"

"Hard to say. Soon if I have any say about it," Mar said.

Mel said, "I recently found out my sister and mother are dead, too."

Mar released her hold on Insol and said, "Mel, I completely forgot about your family's situation. I feel awful. I'm so wrapped up in my own problems."

"I think about them every day. If my father's still alive, I can only imagine how horrific his life is."

Mar said, "My old head of security was ex-military and had connections in the government. My new one might have some, too and he might be able to discover something about your father."

"Whatever you can find out would be appreciated," Mel said.

There was a hard knock at the door. A startled Mel stood up and went to answer it. "All this talk of the GSS is making me jumpy." Mel chuckled nervously and opened the door, then said to the person on the other side, "Yes, she's right here."

Suron stepped into the room. "You told me to remind you of your other appointment when the time arrived."

"Yes, Suron, thank you. I should be ready shortly."

Suron stepped back out of the room and as Mel was closing the door, Insol called out, "Thanks for the heads-up." The she turned to Mar and said, "He's kind of cute."

"Now, Insol, I'm still a partnered woman."

"I know, but. . ." Insol said and nudged Mar with her elbow.

Mar rolled her eyes and said, "So what have you been cooking up, Mel?"

Insol threw her arms in the air and raised her voice. "Mel, why are you involving her? I don't see why we need to put her in danger."

"You see those guards outside, Insol?" Mar said. "They're not following me around for decoration. I've already been in the line of fire and people have died around me."

Insol said, "I just don't want anyone else getting hurt."

"That railcar has left the station, Insol," Mel said. "Or as Yor liked to say, 'In it together.'"

"Yes, I hear you," Insol said. "By the way, before we get down to business, have you spoken to Yor recently, Mar?"

"No, I haven't. Sorry," Mar said. "I hate to rush this reunion, but I do have to get going."

"Basically, our idea is a day of protest worldwide in every dome. We're going to call it Truth Celebration," Mel said. "Workers will take the day off, students won't attend classes, and we'll march down the main streets of every dome city carrying placards stating our sentiments about the Global Assembly's policies. The plan is for a peaceful protest. The militaristic elements of the Movement have been told to stand down."

"Those kinds of protests have been illegal since the DOME riots," Mar said. "You'll get yourselves locked up."

"We're looking at a planetwide mass protest," Insol said. "They can't arrest that many people—we're talking families and children, too. The scope of this sort of protest has never been seen by the Leader. Organizing has been done primarily through our network getting info out to community organizers by word of mouth. The time and date of the protest is a secret and organizers won't know anything about it until a day before."

Mar said, "I don't see how you're going to keep the lid on such a massive event without the GSS finding out beforehand and arresting the network and community organizers."

"As Insol mentioned, it'll happen within a day's notice," Mel said. "This is all at the planning stage right now, and I'm sure Insol agrees with me that you should be kept completely in the dark unless your involvement becomes necessary."

"I do," Insol said.

"You're probably right," Mar said. "Although if they try to stop the protest in the streets and violence breaks out, I think it's naïve to believe that they won't arrest all the suspected conspirators like you two when the march is over."

"There's an escape plan if arrests start to happen," Insol said.

"Still sounds risky," Mar said.

"Is there ever reward without risk?" Mel said and stood up from his chair. "This has to be done sooner than later. Every day we do nothing, Yor's revelations get ground down in the Global Assembly's campaign of lies. Have you seen any of it?"

"I stopped watching. Made me too angry," Mar said.

"Well, our analysis shows that it's solidifying the Leader's base of support," Mel said, "Your son's sacrifice will soon have been for naught if we don't capture the moment now. Yor's words and Yorlik's discovery will be forgotten as lies and trickery, and the lies win over the truth once again. Before its too late, we need to tap into the anger and discontent Yor's actions ignited."

"You sound like my son."

"I'll take that as a compliment," Mel said. "Now, I know you have another appointment and I have a lecture to give."

Mar stood and put her hand on Insol's shoulder. "Contact me. I think my med division can help with your eye," Mar said. "I'm planning on traveling to Shamba in twenty-four days and I may see some of your family. You have any words to pass on?"

"I'm jealous," Insol said. "Just tell them I'm fine. I don't want them to worry."

Mar said, "The three of us should try and get together before this march happens. In the meantime, you two stay safe."

"Be safe yourself," Insol said. "Shamba is beautiful, but it can be a complicated place."

# Lek

When Lek returned home from work, Linara was in the living room lying on the couch watching a viewing-channel with the lights out. She hadn't heard Lek arrive, so he stood in the hallway observing her in the strobing light of the viewing screen.

Earlier, Linara had commed Lek at work and put Ara on the call to say goodnight. Ara had asked why her papa wasn't home to tuck her in. Lek felt guilty, but it wasn't the first time.

When it came to his job, Lek weighed the good against the bad. His GSS position gave his family a better life than ninety percent of the Kodan population, but each day he cringed at the agency's actions while he worked overtime and missed so much of Ara's childhood. There was nothing he could do about it, though, with Director's Thuta's threats of retribution hanging over his head.

He walked further into the room and stood beside the couch. When he did come home to this bungalow, Lek found comfort in his existence with his family. He had fallen in love with Linara for many reasons—strong will, intellect, creativity—including her Mauan features: button nose, long red hair streaming to her shoulders, pale complexion. Tonight, she wore yellow pajamas.

Linara said, "Are you going to keep standing there?"

"I'm enjoying the view."

"That's nice of you, but I'm a fright."

"Far from it."

"Come," Linara said, sitting up and making room for him on the couch.

Lek sat to Linara's right and they kissed, then she went back to watching the viewing channel. Roneh Rayush was being interviewed on a news show. She spoke about her love and admiration for the Leader, her allegiance to the Global Assembly, and how Yor Vanderlord was a traitor to the Kodan people.

Lek said, "Why are you watching this crap?"

"There's not much else on and I find it interesting."

"I don't," Lek said and picked up the viewing screen's controller from the low table in front of the couch. He ran through the channels, and it seemed like Roneh Rayush was appearing on more than half of them, so he turned the screen off. The room was plunged into darkness except for the green glow of the bungalow's control panel on the wall by the front door.

"I was watching," Linara said.

"Not really."

"What does that mean?"

"You were being told what they want you to think."

"I see you're bringing your work home again."

"How can I not?" Lek said.

"Is this about Rajer again?"

"Yes—he had his reunion with Mar today. Makes me sad I can't do more for them."

"You've done enough from what you've told me."

In the glow of the control-panel light, Lek saw worry on Linara's face. He felt bad that his choices were affecting her.

"I don't know, Linara," Lek said. "As far as my job goes, this complication with Rajer might be the thing that breaks the Ashtecki's back."

"And it might be the undoing of this family as well," Linara said, swatting Lek's knee with the palm of her hand and glaring at him. "You could be under scrutiny."

"It would take a serious investigation to discover anything."

"I wish you'd left that job a long time ago."

"We both know why that didn't happen."

"I want you to be happy, Lek," Linara said, "but you need to keep us in mind."

Lek moved closer to Linara and rested his hand on her thigh. "That's exactly what I'm doing, my dear."

"Yes, but…" Linara said and released a long sigh.

"I know it's exasperating," Lek said, moving closer, still holding her thigh. "I feel like I can't sit idly by anymore and enforce Global-Assembly lies every day. What happens when the truth loses all value?"

"Powers-That-Be sake, Lek, I hope you don't say stuff like that when you're not in the confines of this bungalow."

"That's exactly what I'm talking about, Linara. Exactly," Lek said, raising his voice.

"Please quiet down, Lek," Linara said, speaking in a whisper. "You're going to wake your daughter."

"I'm sorry," Lek said, whispering. "But I sit in that office all day and I spend more and more time watching the vid of Rajer tackling that Rayush woman before she's able to shoot Yor. In that moment, Rajer purely defines the kind of life I'd like to lead."

"Being imprisoned?" Linara said. "When I think of Rajer in that moment, I see a man who's lost his mind and isn't thinking about the consequences of his actions."

"I see him defending what he believes in," Lek said, raising his voice again.

Linara grabbed hold of Lek's hand on her thigh and squeezed. "Keep your voice down."

"Sorry, I haven't been able to vent. I've been coming home late and you've been asleep," Lek said, whispering. He could feel the exhaustion from his arduous day at work overwhelming him, but he wanted to make his point. "This is how I see it. People decide what they believe in. Many times, that's a reflection of their flaws or even their strengths. My father is a prime example. I've been think-ing of him a lot lately. He cared for his family, but his devotion to the Global Assembly gave his life meaning."

"Yes. You've said this before."

"He went to war defending the Global Assembly and watched his buddies die in the fight to preserve it. And after the Revolts, he still had to believe in it, believe in its policies, otherwise he would've cracked the foundation of his very being."

"That's a little dramatic."

"You never met my father," Lek said. "My point being, my father firmly latched on to the Global Assembly and believed in it to justify the horrors of war he experienced. I never begrudged him what he believed. The Global

Assembly at that point might've been worth his complete faith."

"I'm not sure where you're going with this."

Lek inhaled and exhaled deeply. "Sorry, I'm tired and meandering a bit," he said. "What I'm trying to say is people make choices about their beliefs and they'll go to great lengths to defend them. Ador believed the Global Assembly was a sham and that their lies were a detriment to the future of the Kodan people so he joined the Movement. He put his energy into debunking those lies masquerading as the truth. Being with Mar and having a family gave Rajer's life meaning. We have that in common. He has no regrets about—"

Lek now saw fear in Linara's eyes. He moved closer and squeezed her hand back. "You all right?"

"Not at all," Linara said. "I'm scared at what you're about to say."

"Yes," Lek said, "it's scary, but would you rather I continue to be complicit in the lies, be miserable while my friends perish around me attempting to do the right thing?"

"The right thing?" Linara said, her voice shaking. "What for the Powers-That-Be sake is that? Taking on the Global Assembly? What good did that do Ador or Rajer?"

"I'm talking about doing the right thing for this family, the one thing on this planet I truly care about, the only thing worth sacrificing my life for."

"Sacrificing your life? Staying alive would be the right thing for this family," Linara said. "Listen to yourself."

"I am listening to myself, and it might be the first time in my life since deciding to partner with you," Lek said. "To be completely honest, I've already crossed the line when it comes to my Loyalty Oath."

"And you didn't think about talking to me first?" Linara said, raising her voice.

"I can't live with myself unless I can make Koda a better place for you and Ara, and that'll only happen if I can make Koda a better place for everybody," Lek said, raising his voice, too. "I can see my chance to make a difference. Mar is the only person in a position to force the Leader's hand and I'm going to help her do it."

Linara yelled, "I can't believe what you're saying—"

"Mama, Papa, what's wrong?" Ara said, standing beside the couch in her orange onesie. She looked confused, scared, and half-awake, rubbing at her eyes.

Lek said, "What do we have here? A squiggle meezer got into the bungalow." He jumped up from the couch and scooped Ara up in his arms, kissing her on one cheek, then the other. "Look, Linara. How did a squiggle meezer get into our home?"

"I'm not a squiggle meezer. I'm not," Ara proclaimed. "I'm not."

"Hmmm…let me taste you," Lek said, giving her a bunch of wet kisses on her cheeks.

Ara squealed, rubbing her cheeks.

"That sure tastes and sounds like a squiggle meezer to me."

"Mama, tell Papa to stop."

"Seems like your papa does whatever he wants, my beautiful girl," Linara said, standing up and walking toward the master bedroom. "Papa will put you back to bed. Good night, my sweetness."

"Night-night, Mama."

Linara closed the bedroom door behind her.

"Let's get you to bed," Lek said, throwing Ara over his shoulder with her squealing once again. He carried her into the dark confines of her room and placed her on her bed, then turned on the night-table lamp.

Ara's room was decorated with the flowers of the Mauan region. She was obsessed with them. The wallpaper portrayed watercolor paintings of flowers. The lamp on the night table consisted of a lampshade covered in more flower images and the base itself was an open flower. Ara's bed sheets and blankets were adorned with a variety of blossoms in different stages of bloom. Linara's parents lived in the Mauan dome, and the lamp, blanket, and bed sheets were gifts from them.

Lek marveled at his beautiful redheaded baby girl. The only thing he wanted on this planet was a superb life for her: a long, happy, and healthy life with the freedom to exist the way she pleased and the ability to express herself the way she saw fit. He felt this sense of mission over anything else in his life. He wished he'd made it a priority sooner when it came to his work.

"Papa, why are you staring at me like that?"

"Because you're the most beautiful and wondrous blossom in this room."

"You always say that."

"Only because it's true," Lek said. "Now get under the blankets."

Ara wriggled under the blankets. "Are you and Mama mad at each other?"

"No," Lek said, tucking her in. "What makes you say that?"

"You were yelling at each other."

"It doesn't mean we're mad at each other. Sometimes adults raise their voices when they're speaking to one another in order to make what they're saying more understandable, but that doesn't usually work so I wouldn't recommend it." Lek laughed at himself, then saw the look of confusion on Ara's face. "Nothing for you to worry about. Mama and Papa still love one another, and we still love you, all right?"

"All right," Ara said and yawned.

"I think it's time for you to get back to sleep," Lek said, kissing Ara's forehead. "Sweet dreams. I love you."

"I love you, Papa," Ara said, kissing Lek on the cheek.

Lek turned off the lamp and made his way out of the room. As he was closing the door behind him, Ara said, "Papa?"

"Yes, dear."

"Please leave the door open a crack."

"Always, my beautiful blossom," Lek said, peeking through the crack between the door and the frame. This was part of their bedtime routine.

Ara said, "Give Mama a kiss for me."

"Will do," Lek said. "Now go to sleep."

When Lek reached the master bedroom door, it was closed. On the floor in front of the door was a blanket, a bed sheet, and two pillows. Lek attempted to open the door, but it was locked. "Linara," Lek whispered, "Linara, let me in, please." There was no answer. Lek didn't want to make a fuss and wake Ara again, so he picked up the bedding and headed for the couch.

He dropped the bedding beside the couch and sat down, then stared at the viewing screen and was reminded of the disinformation campaign he turned off earlier. Lek knew better than most about the suppression of the truth waged daily against the Kodan citizenry and the Leader's plans to permanently eliminate any dissent. That wasn't what he signed up for.

Lek thought about Tas Jerrick and what had finally made him decide to choose the GSS as a career. Nine days after meeting Tas Jerrick, Lek rode a bus back to their rendezvous spot. At that point, he still wasn't convinced a career in the GSS was something he wanted. It definitely wasn't how he saw his future, but he figured it couldn't hurt to hear more. Lek departed the bus at the same stop as before, retracing his steps back to the warehouse. When he arrived, the table and chairs were there, but no sign of Tas Jerrick.

Lek called out a few times, "Anybody here?" The words echoed back to him in the empty warehouse, but nobody responded. He decided to sit down and wait. Never in his wildest dreams could he imagine himself in a clandestine meeting with a GSS recruiter. The longer he sat there, the more he became uneasy. It was clear they wanted him to take the job. Was he afraid of what Tas Jerrick might do if Lek rejected his pitch? Or was he scared of his future if he didn't take the position? He decided he was overthinking the situation and he wasn't going to wait around any longer.

That's when Tas Jerrick appeared where a hallway met the warehouse space. "Lek," Tas Jerrick said. "You made it."

"You sound surprised."

"I had a bet with a few friends. They were sure you wouldn't show. I just made a pile of units."

"I'm glad I could do that for you."

Tas Jerrick sat down at the table and pounded out a rhythm with his palms. That reminded Lek of one of Rajer's habits.

"It's good to see you," Tas Jerrick said. "I'm not gonna lie. If I sign you, I get a bonus."

"That's nice."

"Yes, it is," Tas Jerrick said. "Now, what questions do you have for me?"

"I'm curious about the training."

"For starters, there'll be interrogation training."

"Before, you said you see me as an analyst rather than an interrogator."

"Yes, you're more suited as an analyst being university educated and you don't have the profile of an interrogator. They're typically ex-Global Guard who already know how to get the job done, so to speak. No need to get into the gory details. You'll be given interrogation training so you understand the techniques. You'll also receive physical training and are expected to be competent in hand-to-hand combat, but I don't see that being a problem for you. According to your file, growing up on a ranch in a small town, you got into a few scrapes. Am I correct?"

"That's true." Lek was astounded his file included such detail.

"What else? Of course, you'll have classes in analyzing data," Tas Jerrick said. "You already speak two languages. We'll probably put you through training to speak Shamban, which is a language you'll need to know if you're going to be an analyst."

"I can do that."

"Of course you can, and you'll probably enjoy it," Tas Jerrick said. "What else is on your mind?"

"Well, to be completely honest with you, I'm not too crazy about violating people's privacy. Seems like we're taking away basic rights by setting up all that surveillance."

"You're looking at it the wrong way," Tas Jerrick said, scooting his chair closer to Lek. "This is about violating the privacy of those who wish to do harm to the Kodan people."

"Seems rife for abuse. How do we spot the people who need to be watched?"

"It'll be your job to make sure we target the correct citizens."

"But in the process, we're violating innocent citizens' rights in order to locate the guilty."

"You'll be at the front lines protecting the innocent citizens of the planet by removing suspicion from them and targeting the guilty parties."

"I don't know—"

"Before you go any further with that thought, let me tell you about your compensation package." Tas Jerrick told him the GSS paid better in the first year than most private sector jobs. Lek would be housed in new hi-tech apartments for single government employees until he had a family, then he would qualify for a bungalow. Annual pay increases keeping up with inflation would be built into the contract he'd be asked to sign.

"Can I stay in Capitol City?" Lek said.

"Yes, we can work that into the contract. Most GSS analysts will be housed here anyway."

"That's all extremely generous, but I still have reservations."

"I'm fine with answering more questions. Don't be shy," Tas Jerrick said. "I've also been authorized to offer one more thing to entice you to take this position. Would you like to hear it?"

"Sure."

"We did some research on your family, of course— normal procedure for security purposes—and I came across more than a dozen loan applications your father submitted for his ranch."

"Yes, he's stubborn about saving that place. I told him—"

"Well, we can help. As part of the contract, we can give your father a loan at a favorable rate," Tas Jerrick said. "Of course, he'll have to pay it back or lose the ranch, but seems like he wants it."

"That ranch is a lost cause."

"Nevertheless, we can make it part of your contract if you're interested. It'd be a nice gift from his son who'll be taking a job he'd certainly approve of."

"I don't know what to say."

"Say you'll take the job."

"I'll have to think about it."

"We'll give you five days, then the offer is off the table. I'll digi-mail you the details later today," Tas Jerrick said. "My comm number will be in the mail so feel free to contact me with any further questions, day or night. The Kodan people need you, Lek. The Global Assembly needs you. It'll be a better planet with you onboard. For the good of the globe."

Tas Jerrick stood, smacked Lek on the shoulder, and departed down the hallway. Lek's shoulder throbbed.

As Tas Jerrick promised, the offer arrived in Lek's digi-mail later that day. All the points he mentioned were there, including the loan to his father which detailed the amount and interest rate. Both were generous and his father would be pleased. The part of the offer Tas Jerrick failed to mention was the Loyalty Oath. It explicitly stated that any actions ruled seditious by the Global Assembly and its duly appointed magistrates would bring the sentence of death without appeal. The Oath gave Lek further reservations about taking the offer.

He needed a sounding board to make his decision about the position. He had a few good friends, but none he trusted more than Rajer to affirm or refute his thoughts regarding this job prospect. But Rajer wouldn't return from his trip until seventeen days beyond Tas Jerrick's deadline and he had turned off his comm for everything but emergencies.

So Lek spent a few days taking walks around Capitol City, considering his future. He toured the Royal Palace and strolled around the Old Quarter. He observed demolition crews knocking down an office complex and a Malrap brewery to start construction on the Arena and the GSS building. These buildings would complete the Global Plaza. If he took the job, Lek would come here for work every day.

He sat down on a bench outside the Global Assembly building and thought about the time he visited with his parents when they took him to the University for orientation. They'd never been to the Plaza and his father's loyalty to the Global Assembly was on full display. He insisted on "dressing up" for the occasion, out of respect for the Global Assembly. Over his usual button-down green work shirt, he wore his blue suit jacket, which he hadn't taken out of the closet in years, with his lapel pin displaying the insignia of his Separatist Revolt military unit.

When they reached the steps of the Global Assembly building, Lek's father removed his sweat-stained wide-brimmed hat, smoothed out his thinning grey hair with his right hand, and stared at the Global Assembly flag flying from a pole. Then he snapped to attention, put up his hand to salute the flag, and said, "For the good of the globe." The words tripped off his tongue full of devotion like a prayer. As his father saluted, a government worker about his father's age was passing by and stopped in his tracks beside him.

"Powers-That-Be bless you," the man said. "Thank you for your service. For the good of the globe. What was your unit, soldier?"

It turned out they'd both fought in Shamba at the same time and in the same military campaign. Lek's father was enthralled as they discussed their shared past defending the Global Assembly. Lek couldn't recall the last time he'd seen his father this engaged and spirited. Lek's mother was smiling. She was happy for her partner. Viewing this scene, Lek truly understood what his father's connection to the Global Assembly meant to him.

As Lek sat on a bench outside the Global Assembly building, pondering his future as a GSS analyst, he realized he had no connection to anything like the one his father demonstrated that day. Maybe he could find it in the GSS. He revisited his reservations about the position and saw his path forward. There would be rough days ahead as the domes were built and the Selection Process began, but people were needed inside the Global Assembly to uphold the ethics of Kodan society. The temptation to misuse those instruments of surveillance, those instruments of power, was great. That's why his employment within the GSS was necessary. *Yes*, Lek thought, *for the good of the globe*. He'd accept the job and the topper would be his father receiving a loan from his beloved Global Assembly.

In the first few years of his GSS tenure, Lek's fears about the job came true. He was haunted by what he saw every day. He observed average citizens being spied on for speaking their minds against the Global Assembly. He witnessed interrogators torturing citizens and obtaining false confessions. All of this immorality to maintain power, but Lek stayed. He was still convinced he could make things better by being on the job.

When he did criticize the GSS's actions, his words fell on deaf ears. His superiors finally told him to keep his thoughts to himself, and that his statements came close to sedition and violating his Loyalty Oath. Hope of any oversight faded with the DOME riots, but soon afterward, he met Linara. They partnered. She became pregnant and the day Ara was born, his life was given true purpose. His job became a way to provide for his family. They moved into a deluxe bungalow. He earned more units than they could spend, and they were afforded the best early schooling for Ara.

If he left his GSS job, all of those benefits would be taken away, so he remained the good soldier. He overlooked what he would have bristled at before, and as he moved up the GSS ranks, those perks became ever sweeter. The one time he threatened to leave, Director Thuta reminded him of the secrets he possessed and how the GSS would never let him return to civilian life. They'd take away his freedom on some charge and his family would be left in ruin.

Lek had no choice but to stay put. Then Ador was murdered for his words. At Breeze Celebration, Yor Vanderlord revealed that the GSS's cruelty was based on a lie. Rajer was imprisoned, and in the near future, the Leader was planning a planetwide purge. When he watched the vid of Rajer tackling Roneh Rayush, he asked himself, *What kind of world am I building for my daughter?*

Now, sitting in the dark in his living room, Lek looked down at the bedding by his feet. Tomorrow, he'd wake for work and soldier along the best he could within view of his superiors, but he intended to make a better life for his family and Koda.

# VIDOR

In his Global Assembly office, Vidor read a GSS digi-report regarding Joro Camtur's interaction with Mado Prevor at Breeze Celebration, then reread the one from Lek Valsted about the Jeps' meeting for the third time. In the transcript attached to the Valsted report, Mar Jeps' statements about consciously outwitting him were laughable and there was some suspicious conversation, but he couldn't get past how Mar Jeps had the gall to speak harshly about him after she had the audacity to demand under threat that Vidor arrange her meeting with Rajer Jeps.

*Such insolence.*

Vidor recoiled at Mado Prevor and now Mar Jeps thinking they could take such liberties with him. That type of behavior ended years ago when Vidor took his rightful place as Leader of Koda and became the final word in governing the planet. In the first three terms of his Presidency, though, Vidor had surrounded himself with sycophants and incompetents who attempted to advise and influence his decisions, thinking they knew better than him and could tell him what to do, but the DOME riots changed that forever.

The DOME riots were a slow-moving disaster at first, starting with the planned domed cities filling with migrant camps. Homeless encampments had existed on the outskirts of these cities before as the environmental crisis increased unemployment by accelerating the loss of manufacturing and agriculture jobs, but these new camps were larger and growing exponentially. People were hoping to move into the cities before the domes were finished. Vidor watched this happening for hundreds of days, then wanted to use Global Guards to clear them out. He believed the migration had to stop. A clear message was necessary to deter others from doing the same thing, otherwise it would become a major problem before the Selection Process was completed and the domes were sealed. At the time, all his advisors were political appointees rather than his ex-military colleagues. They told him the migration would end soon when people saw the hardships they'd have to endure. They told him to wait and see, and against his better judgment he capitulated to their advice.

The problem careened out of control when viewing channels began covering the thousands of Kodans camped around the planned dome cities, which triggered a planetary panic. Hundreds of thousands began heading toward the cities as most people didn't want to risk being shut out in the deteriorating environment. This would mean becoming outer-Kodans—the portion of the planetary population who would reside outside the domes—which everyone presumed was a death sentence.

Gridlock seized Koda's roadways into the planned domed cities. In some regions, the traffic jams stretched as far as 145 kilometers from the cities. Water and food became scarce inside the cities as the road blockage hindered the movement of supplies. As the dilemma worsened Vidor's advisors advocated against the military again, so Vidor ordered airdrops by military cruiser.

When the riots broke out, the city police were overwhelmed. Vidor called his advisors into his office and said, "This is all your doing. You advised me to wait and see. Well, look at what your shortsightedness has produced. I'm calling for an aerial bombardment of the roads, then sending troops into the cities."

Tak Rork, Vidor's Global Security advisor, said, "That'd be political suicide."

Vidor's Secretary of Global Affairs Min Tohk added, "The sheer number of deaths would sway public opinion forever against you, Mister President."

Davik Atmar took the middle ground, saying, "There would be a drop in approval but if nothing is done, the results will be worse."

None of Vidor's other advisors wanted to speak up so he told them all, "This is why I was elected President three times. The Kodan people expect me to make the tough decisions, no matter what the cost. None of you has the nerve to do what needs to be done. It's time for me to take control. I know what's best for the Kodan people."

Vidor took action. He told Supreme Commander of Global Forces Nar Falojin to make plans for the bombardment of the roadways and clearing them, then gather the army for a full-scale assault on the cities to wipe out the rioters and migrant camps. He arrested Tak Rork and Min Tohk and ordered Orn to take care of them. He exiled his other advisors and their families from the planned domes and brought his ex-military colleagues onto his staff. He encouraged his wealthy friends to buy up the major viewing channels and digi-media outlets and placed his public relations division in charge of news content.

By the time the Global Assembly passed the edict making him Leader, Vidor was in complete command. Koda was his planet to control, his planet to shepherd into the future. Nobody could guide the Kodan people better than him, and the DOME riots taught him there were few around him who weren't seeking to undermine his position as leader of the planet.

In those days, Mado Prevor was one of the few people he trusted. Mado had been a friend to Vidor and the Kodan people. He'd been invaluable in affirming Vidor's ideas and was a believer in his leadership, but Vidor recalled a few events, starting over a decade ago which began raising doubts about Mado's fealty.

The first was Mado mentoring the Vanderlord boy. Vidor found Mado's interaction with the boy disturbing. After the Great man passed, Vidor tasked Orn to keep an eye on the boy. Orn told him the boy continued to demonstrate a dangerous level of curiosity about his great-grandfather. Mado said their relationship had nothing to do with the Great man. He was simply fulfilling an obligation he made to Yor's father before he died to watch over the boy and keep him out of trouble. Mado assured Vidor that his loyalty had never been stronger, so Vidor decided to let it go until it became a problem.

Then, years later, Vidor received a request from a Global Assembly rep regarding Mado Prevor's desire to restore the WAEF for the new Museum of Global History and Information. When Vidor heard this news, he was furious. Mado was still working with the Vanderlord boy, too. He commed Mado again and again, and each time he was rerouted to Mado's assistant who told him that Mado was busy and would get back to him. Vidor also realized Mado hadn't attended a Global Assembly political rally in support of him or come to a banquet at the estate in a while. Suspicion rose in Vidor. He was the Leader and he wouldn't be disregarded. For days, he chastised himself for trusting Mado and bringing him into his home. Finally, he commed Mado again and as usual was rerouted from Mado's personal comm to his assistant. This time, Vidor insisted on Mado's presence at his home at a specific time and date.

That day, waiting for Mado, Vidor stood on the terrace of his estate watching his boys play below him on the lawn. He plotted how he would punish Mado and his corporation if Mado failed to appear, but when Vidor heard the Prevor Industries cruiser approach, he felt his burden lift slightly, and he hoped Mado would prove his concern ill-conceived. Although he had explaining to do, Mado had become close with Vidor's family and Vidor always looked forward to spending time with him.

The boys ran down the path in the direction of Mado's cruiser and disappeared into the trees. A few moments later, the boys were running back toward the house. Vidor's eight-year-old Carz was carrying a package with six-year-old Minok sprinting beside him, pawing at the bundle and yelling at Carz when he pulled it away. Although Vidor had spoken to Mado about spoiling his boys, whenever "Uncle Mado" came to the estate, he brought some sort of gift for them.

Vidor waited for the boys as they scrambled up the stairs. When they reached the top, they halted in front of their father, panting.

"What did I tell you about teasing your brother, Carz?" Vidor said. "He may be smaller than you now, but someday he'll be your size or larger, and he might be doing the same to you."

"Yeah, right," Carz said as Minok took a swipe at the package and Carz lofted it above his head where Minok couldn't reach it.

"What was that?" Vidor said in an angry tone.

Carz's demeanor changed immediately. "You're right, sir. Sorry, sir. I promise not to do it again."

"This is the last time I will warn you," Vidor said. "You know what that means, correct?"

"Yes, sir. Sorry, sir."

"Now give your brother the package."

Carz hesitated for a moment, looking at his father.

"Well…" Vidor said and took one step in Carz's direction.

Carz handed the package to his brother who clutched it and snickered.

"Minok, what do you say to your brother?"

"Thanks, Carz."

"Now, what has Mado brought you this time?"

Carz said excitedly, "The newest version of HGD, Father. Nobody else on the planet has it."

Vidor heard Mado coming up the stairs. Mado had a distinctive way of walking, always hesitating before every third step. Vidor filed away that eccentricity along with Mado's others. The boys turned as Mado came up behind them and wrapped their arms around his waist.

"Mado," Vidor said.

"Leader, sir," Mado said.

"I see you brought my boys another gift. You're going to spoil them, and you know how I feel about them playing instead of doing their schoolwork," Vidor said. Mado was carrying a large case with him. "What do you have there?"

"I couldn't come empty-handed for you and Flomina," Mado said, putting the case down with a loud thud.

"That's too kind of you," Vidor said. "Very thoughtful. Boys, what do you have to say to your Uncle Mado?"

Carz and Minok said in unison, "Thank you, Uncle Mado."

"Now, you boys go do your homework, then you can play with Mado's gift," Vidor said. "I'll be up in a while to make sure you've done all your homework properly. And what is it I always say not to forget?"

Carz and Minok chanted, "We always have each other so we should always be good to one another."

"Very good," Vidor said, then pointed to the building. "Now go and don't make too much of a ruckus—your mother is under the weather. You're dismissed."

"Yes, sir," the boys said as they ran across the terrace, past the security guards, and into the house with Minok still holding tight to the package.

The Leader said to Mado, "You're good with them."

"Something I've learned over the years."

"Well, someday you'll have one of your own."

"We'll see about that," Mado said, picking up the case. "Where would you like to talk?"

"Out here, I think. Nice day," Vidor said. "I keep forgetting—it's always a nice day in the dome, isn't it?"

"Yes, it is, thanks to you."

"Lots of other people made it happen, including yourself," Vidor said, walking toward the glass-top table set up with a carafe of Malrap and one of water alongside two empty goblets. He sat down. "I'll take credit, though. Couldn't have happened without me."

Mado seated himself at the table and placed the case next to him. "My assistant said you called personally and were adamant about seeing me."

"I have some concerns about your recent activities and you weren't responding to my calls, so I decided to make my request perfectly clear to your assistant. If I'd gotten you on the comm, I would have used the same tone," Vidor said. "I'm the Leader of the planet, aren't I?"

"Nobody is questioning your authority. I wasn't avoiding you—I've been busy running my corporation. I apologize if I didn't get back to you sooner. I thought we'd moved beyond your concern for my loyalty. I thought we were friends," Mado said. "By the way, the estate looks beautiful these days. The landscape architect has done a magnificent job. You can see his plan unfolding now that everything has grown in, and the energy field still appears to be holding up quite well."

"Yes, it's operating well, but that's beside the point," Vidor said. "Whether we're friends or not, I'm still the Leader, and when I call, I expect a prompt reply."

"You're absolutely right. I'll keep that in mind. Whether you're Leader or not, that's the respectful thing to do. I just get wrapped up in my work," Mado said. "Sorry to hear Flomina isn't well."

"Oh, it's woman's stuff and we had a spat," Vidor said, thinking about his argument with Flomina. She was unhappy that he'd invited Mado over to the estate without consulting her first since she wasn't feeling well. "Just marital bliss in full bloom."

"So why did you summon me?"

"I'm…" Vidor couldn't get his mind off his argument with Flomina. He was Leader of the planet and he could invite whoever he wanted to his home, whenever he wanted to. "I'm sorry, Mado." When the words left his mouth, he didn't know why.

"Nothing to be sorry about, sir," Mado said. "If I might be so bold, you seem a little out of sorts yourself."

"No, I'm fine," Vidor said. He needed to pull himself together. He'd been through military campaigns and here was Flomina knocking him off his game. "I called you here, because I'm having second thoughts about the restoration of the WAEF."

"Yes, I talked to the Global Assembly rep the other

day and he said you hadn't approved the WAEF's move to the Complex yet. What's the holdup?"

"I'm concerned it could resurrect Yorlik the Great in the Kodan consciousness and upset the calm that's come over Koda since the domes were sealed."

"That…again," Mado said. "Now that you're the Leader of the entire planet, you should be over feeling threatened by the Vanderlords."

"So you're dismissing my concerns."

"I would never presume to do that, sir," Mado said. "I have the utmost respect for you and your office, but can you explain your concerns in greater detail so I can address them properly?"

"I'm not required to explain myself to anybody," Vidor said, then watched as Mado cocked his head in a questioning manner. Vidor peered over Mado's shoulder at the beauty of his estate. He wouldn't have any of this if it wasn't for Mado. "But since it's you, I'll do the best I can."

"I appreciate that."

"I appreciate you appreciating that," Vidor said, and he chuckled along with Mado who made that weird smile of his, too.

"So, you're concerned about Yorlik Vanderlord gaining some sort of traction in the Kodan consciousness again?"

"That's part of it," Vidor said, pouring a goblet of Malrap for Mado and one for himself.

"You do realize you'll never be able to wipe the memory of Yorlik the Great from Kodan consciousness. Schoolchildren still sing nursery rhymes about him."

"That's my point. Why lift his image up anymore? I could ban the nursery rhymes but how would that look? The legend is fine, but by restoring the WAEF, you're inserting the Great man back into mass culture and reigniting interest in his voyage and its outcome," Vidor said. "That will lead to civil unrest."

"Understandable conclusion, but you should look at how it could work for you." Mado took a sip of his Malrap.

"Enlighten me," Vidor said, then slugged down his entire goblet of Malrap.

"First off, wouldn't you agree that Yorlik the Great is already the most popular figure in Kodan culture? A man vaunted as the savior of Koda who for over a hundred years caused the population of the planet to look up at the night sky, waiting for him to bring news of their salvation. His return may have been anticlimactic, but his legend lives on just the same."

"Sounds like you're making my argument for me."

"You remember a few years back the Royal University did a 'Most Popular Kodans in Modern History' poll? Yorlik and you were one and two with the next person a distant third," Mado said. "We could use the restoration of the WAEF to ensure your place as the most popular person in Kodan history."

"How would that work?"

"It'll take years for the WAEF to be ready for launch, so to speak, but in the meantime, you and your people spin the WAEF's restoration as your inspiration. Solidify your similarities with the Great man, like your love for the Kodan people and your desire to overcome the crisis. Just like Yorlik rallied the Kodan people behind the SEEDER program for a new and better future, you've done the same with the DOME project. After a century of the Global Assembly spending quadrillions on a prospective DOME project, you got the entire thing off the ground. You mustered the Kodan people to build the domes as their ability to exist on the planet's surface waned. That took true leadership."

"I've always felt that way," Vidor said, pouring himself another goblet of Malrap.

"By the time we roll out the restored WAEF, you'll no longer fear Yorlik's popularity because this promotional campaign will boost you to a legendary status like the Great man's. Maybe we roll out the WAEF at a Breeze Celebration as the grand finale."

"I do like the sound of that," Vidor said. "It's plausible, but were you thinking about this when you concocted your pitch to the rep for the restoration?"

"To be completely honest, I was thinking how much fun it would be to take on the project and do the job with Yorlik's great-grandson by my side. This entire idea for boosting your popularity came to me later," Mado said. "If you look at the addendum at the end of the pitch to the rep, this idea is there."

"I haven't seen it."

"Well, now you know."

"Sounds like you've given this some forethought."

"Just attempting to address my friend's issues," Mado said and finished off what was left of his Malrap. Vidor took hold of the carafe to pour more for Mado, but Mado put his hand over the top of his goblet.

"No, thanks," Mado said. "I've still got CEO-ing to do today and the Malrap is already swirling around in my brain."

"What if I gave you a direct order?"

"I'd have to comply…under protest." That weird smile crept across Mado's face again. He took his hand off the top of the goblet and slid it over to Vidor, who laughed.

"I'm just kidding. I completely understand if you have more work to do today."

"Appreciate it," Mado said, sounding relieved. "If we're all in agreement about the WAEF restoration, then I have something for you."

"I'm satisfied, but if projects like this one come up in the future, I want to hear about them directly from you before I have to comm you or order you here."

"I'll be more diligent in the future," Mado said, then he reached down beneath the table and Vidor heard the sound of the latches on the case being thrown open. Mado looked up at the table and said, "Can you move the glasses and the carafe to your side of the table? I think you're going to like this gift."

Vidor moved the items. Mado reached down again and emerged holding an object Vidor recognized immediately, although he couldn't believe he was seeing it at his home. It was Leen the Magnificent's war hammer. The entire weapon had been forged as a single piece using metal from the Mlimoan mountains. The handle was over half a meter long and wrapped in petrified vines so it was easy to grip when wielding the head, which was about one-third of a meter long and half that wide. Mado placed it on the table with a thud, rattling the glasses and the carafe.

"Whoa!" Vidor said, standing and picking up the hammer. He thought it would be heavier. When he stepped away from the table and swung it back and forth, he was amazed by how easily he could control it with one arm. "That's incredible. I've heard myths about the weight of the hammer and how it was engineered by the weapon designers a thousand years ago so it could be whirled through the air without effort and cause maximum damage on impact."

"I've heard the same myths," Mado said, still sitting and observing Vidor.

Vidor was thrilled. "Would you like to try?" He held the hammer out to Mado.

"No, thank you. I actually tested it before I brought it here. I wonder if the design is part of what gave the owner his name? He must've been magnificent in battle with that thing. Since Yor is a historian, I was going to ask him, but never got around to it."

The mention of a Vanderlord in the moment spoiled it for Vidor, but that quickly passed. "So this is a gift for me?"

"Yes, sir."

"It should be in a museum."

"Where better to display it than the Leader's home?"

"I can't argue with that," Vidor said, swinging the hammer with one hand, nicking the terrace's railing and taking a chunk out of the wood. "Damn it! Flo is going to have my head for that, but maybe she won't notice." Vidor planned on calling the handyman as soon as Mado left.

"So you like it?"

"Like it? I'm…speechless. I heard it sold for an exorbitant amount to an anonymous buyer at a private auction."

"I saw it going up for auction and thought the Leader should have it."

"I don't know what to say," Vidor said, gently placing the hammer down on the table. Vidor couldn't recall the last time somebody outside of his family had given him a gift without an ulterior motive. "Really. Thanks. You're a good friend."

"I have something else," Mado said, reaching down again and revealing a vase covered with intricate colorful drawings of life on Koda about 700 years ago. "Second Kodan Dynasty. I thought Flomina might appreciate it. She can add it to the collection. If you like, you can tell her you bought it for her." He placed it on the table beside the hammer.

"She'll never believe me, but I'll give it a try," Vidor said. "This is so considerate."

"It was up at the same auction and I thought it went with the hammer, being an antiquity."

"Can you stay for evening meal?"

Mado reached down and Vidor could hear him shutting the case and latches, then he stood with the case in hand. "If I don't get going, I'll be late for an important meeting. I appreciate the invite, though—maybe another time?"

"Anytime."

"And please," Mado said, walking up to Vidor and patting his arm, "if you want me, comm me and I'll be sure to pick up. I apologize again for being so absent lately." Mado waved goodbye and descended the terrace stairs.

Now, years later, as Vidor sat in his Global Assembly office, he opened the daily security briefing on his viewer and was reminded again why he needed Mado Prevor. Part of this briefing was a report on planetary environmental conditions. They were deteriorating faster, which meant in turn that the structural integrity of the domes would become untenable sooner than predicted.

Back when the first dome collapse occurred, Vidor presumed it was an isolated incident and it had worked out politically to send Orn to the disaster site and pin the blame on anti-government terrorists. When further collapses began happening one after another, it was easier to dispatch Orn each time than admit the reality of the situation to the Kodan people.

Vidor discovered the truth by sending a team from the Global Assembly Corps of Engineers (GACE) to assess the rubble from the first collapse. GACE was composed of ex-military men who understood that the preservation of the Global Assembly depended on their discretion. They were aware of the consequences if they leaked their findings.

In their calamitous report, they found the metal in one out of twenty-two pane frames to be deficient and the frames were disintegrating in the increasing temperatures outside the domes. The dome's structural integrity was reliant on the pane frames. If multiple frames fractured within close proximity, then the imbalance on that section of the dome would generate a substantial collapse.

The report concluded that the malfunctioning of the frames would increase and the collapses would happen with greater frequency as the planetary conditions worsened. GACE recommended inspecting every dome and every pane frame, then replacing the faulty frames, but it wasn't safe to open the domes to the toxic environment in many regions, and this would only bring Vidor's administration under public scrutiny and confirm anti-DOME rhetoric.

Vidor directed GACE to evaluate the domes and come up with a predictive model for complete failure, taking into consideration the faulty part and deteriorating environmental conditions. The report was sobering. He was told by the engineers that the majority of the domes had a 24% likelihood of complete failure in 30 years, a 47% chance in 42 years, a 69% chance in 60 years, and 92% chance in 78 years. Vidor was appalled. When the DOME project was launched, the domes were projected to last 1,000 years despite the rising temperatures. They were touted as the greatest architectural achievement in Kodan history.

Vidor felt betrayed, and there was plenty of blame to go around. He wasn't stupid. The corporate builders had bilked the Kodan people, siphoning off the research, development, and construction funds and creating a defective final product. Only a conspiracy could have enabled this treachery. Execs, techs, inspectors, factory foremen, and even workers must have been paid off to keep silent about the flaws. This was fraud on a global level that was simply hard to fathom, but Vidor couldn't take the corporate builders—the truly guilty—to task. He couldn't drive them out of their mansions, placing the spotlight on them, because these were the people who had put him in power and kept him there. When he thought of all those who had perpetrated this debacle, he wondered what they were thinking. They'd placed the entire planet in jeopardy to fill their already bountiful coffers.

*Those spaceships must be ready*, Vidor thought, staring at the digi-foto of his family on his desk.

Mado needed to be found. It now occurred to Vidor that he'd been sullen since Breeze Celebration because he hadn't come to grips with the fact he felt duped by someone he considered one of his closest friends and allies. Mado had betrayed him. Vidor had clung to his idealized notion of Mado because it was rare to have someone like him in his life, but he was through brooding. It was infecting his ability to govern effectively.

And Mar Jeps was an extension of that problem. He was allowing her to dictate policy, because he required what Mado possessed. If Mado was truly unavailable, then he was going to put an end to that, too. She was just another Vanderlord, and it was time for the Leader to make the hard decisions once again.

The GSS had notified him that Mar Jeps was traveling out of the dome soon. That was perfect because it would give him plenty of time to organize his plan before he rolled out his forces. He'd wait until Mar Jeps returned from her trip to comm Director Thuta about scheduling a meeting with Lek Valsted, but for now Vidor intercommed Kel. He told her to set up comms between himself and the Supreme Commander of Global Forces, the Head Director of the GSS and the Lead Commander of the Global Guard. As far as Joro Camtur was concerned, Vidor would deal with him. He'd reach out to him tomorrow and invite him to the estate so they could speak in private as soon as possible.

# MADO

Yor said, "So you held the Leader at bay by coddling his ego with gifts?"

"I also went out of my way to be supportive politically," Mado said, shifting his weight on the crate in the storage room. He'd been sitting there for quite some time explaining his relationship with the Leader. He and Yor hadn't met in this room to discuss the past for awhile. The engines had been their priority, but Mado thought it might be beneficial to take a break and Yor was taking full advantage of it. Mado adjusted his place on the seat again. He noticed Yor had kept the tally marks up to date. They were seventy-eight days from Breeze Celebration.

"You all right?" Yor said.

"I might need another pillow, but I'm good for now," Mado said. "Aren't you hungry? Tired?"

"No, I'm fine," Yor said, standing up and stretching, then sitting down again.

"I'll keep going from where I left off then." Mado was well aware that if Yor latched on to a subject, he wouldn't stop until he'd wrung it dry. In addition to his intelligence, this tenacity had made Yor so successful at such a young age.

"I attended parties and planetary functions at the Leader's estate," Mado said. "The Leader invited me to them all and I attended the vast majority of them, unlike the other corporate heads. I was supportive of the First Lady's charities too.

"At the time, the Leader spearheaded a political initiative fomenting fear to cover up the shoddy dome construction. Arousing fear had always been a successful strategy for him. When he was first elected, as a cornerstone of his administration, he stoked the idea that the anti-DOME movement was the enemy of all Kodans and he kept repeating it, so it was easy to convince his followers that the Movement was behind the DOME riots. He built on this fiction to deflect any blame for the collapses by claiming the anti-DOME terrorists were causing them. It wasn't difficult with the viewing channels being purchased by his political allies and backing his story."

Yor said, "Were you supportive of this policy?"

"It was difficult to watch. He was arresting and torturing innocents so they'd confess to crimes they didn't commit. I sat through many public addresses in the upper gallery of the Global Assembly chamber as the Leader told lies to keep the Kodan people from learning the truth about the faulty domes."

"Wasn't it hard being around the Leader knowing what he was doing to innocent people and the lies he was telling Kodans?"

"Painfully so," Mado said, adjusting himself on the crate. "But I had to keep up the masquerade. We'd begun working on the WAEF. You were building your network and researching *Power Over the Future*. So, as you said, 'coddling' the Leader was a constant chore."

"Sounds like it. That hammer must have cost a fortune."

"It was worth it," Mado said. "As for the domes, I have to admit their failure is happening faster than I predicted and the date for complete collapse will be sooner as well. I guess I didn't calculate the complete incompetence and greed of the corporations involved. One wonders how they valued units more than the future of their genetic lines. So what happened was, Joro—"

"Wait," Yor said, looking up from his viewer at Mado. "How soon is the complete collapse of the domes?"

"A greater than fifty percent chance in fifty years."

"You didn't think that was important enough to tell me? That it would've been good for others to know?"

"Who? Mel or Insol or the Movement in general? Think of the furor that would be unleashed. The fighting and bloodshed caused by the indignation resulting from being conned out of continued existence."

"Well, when you put it that way—"

"Exactly. Please, Yor, when you read these notes back to yourself, learn something from what your great-grandfather set in motion and what I've done to keep it going. You're a brilliant young man. I'm proud of all you've accomplished, but just when I think you understand what I've been doing for decades, you say things like you just said. Consequences exist beyond the moment of emotional response. Please let your intellect take primacy over your impulses before you act. I understand it's easier said than done."

"I'll keep that in mind. Please continue."

"Well, let's see…Joro commed me late one night. He said, 'Mado, you won't believe it. I mean, I can't believe it and I was there…' I told him to calm down and say what was so unbelievable. That's when he told me he'd attended a dinner party at the Plemso estate for a regional ambassador, one of the few events I missed over the years. During a late-night Malrap drinking session with several of the Leader's close allies, the Leader yelled and screamed about the frequency of the dome collapses and the engineers' prediction of complete failure. He threw a full carafe of his precious Malrap across the room, smashing it to pieces against the wall.

"Joro said to me, 'You know what that means?'

"'The Leader wasted some fantastic Malrap.'

"'Very funny,' Joro said.

"I said, 'I have a good idea, but you sound like you want to tell me, so go ahead.'

"'It means we're finally moving closer to our goal after all these years of waiting.'

"I said, 'I've been working more than waiting, but I understand what you're saying. I still have to convince him to do it.'

"Joro said, 'I don't think it'll be that hard. I wish I could convey his rage at being known as the Leader who oversaw the end of the Kodan species. He even talked about executing the corporate heads who constructed the domes, except for you. He mentioned you specifically. His disappointment in them and his dissatisfaction with his leadership was on full display. Of course, we all told him it wasn't his fault but he became close to despondent—or maybe that was the Malrap. He was at a complete loss about how to rectify the disaster. The SEEDER program was brought up which only further angered him, but I think our time is now.'

"'Yes,' I said. 'It's finding the right moment, though.'

"So, I waited. The Leader loved his late-night Malrap drinking sessions after Global Assembly functions at the estate. He called them 'think tanks.' He felt like he needed to unwind after being social and stately for his constituents. The night I decided to make my move, Joro ran interference and told the few people the Leader had invited to his think tank that I had a subject of great importance to discuss with the Leader alone. Being invited to these sessions was a big deal because it was a way to curry favor with the Leader, so Joro told the Leader's guests that I now owed them and they left.

"The Leader was surprised I was the only one to take up his invitation, but I told him what I'd done and he was clearly pleased to be alone with me. I surmised he wanted to talk to me about his dome quandary, so this was the opportune moment to bring up the spaceship initiative.

"By the time I wrapped up my pitch to build spaceships for the survival of the Kodan people and showed him the blueprints on a memory wafer, the Leader had consumed a few glasses of Malrap and was sitting there in silence staring at me. I wasn't completely sure whether it was a good sign as I waited for him to respond. I did mention in my presentation that I'd learned a thing or two about space travel from your great-grandfather and could use that knowledge to make faster ships. That my med techs had been working on cryotech which would be perfect for this journey, given that we didn't have the coordinates for a new home. If we launched with hundreds of thousands Kodans onboard and limited resources, we could still travel for a century, searching for a new planet.

"Eventually, a grin formed on the Leader's face and he yelped in joy so loudly that one of his guards entered the room to see if everything was all right. Once the guard left, the Leader jumped out of his chair and literally walked laps around the room saying, 'This is incredible. I've been eating my heart out for days worrying about the failure of the domes and how the Kodan people might become extinct because of blunders made on my watch, and then of course I was concerned about my boys growing up with this disaster looming over their heads with no solution in sight.'

"He was stymied because Kodan scientists would need to learn about space travel from scratch. No space travel had occurred in over a hundred years and Plemso had banned and destroyed much of the tech know-how surrounding it. Nobody had a clue how long it would take to build functional spaceships for the population of the planet or whether it could occur in time to save the Kodan species.

"Then he stopped walking around the room and approached me, saying, 'Now, you're telling me you understand the concept of space travel. That constructing a workable spacecraft is within your intellectual grasp. I would have come to you sooner if I'd known. I still don't want to give Yorlik the Great any credit for making space travel a reality again for Kodan survival, but that's something I'll need to get over.'

"The Leader stood in front of me and grabbed me by the shoulders, and in reflex, I stood and did the same. I could sense the sheer joy he was experiencing in the moment, then a dark wave of emotion streamed from him. He let go of me, sat down, and poured himself a goblet of Malrap. He was in deep contemplation. I seated myself and asked him what was wrong.

"He said, 'I'm not sure what just happened, but when we were embracing, I had the distinct feeling you're deceiving me somehow.' I told him that made no sense. Why would I be misleading him, for what reason? He told me it made no sense to him, either, but he'd need to think about my proposal."

Yor said, "Did you transfer your emotions to him somehow?"

"That's what must've happened. I was so out of practice, and when I sensed his emotions, I must've let mine go out toward him in response. Lack of concentration on my part. Maybe I was tired. It'd been a long day. Maybe I was excited myself about how well my overall deception was going over and it leaked out. I changed the subject and we chatted some more before I departed.

"I decided not to comm him about the proposal. I didn't want to appear too anxious and assumed I'd hear from him soon enough. Not that I was thinking about it too much or beating myself up about it, but at least once a day I considered how I might've destroyed close to twenty years of planning in one moment.

"Hundreds of days passed. The Leader and I spoke of other things like the dome power source or how the WAEF restoration was coming along. I had dinner at his estate with his family. I saw him at Global Assembly functions. He never mentioned building spaceships. I felt like he was testing me to see if I'd bring it up so he'd catch me being overanxious about it. All was silent on Joro's end, too. He hadn't heard anything from his leakers inside the Leader's inner circle and I told him not to bring it up, either.

"My daily obsession with my mistake at the Plemso estate faded. Not that I wasn't still worried, but I calculated another dome collapse was imminent so there was no reason to fret about it. And then the Great Norian Collapse happened. A major disaster. Over eighty thousand dead. All the viewing channels and digi-media covered the tragedy for days. There were tearful interviews with Norians who lost loved ones. Tens of thousands injured. The population was evacuated to an area in the dome where the air circulators were working and food and water could be supplied. Everyone on Koda was devastated. Of course, you remember that one—you were about to head for a book signing when all flights were cancelled."

Yor said, "I remember you being overwhelmed emotionally by the event. You were engrossed in the tragedy and even donated a generous number of units to the relief effort. I was honored to know you."

"It was a horrifying moment in Kodan history and I'd never seen such a loss of life in my existence," Mado said. "I recall the Leader's receptionist commed me exactly

nine days after the incident because the viewing channels
started running those banners every day on-screen counting the days since the disaster and retabulating the loss of
life. The receptionist told me when to meet the Leader
at his Global Assembly office, which would make our
conversation an official one, but it was after office hours.
The receptionist didn't tell me what the Leader wanted,
but I assumed it was about the spaceship project and I
brought the updated blueprints of the ship's design just
in case I was correct.

"When I arrived for the meeting, the receptionist had
gone for the day and the Leader's office doorway was wide
open. A guard standing in front of the entrance stepped
aside as I approached. When I was fully in the room, the
door slid closed behind me. The Leader was standing,
peering out the window, and without turning around, he
said, 'Mado, seat yourself on one of the couches, please.
I'll be right with you.' I sat down and when he finally
turned around, the Leader looked horrible, like he hadn't
slept in days and had lost weight.

"I said, 'Are you all right?'

"The Leader said, 'I look that bad, huh?'

"I said, 'You've looked better.'

"'This dome collapse has been a horrible burden. I
wanted to wait the proper amount of time before talking
about it with you, plus every day brings another logistical
nightmare in dealing with the victims…and the dead. We
have tens of thousands of corpses to excavate from under
the rubble and remove from the dome quickly enough to
avoid a health-related problem and do it respectfully at

the same time. That doesn't even include making sure the survivors get the necessary supplies. You've probably heard the Global Assembly voted to create a special security and disaster division to act expeditiously in these kinds of scenarios. This is a blemish on my leadership capabilities. I've been battling Global Assembly reps who want to launch an investigation into the domes' structural integrity and finally convinced them it's all a matter of terrorism.

"I knew when he said 'battling' he meant 'intimidating.' I listened to his rant and remained silent. He told me many times that my ability to listen was one of the qualities that endeared me to him. My listening started out as an attempt to understand him and the motivations behind his actions, but it produced this unexpected benefit. As he moved toward me from the window, I could smell he hadn't bathed in days. I wondered the last time he was home, then I noticed an unmade cot in the corner of the room and a suitcase on a stand next to it with unfolded clothes piled inside it.

"The Leader said, 'I know I'm a sight.' Then he seated himself on the couch across from me.

"I said, 'You haven't been home lately?'

"'No,' he said, 'and Flo is not pleased with me.'

"I realized the field commander in him had kicked in and he didn't want to leave the front lines until the job was done. Silence filled the air and the Leader appeared to be daydreaming. Maybe he was thinking of home and his family or contemplating his next logistical move for the disaster. I finally said, 'So you asked me here because…?'

"The Leader threw his head back and sighed, then launched into a long-winded, meandering speech about the spaceship project and our relationship which was so incoherent at times, it's hard for me to recall exactly what he said. Basically, he confirmed my fears.

"He liked the spaceship project idea when I first told him about it, but he couldn't get the feeling of distrust out of his system. He called it his instincts, but I knew better. He told me he enjoyed our relationship and decided to continue it without talking about the spaceship project. Then the collapse happened and after the initial shock, he began to consider the project again and put his misgivings aside. He was ready to entrust me with bringing the project to its successful completion.

"The Leader had invested his 'reputation' in the DOME project. This was how he intended to make his mark on Kodan history. He saw the domes as the only way for the Kodan people to survive, which is why he felt compelled to act so severely during the DOME riots."

Yor said, "You did back him on the DOME project, so aren't you complicit in those deaths, too?"

"That's not fair, Yor. His actions were horrific, especially the aerial bombings of the roadways. It was far more violent than what I was expecting at that moment in history from the President of Koda. I agreed there was no way for the Kodan people to survive without the domes at that point in time, but I never condoned the way Vidor Plemso dealt with the DOME riots. In retrospect, he was a military man who saw the extreme use of force as necessary to clear the way so the domes could go up without any contention. I've found on Koda that in many scenarios, violence is easy to inflame and used to generate a specific outcome. It's just the way it is. I don't condone it. You didn't think your Breeze Celebration speech would cause violence?"

"I had no idea that—"

"Your speech had good intentions, but people were killed and injured in the post-Breeze Celebration riots. So, were you complicit in their deaths? That's definitely an argument we could have. I backed the DOME project, but I had no clue about the violence the Leader would bring down on the citizenry to make it happen. So think before you judge what I'm telling you." Mado made an effort to control his outrage. He wanted to believe Yor would understand someday.

"To continue," Mado said, "the Leader laid out how he wanted to proceed. He demanded the project be accomplished with the utmost secrecy, so the shipbuilding had to happen in a remote area of Koda where only the people working on the project would know about it. The workers would be given lengthy contracts and sworn to secrecy. To divulge the project would mean death. Why the airtight secrecy? The Leader said he didn't want to cause panic in the Kodan population by building space-ships in the public eye. The real reason: he couldn't get past his own ego and having to explain why the domes were failing under his leadership. He'd spent immense amounts of political capitol suppressing the anti-DOME movement, the truth about Yorlik the Great's voyage, and constructing the domes, and he wasn't going to admit he was wrong on any of those counts because that would tarnish his legacy."

"Legacy?" Yor said.

"Yes, the Leader has always focused on what the history books will say about him when he's gone."

"Eventually, history will catch up with his lies. We proved it at Breeze Celebration."

"As you've seen on the viewing channels, the Leader is attempting to create doubt around what you presented. He's convinced he can shape what the historical record will say about him. If his followers are the only ones on the spaceships, then his legacy will be whatever he wants it to be. On the face of it, he wants to limit the number of spaceships and passengers due to the financial budget, but he has a clear idea of how many Kodans he wants to transport off the planet based on handpicking the Kodans most loyal to his rule. When he asked me the passenger capacity of two ships, I told him 75,000 people with cryotech units."

Yor said, "So these ships are massive?"

"The ones being built in the caverns are much larger," Mado said. "When I told him the capacity, he said, 'That'll do.' When the time comes, he will select his steadfast supporters which will include his wealthiest benefactors and their extended families and the Global Assembly reps and their families. The next chosen will be the most devoted men and women in their childbearing years and their children, according to their GSS files.

"Then he told me he'd pay for it with the units from the Malrap tax stashed away in a blacked-out account.

Only a few people with clearance were aware the account existed or how much was in it. The account had originally been set up as a way to bolster the military if rioting broke out again. He told me that he could start the project anytime with those funds, then asked me how long it would take to build the ships. I told him twenty-five years to create and test the necessary tech, build the ships, and train the personnel.

"I said, 'Shouldn't we build more ships? We're leaving the majority of Kodans behind.'

"The Leader said, 'Why should I care about them?'

"I said, 'You're their Leader.'

"The Leader shook his head and sneered in derision, 'They're mostly disloyal in their hearts. Now get started with my ships. I have a site in mind for the facility and I'll set up security.'

"I sent some of my more diplomatic and empathetic staff to Shamba to discuss building spacecraft for the rest of the Kodan population, or as many ships as we could build in the time remaining before the Big Collapse, as I like to call it. The idea was to build in the caverns beneath the Elysian mountains where a large number of Shambans survived outside of their dome. Since it's such a substantial project, I thought it would be problematic instilling the proper degree of secrecy there. I underestimated the Shambans. They're up to the task since secrecy has been the basis of their society for centuries in order to survive as enemies of the state.

"As for the Leader's project, I've sprinkled major setbacks with minor successes in building the ships' hulls and basic interiors to keep the Leader happy, and I continued to massage his ego to make him forget that lapse in our relationship."

"Well," Yor said, "this is a lot to take in. The Leader's attitude is horrendous. I knew he was terrible, but this confirms my worst fears about him."

"Yes, it's hard to believe he can be so callous toward the citizens he swore to protect."

"What I said before about you being complicit? I was out of line. I didn't mean anything by it."

"Sure you did," Mado said. "I can forgive you, though."

# RONEH

R oneh Rayush sat on the government-issued couch in her government-issued apartment in a building where the single government employees without families lived. She shared the residence with two of her former officemates at the Department of Education and Well-Being.

Earlier today, Roneh had been offered her own multi-occupancy bungalow in a housing development as a bonus for her new job as Public Relations Liaison to the Leader. As she was finalizing her employment transition papers, the person at Human Resources reminded her, "According to the digi-docs received by the Leader's office, you were assigned this bungalow. It's yours."

"Yes, I know, but I'll stay where I am," Roneh said.

"Maybe you don't understand. The bungalow goes with your new position."

"It must be a clerical error," Roneh said. "I'm a servant of the Global Assembly and I live by the edicts of the Global Assembly. Those state that I'm not permitted to live in my own multi-occupancy residence until I'm partnered and have a child. For the good of the globe."

The HR person mumbled under her breath, "Oh, you're one of them."

"What was that?" Roneh said, banging her fist on the Active Glass partition between them.

"Nothing," the HR person said. "Here's the memory wafer stating your raise in pay and you can contact the housing department and reject the bungalow if that's your wish." She handed Roneh the wafer through the slot in the glass.

"What's your name?" Roneh said, examining the HR person. She wore the usual clothing of a government worker—white button-down shirt and Global-Assembly-blue pants—but Roneh could tell she was hiding a seditious nature and could do damage to the good of the globe.

"Why?"

"Because I intend to report you for violating government policies," Roneh said and spotted the HR person's ID tag. She noted the name and ID number in her digi-tablet.

She had considered letting the HR person's violation slide, but then Roneh would've been disparaging the Global Assembly. She'd made a mental note to send a message of complaint to the GSS before she went to sleep this evening.

Now, her comm buzzed. Her roommates were on the line and asked her to meet them at a Malrap bar with other employees from their department. These after-work get-togethers at a bar were as much about hooking up with other government employees as they were about drinking. For a moment, Roneh considered the invitation, but she was too tired from her day and was enjoying being alone in the apartment, so she passed on it. She prepared herself a protein meal and opened her viewer to compose a digi-mail to the proper authorities about the HR person's insubordination. As she typed the message, she felt pride in doing what was expected of every loyal Kodan citizen. She'd learned her duty at an early age attending Allegiance Camp every year during school break.

Due to Roneh's parents' Global Assembly military service, Roneh went to Capitol City Allegiance Camp (CCAC) for free. She was eight years old when she attended her first CCAC girls' camp. She'd never been separated from her parents and away from home before, and she cried hysterically when her parents placed her on the bus. She didn't want to go and couldn't understand why her parents were sending her. The other passengers were strangers ranging from Roneh's age to sixteen years old. She refused to engage in conversation with them, even though many of the older campers attempted to console her, telling her the experience would get better.

In those days, the environmental crisis hadn't reached the stage where being outside for too long was hazardous to one's health. The camp was located outside the city limits in what had once been a pristine setting. The lake was little more than a mud puddle now, while half the trees were bare of leaves and dying due to the lack of rain and the unrelenting heat of the crisis. Rumor was the camp had been a training facility for the Global Monarchy Army.

Although Roneh perceived the beauty in her surroundings, she couldn't see how the old ramshackle wooden barracks and outbuildings and the rusty military vehicles parked on the perimeter of the camp were conducive to having fun. Roneh found her assigned barracks and lay down on her bunk, feeling the wooden slats beneath the worn mattress jabbing her. Her mother had told her to be patient, that she'd enjoy herself in time. She buried her face in the moldy pillow, but she couldn't see how her mother's prediction would ever come true.

Then she felt a tap on her shoulder and opened her eyes to see a girl about her age, dressed in a blue CCAC T-shirt featuring the images of a barracks, a rusted-out tank from the edge of the compound, and a flagpole bearing the Global Assembly flag.

"This is for you," the girl said. Her dark hair was in two long braids that hung below her shoulders. She smiled as she handed Roneh a T-shirt like her own. "This is yours. You'll get more than one, but this is from me. Put it on. See how it fits."

That girl was Zeela Ajetuh, and she became Roneh's best friend at camp. Zeela was a year older than Roneh and had attended the camp for the first time the year before. She made it her duty to acclimate Roneh to camp. Zeela possessed a cheery demeanor which Roneh found infectious. It overrode her own gloomy nature.

At home, anger was always present. Her mother swore out loud, blaming the Separatists every day for her injury. Her father's salary from working double shifts combined with her mother's meager disability payments barely covered the rent or kept food on the table. So Roneh's parents argued incessantly over their paltry income and how being together was a curse.

Roneh had never experienced anyone as upbeat as Zeela. Her penchant for camp inspired Roneh to focus on the activities which explained how her parents' financial plight would soon be mended by the DOME project, and how her mother's resentment of the Separatists was actually fueled by her fealty to the Global Assembly. As each day passed at camp, Roneh began to comprehend the importance of the Global Assembly in her life. She understood the struggles of the Global Assembly against the forces out to destroy it and its mission to protect and nurture the Kodan people.

At morning meals, the campers stood and faced the Global Assembly flag while the anthem played over a public-address system. Then they sat down and chanted "For the good of the globe" over and over again while pounding their eating utensils in rhythm as morning meal was passed out. The food was fresh, actually grown at nearby farms where the livestock for the meat was raised as well. Roneh's meals at home consisted of processed protein drinks. The campers were told their meals were typical of life before the crisis, and that they'd return to this bountiful life once the Global Assembly helped them pass safely through the difficult times ahead and the planet was healed. For the good of the globe.

Morning meal was made more appetizing by exercise beforehand. All the campers ran five kilometers along a trail through the silent, dying woods, then climbed two six-meter walls by rope and crawled in the dirt under netting. Those who didn't make it over the walls were assigned to clean the kitchen after meals and shovel out the latrines, and they were chided by the other campers passing by who yelled at them, "You failed, you failed, you failed the Global Assembly!" After a few weeks of this, those who couldn't make the run or the climb usually went home in humiliation.

After morning meal, scheduled activities occurred throughout the day. They watched documentaries on Global Assembly military victories, the wonders of the DOME project, how to spot a person committing sedition or the false prophecy of the anti-DOME movement. Graduates of the camp who attained high rank in the military or influential employment in the GSS or another Global Assembly agency gave lectures. They talked about their jobs defending, protecting, and safeguarding the Global Assembly so it prospered. They discussed how serving the Global Assembly filled their lives with satisfaction.

Arts and crafts sessions consisted of drawing military vehicles or how they imagined the domes would look. Every day, the members of each barracks were allotted time to work on their presentation for the competition on the final day of camp. Each barracks' exhibit would portray the glory of the Global Assembly and how it brought a better life to the citizens of Koda. The winning barracks, judged by the camp staff, would be awarded the honor of their T-shirt design being next year's camp uniform.

Roneh and Zeela hit it off that first year and their barracks won the competition hands down with a presentation on the military exploits of Vidor Plemso and why he was an insightful President. When camp ended and they returned home, they didn't know how they could exist without one another. Zeela lived in a farming community over a hundred kilometers from Capitol City. Roneh's and Zeela's parents worked paycheck to paycheck and didn't have the time or money for their children to visit one another, so Roneh and Zeela communicated by digi-mail or comm. That kind of contact was frequent immediately after camp and tapered off to nothing as life outside of camp resumed its daily rhythms, but as anticipation for a new camp season approached, the digi-mail and comms between them picked up again. They plotted for the competition in the coming year, and for four years in a row, each year they attended together, they won.

Then, in their fifth year at camp, Zeela began displaying sullen streaks. Her home life had begun to change. Zeela's parents were forced to move off their farm when the crops in their community failed for the second year and they were required to find another way to make a living. Her parents, who were botanists, had become factory workers in the city. They hated their jobs molding steel beams for the domes, fueling discontent in their household.

One day, as they sat on one of the rusted-out assault vehicles on the edge of camp waiting for arts and crafts to begin, Zeela told Roneh that her parents didn't want her going to CCAC anymore. They considered alternatives like having her stay at home or join an academic camp which might increase her chances of a university scholarship.

"I don't understand," Roneh said. "Why are they so against camp?"

"It's not exactly camp."

"Then what is it?"

"They think what they're teaching here is wrong," Zeela said, jumping down from the vehicle and walking back into camp.

Roneh followed her. "What's wrong with what we're learning?"

Zeela threw up her arms and walked faster. "I don't want to talk about it. I've probably said enough."

Roneh ran to catch up, stopping in front of Zeela and cutting her off. "Zeela, how long have we been friends?"

"Over four years."

"You're my best friend, which is saying something since we only see each other for a short time each year."

Zeela didn't respond.

Roneh said, "We're best friends, aren't we?"

"Yes," Zeela said. "Yes, of course."

"And we've never kept secrets from one another, have we?"

"No," Zeela said. "But I know you and I can't tell you what you want to know."

"Why not?"

"Because."

"Because why?"

"Because…" Zeela said. "Because you love the Global Assembly."

"You do, too."

"But you care about it more than anybody I know, even me."

"I don't know if that's true."

"It is," Zeela said. "And I can't tell you because I know how you'll react and it won't be good."

"How bad could it be?" Roneh said. "Like they think Tetrick Vanderlord is right?" Roneh laughed.

Zeela bowed her head.

"Look at me," Roneh said.

Zeela kept her head down.

Roneh said, "Look at me. Is that what you're telling me?"

Zeela looked up. Her eyes were full of tears.

"Powers-That-Be, I guessed right?" Roneh said. "Tell me, Zeela." Roneh grabbed her and shook her. "Is it true?"

Zeela began weeping. "Yes, it's true."

"How? How could that have happened?"

"I don't know. When they lost their jobs at the farm and we moved into the city and they began working at the factory, they became angry and sad. They began saying, from their observations of the soil degradation, they could see the planet never recovering."

"That's blasphemy."

"They're scientists."

"It's blasphemy."

"See, I shouldn't have told you anything," Zeela said and attempted to maneuver around Roneh, who blocked her path and shoved her.

"I want to know everything." Roneh shoved Zeela again.

"Leave me alone. Stop doing that."

"Not until you tell me everything."

"No!"

Roneh shoved her again.

Zeela shoved her back and said, "They went to one of Tetrick Vanderlord's rallies and they returned in a different mood."

"What kind of mood?"

"A better mood. I asked what happened at the rally and…"

"And?" Roneh said and shoved Zeela again.

Zeela took a deep breath. "They told me what Tetrick Vanderlord said and how it confirmed their appraisal of the environment. They said the rally made them understand how the domes were a scam on the Kodan people. They said the rally gave them hope that there were other like-minded Kodans who could make a true difference," Zeela said, wiping the tears from her eyes. "They started going to anti-DOME meetings and even had a meeting at our apartment."

"In your home? What were the traitors like?"

"Just regular people, normal people, kind of nice, who wanted the best for their families."

"Listen to yourself," Roneh said, shoving Zeela again. "They're not normal. They're a stain on Kodan society."

"I don't know. Some of the things they said made sense."

"Made sense? Are you one of them now? Is that why you avoided my comms this year?"

Zeela bowed her head again. "Yes. I didn't know what to say, what to tell you. Look how you're reacting right now."

"I…I'm reacting like any good Kodan would react. I'm reacting like a concerned citizen who is learning about seditious activity."

"It's not sedition. They're concerned citizens, too."

"I don't know what else to say," Roneh said. "I need to think about this." She began to walk away and Zeela grabbed her arm.

"Don't go, Roneh. Don't go. Let's talk about this," Zeela said. "I know you. We need to talk. That's what we do, right? We're friends. Best friends, right?"

"I don't know. I'm not sure," Roneh said, yanking her arm free of Zeela's grasp and storming off.

In the following days, Roneh avoided Zeela. She even put in a request and moved into a different barracks. This attracted questions from the camp counselors. They were aware of the close relationship between Zeela and Roneh: their domination of the competition had become legendary and both of them were held up as shining examples of the Global Assembly's future. Roneh overheard Zeela telling the counselors she had no idea why Roneh made the request. When the counselors asked Roneh what was happening between her and Zeela, she told them she didn't want to discuss it.

Roneh was torn. She was ashamed Zeela hadn't reported her parents and sounded sympathetic to their treasonous turn. Roneh knew her duty to the Global Assembly, but Zeela was her best friend. How could she report Zeela and her parents? Were they really a threat to the future of Koda? From what Zeela had told her about them, they seemed like peace-loving people, but Roneh had been lectured incessantly by Global Assembly vids that sedition was like a virus. Once it infected an individual's spirit they were never the same.

Then came news of the DOME riots. Each camper was allowed to comm their parents to confirm they were safe. A handful of campers were sent home immediately when they discovered their parents were critically injured or killed or displaced by the riots. The remaining campers including Zeela gathered around a viewing screen in the dining hall for a planetary address by President Vidor Plemso, who had just been decreed Leader by the Global Assembly. In his speech, the Leader spoke of the loss of life and the devastation wrought by the rioters across the planet and how it was a sad day of mourning for so many Kodans. He called the rioters misguided citizens who had been led astray by traitors spreading lies about the Global Assembly's efforts to guarantee the survival of the Kodan people. He reminded everyone how the Global Assembly made the decision to build the domes almost a century ago but their efforts to snuff out the seditious untruths infecting the population weren't foolproof. Citizens were asked to remain vigilant, to keep an eye out for those ready to do harm and report them to create a better peaceful future. For the good of the globe.

As Roneh sat in the Allegiance Camp dining hall, listening to the Leader, she looked over at Zeela every so often and when the speech ended, Zeela turned toward Roneh. She was scared. Roneh ran from the hall to the assault vehicle where Zeela had told her about her parents' transformation. If she turned them in, Roneh was fully aware of what would happen to Zeela and her parents, but she also understood the dire consequences of inaction. She sat there for she didn't know how long, contemplating what she should do.

That's when Roneh saw the girls' head counselor coming across the field toward her. The head counselor was a tall woman with muscular arms and a short haircut, wearing a camp T-shirt, hiking shorts, and military boots. She was a former member of the Global Guard who many girls in camp including Roneh admired and hoped to emulate as adults. She was strong in body and will, never wavering from her loyalty to the Global Assembly. She reminded Roneh of stories she'd heard about her mother as a young woman.

"Roneh!" the head counselor called out.

Roneh jumped off the vehicle and stood at attention as the head counselor approached. "Yes, Head Counselor. I'm here."

"We've been looking all over for you. Zeela said this is where you might be hiding."

"Not hiding, Head Counselor," Roneh said. "Thinking."

"Yes, this has been a trying time, but the Global Assembly shall overcome. Don't you agree?" she said, stopping in front of Roneh.

"Of course, Head Counselor. I believe it."

"I thought so. You're one of the best soldiers we have, one of the bravest. I'm here because we've received news that your father was critically injured in the riots and your brave mother has requested you come home. A bus is waiting to take you and a few others back to the city."

"My father?" Roneh said, feeling tears welling in her eyes.

"Yes," the head counselor said. "Now pull yourself together, soldier. I know you're strong and your mother will need that strength at home."

"What happened?"

"I don't know, but you'll find out soon enough. Now go pack—you're holding everyone up."

Roneh raced back to her barracks and was out of breath when she arrived. She quickly pulled together her belongings. When she exited the barracks with her satchel, Zeela was waiting for her.

Zeela said, "I'm sorry to hear about your father."

"You are?" Roneh said. "You are? Your parents conspired with the rioters who did this to my father. I don't accept your apology." Roneh slapped Zeela across the face. Her palm stung as she headed for the bus and she could hear Zeela weeping behind her.

The head counselor was waiting for her at the bus. "You ready to go, soldier?"

"Yes," Roneh said. "But can I ask you a question before I leave?"

"Of course, Roneh. Anything."

Roneh could hear the sincerity in the head counselor's voice. Roneh believed the Global Assembly cared about her and her family, and the head counselor was an extension of the Global Assembly, teaching her the difference between right and wrong.

The head counselor said, "What is it, soldier?"

"Nothing," Roneh said. "I think I know the answer. Thank you for everything."

"My pleasure," the head counselor said. "For the good of the globe."

"For the good of the globe," Roneh said, clicking her heels together and saluting the head counselor.

The bus was half-empty on the ride back to the city so Roneh had a two-person seat to herself. When the bus exited the forest into a landscape of open fields, the four-lane road tapered down as the lane to the right of the bus was blocked off by barricades. Burned-out vehicles packed the right lane and shoulder. Chunks of the vehicles' chassis were missing, and their windshields and windows were busted out. On her way to camp, none of these vehicles were here. Although the windows of the bus were shut, the smell from outside was putrid and when Roneh peered closer into the vehicles, she saw charred, half-skeletal corpses inside. Many of them were children.

The Global Assembly was the only power on the planet that could wreak such devastation. Although she felt sorry for the dead and was horrified by the scene before her, Roneh had faith in the Global Assembly's reasons for their actions. She recalled the Leader's speech, and she understood that this violence was perpetrated to keep the peace, to stop the agitators from disrupting the Global Assembly's agenda.

When she wasn't looking out the side window, Roneh watched the stop-and-go traffic. She worried she'd arrive home too late and her father would be dead before she was able to tell him how much she loved him and say goodbye. Roneh was convinced that Zeela, her parents and their kind were to blame for the horror outside her window and her father's injuries. Once, she'd loved Zeela like a sister, but she was dead to Roneh now.

Roneh lay down on her seat and fell asleep. She awoke to the other campers on the bus gasping in disbelief. Traffic had completely halted on the flatlands. It was twilight and the sky had a dark-red hue. In the distance, smoke was streaming from Capitol City in great plumes as if the entire city was on fire. All the campers gathered at the front of the bus to observe the spectacle until the traffic started up again and the driver ordered them back to their seats for the remainder of the journey.

Roneh had lost track of time and one camper told her they'd been on the road for five hours. Usually the trip from camp took less than two. A sea of burned-out vehicles now reached to the horizon on either side of the road and Roneh's eyes teared from the smoke even though the bus windows were shut. Global Assembly soldiers wearing breathing masks were walking along the shoulder on both sides of the road, examining the rubble. A few fired their weapons into the vehicles.

Roneh was filled with anger over the scene. She removed her digi-tablet from her satchel and wrote a digi-mail to the GSS Office for Concerned Citizens (OCC). This agency existed so loyal citizens could expose Kodans who might be a danger to the greater good. In Allegiance Camp, they'd attended workshops where they'd practiced writing letters to this agency. Roneh typed in a fury, writing an impassioned letter about Zeela's family who had been turned by the anti-DOME movement.

Roneh finished her letter by saying, "Immediate action is required against these enemies of Koda." She possessed Zeela's city address and directed the GSS to locate the family there. She read the letter over once and sent it without a second thought, then turned off her digi-tablet, placed it back in her satchel, and fell asleep.

When Roneh woke again, the bus was standing still with the engine off. They'd moved closer to the city, maybe half the distance than before she fell asleep. The sun had set and the night sky above the city glowed red from the fires. Roneh thought she could almost see flames licking at the buildings. She had no idea what time it was, but all the other campers were asleep.

She left her seat, walked up to the driver and asked, "What's going on?"

The driver was startled and grabbed his chest. "You shouldn't sneak up on people like that, young lady, especially with what's going on outside."

"It's horrible."

"I was in the military and I've seen some bad stuff, but this is something else," the driver said. "Why aren't you asleep like the others?" He peered over his shoulder at Roneh. He was an older man with a patch covering one eye and a deep scar across his cheek.

"I don't know," Roneh said and squatted beside him. "I've slept a lot and just woke up. How much longer before we get to the city?"

"Your guess is as good as mine," the driver said. "We haven't moved for a while. They're clearing the road up ahead—cruisers were lifting cars from the roadway earlier and dumping them on the side." He pointed to the far right and Roneh noticed his hand was missing a few fingers. She would've asked him about his military service, but her mother had chastised her once for asking a veteran about his injuries.

The driver said, "At this rate, we probably won't get there till sunrise."

Roneh pointed at the city. "Those must be some kind of fires to see them from here."

"I can only imagine," the driver said, looking out through the windshield. "So, are you here because of your parents?"

"Yes," Roneh said. "My father was injured in the riots."

"It's unfortunate. The riots are hurting lots of people on both sides."

"Both sides?" Roneh said. "Who cares about the other side? This is their fault."

The driver chuckled. "I know you attend Allegiance Camp, young lady, and I respect being loyal to the Global Assembly. I paid with my fingers," the driver said, turning toward Roneh and removing the eye patch to reveal a gaping hole where his eye once resided. "And my eye. But the men, women, and children in these charred vehicles we've been passing were innocent bystanders in this skirmish. They just happened to be in the wrong place at the wrong time."

"So are you saying the Global Assembly was wrong to do what they've done?"

The driver put the patch back over his eye and leaned toward Roneh, examining her, then chuckled again. "What I'm saying is that the story isn't always as black and white as we'd like it to be. Did all these people deserve what they got? Absolutely not. Did the Global Assembly do what they thought was right in bombing these people? Absolutely. Sometimes in war there's collateral damage. You don't mean for innocent people to get hurt, but it happens. It's sad but it's true. There's always blame to go around. Nobody likes it, but it's part of life and we have to live with it and carry the burden around with us," the driver said. "You're too young to understand. Maybe someday you will."

Traffic started forward and a helmeted soldier with a blue flare in hand waved the bus forward. The driver said, "Looks like we're moving again. Now please get back to your seat."

As the bus drew closer to the city, the number of burned-out vehicles increased on both sides of the road. They were now piled on top of one another, sometimes four high. The roads leaving the city were gridlocked, probably with people fleeing the mayhem and attempting to get their families clear of the violence. Cruisers from the city roared overhead at a low altitude one after the other, leaving the bus shaking in their wake. The red glow above the Capitol appeared to be subsiding, and Roneh saw this as a sign that the Global Assembly had prevailed.

She thought about what the driver had said as she peered at the devastation. *Collateral damage*, Roneh thought. *But necessary to guarantee Koda's survival.* The Global Assembly only had the good of the globe in mind. The wreckage of Zeela's life would become collateral damage as her parents were dealt with by the proper authorities. It was too bad, but as the driver said, it was part of life.

As they entered the city, the sun was coming up, but the air was so thick with smoke that they couldn't see any damage from the riots. Roneh was being dropped off first since she lived close to the outskirts of the city. When the bus arrived at her home and the driver opened the door, Roneh grabbed her satchel and hurried to the front of the bus. The driver wished her good luck and she thanked him for the advice.

The driver chuckled. "Oh, don't take what I said too seriously. I was pretty tired."

"You may have been tired," Roneh said, "but I found it helpful."

"Is this one yours?" the driver said, looking past Roneh out the open bus door.

Roneh turned around as her mother rolled up in her wheelchair. Roneh ran out of the bus and hugged her.

"Yes, this is mine," Roneh's mother said.

"She is a serious one."

"Yes, she is, and I love her for it," Roneh's mother said, then her father exited their home. His head was wrapped in bandages and Roneh ran to him and began crying.

"What's this, my little soldier?" Roneh's father said.

"I was worried about you. Thought you might be…" Roneh said, embracing him.

"Oh, yes—the doctor initially thought it was much worse than it was, and that's why your mother called you home. By the time we found out it wasn't serious, you were already on the bus heading back here," Roneh's father said, hugging her back.

"I thought…and I…" Roneh said, crying some more.

"I think someone's exhausted," Roneh's mother said. "Let's get her fed and into bed."

In the days that followed, Roneh's father stayed home and recuperated. The factory reopened after the damage from the riot was repaired and Roneh's father went back to work. CCAC was closed for the season.

Since she'd returned home, Roneh had received a reply from the OCC, thanking her for performing her civic duty and saying they'd look into her concerns, but Roneh had a change of heart. She began writing back, explaining why Zeela was innocent and her parents were the real traitors, but she found herself staring at her half-composed mail.

When she grew frustrated, she left her room with her digi-tablet and found her mother sitting in the living room watching a viewing-channel news show. Roneh stood in place, waiting for her mother to notice her.

Roneh's mother finally looked over at her and said, "Something wrong? I can see it all over your face. Come sit by me and tell me what's on your mind."

Roneh sat on the couch beside her mother and told her about the falling out with Zeela and what the bus driver said to her. She read her mother the digi-mail to the OCC and their reply.

Roneh said, "I feel terrible about what I've done to her."

Roneh's mother stared at Roneh, beaming. "I'm so proud of you."

"But mother…I—"

"Yes, you feel bad for how you've impacted your friend's life, but let me ask you something," Roneh's mother said. "If you saw me or your father consorting with anti-government types, what would you do?"

"I'd talk to you about it."

"Yes, of course. As an intelligent young woman, you'd want to know why your father or myself had turned against the Global Assembly."

"You haven't, have you?"

Roneh's mother laughed. "Of course not, this is all hypothetical, but what if we did and we told you that as perverse as our reasons might be, we weren't going to change our minds?"

"I'd have to turn you in."

"Exactly. Why?"

"What do you mean, why? For the good of the globe."

"And how would you feel about it?"

"I'd feel horrible, but it's my duty as a citizen."

"That's my girl," Roneh's mother said, leaning toward Roneh and kissing her on the cheek. "Zeela is as guilty as her parents for being complacent and you've done the right thing. Stop eating yourself up about it."

Zeela didn't return to Allegiance Camp the next year. Roneh never saw Zeela again, but after her conversation with her mother, Roneh never wavered from doing her duty as a citizen.

Now, as Roneh sat in her government-issued apartment, she knew her parents would be proud of her, working at the Leader's side. They'd take it as an affirmation of the Leader's wisdom. She wished they could see her, spreading his word, but due to the Global Assembly's judiciousness, her parents were rejected in the Selection Process and sent to a relocation camp while Roneh was chosen to survive in the dome.

Roneh pressed send on her digi-mail to the OCC about the seditious HR person and closed her viewer, then decided to celebrate her day by drinking a few Malraps with her roommates.

# MAR

Mar gazed out the window from her seat in the commercial cruiser which had just landed at the cruiserport in Mafanikio, a non-domed Shamban city. Mar touched the window and pulled her hand back from the blistering heat. The landing crews were wearing air-cooled suits from head to toe, scrambling around the cruiser connecting tubes to its chassis to keep the inner workings cooled. Mar observed the sixty passengers waiting to disembark. The majority were uniformed military including the baby-faced private, maybe eighteen years old, seated next to her. He looked afraid.

Mar said, "First assignment?"

The Private didn't hear. His eyes were vacant and his mind was somewhere else.

"You all right?" Mar tapped him on the shoulder.

The private leapt in his seat and said, "I'm fine."

"Sorry," Mar said, "I didn't mean to frighten you. First assignment?"

"Yes. Is it that obvious? I just don't know what to expect."

"Take it from someone three times your age, don't fret about it because you'll never know until you get there." Mar thought that was good advice, even for herself.

The young soldier chuckled. "Thanks. Looks like we're disembarking."

    *Howard Libes*

The passengers rose from their seats, removing bags from the overhead compartments. Other than the military, there were businesspeople wearing jewelry—watches, rings, pendants—only the wealthiest Kodans could afford.

Mar grabbed her viewer case from under the seat in front of her. "Good luck."

"You as well," the private said, standing and joining the line of passengers leaving the cruiser.

"Thanks," Mar said, then said to herself, "I'll need it."

She decided to wait until the other passengers left the cruiser before tightening her grip on her viewer case and leaving her seat. She exited onto a walkway which was scalding hot even though she could hear the whir of an air-cooling system. She hurried through the walkway and into the cruiser terminal where the transparent ceiling looked stopgap, as if the terminal had been open to the elements at one time and this was the locals' makeshift solution to keeping out the intolerable weather.

Mar didn't fly often, but her surroundings made her feel like she'd stepped back in time. The flights weren't listed on viewing screens but rather posted on boards manned by a local young man with a box of letters and numbers, a small ladder, and a letter-changing pole which he used to update the flight status for each arriving and departing cruiser.

On the way to baggage pickup, instead of the customary gift shops and restaurants, there were vendors with metal carts, pitching local cuisine and totems constructed from junk metal and tech left behind by the military. Mar had seen these same objects in museums carved from the wood of trees. The brown-skinned Shambans manning the carts were beautiful yet thin to the point of being unhealthy. They wore their traditional garb of colorful robes.

The wealthy-class passengers rushed past the vendors, paying them no mind. They were clearly well-fed, wearing clothing—tailored suits, expensive dresses—which distinguished them from the locals, as did the pilots' and flight attendants' outfits.

The baggage counter wasn't automated like the one in Capitol City where a machine scanned your baggage ticket and the bag appeared at your feet. Here there was a Shamban baggage handler in cruiser-company uniform. He took Mar's tickets and hurried through a door behind him, then returned through a side door with Mar's personal bag and four crates piled on two trolleys.

The attendant pushed one trolley and Mar took the other. Back in Capitol City, her security personnel had taken the crates to check-in so she had no idea how much they weighed. They were heavier than she realized, and it took her a few moments to gain forward momentum toward the terminal exit. In the distance, she spotted a young woman who looked like Insol, wearing a business professional's grey skirt and white blouse, holding a sign reading *Mar Jeps—Prevor Relief Foundation*. This was Insol's sister. Mado hired her on Yor's recommendation as the liaison between the Foundation in Shamba and its headquarters in Capitol City.

Mado created the Foundation as a relief effort for outer-Kodans. The Foundation raised billions of units in donations planetwide to feed and house outer-Kodans who received little relief from the Global Assembly. The Foundation was also a cover for Project FoFu. Techs arrived in Shamba as volunteers for the Foundation, accompanying meds, nurses, and relief workers. They brought tech for the project inside crates containing real relief—food and water—and stayed to work on the project.

Insol's sister embraced Mar, surprising her. Mar wasn't expecting the hug or the sincerity with which it was given by this complete stranger. Mar returned the embrace.

"So good to finally meet you," Insol's sister said, releasing her hold on Mar. "I am—"

"You're Najubo, Insol's sister. My assistant Gols told me all about your work for the Foundation. He speaks highly of you."

"That's nice to hear," Najubo said. "I've only heard wonderful things about you, mostly from my sister."

"I'm fond of her," Mar said. "As is my son."

"Yes, yes, so I've heard," Najubo said.

They both laughed.

People were backing up behind them, attempting to get around Mar and the trolleys. "We should probably move," Mar said.

"I agree. We'll have plenty of time to talk. I have a vehicle waiting," Najubo said. "Let me take that from you." She got behind Mar's trolley and began pushing it through the baggage area. Mar tipped and excused the attendant who told her to leave the trolleys outside when she was finished with them and they'd be retrieved. Mar trailed behind Najubo with the other trolley.

Outside, the walkway was air-cooled. On one side was the outer wall of the terminal with vents pumping cool air. On the other was a translucent sheet with thin slits cut in it, draped between the curb and roadway, serving as a barrier to keep the cool air trapped in the walkway. Mar followed Najubo through the crowd who were waiting for their rides.

The military presence was large. When a sergeant barked out their names, low-ranking soldiers disappeared one by one through the translucent sheet and boarded a large military transport. Mar noted a few officers milling about for their staff cars and wealthy businesspeople passing through the barrier to their waiting limousines. Locals in cruiser-company uniforms served as valets.

Mar was falling behind Najubo who stopped and waited for her.

"Sorry," Najubo said. "They make us park at the far end. The military and the wealthy have priority."

"That's fine," Mar said. "I don't mind stretching my legs. I've been sitting for hours."

They continued moving in the same direction for a while until the crowd thinned and no vehicles were parked along the curb. The walkway ended and Najubo stopped. Mar pulled up beside her.

Najubo said, "Wait here with the baggage while I get the vehicle. The heat out there doesn't sit well with the uninitiated."

"I'm sure I'll be fine."

"Please stay. Trust me," Najubo said. "Plus somebody needs to watch the baggage—this is a poor city and unwatched items tend to go missing." Then she passed through the barrier. A few moments later, Mar observed an old four-seat vehicle pull up. She hadn't seen a vehicle like it since her youth and it appeared to be in impeccable condition. Najubo exited the front passenger seat, closed the door behind her, and peeked through the barrier.

Najubo said, "We can get settled in the back seat while the driver loads the baggage. I suggest you hurry—you'll understand once you step outside."

"Lead the way," Mar said, removing her viewer case from the trolley.

Mar wondered how outside could be any worse than the day of Yorlik's landing, but as she moved from the air-cooled walkway to the outdoors, the heat struck and her legs withered under her. Somebody caught her from behind. She gathered her wits the best she could as a tall, thin Shamban man in traditional garb helped her into their waiting vehicle and shut the door. Najubo was already inside and sitting next to her. Mar crumpled onto the seat, resting her head on Najubo's thigh staring up at her. In her light-headedness, as she recovered in the air-cooled vehicle's interior, she thought Najubo was Insol and mumbled something she couldn't quite remember after she said it. Najubo giggled, then handed Mar a bottle and said, "Drink."

Mar sat up and drank the sweet substance without asking Najubo what it was. She'd never tasted anything like it and not only did it quench her thirst, but energy returned to her body. "Whoa," Mar said, handing the bottle back to Najubo. "What's that?"

"That's Laylu," Najubo said. "Seems to have brought you back to life."

"Yes, sorry about that."

"Believe me, I've seen worse reactions from dome dwellers," Najubo said as the driver entered the vehicle and closed his door. "When was the last time you were outside the domes?"

"Eight years ago. Before the Capitol City dome was sealed," Mar said, feeling like she was regaining her bearings. "By the way, what did I say to you when I was semiconscious?"

Najubo giggled as the vehicle began moving forward. "You said, 'I love you, Insol. You're beautiful inside and out.'"

"I apologize."

"Why? I feel the same way about my sister."

"There's an uncanny resemblance, although you're not twins, are you?"

"No, but I've heard that before," Najubo said, pulling out a case in front of her legs.

"Where's my viewer case?" Mar said in a panic, looking around her.

"Right here," the driver said, holding up the case and handing it back to Mar. "You dropped it when you fainted."

"Thank you for rescuing it and me," Mar said, placing the case by her feet.

"My pleasure," the driver said.

"This is my brother, Nabo."

"Nice to meet you," Mar said. She noticed Najubo was still holding the bottle and reached out for it. "May I?"

"Just take a sip," Najubo said, handing Mar the bottle. "Too much will make you jittery."

"This drink is remarkable," Mar said, taking a mouthful and feeling another rush of restorative energy. "Is this easy to make? I'd love to analyze it for a Prevor Industries product and for the proj…Foundation."

Both Najubo and Nabo laughed as Mar handed the bottle back to Najubo.

"Nabo knows about the project," Najubo said. "I'll make sure to get you a sample before you leave. It comes from a local plant. Plans have already been made to grow it in the spaceships' hydroponics bays."

"Hydroponics bays? I have lots to learn about the project. I've seen the schematics, but I guess I need to study them some more."

"The ships are quite vast. My brother and I have spent many years involved in the project one way or the other. Nabo is an expert at building the interiors. He learned it from our father. Our mother is the supervisor at the site."

"I had no idea. Insol never speaks of it."

Both Najubo and Nabo laughed again.

"Well, it's a secret," Najubo said. "Nobody speaks about the project outside of it."

Mar laughed. "Yes, of course. I must still be affected by the heat."

"I wouldn't doubt it, and Insol doesn't know about the project. She left here before it began and there's the risk of her being interrogated because of her anti-government activity so we've kept her in the dark about it," Najubo said, opening her case and removing two colorful Shamban robes and handing one of them to Mar. "You can simply wear this over your dome-dweller clothing. You need to blend in once we get out of the cruiserport and into the poorer part of the city. Military checkpoints pop up all over the place and they'd be suspicious of a person who looks and dresses like you. I believe Gols has given you paperwork, but still best to blend in. When you leave the vehicle, I suggest you put the hood over your head and look down until I tell you it's safe."

"Got it," Mar said, placing the one-piece robe over her head and slipping her arms into it, then working the garment down the rest of her body. Najubo did the same. "Where to next?"

"A safe house. It's cooler there. We'll leave at night for the project site when the weather is better and the vehicle can make it there without overheating," Najubo said. "If you don't mind, I'm going to close my eyes. Long day ahead of us and the city is congested. It'll take some time to reach our destination. If you have any questions, feel free to ask Nabo."

Nabo raised his hand, smiled at Mar via the rearview mirror, then looked back at the road. His teeth were stained brown and he was missing a few. Najubo was already asleep with her head tucked in the upper corner of the sofa-like back seat and her legs stretched out. The vehicle reached the cruiserport exit in no time, but hit a traffic jam the instant they pulled onto the main eight-lane highway.

"So, no rail cars here?" Mar said to Nabo.

"No, no," Nabo said, keeping his eyes on the road.

"This is a poor city, a poor country. The Global Assembly only spends their units on the military here."

"Hasn't it been relatively peaceful here for decades?"

"President Plemso, or the Leader as you call him, thinks we're all terrorists and has a hard-on for us."

"Oh," Mar said and chuckled.

"Sorry," Nabo said. "Shambans don't beat around the bush when it comes to saying what we think."

"Yes, I've met your sister."

The vehicle moved a few meters forward, then halted in traffic again.

Nabo laughed. "Yes. I miss my big sister. How is she? She comms when it's safe but that isn't very often. Last time, she said everything was fine, but none of us believed her."

"No viewing-screen comms, I guess."

"No."

"She'll be up and walking again soon," Mar said, leaning forward and placing her hand on the top of the front seat. "The fire hasn't left her. It was only stoked by the accident."

"Accident? You're too diplomatic," Nabo said. "Those GSS bastards did this to her. There's no doubt."

"Probably right."

"No doubt," Nabo said, anger rising in his voice. "No doubt. Those bastards. It'll take more than a beating to silence my sister."

"That's for sure. She's remarkable," Mar said, deciding to change the subject. "How many children did your parents have?"

"Eleven."

"Eleven?" Mar said. "So much for the one-child-per-family mandate."

"Not around here."

"Where are they now?"

"All here except for Insol, working on the project in one way or another."

"Oh my," Mar said, suddenly worried. "Is the tech in the trunk all right? The heat might damage it."

"It's fine," Nabo said. "We've done this many times. The trunk is air-cooled and lined so it won't get too hot. This is my vehicle and I'm the only who's allowed to drive it. I repair it myself and keep it in tip-top shape. No need for concern."

"Good to know."

"If we take this road my sister likes, we'll never get where we're going. Lucky for you, I know this city like nobody else."

Nabo nosed the vehicle in front of a military transport in the right-hand lane, then did the same to a shiny limousine in the furthest right lane. The limo driver rolled down his window, yelling in Shamban at Nabo who waved and smiled at him. Then Nabo peered over his shoulder at Mar and said, "Hold on!" as he cut the wheel to the right and the vehicle veered down a dirt incline onto a service road. Mar grabbed the seat in front of her with both hands otherwise she would have been hurled forward.

Najubo mumbled, "Be careful, brother."

Nabo said, "When am I not, sister?"

Najubo said, "Haha," then curled up again in the corner of the seat.

The vehicle accelerated down the one-lane road until they were passing between brown single-story buildings with horizontal slits rather than windows in the walls.

"You should put on your seat belt," Nabo said as the vehicle bounced in and out of holes and Mar's head practically struck the ceiling. The condition of the road didn't slow Nabo down. He drove even faster and the vehicle skidded into a left-hand turn down a similar street. Mar didn't see any people.

"Where is everybody?" Mar said, securing her seat belt.

"Most of these buildings are empty. This used to be a city of five million people, now it's around three hundred thousand," Nabo said. "It's too hot during the day to be outside so everyone is asleep inside now. The city comes alive at night when the temperature is barely manageable."

In the distance, out her side window, Mar observed a small city skyline. "Is that where we're going?"

Nabo turned his head slightly and glanced out of the corner of his eye to note what Mar was observing. "Oh no, we're headed around it. We don't go there if we can help it. The GSS is stationed there."

"I haven't noticed any surveillance cams since we left the cruiserport."

"The GSS watches us, but no cams. The cams are for the domes. They don't see us as worth the investment. They're just waiting for us to die out."

"That's kind of bleak."

"The truth is bleak. Look around you."

"Is most of the city like this?"

"Yes. The downtown area around the GSS and Global Guard headquarters is the exception. It's funded by Global Assembly units." The vehicle turned sharply right down another one-lane road, still bouncing in and out of potholes.

Mar braced herself with her legs. "Don't they ever pave around here?"

Nabo laughed. "No units. No paved roads. The only paved roads are downtown and lead to the military bases. That's it."

"Lots of military bases in the area?"

"The Global Assembly likes to test their weapons in the fields and mountains outside of the city and sometimes on the people. Shamba is their proving ground."

"So who were all those wealthy men and women at the cruiserport?"

"Mostly military contractors," Nabo said. "The people in these houses service the people with Global Assembly units. They clean and maintain their homes. Make their meals. Drive their vehicles. That's how the regular people feed themselves. It's more surviving than living around here."

Then the vehicle skidded to a halt. Mar would have been hurled through the windshield if she wasn't belted in. Najubo shot up from her slumber.

A young boy, maybe seven years old, barely as tall as the vehicle's hood, crossed in front of them and waved to Nabo who waved back. The boy's clothing was tattered and he was barefoot and gaunt. Mar could see the malnourishment from this far away.

Najubo yelled, "Nabo! This is an important passenger. The only person you're impressing is yourself. Slow down and be careful."

Nabo rolled down his window and the hot air rushed in. Mar began sweating as the temperature inside the vehicle rose. Nabo called out to the boy, "I almost hit you."

The boy waved back, giggling, and hurried into a building.

"Nabo," Najubo murmured, nestling into her corner of the seat and closing her eyes. "Shut the window."

Nabo rolled the window up, the wheels spun out, and the vehicle shot forward. Nabo didn't seem to care about his sister's complaints. He was emboldened to drive faster as the vehicle wound through the city streets. Mar didn't engage Nabo in conversation anymore, not wanting to divert his attention from driving. She closed her eyes, feeling nauseous from the constant jarring of the holes in the road.

Then Nabo said, "We're here." The vehicle skidded to a halt and Mar was thrown forward, the restraint again saving her from injury.

"What're you thinking, Nabo?" Najubo said. "I'm going to tell Uncle Gnivri about your recklessness."

"Go ahead," Nabo said. "I'm not afraid of the old man. What'll he do? He can't drive us to the site and you don't drive, either."

"So disrespectful."

"We got here safely, and that's what matters," Mar said, attempting to lighten the mood. "Where are we, by the way?"

"Our destination. The safe house," Nabo said, turning off the engine.

The vehicle's interior immediately began to heat up.

"We should get inside," Najubo said. "Don't forget to put the hood over your head. You never know who's spying for the GSS."

"What about the crates?"

Nabo said, "I've got them."

"Follow me," Najubo said, placing her hood over her head and exiting the vehicle.

Mar was sweating profusely already. As she undid her seat belt, her midsection ached from the force of the last stop. She put the hood over her head and followed Najubo across the street, where they entered a building much like all the others they'd passed on the journey here. Nabo was behind her carrying two crates which he placed just inside the doorway and went back outside. Najubo removed the robe and Mar followed suit. In the walk across the street, she'd sweated through her regular clothes under the robe.

Mar stood in a room where the light was low, and it smelled of sweat and possibly a sweet substance burned to make the scent of the room tolerable. A man who emerged from a side room was missing his left leg and walking on crutches. His brown button-down shirt with stains under the armpits fit loosely on his tall, lean frame. He wore similar colored brown pants and combat boots. He appeared to be in his sixties, had a short grey beard and was bald. He was missing his left ear, and there was extensive scarring on that side of his face. Najubo introduced him as Uncle Gnivri.

"It's a pleasure to meet you," Mar said.

"The pleasure is all mine," Uncle Gnivri said. He had a much thicker Shamban sing-song accent than Insol, Najubo, or Nabo. "I once met the Great man. He spoke highly of you, your late partner, and your boy. He was very proud of your son. We are all proud of him for revealing the truth to all Kodans. I'm saddened by his demise and my heart goes out to you."

"I…that's very kind of you to say."

"I mean it sincerely."

"I appreciate your kind words."

The door opened behind them and Nabo entered, carrying the final two crates with Mar's baggage and viewer on top. He put down the crates and handed Mar her viewer case, saying, "You left this in the car," then closed the door behind him. Mar noted how pleasant the temperature was in the building, and she didn't hear the whirr of an air-cooling device.

Najubo approached her uncle and began talking to him in Shamban. In all the rush and most everyone speaking the language of the Capitol City region, she forgot Najubo, Nabo, and Uncle Gnivri were speaking a second language as a courtesy to her. At first, it sounded like Najubo was greeting her uncle, then her tone became angrier and she pointed her forefinger at Nabo who was removing his robe. He wore the exact same clothing and boots as his uncle underneath. When Najubo stopped speaking, Uncle Gnivri's face became stern. He advanced toward Nabo on his crutches until he was face-to-face with him and began yelling in Shamban. Nabo stood there absorbing the tirade.

Najubo said to Mar, "Let me show you to your room."

"What's happening?" Mar said, pointing to the confrontation.

"I told my uncle about Nabo's reckless driving and he's reprimanding him."

"That's not necessary," Mar said. "We arrived safely."

"You're lucky," Najubo said, waving for Mar to follow her. "Not all of his passengers have been as fortunate. A tech from your corporation was seriously injured although I heard he'll make a full recovery."

Mar had seen a worker's compensation claim come across her desk from a tech injured in a vehicular incident in Shamba. She signed off on it since Gols had already cleared it, but now she knew how it happened. The claim reported broken bones, a concussion, and internal injuries. From what she'd experienced of Nabo's driving, she wasn't surprised.

Mar grabbed her bag from beside the pile of Relief Foundation crates with her free hand, then followed Najubo down the low-lit hallway. It was cooler the further into the house they went, and she noted there was still no air-cooling system. Uncle Gnivri's yelling continued behind her.

Najubo turned into a room with two mattresses on the floor against opposite walls, blankets on top of them. There was no other furniture in the room.

Najubo said, "You can rest here before we leave for the mountains. The sun sets shortly. We'll eat before we go.

The drive will take us most of the night, so you may want to stay up now and sleep on the drive. I'll be back soon."

Mar put down her case and bag, then lay down on a mattress. She closed her eyes, felt herself falling asleep, and sat up again. She placed her hand against the wall and found it cold to the touch, as was the stone floor. Then she rose from the mattress and touched all the walls in the room, including an outer wall. They were all cool. Given the heat outside and the lack of an air-cooling system inside, things didn't add up. Mar was standing with both her hands and her face against a wall when Najubo entered the room.

Najubo said, "Is everything all right?"

"This must look odd," Mar said, removing herself from the wall.

"Yes." Najubo laughed.

"Why are these walls cool when it's scorching outside?"

"You don't know?" Najubo said. "It's a substance called Frezon, patented by Mado Prevor, mixed with the plaster. He gifted it to the Shamban people about eight years ago. We're the only region with the rights to use it and he charges one unit a year. He told me once he gave it to us because the DOME project was building the smallest dome here as punishment for the Separatist Revolts. Many have survived because of this gift. Mado Prevor is revered here."

"I've never heard of it. As CEO of Prevor Industries, I wish somebody had told me," Mar said, touching the outer wall again. "I suppose Mado has already figured out a way to use this in the project."

"Yes, Project FoFu uses it in the outer hulls of the ships."

"Project FoFu. I'll never get used to that."

"How so?"

"Oh, it's an inside joke between myself and the Great man. I'll tell you the story sometime."

"I'd like that," Najubo said. "Rest for now."

"I'm going to take your advice and save sleeping for the ride and get some work done."

"I suppose your job keeps you busy."

"My work is never done. Unfortunately, this isn't a vacation for me."

"We'll have food ready in a short time. Do you need a table and a chair for work?"

"No, thank you. I'll just stretch out here."

"One last thing—I want to apologize for being negligent before in not offering my condolences on the senseless death of your son. We're all heartbroken at his loss after his courageous speech," Najubo said, her voice shaky with emotion.

"Thank you." Mar sat down on the mattress, reaching out to grab her viewer's case.

"I'll leave you to work." Then Najubo exited the room.

Mar removed the viewer from the case and closed it, then set the viewer on top of it. She sat cross-legged on the mattress and activated the viewer, thinking about Najubo's display of sadness and her uncle's statement about her son. Mar was moved by them even though she was aware Yor was still alive.

Since Breeze Celebration, she hadn't spent much time

in public except for her interaction with the Leader and her visits to campus. Her employees at Prevor Industries had stated their sympathies regarding Yor's death, but it always felt more like a professional courtesy. They were programmed not to be too saddened by Yor's supposed death in their daily lives, because somebody might overhear and take what they said as a seditious act and report them.

Mar plunged herself into her work, making her way through digi-mails containing messages and memos from different Prevor Industries departments detailing problems and progress on specific projects. She'd discovered in her brief stint as CEO that Mado ran a productive corporation with employees who loved their jobs. Mado paid them better than most Kodans and gave them a share of profits on their projects. They took pride in their accomplishments and personal responsibility for failure. She was impressed daily. As CEO, she thought her best strategy was to keep a distance, and she only weighed in when she was asked to, or if it seemed in the corporation's best interest.

She found herself invigorated by the coolness of the room. Najubo brought her a warmed Relief Foundation protein dinner on a tray. Mar was famished and devoured the meal, which was better than she'd expected, then she continued working.

A little later, Uncle Gnivri entered the room and said, "The sun's setting and we'll be on our way shortly. We're packing up the vehicle now. I assume you have your papers."

"Yes, the papers," Mar said. She stood and reached into her case, removing her ID and a GSS travel-papers memory wafer.

"Your ID is worthless here. It's a dome-dweller document," Uncle Gnivri said. "The papers are the ID of the outer-Kodan. It'll save you where we're going. Can I take a look?"

Mar handed it to him, then he removed a GSS mini-tablet from his pocket and inserted the memory wafer. Mar had heard about these hand-sized devices and seen fotos of them. They were rarely used inside the domes and only GSS security officers and Global Guards were allowed to possess them by law.

The glow from the mini-tablet's screen lit Uncle Gnivri's face in the low light of the room, giving Mar a closer look at the brutal nature of the scarring on the side of his face.

"Where did you get a mini-tab?" Mar said.

"We have our ways," Uncle Gnivri said. "It all looks perfect, down to the security chip on the side of the wafer. Your people always do fine work and I'm sure this is backed up at the GSS mainframe."

"Gols told me to tell the person who examined the document that 'All necessary measures have been taken.'"

"You know your cover story?"

"My name is Mara Lensa and I'm a military contractor from Capitol City on my way to the Magri facility."

"You've got the basics down. That's all you'll need. I'm sure the birthdate and place of birth are the same as your own to avoid confusion," Uncle Gnivri said. "No need to wear the robe anymore. Normally, relief workers travel in vehicles like Nabo's and wear robes as a sign of respect to the locals and are ignored by the GSS. If you were stopped wearing dome-dweller clothes in Nabo's vehicle in the city, the GSS would've found it suspicious and taken you into custody regardless of the wafer. On the other hand, locals transport contractors to their work sites outside the city all the time in vehicles like Nabo's. It's part of the local economy so the GSS will be less suspicious if you're wearing your dome-dweller clothes when we leave the city. I understand the bureaucracy probably seems arbitrary to an outsider's perspective."

"No more arbitrary than the bureaucracy in the domes," Mar said. "I just remembered I was supposed to check in with my head of security when I arrived. He wanted to come with me, but your people advised against it."

"We have nothing against Colonel Suron. He and Commander Warver helped us a great deal to set up security for the project, but with all the military officers and contractors around the city, there's a good chance he'd be recognized, so he's too much of a security risk," Uncle Gnivri said, removing the wafer from the mini-tab and handing it back to Mar before putting the tab back in his pocket. "Suron has already reached out to our people. He was concerned when you hadn't checked in, but we told him you're fine."

"I'll hear about it when I get home," Mar said, placing the wafer in an outer compartment of her viewer case.

"Undoubtedly," Uncle Gnivri said. "And I'm sorry to hear about Commander Warver. He was a honorable man and an asset to the project. He'll be sorely missed."

"I appreciate it," Mar said. "I didn't get to know him that well, but he did make me feel safe."

"That was one of his skills," Uncle Gnivri said. "Gather your belongings. We'll be leaving shortly." Then he turned on his crutches and exited the room.

Before leaving Capitol City, Mar received a detailed memo from Suron about the dangers of traveling in Shamba and how to avoid them. Gols had said the Shambans understood the hazards of their region and she'd be fine without Prevor Industries security. Mar was glad when Suron couldn't come with her. She wanted to make this trip on her own. She needed to start asserting herself with confidence in her current role without being scared of the consequences.

For the night's journey, Mar changed out of her traveling clothes which were still damp with sweat into something less business formal, a pair of slacks and a comfortable top, then carried her bag and her viewer case into the room where they'd entered the house. Najubo was standing by the door. She was wearing her traditional robe and applying pressure to her right side with her hand.

Mar said, "Are you all right?"

"I am," Najubo said. "Are you ready to go?"

"Yes," Mar said. "Where's Nabo and your uncle?"

"Waiting for us in the vehicle," Najubo said, then opened the door. "After you. I'll put your bag in the trunk." She took Mar's bag with her left hand, still pressing her right side with the other.

Outside, the weather was hot but not scorching. Mar noticed Uncle Gnivri's crutches loaded in the trunk with the Relief Foundation crates as she walked behind the idling vehicle. Mar climbed into the passenger-side back seat and closed the door. Nabo was behind the wheel with his uncle beside him in the passenger seat.

Najubo settled herself in the back next to Mar. "Probably should strap yourself in."

Uncle Gnivri said, "My nephew will be less reckless, but best to be cautious. Isn't that right, Nabo?"

"Yes, Uncle," Nabo said, turning in his seat to face Mar. "I apologize for my driving before."

"Apology accepted. No harm. No foul."

Nabo laughed. His uncle punched him in the arm and Nabo yelped in pain.

"That doesn't justify your actions, Nabo," Uncle Gnivri said. "Najubo, you have something for me?"

Najubo reached under her robe and removed an antique gun which released thumb-sized projectiles at high velocity. As a child, Mar had seen this kind of gun in a museum. She had read Shambans used them back in the early days of the Separatist Revolts while Global Assembly forces were employing stun-and-kill weapons. That was until Shambans found arms dealers willing to sell them modern weapons. Najubo handed the gun to her uncle who placed it on the floor by his feet.

Mar said, "Is that necessary?"

"If your life is in danger, yes," Uncle Gnivri said. "Let's go, Nabo. If we leave now, we may avoid a few patrols along the way."

Nabo drove at a slower rate than earlier yet the holes in the road were still jarring. The streets were well lit. AID illuminated even the outer-Kodan cities.

Nabo stopped often for men, women, and children to cross the street, wearing robes and carrying cloth bags which Mar assumed were filled with groceries from the open-air marketplaces lit by strings of lights along their route. The vendors manned what appeared to be home-made carts constructed from scrap wood and pieces of old billboards. The carts were filled with produce of all varieties.

Mar said, "Where do they grow this stuff?"

Nabo said, "They turn rooms in their homes into greenhouses with grow lamps, dirt, and whatever water they can scrounge. A friend of mine has a cart in a market around here."

"Many do it," Uncle Gnivri said. "It's a way to make a living and there's so many of them, it drives down the prices a little. People get their protein from the relief packages, though."

Mar said, "I mean no disrespect, but all these people appear malnourished."

"That's been the state of Shambans for decades," Uncle Gnivri said.

Before she became CEO, Mar was aware that outer-Koda was in a health crisis of disastrous proportions because her coworkers—nurses, meds—traveled to outer-Kodan cities and encampments with Mado's relief effort. Malnutrition was only a small part of the problem here. The infant mortality rate was many times greater than inside the domes, and the death rate for those with even minor infirmities was off the charts due to lack of antibiotics. Outer-Kodans had a much shorter life-span than dome dwellers, too. These statistics weren't reported on viewing channels or digi-media, so the vast majority of dome residents were unaware of this calamity's magnitude. Also, dome dwellers had no legal way of communicating with any outer-Kodan family members, so many of them had no idea of these living conditions. Although Mar now ran the Foundation as part of her CEO duties, she felt guilty for her complicity in not helping her fellow Kodans earlier.

When they reached the outskirts of the city, the road changed into a well-paved two-lane highway and they were plunged into darkness except for the vehicle's headlights.

Mar said, "Nice road."

"Paid for by the Global Assembly so their weapons and personnel can reach the bases they've built for weapons testing," Uncle Gnivri said. "It's the smoothest part of our ride and the most patrolled. Might be advisable to get some sleep."

Najubo was already asleep with a pillow under her head.

"Probably a good idea," Mar said.

"By the way, if we're stopped and asked our relation-ship, I'm your guard. Najubo is your translator and Nabo is your driver, obviously," Uncle Gnivri said, not turn-ing around. "If we're stopped, it'll be between now and when the road gets rough again. After that, there won't be a problem."

At that moment, they raced past a stationary two-seat military vehicle with headlights on and two armed soldiers leaning against the chassis. Nabo and his uncle looked at one another and shrugged.

Nabo turned to Mar and said, "One down."

Mar laughed nervously. "How many more are there?"

"Depends," Uncle Gnivri said. "If they're doing any weapons testing up the road, then security will be tighter. On average, there are four or five patrols along the way."

Mar stared out the window at the landscape revealed by the headlights—bare trees, clumps of dead bushes—as the vehicle raced down the road. She found it hypnotic and began to feel drowsy. Somebody had put pillows in the back seat of the vehicle. Mar placed one under her head, stretched out her legs, and closed her eyes, falling asleep immediately.

She woke later to the sound of the vehicle's engine straining as they climbed what must have been a mountain pass with sheer walls on either side of the two-lane highway.

"How much further?" Mar said.

Without taking his eyes off the road, Nabo said, "A long way."

Mar closed her eyes again, the whine of the engine lulling her back to sleep.

She woke again to Najubo poking her and saying, "Wake up, Mar Jeps."

The vehicle was slowing and up ahead through the windshield, Mar saw the taillights of a military two-seater on the side of the road. One soldier stood in the middle of their lane and the other in the oncoming one so they couldn't pass. The soldiers raised their hands to signal the vehicle to halt, and as they slowed, the soldiers waved them over to the road's shoulder with blue flares. They were no longer in the mountains and the landscape outside looked similar to when they left the city.

Uncle Gnivri said, "Just act normal," as Nabo stopped their car behind the military vehicle.

Mar said to Najubo, "How often does this happen?"

"Not too often," Najubo said.

"Lucky me," Mar said.

One soldier approached the driver's door and the other moved toward the passenger-side front door. Nabo rolled down his window. Uncle Gnivri cocked the gun.

The soldier outside the driver's door was late thirties, early forties, well groomed and wearing sergeant's stripes. He carried himself with confidence as if he'd been in this situation before. The soldier at Uncle Gnivri's door was younger than Yor and appeared nervous.

The sergeant said, "Papers, please. Where are you coming from?" He shone a light into the vehicle, resting it on each face one by one.

"Mafanikio," Nabo said.

Najubo had taken out her memory wafer and was holding her hand out for Mar's. Nabo took Uncle Gnivri's wafer and extended his right hand toward the back seat for Najubo's and Mar's.

"That's a long way from here," the sergeant said.

Mar searched for the wafer in the outer compartment of her case but couldn't locate it. The longer it took, the more nervous she became.

"What's the holdup on the papers?"

Nabo reached further toward the back seat and wagged his hand. Najubo placed her wafer in it and Nabo handed the three wafers he possessed to the soldier.

"You're one short," the sergeant said, shining the light into the vehicle again and pausing it for a longer period of time on each of the passenger's faces.

When the light landed on Mar, she waved to the soldier and said, "Sorry, sir. I'm looking for it. I've been traveling all day and just woke up. It's here. I'll find it."

"You're a little pale to be from around here," the sergeant said, still shining the light on Mar as he waved over the younger soldier. "What brings you to the ass end of Koda? Where you from?"

Najubo's body stiffened at the soldier insulting her region. Mar continued digging through her case. She began wondering if she'd put the wafer in the pocket of the pants she'd removed which were in her clothing bag in the trunk.

Mar said, "Capitol City."

The sergeant handed the wafers to the younger man, then said something to him. At the same time, Mar saw Uncle Gnivri raising the gun up from the seat, then the younger soldier walked off toward the military vehicle and Uncle Gnivri lowered the weapon.

Mar panicked and went back to searching for the wafer. Her heart was racing.

"So, what brings you here?" the sergeant said, leaning in through the driver's window and scanning the interior with the light. Nabo shielded his eyes.

"I'm a military consultant on my way to the Magri facility," Mar said, fear gripping her.

"Are you helping to perform the energy field test?" the sergeant said. Mar was now the center of his attention and he shone the light beam on her only.

Mar continued searching for the wafer. She removed her viewer and checked that compartment, too.

As CEO of Prevor Industries, she was aware that the energy field was proprietary tech owned by her company and the military was constantly haranguing them to utilize it. She'd even had a conversation about it with the Supreme Commander of Global Forces a few days ago. He had attempted to persuade her that the security of the planet hinged on the military obtaining the tech, and allegedly Mado Prevor had decided to allow the military to use it before he disappeared. She placed him on hold and asked Gols about the commander's statement. Gols said, "Absolutely not," and told her that Mado had denied the military and the Leader's personal requests a number of times already. Mar did the same. *Could they have stolen the tech or is this a bluff by the sergeant to catch me in a lie?* Mar thought.

Mar peeked up at the sergeant, who was still holding the light on her. She observed his pressed uniform, buttoned up to the collar, his short haircut, and his face probably shaven before he took his post. He wore a handful of ribbons proudly on his chest. Mar recognized one of them as a commendation for being a veteran of the Separatist Revolts. She recalled his earlier remark about Shamba.

"Not my area of expertise," Mar said, shading her eyes from the light and peering directly at the sergeant. "And your rank wouldn't afford you the privilege of confidential information regarding a weapons test, so why are you asking?"

"I don't think—" the sergeant said.

"You don't think what?" Mar said. "That I couldn't take down your name and rank and have the GSS investigate your unsanctioned snooping into the Global Assembly's affairs? Let me find my digi-tablet and get that information from you. Hold on."

"No need for that," the sergeant said, turning his light off.

"No. Hold on," Mar said, knowing she was in control now.

The younger soldier returned to the vehicle and said something to the sergeant, who handed the wafers back to Nabo. "You're cleared to go," the sergeant said. "Have a safe trip."

Nabo started the vehicle and headed back onto the road.

Mar opened her window and called out to the soldiers who were behind them now, "For the good of the globe."

"For the good of the globe," the sergeant said.

"For the good of the globe," the younger soldier repeated.

Nabo accelerated, moving past the military vehicle and rolling up his window. Mar looked back as the military vehicle's headlights faded into the darkness and then shut her window.

Najubo said to Mar, "That was impressive."

"I guess I have a few tricks up my sleeve."

Najubo, Nabo, and Uncle Gnivri laughed. Nabo handed the wafers to his uncle. Mar dug further into the outer compartment of her case. She was sure that's where she'd put her wafer.

"I have to agree with my niece. Impressive. The fear in that soldier's eyes was enjoyable."

"Unfortunately, I've had unpleasant encounters with the GSS before," Mar said. "Anyway, thanks, it's always gratifying to rise to the occasion." She did feel thrilled with the run-in. She hadn't felt this way since she'd been a med. This was an emergency-room rush.

Uncle Gnivri said, "Good to know we can count on our leader in a tight spot."

"I'd prefer not to be referred to that way."

"If that's your wish," Uncle Gnivri said.

Mar decided to take Uncle Gnivri's statement as a compliment, though. Najubo smiled at her and patted her knee, then curled up in her corner of the seat. In a short time, her breathing changed and she was asleep.

Mar finally found the wafer wedged in the bottom corner of the outer compartment. She was annoyed at herself. She didn't know how she missed it. With that off her mind, she relaxed in her seat, closed her eyes, and easily fell back to sleep.

Mar was jarred from her slumber as the vehicle hit a bump in the road. The headlights illuminated an unpaved dirt road lined with boulders on either side of them. Najubo smiled at her. Mar's ears were clogged, presumably from the altitude. She felt well rested like she'd been asleep for a long time.

"What's happening?" Mar said.

"Almost there," Najubo said. "We just left the pavement. We'll get out soon, then a short walk."

"Short walk?" Uncle Gnivri said. "If you're not on crutches."

Nabo's window was open halfway. The air blowing into the speeding vehicle was cooler than when they left the city, although still warm. It was refreshing nonetheless and  occasionally carried a strong, sweet scent. Mar had never experienced anything like it.

Mar asked Najubo, "What is that wonderful smell?"

Najubo sniffed at the air. "You mean the ubani? This is the last place in Shamba where it grows. There are still some natural springs at this height. You'll see."

As they traveled further down the road, the bumps got worse and Nabo slowed until they were creeping along. Eventually, they stopped and Nabo turned off the headlights and the engine. They sat in silence except for the ticking of the cooling engine.

Mar began to ask what was happening, but Najubo put her forefinger to Mar's lips. Uncle Gnivri rolled his window down and stuck out his hand, holding a light that was turned off. Then he flashed the light ahead of them in a sequence, turning it on and off six times, waiting a few beats, and doing it again.

The sound of footsteps could be heard coming their way. Uncle Gnivri cocked his weapon. Up ahead, a light flashed eleven times, then six. Nabo turned on the headlights, then Nabo and Uncle Gnivri exited the vehicle.

"Come," Najubo said, patting Mar on the knee before following Nabo and Uncle Gnivri outside.

Mar joined the rest of her party in front of the vehicle. Two men approached, wearing combat boots and the same uniform as Nabo and Uncle Gnivri with stun weapons slung over their shoulders.

"Good to see you," one of the men said. He was a broad-chested, powerful-looking man, standing a head taller than all of them. "You're late."

Uncle Gnivri said, "We ran into a patrol about a hundred and fifty kilometers from the city, but our guest put them in their place."

"Glad you made it. Mother was concerned," the other man said. He looked like Nabo. "You're carrying precious cargo." He put his hand out toward Mar.

"Where are my manners?" Uncle Gnivri said. "Mar Jeps, this is my nephew Islo, and this is Kubwa, an old platoonmate of mine."

"Not so old and Kubwa's not my real name," Kubwa said. "It's a nickname Gnivri gave me. I owe him my life many times over. I was a young, wet-behind-the-ears soldier when we met. He taught me everything I know."

"Not everything," Uncle Gnivri said. "Most everything." They both laughed.

"These two are incorrigible," Najubo said. "We should get a move on."

"You're right as always, sister," Islo said and hugged her.

Uncle Gnivri said, "Yes, your mother will be worried sick and I'll be blamed. Let's get on our way."

Kubwa said to Uncle Gnivri, "Would you like me to carry you? We'd move faster."

"That day will come soon enough, but not today," Uncle Gnivri said and patted Kubwa's arm.

Nabo opened the trunk and removed Uncle Gnivri's crutches, then climbed behind the wheel and started the vehicle. They all moved to the side of the road and he drove past them. Kubwa and Islo jogged behind the vehicle. Najubo hooked her arm around Mar's and said, "This way." Uncle Gnivri trailed behind them on his crutches, lighting their path.

When they reached the vehicle, it was parked perpendicular to the road between two boulders, and all the crates plus Mar's bag and viewer case had been unloaded. Kubwa and Islo were draping a brown tarp the same color as the two boulders over the vehicle. Nabo held a light in each hand to illuminate their work while they staked the tarp around the vehicle. When the brown stakes were deep in the ground, Kubwa and Islo kicked dirt over them.

Mar said, "Camouflage. Smart."

"We have a few tricks up our sleeves, too," Nabo said, juggling the lights.

Kubwa said, "Stop fooling around, Nabo."

Uncle Gnivri walked up behind Nabo and smacked him in the back of the head. Nabo stopped juggling and shone the lights on the work again.

When they finished securing the tarp, Kubwa and Islo walked in opposite directions around the entire vehicle, tugging at the tarp to ensure it was firmly in place.

Kubwa said, "All set."

Mar grabbed her bag and her viewer case.

"We can take those for you," Islo said.

"That's kind of you," Mar said, "but I prefer to carry my own weight."

"I like this one," Kubwa said.

"She's impressive," Uncle Gnivri said. "Shall we go?"

Nabo handed one of his lights to Najubo.

Islo and Nabo lifted one crate each and Kubwa took two and they began marching up the road. Mar walked beside Najubo. She hadn't experienced anything like this mountain air in decades. The dome atmosphere picked up a metallic scent as it passed through the air circulators. Before the domes, the air was polluted and it became harder to breathe without coughing as the years passed. This air was fresh. There was no other way to describe it. She inhaled it deeply. It was invigorating.

As they climbed higher, the road narrowed into a steep trail of gravel and larger rocks. From hiking in her past, Mar assumed this was an old riverbed. The trail kept getting steeper and Najubo stopped Mar every once in a while to wait for her uncle to catch up. A momentary smile brightened the older man's face as he reached his niece, then he would say, "Go on, go on. Don't wait for me." Uncle Gnivri appreciated the sentiment, regardless of what he said. Mar imagined this was a game they played on this trail when Najubo was a young girl and they climbed up here together. Due to this ritual, though, they lost sight of the three men up ahead.

In a while, the trail flattened out and a sheer rock wall loomed in front of them. They waited for Uncle Gnivri to catch up, then turned to the right with the wall on their left. Mar peered upward, but she couldn't estimate the height of the wall before it met the sky.

"Stay as close to the wall as possible," Najubo said. "There's only room for one person at a time."

About ten or twenty meters later, the trail had become a ledge and to her right was a precipitous drop. Mar's heart raced. Unlike the penthouse terrace, there was no railing, so she kept her eyes looking down at her feet.

Now, each time Najubo stopped for her uncle, she tapped Mar on the shoulder and Mar leaned against the wall, still holding her bag and case, staring straight ahead. During one of the pauses, Najubo said, "Are you all right? Would you like to rest?"

"No," Mar said. "The sooner we get there, the better." Mar was glad she'd slept in the vehicle.

"We're close," Najubo said. "Very close. The men will be waiting for us at the mouth of the tunnel."

They continued walking until Mar heard voices up ahead and approached the men standing inside a cave entrance.

Kubwa said, "Where's Gnivri?"

"He's right behind us," Najubo said. "Let's get the lights on."

"Come on in," Nabo said to Mar. "You look a little peaked. Are you all right?"

"I wasn't crazy about walking on that ledge."

"We're all done with that," Nabo said, turning on his light, taking her by the arm, and leading her into the cave where the crates were lined up. "Wait here."

Mar put down her bag and case. Nabo walked a short distance further into the tunnel, then pointed his light at a small box mounted on the cave wall, opened it, and flipped a switch inside. Mar's eyes were stung by the sudden light. She closed them and held her hand over them.

"Sorry," Nabo said. "I should've warned you."

When Mar's eyes adjusted, she looked around. The crates were lined up on a conveyor belt that snaked down a tunnel. Lights were strung up along the cave walls like the lights on the vendors' carts in the market.

Uncle Gnivri made his way toward her on his crutches. "Welcome to Project FoFu."

"Glad we made it," Mar said. "Where's the power for these lights coming from?"

"Those miraculous boxes from your corporation power this entire facility."

"Right. That was a silly question."

"It's wondrous," Uncle Gnivri said. "After you."

Nabo threw a switch at the base of the conveyor belt and the crates began moving down the tunnel along the conveyor belt. Mar placed her bag on the belt but kept hold of her case, then hooked her arm around Najubo's and said, "Shall we?"

Najubo smiled and said, "I can't wait for you to see everything. We passed a hidden surveillance cam a few kilometers back. My mother will be waiting."

"I noticed none of you have comms. Suron had me leave mine at home."

"The military is always searching for comm signals to track," Najubo said as they strolled arm-in-arm down the tunnel, which curved left, then right. They walked further than Mar had anticipated. She figured they'd gone about one or two kilometers. The crates and her bag had disappeared out of sight on the conveyor belt and it had stopped running at one point.

To break the silence, Mar said, "This is something."

"This is nothing," Najubo said.

Finally, in the distance, Mar saw a woman standing between two men armed with the latest Prevor Industries stun weapons.

Najubo hollered, "Mama!" and ran down the length of the tunnel into the woman's arms. The two men slung their weapons over their shoulders. Najubo kissed one of the men on the lips. The conveyor belt ended where the men and the woman stood. Mar's bag was still there, but the crates were gone.

The woman wore a brown dress that hugged her svelte figure. She was an older version of Najubo and Insol. She possessed a powerful presence and Mar figured she was about her age.

When Mar was within a few meters, the two men clicked their heels together, stood at attention, and placed their right fists over their hearts. They wore the same brown uniform as the men traveling with her, but their clothes were recently cleaned and pressed. They appeared unrelated to Nabo or Najubo.

Mar understood that the act of placing one's fist over one's heart was a Shamban salute of respect and gratitude. "I appreciate the sentiment," Mar said, putting down her case.

The woman stepped forward and embraced Mar, who hugged her back. At this point, Mar assumed this was the customary greeting here, then the woman kissed Mar on the cheek and stepped back.

"I'm sorry. I feel like I already know you. I'm Rika, and this is Melo and Hefi," she said, " I have to say, it's marvelous to finally meet you. Insol speaks so highly of you and since I'm so far away, I'm happy you're in Capitol City for her. She loves you very much."

"I feel the same about her. She's a phenomenal young woman. She's family," Mar said, feeling emotional.

"And our deepest condolences for your son. He was a brave and honorable man. His courage is unsurpassed on Koda," Rika said and embraced Mar again.

The two men said together in a solemn tone, "Yes, yes."

Rika stepped back and Mar wiped tears from her eyes, then Rika pointed down the tunnel past Mar and said in a stern tone, "What took you so long? You had me worried, you old *mtunga shida.*"

Uncle Gnivri walked up behind Mar. "Good to see you, too, sister. We had a run-in with a patrol. I'll tell you about it later, but right now I need to relieve myself. It's been a long trip. Excuse me, Mar Jeps. I'll see you later." Mar stepped aside and Uncle Gnivri hurried past on his crutches. At the end of the tunnel, he turned left and was gone.

"I hope my brother treated you well," Rika said. "He can be a little rough around the edges."

"He was a gracious host."

Rika chuckled. "That's kind of you, but I know my brother."

"Mama…Mama…Rika," Najubo, Islo, and Kubwa said as they came up behind Mar.

Rika said, "Then there's these three."

Kubwa said to Rika, "The outer door is locked."

"Thank you, Kubwa."

Then Rika said to Mar, "It's been a long journey. You must be hungry? Tired?"

"How about a tour of the facility?"

Everyone laughed.

Mar said, "Why is that funny?"

"I'm sorry," Rika said. "We laughed because a tour will take an entire day or two. You'll understand soon. How about a short stroll and we can start on a tour tomorrow?"

"Sounds great," Mar said, picking up her viewer case and her bag.

"No need to bring those," Rika said, pointing at the bag and case. "I can have them taken to the room we've prepared for you."

"That's fine for the bag," Mar said, "but I'd like to keep this case with me."

"As you wish," Rika said. "Hefi, please take the bag."

Hefi took Mar's bag from her and walked down the tunnel, then turned to the left and was gone.

Rika said, "I sent a patrol earlier to smooth out the vehicle's tire tracks and your footprints. They won't be back until morning so the rest of you shut down the tunnel. You four know the drill. Turn off the lights and make sure the inner door is bolted, too. Najubo, you have your shift. You come with me."

Najubo said, "Can't I—"

"No," Rika said. "You'll see Melo later."

Rika took hold of Mar's empty hand. They headed down the tunnel about ten meters, where it ended and intersected a tunnel running perpendicular to it, and turned in the opposite direction from Hefi and Uncle Gnivri. The passageway Rika led Mar down was lit by blocks of overhead lights mounted in the ceiling.

Mar said, "What does 'mtunga shida' mean?"

"Oh, that," Rika said and chuckled. "It means trouble-maker. I love my brother. I was just ribbing him."

"I appreciate all of you speaking my language for me."

"That's mostly what we speak around here. Makes it easier for the visiting techs and we're aware most Kodans speak it. Everyone assumes that's what we'll be speaking on the ships."

As they continued down the tunnel, it widened and became busier. There were Shambans wearing brown uni-forms and Project FoFu ID tags interspersed with Kodans from other regions wearing dome-dweller garb and ID tags. As people passed, they said hello to Rika and their eyes widened when they recognized Mar. Some placed their fists over their hearts. Rika smiled and nodded at them but was silent.

Rika said, "The tunnels get jammed this time of day—it's break time for the third shift."

Up ahead, Mar heard the buzz of many people chat-ting, then she and Rika stopped at the entrance of a large room to their right carved out of the tunnel where maybe two hundred people were sitting at long tables eating and talking. The smell of cooking food emanated from the room. People were lined up with trays behind others being served food at a long counter. The occupants of the room were a mixture of Shambans and dome dwellers.

"This is incredible," Mar said, standing beside Rika.

Rika looked over at Najubo and they chuckled. "Yes, they're hungry. They work hard," Rika said. "Are you sure you don't want a bite?"

"No, I'm fine," Mar said. "So this is the cafeteria for the project?"

"One of them," Rika said.

"How many are there?"

People at the tables began to notice Mar, Rika, and Najubo and pointed at them, then spoke excitedly among themselves. This activity soon spread throughout the cafeteria.

Najubo said, "We have three."

"We're thinking about installing a fourth, depending on future funding," Rika said. "Something we'll talk about later."

The people at the tables began to stand up one by one and face Mar, Rika, and Najubo. Those in line and at the counter turned and faced them, too. Kitchen workers emerged, then one by one they all placed their fists over their hearts.

Mar said to Rika, "They have a lot of respect for you."

Rika released Mar's hand, then turned toward Mar and put her fist over her heart. Najubo did the same.

Rika said, "No, my dear. This is for Yor." Then she called out, "For Yor."

The hundreds of people standing in the cafeteria shouted in unison, "For Yor…For Yor…For Yor…" Rika and Najubo joined them. "For Yor…For Yor…"

Mar couldn't help herself as emotion washed over her and she began to cry. It didn't matter that Yor was still alive. This salute was for what he had achieved. She was as proud as the day of Breeze Celebration with her son standing on the stage in front of the crowded Arena, in front of the entire planet, calling out the Global Assembly on their lies.

"Thank you," Mar said to the crowd, wiping away the tears. "Thank you."

They continued chanting, "For Yor…For Yor…"

"Thank you," Mar said louder. "Please sit and enjoy your food."

The chanting gradually diminished and the people in the cafeteria began to sit down and return to their meals. A Shamban woman about Yor's age ran out from the cafeteria and hugged Mar, then released the embrace and stood in front of Mar with tears in her eyes. She placed her fist over her heart and said, "For Yor. He was a brave man. We'll never forget." Mar hugged her back.

"Thank you," Mar said and released the embrace.

"Thank you," the woman said and returned to the cafeteria.

Mar said to Rika, "Well, that was something." She wiped the tears from her eyes again.

"You deserve it," Rika said, taking Mar's hand.

"I deserve it?"

"You're his mother. You raised him. You made him what he is."

"You obviously don't know my son," Mar said. "I mean, you didn't know my son."

Rika squeezed her hand. "In our culture, we believe the mother molds their child into the person they become."

Najubo said, "Mother, would you mind if I got something to eat?"

"Go on," Rika said. "Then do your shift before seeking out Melo."

Najubo hurried into the cafeteria line.

"It's just you and me," Rika said. "Let me show you something beautiful."

They continued down the tunnel, passing what looked like a large break room with groups of people watching viewing screens or playing board games. People continued saluting Mar as they passed.

"How do they know I'm here?" Mar said.

"This is a big place but a small community," Rika said. "Word gets around fast."

They veered left toward a lift descending with two people on it. The lift's shaft was cut into the cave wall and open to the tunnel hallway for about twenty meters before it disappeared into the ceiling. When the lift touched down and the two people stepped out, they saluted Mar who smiled and thanked them.

Mar entered the lift with Rika who let go of her hand and pressed a button with an upward-pointing arrow. As the lift's gate was closing, a man dressed in what Mar identified as Capitol City attire dashed toward them and shouted, "Hold the lift." Rika stuck out her foot and blocked the waist-high gate from closing.

"Thanks," the man said. "I'm late for a meeting."

Mar stepped aside to make room for him, and Rika pressed the button again.

"I'm sorry," Mar said to the man, "but for some reason, you look familiar."

As the gate closed and the lift began to move upward, the man gazed at Mar and a smile formed on his face.

"My apologies—I'm in such a rush that I didn't recognize you," the man said, "I actually work for you. I mean, technically we all work for you here, but I live in Capitol City and work at the Complex. We've been in a few meetings together since you took over. I'm Tosh Reem."

Mar examined Tosh Reem's face. He was in his mid-fifties, with a full head of grey hair but a youthful demeanor.

"Yes, that's right," Mar said. "I had a meeting with you and a few others about the cryotech units."

"Yes, and you had some fantastic insights."

"Thank you," Mar said, gazing up. The lift didn't have a ceiling and they were now traveling through a tube of stone. "How long have you been here?"

"About eleven days, I think. I lose track of time here. I'm usually told when it's time to leave."

The lift stopped and the gate opened onto another tunnel with workers scurrying one way or the other, some of whom wore brown coveralls.

"I have to run," Tosh Reem said. "We're actually working on the attenuator as you suggested. I'd like to pick your brain further about it if you have time while you're here."

"I'd love that, but I'm not sure how I'll find you."

"Oh, did you just get here?" Tosh Reem said, looking over at Rika and stepping out of the lift.

"We'll make that happen," Rika said.

"Great. I look forward to it. Gotta go." Tosh Reem waved goodbye and ran down the tunnel to the right.

Mar said, "Small world."

"Certainly is," Rika said. "You ready?"

"I'm in awe of this place."

"You've seen nothing yet," Rika said. "People always remember their first view of the project. Come along." She didn't take Mar's hand this time, but exited the lift and turned to the left, performing a few skips then waving for Mar to follow, like a child eager to show a parent what she'd done. "Come along."

"I'm right behind you," Mar said.

Rika hurried ahead down the tunnel. Mar took long strides, practically running to catch up, but she lost sight of Rika as the tunnel curved to the left. Mar was a little winded. She assumed it was the altitude. She noticed the air was bracing, at least twenty degrees cooler here than in the tunnel downstairs.

Mar caught up to Rika, who was standing in place and pointing ahead of her. Mar looked where Rika was directing her, and the sight was breathtaking. The cavern before her was maybe twice or three times the size of Capitol City's Arena and stretched into the distance. Water trickled down the rock walls to a lake below.

The natural beauty was astounding, but the contents of the cavern were magnificent as well. In sight, there were six spaceships, maybe forty stories at their tallest point and 250 meters across. Three looked finished on the outside and the other three were at different stages of construction from skeletal to half-finished. Workers were stationed all over the ships accompanied by the sounds of hammering and the whirring of compressed air tools. Sparks from blowtorches floated down toward the lake and dissipated. The ships were mounted on stanchions protruding from the rock walls and out of the lake below. Lights mounted in the cavern walls gleamed off the smooth silver hulls of the finished ships. There were more ships lined up further down the cave.

Mar had never seen anything like these spaceships. While the WAEF was a spin-off of the flying machines and cruisers that pre-dated it, these ships embodied a completely new design. The closest approximation to their appearance was a drop of water falling from a spout, but on its side.

Mado Prevor had outdone himself once again. Mar stared in disbelief.

"Well?" Rika said. "Well? You haven't said anything, what do you think?"

"I'm speechless," Mar said. "It's out of this world."

***

AFTER THE CRYOTECH MEETING ADJOURNED, MAR was approached by Tosh Reem.

"Thanks for meeting with us," Tosh Reem said. "Your input was invaluable."

"I thought approaching the problem from a completely different angle might be useful," Mar said, tucking her digi-tablet under her arm.

"Hopefully we can make more headway before I go home."

"There are good people here working on the problem, and we can always pass along ideas from home by courier." Mar noticed Rika in the hallway outside the meeting room. "It's been a pleasure, but I've got another engagement and I don't want to be late."

"Yes, I know," Tosh Reem said. "I wouldn't miss it."

"Oh—see you there, then," Mar said, exiting the meeting room.

Rika smiled as Mar neared and said, "How did it go?"

"This is a nice surprise. I wasn't expecting to see you here," Mar said. "I believe we're closer to getting the cryo-units up and running."

"Too bad you have to leave tomorrow. We're going to miss you. I'm certain you could help on so many other things."

They headed down the hallway side by side. "I've been here ten days and people will be missing me back in Capitol City," Mar said. "And I think the project is doing fine in your competent hands."

"Kind of you to say."

"I mean it."

"There's a lot to deal with here and the clock is always ticking."

"I could always send more people to help."

"I discussed the prospect with Mado," Rika said. "He was concerned about blowing our cover with too much traffic."

"We'll see how things work out in the days ahead."

"Sounds like trouble."

"It's politics. I find surgery easier," Mar said as she stopped in front of a lift shaft and pressed the button to summon the car.

"Do you need to freshen up before your final presentation?"

"About that," Mar said. "I thought this was an overall evaluation for the admins of each division, but I've heard other people saying they're looking forward to it."

"Yes, that's what I came here to tell you. I heard the rumor a few days ago that people were excited to hear what you had to say, then Islo told me today that the entire facility will be showing up. As I said, word spreads fast around here."

"The entire facility. What does that mean?"

"Everyone who's not on guard duty."

"I see," Mar said as the lift stopped at their floor.

The gate opened, revealing a young woman standing inside. She was in her thirties, with long, straight hair down to her shoulders, wearing a brown uniform with her shirt buttoned up to the collar. She recognized Mar and placed her fist over her heart. After ten days here, Mar was used to it.

"Thank you," Mar said to the young woman who was frozen in place, staring.

Rika said, "Are you going down, young lady?"

"Uh…yes…" she stammered, shifting her feet. "I'll be at the speech. I have an errand to run first, though." Then she sidled past Mar and Rika and dashed down the hallway which Mar noted was now empty of people.

Rika said, "Shall we?" She held her arm out for Mar to enter the lift first.

When the lift headed downward, Rika said, "We can cancel. It's easily done." She smiled at Mar.

*Rika is a good judge of character*, Mar thought. *She already knows what I'm going to say.* "I don't want to disappoint."

"I had a hunch," Rika said and giggled. "I thought I'd give you the choice, though."

"I wish I'd known about this change sooner. I'm kind of unprepared."

"I'm sure they'll enjoy whatever you say."

The lift emerged from the rock tube and Mar immediately heard the buzz in the passageway below which was packed with people.

Mar said, "Is this for me?"

"There's no other reason," Rika said. "I'll escort you to the tunnel that leads to the lectern."

They made their way through the crowd and when they reached the entrance to the tunnel, Rika said, "This is where I leave you."

Mar said, "You're not coming with me? Won't the crowd be expecting you to present me?"

"You need no introduction," Rika said. "I'll be in the front row with my children. They're excited to hear what you have to say."

"Me, too," Mar said, chuckling nervously, still clutching her digi-tablet.

Rika placed both her hands on Mar's shoulders. "Embrace the moment. These people want your leadership. It's needed around here after the death of your son, and there's a rumor circulating that Mado's dead as well, and it's making people worry about the future. They need someone to inspire them." Rika let go of Mar's shoulders.

"I've never been the most inspirational speaker. I'm better at lectures about bowel resections."

Rika laughed. "I'm sure you'll rise to the occasion."

"I guess I'll just make things up as I go along."

"Isn't that life, though?" Rika said. "I have confidence in you. Mado had confidence in you, and from what you've told me, the Great man had confidence in you. What other endorsements do you need?"

"You're right. I'll be fine."

"I know you will," Rika said and smiled. "See you soon." Then she walked away.

As Mar moved down the tunnel by herself, she thought about how dramatically her life had changed since Breeze Celebration and how this trip made her path ahead crystal clear. Even though she had been scared and reluctant to admit it, her job had become the survival of the Kodan people. She was left this task by Tetrick, Yor, Mado, and the Great man himself and now was the time when she needed to fully embrace her role. There was no running from it.

Mar emerged from the tunnel on to the shore of the cavern's lake. The spaceships in their various states of construction were looming in the distance and the chilled air made her clutch at herself. The water which seemed to be dripping down the walls from a distance sounded more like waterfalls from this vantage point.

A female voice said, "There she is," and a smattering of clapping built into a wall of cheering and applause. The people in the crowd were seated in what appeared to be an amphitheater carved out of the slope leading to the shore. There were at least a few thousand people jammed into forty or fifty horizontal rows. People stood at the top of the amphitheater, straining to get a glimpse of her. It was all rather humbling.

She waved to the crowd and stepped onto a platform with a lectern where a wireless mic was waiting. She picked up the mic and put her digi-tablet on the lectern. Her first impulse was to turn on the mic and launch into a speech, but the one she'd written for the admins was not the pep talk this crowd was expecting from her.

As Mar waited for the crowd to simmer down, she saw Rika descending an aisle cut perpendicular to the rows. In the front row, Melo, Najubo, Nabo, Islo, and Uncle Gnivri were sitting next to one another. When Rika reached them, Melo stood along with Rika's children to make room for her to pass so she could sit beside her brother.

Mar turned around to observe the spectacle of the cavern and collect her thoughts. In the ten days she'd been here, this sight had never gotten old. The sheer vastness of the cavern and the project itself were awesome to behold. In fact, when she'd learned her way around the facility and had time between meetings, she came to the place where she first saw the spaceships and gazed out at them. Not only was it a magnificent sight, but it brought home the magnitude of the mission before her.

The crowd began chanting, "Mar Jeps," clapping twice, then pronouncing her name again. She waited until it sounded like the entire crowd was involved and then turned back to them. They burst out into applause and cheering. Mar turned on the mic and said into it, "Hello, Project FoFu." Her voice booming out from speakers around the amphitheater sounded unfamiliar. The crowd somehow got louder. All of a sudden, she thought of Tetrick and his years of touring the planet attempting to inspire the crowds who thronged to his speeches.

Mar held the mic in her right hand and raised her open left palm toward the crowd, who seemed to settle a little, and said, "Please, I should be applauding you." The crowd began chanting her name and clapping again. "Thank you," Mar said. "I should be calling out each and every one of your names. You are the true heroes here."

The crowd broke out into thunderous applause and cheering again. Mar held up her mic arm, too, and waited a few beats to let the crowd get it out of their system. She thought about all of these people carrying the future of their species on their shoulders, and she thought of Yor, and then the theme of her address dawned on her.

Mar dropped her arms and said into the mic, "Now, now…" attempting to get them to calm down. "We don't have much time together here so let's make the most of it, shall we?" The crowd laughed. "Mutual admiration has its place, and right now we all understand the urgency of the monumental task before us. And you've all made a wonderful start of it."

She partially turned in the direction of the construction and said, "The reality of what we're facing is unimaginable. That we must abandon our planet, our home, where our species crawled out of the primordial ooze, basked in the riches of Koda, and thrived."

Mar turned back toward the crowd. "Somewhere in the course of our history we began taking our planet, our home, for granted, and as I look out at all of you, seeing all your faces, from all the different regions of Koda who have been divided politically, who have been manipulated by our leadership to despise one another, we have to remind ourselves that we're all in this together." The crowd broke into applause.

"Spending time here with you, I see a future where we place those divisions behind us, work past the prospect of our extinction, and arrive on a new planet where we thrive again as one people under an open sky without the domes and air circulators to keep us alive.

"Attaining this future will be difficult, but I am confident seeing what's happening here in this place at this time that the future will be brighter than it has ever been in recent Kodan history. But we must not waver in the task ahead of us. We must persevere for the Kodan people, not for Shamba, not for Msitua, not for the Capitol region, not for Nor, not for Mlimoa or Maua. We must persevere united as Kodans. If we're going to salvage the Kodan species, we must replace hatred and anger with love and mutual respect.

"During my visit here, as I've marveled at the cavern behind me, I've seen a wonderful new beginning toward that future. I guarantee the tech know-how and the resources for that future, and I pledge myself to making the foreseeable future a reality. Will *you*?"

Rika bolted up from her seat and yelled out, "We will." Then the rest of the crowd immediately took up her cry.

Mar turned off her mic, stepped down from the platform, stood in front of it, and shouted, "Will you?"

"We will," the crowd yelled back in unison and surged to their feet.

"Will you?" Mar screamed, feeling her vocal cords straining.

"We will," the crowd called, louder this time, creating an echo in the cavern which made the crowd cheer.

"Koda thanks you. I thank you," Mar said, moving closer to the seats. "Now I take my leave of you. My thoughts and prayers will be with you and our noble endeavor. Powers-That-Be bless us. And I will see you again soon."

The crowd applauded and cheered, and somebody yelled out, "Kuvutia," then a few others repeated the word until the entire crowd was chanting, "Kuvutia…Kuvutia…." The din continued as Mar waved to the crowd and headed toward the tunnel, where she waved to them one more time before leaving the shore. She walked slowly up the tunnel wondering whether her words had been what these people needed, whether they were inspired by them.

Rika was waiting for her with Uncle Gnivri at the end of the tunnel. They were both smiling.

Mar said, "How did I do?"

Rika said, "You met everyone's expectations and more."

"Good to hear," Mar said, feeling relieved. "What were they chanting at the end?"

Uncle Gnivri said, "Kuvutia means 'Impressive One.'"

"I wonder where they got that from?" Mar said as she hugged him.

He returned her embrace and said into her ear, "I started it, but when people met you, it easily caught on around here as your nickname."

Mar said, "Thanks, mtunga shida."

"You're very welcome."

When they stepped out of the embrace, the main passageway was completely empty. "Where is everybody?" Mar asked.

"Where else?" Rika said and smiled. "Working to make the foreseeable future a reality."

# LEK

Lek was sitting in the waiting area outside the Leader's office. He looked over at the receptionist who smiled at him and shrugged. The Leader was running late.

The receptionist said. "Sorry, I checked again, and he told me again he wants to see you and you shouldn't leave."

"Not a problem," Lek said.

The receptionist resumed working at her viewer.

When Director Thuta told Lek the Leader had requested him, Thuta was excited, predicting a promotion might be in the works. Lek didn't share Thuta's delusion. He was actually stupefied by the Leader's summons. He thought it would take longer for the GSS techs to notice that the high-security server had been hacked and that Lek had downloaded sensitive data. He also assumed if he was caught he would be jailed, not ordered to the Leader's office. Lek decided he'd enter the interaction with the Leader as if nothing unusual was happening, assuming that the Leader had called him in to discuss his progress on Rajer's interrogation. He'd take it from there and, just in case, he'd brought a memory wafer with the hacked materials to beg leniency for his family.

Lek observed the waiting room. After graduating with high honors from the GSS Academy and being awarded his GSS job, he had been brought here with another grad for a public-relations viewing-channel spot, to be filmed shaking the hand of then-President Vidor Plemso. Lek's Academy class was the first in a GSS recruitment drive to staff the massive increase in surveillance around the planet.

Now, he was experiencing the oldest tactic in the book: keep the subject waiting, because if they're guilty of something, then all their doubts and fears will creep closer to the surface and can more easily be exposed. Lek learned this move in his first year at the GSS Academy and was astonished that an interrogator of the Leader's legendary stature and founder of the Global Guards would try to use this ruse on him. From Lek's extensive file and Academy records, the Leader should've known Lek wouldn't fall for such an obvious trick.

The receptionist's intercom buzzed. By this point, Lek had heard it buzz so many times he had no expectation it was for him.

"He'll see you now," the receptionist said.

Lek felt a rush of nerves, then paused for a moment, reminding himself to stick to his plan.

When the door slid open and he entered the Leader's office, he took it all in. The room didn't look much different from his visit twenty years ago except for the image of the completed dome hanging on the wall. The Leader sat behind the desk, observing his viewer with Davik Atmar who looked up and nodded to Lek. "Be with you in a moment. Please have a seat in that chair."

Lek sat down in the wooden chair in front of the Leader's desk. It was highly uncomfortable. Lek had learned about this chair when he studied the history of torture at the Academy. It was a Global Monarchy relic built from the wood of the Clack tree, which hadn't existed for over a century. The chair was designed to tighten its grip on the person seated in it. Each time Lek adjusted himself in the seat, the chair bound Lek's torso tighter. He'd been asked to sit here for a reason, instead of the couch where he sat on his last visit. The Leader was telling him this was a different kind of encounter.

The Leader closed his viewer, beckoned Davik Atmar closer with his forefinger, and said something into his ear, then Davik Atmar hurried out a side exit, the Leader watching him go. The Leader adjusted the placement of a digi-foto on his desk and finally looked up at Lek as if he had no idea a person was sitting right in front of him.

Lek decided to cut through the act and said, "Your office hasn't changed much since the last time I was invited here."

"I've never invited you here," the Leader said in a tone of complete conviction.

"I'm sorry, sir, but I was here twenty years ago as a recent Academy grad."

"Yes, I remember you, of course, but I didn't invite you, did I?"

"Technically, it was part of a public-relations campaign for the Academy."

"See! So I'm correct."

"Yes, sir," Lek said. He cautioned himself not to argue.

"Do you know why I asked you here today?" the Leader said, walking around his desk to stand directly in front of Lek.

"I assume this has to do with Rajer Jeps."

"You always were a sharp one." the Leader said, pointing down at Lek and stepping so close his knees almost touched Lek's. "I've been reading your file. Did you know the Academy had reservations about recruiting you? But this Jerrick character said, and I quote, 'Valsted is brilliant and his recruitment can only make the GSS a better, more insightful organization.' You proved him right. High commendations throughout your career."

"I've always given the GSS my best, sir."

"Yes. Yes. Your best, I'm sure, but what does that really mean?" the Leader said, not moving from his position. "I find your handling of the Jeps affair—or the Jeps–Vanderlord affair, as I like to call it—highly questionable."

Everyone knew how the Leader felt about the Vanderlords. This increased Lek's nervousness and the Leader was trained to note such things and take advantage of it.

"I'm sorry, sir. I don't understand. Can you be more specific?"

"One wonders whether there's a hidden agenda here."

Lek didn't know how to reply. The Leader was staring at him with a look on his face as if he was flabbergasted Lek wasn't confessing already. Lek recognized the tactic. It was employed to make a person feel concerned that he'd already been caught.

"The only agenda I have is the good of the globe, sir."

"Interesting to hear you say that," the Leader said. He walked back to his desk, sat down, and opened his viewer. "I see here it took you the entire time this Jerrick character gave you to accept your position, and he threw in a loan for your parents to seal the deal. Makes it sound like your agenda was more than the good of the globe. What do you have to say about that?"

"That was twenty years ago. I was a young man attempting to figure out my future and I didn't ask for the loan. Tas Jerrick offered it as compensation for signing the contract."

"Did you think that was normal?"

"I assumed so."

"Jerrick was known to stretch the rules to get his signing bonus," the Leader said. "At least, that's what I've been told, and in those days, they let him get away with it because the GSS required qualified recruits."

"I had no idea, sir. Again, that was a long time ago. With all due respect, if you look at my record over the years, you'll see I've been productive and loyal," Lek said. "I'm unsure how my interaction with Tas Jerrick is relevant."

"You don't? I see a history of selfishness and reckless affiliations. Subterfuge usually follows, and that behavior continues to this day," the Leader said, closing his viewer and coming around his desk again. "You were seen attending a memorial service for a known member of the Movement at the Royal University. This was reported by an agent and a citizen." The Leader leaned back against his desk as if he was confident he had cornered Lek.

*Citizen? Had to be Harmin*, Lek thought.

"My presence was authorized by Director Thuta otherwise going there would have violated my Loyalty Oath," Lek said. "I was acquainted with Professor Wint as a young man, but I denounced my association with him when I became a full-fledged GSS agent."

"Director Thuta clearing you is another matter. You still felt the need to appear at this memorial service which was attended by a good number of Wint's associates in the Movement. You still felt a need to pay your respects to an enemy of the Global Assembly."

"I'm not sure what to say, sir."

"What? No smart retort?" the Leader said, then he pointed at Lek. "Isn't there an association between the deceased terrorist and Rajer Jeps?"

"Yes, sir."

"Tell me about it."

*He already knows*, Lek thought. *He just wants to hear how I candy-coat it.*

"We all attended the University together," Lek said. "Ador went on to become a professor and Rajer took a position at Budgetary Standards. Ador introduced Rajer to Mar Vanderlord. The last time I saw Ador was at Mar and Rajer's partnering ceremony. Again, I made sure I received permission from my superiors to attend the ceremony because I was aware Ador would be there."

"How did you feel when you heard of Ador Wint's death?"

"Untimely. Unfortunate."

"That's it. So clinical. So dispassionate. Yet you still felt the compulsion to attend his memorial," the Leader said. "Shall we cut through the pretense? Obviously, you did something else while you were there, and if I have to pull it out of you, then this interview can be done in an interrogation room, and you understand the pain that will entail. So simply tell me what you were doing there and stop wasting my valuable time."

Lek was certain now that his next words would determine his future. It was more than obvious the Leader had him in a compromising position, just not the one he surmised earlier. "I was there to tell Mar Jeps about Rajer Jeps' situation."

"See. That wasn't hard at all, was it?" the Leader said, positioning himself in front of Lek again. "Was it?"

"No, sir."

"So here we have a violation of protocol. How do you think we should proceed?"

"Procedure would require me to be stripped of my job and executed for violation of my Loyalty Oath."

"See you are a smart one. You don't disappoint," the Leader said. "I actually directed my Chief of Affairs to summon a few Global Guards to arrest you at the end of this interview. They're probably standing in my reception area as we speak." The Leader moved closer, bumping knees with Lek and placing his right hand on Lek's left shoulder, then stood there in silence, staring at Lek in condemnation and moving his head back and forth.

Lek hung his head. He was ashamed of himself, and meeting with Mar had nothing to do with it. He was deeply regretful that he had waited so long to act on his morals when there'd been so many times over the years when he'd done his job coldheartedly without considering the impact of his actions on the alleged enemies of the Global Assembly. Being an analyst, it was easy to keep a distance from any personal damage done to an individual or their lives, but that was no excuse. He deserved to be punished one way or another and he felt relieved that the time had finally come. "I'm ready to be arrested," Lek said, feeling himself welling with emotion.

The Leader stepped back and said, "I'm glad you see the error of your ways, but I have plans for you. If you perform them properly, then it might make me consider letting you keep your life and your job."

"I don't know what to say, sir." Lek didn't believe him, but he'd play along and see what kind of deal he could secure for his family. "I'll do what's necessary."

"Perfect," the Leader said. "I assume you've received no usable intel from Rajer Jeps?"

"Correct, sir," Lek said. "His stepson was concerned about incriminating him and told him nothing."

"And I assume he refused to obtain the information I want from his partner about Mado Prevor's location?"

"I received your memo. I told Rajer that your promised pardon would be finalized if Mado Prevor was located. I asked him more than a few times to speak with Mar Jeps about it," Lek said, "You're correct. He refused. As with his actions on Breeze Celebration, Rajer is more than happy to play the martyr."

"Honorable and suicidal on his part, but so be it," the Leader said and took another step back, leaning on his desk. "But we can make that work for us."

"How so, sir?"

"I want you to visit Mar Jeps at Prevor Industries and tell her if she doesn't present Mado Prevor in the next thirteen days, then I will execute Rajer Jeps in front of the entire planet. You will be executed as well, and I will take control of Prevor Industries with hostile force and arrest her," the Leader said. "If she comes through, I will commute Rajer Jeps' sentence to prison for life. You'll be cleared of charges and returned to your job and family, and I'll leave Prevor Industries untouched, of course."

"So I—"

"Global Guards will escort you to a cruiser that will take you to Prevor Industries," the Leader said. "After you speak with Mar Jeps, you'll relay her reply and be escorted to a holding cell at the GSS to await your sentence. Do I make myself clear?"

"Yes, sir."

The Leader pressed a button on the intercom. "Tell the Global Guards that Lek Valsted will be joining them in a moment."

**BEFORE THE MILITARY CRUISER TOUCHED DOWN** at the Prevor Industries Complex, the landing pad was surrounded by a contingent of well-armed security guards wearing helmets and stun-proof armor. Lek had never seen anything like their military-grade weapons, which were newer tech than the Global Assembly's. There had been rumors inside the GSS that Mado Prevor was working on a innovative weapon said to be more effective at stunning for longer periods of time and, if necessary, killing more efficiently. Lek could tell by their movements that the security guards were ex-Global Assembly forces, too.

When the cruiser's wheels hit the ground, all the guards drew their weapons simultaneously, then one man entered the circle with his weapon slung over his shoulder, strolling toward the cruiser with complete composure. The Global Guards sitting on either side of Lek were fascinated by the person moving toward them. The Global Guard on Lek's right leaned across Lek and said to the other, "That's Kush Suron. I told you he worked here."

"No shit," the other Global Guard said. "I think you're right. He looks pretty alive for a dead man."

Colonel Kush Suron was a famous figure in Koda's military history. His strategy in the Separatist Revolts was renowned and studied at the military academies. He had been trained by Commander Wel Warver and the Leader. Both Suron and Warver were reviled by many inside the military hierarchy because of their highly publicized court-martial resulting from their actions during the Shamban Massacre, although many considered them heroes for taking a stance against the inhumane orders of their superiors. Obviously, the Global Guard who called Suron a "dead man" held the former position, but that's why he was a Global Guard. "Orders are orders, no matter the cost," was their credo.

As the cruiser powered down, Kush Suron reached the pilot's window and knocked on it. Lek heard him shout over the engines, "Release the prisoner into my custody with one of your men in tow or feel free to leave."

The pilot turned around to the Global Guards and said, "How do you want to proceed?"

"That's fine," said the Global Guard to Lek's right.

"We're supposed to stay with the prisoner at all times," the other Guard said.

"I think one of us can handle this," the Global Guard to Lek's right said, glaring at Lek.

"Yeah, you're right," the other Guard said.

Both Global Guards were maybe twenty years younger than Lek. A few hours ago, he was their superior. He doubted they had any idea why they were transporting him, other than he was an enemy of the Global Assembly. He was in their custody and therefore a figure of derision. Lek didn't take it personally. He understood his predicament.

The Global Guard to Lek's right slid open the door beside him and said, "Let's go," yanking Lek out of the doorway by his shackles. The pain was excruciating.

Colonel Suron stood beside the doorway. "Do you think this kind of manhandling is necessary?"

"My orders are not to let the prisoner out of my sight, Colonel," the Global Guard said.

"First of all," Colonel Suron said, "no need to address me as colonel. I'm a civilian. Sir is fine. Second, I don't think you need to literally keep ahold of him. You have my word the prisoner will remain in your custody."

The Global Guard glanced at his companion in the cruiser, who scooted over to the open door and said, "It's on you."

"He's in shackles, what's he gonna do?" the Guard said, releasing the shackles from his grasp, then putting his face up to Lek's. "No funny business."

"Now that's out of the way," Suron said, "can we proceed?"

Lek noted Suron was a tall man, exuding strength and confidence. He could see why soldiers followed him so readily and successfully into battle. Lek imagined some of the men encircling the cruiser were soldiers who were once under Suron's military command and had followed him here with Warver.

The Global Guard grabbed the back of Lek's shirt and steered him toward the building. One of the security guards in the circle stepped aside to let Suron, Lek, and the Guard by. Lek peered over his shoulder after they passed and the security guard had resumed his former position so the cruiser remained encircled by the armed men.

"Eyes forward," the Global Guard said and shoved Lek.

Lek had never visited the Prevor Industries Complex, which was considered the center of tech innovation on Koda. They were now outside the Complex's renowned administrative building. Its architecture was considered unique and recognizable to every Kodan. Under different circumstances, he would've been excited to be here.

Lek spotted an upscale red cruiser parked in the landing zone area and slowed to get a look at it. The Global Guard shoved him again, surprising Lek who stumbled and almost lost his footing, then regained his balance.

"Is that really necessary?" Suron said to the Global Guard.

"Mind your own business."

Suron shook his head and snorted in disgust. "Have it your way."

They entered the admin building and took a lift up to the twenty-fourth floor where the doors opened on a reception area. The walls displayed promotional ads for Prevor Industries products spanning more than nineteen years since the first HGD was released. Lek recalled buying the device with units from one of his first GSS paychecks.

The person behind the desk hurriedly approached as they entered the reception area. "Mar Jeps is on her way," he said nervously.

The Global Guard said, "We're here on an urgent mission from the Leader."

The nervous receptionist said, "Yes, we received the Leader's comm. Mar Jeps is coming from another part of the Complex."

"You don't need to explain yourself to him, Gols," Suron said.

The lift opened behind them and Mar stepped out of it. "Looks like I'm late."

"You're actually right on time," Gols said.

"It's good to see you," Mar said, approaching Lek to embrace him.

The Global Guard put out his hand to stop Mar from getting near Lek, saying, "No touching the prisoner."

But before the Guard could touch Mar, Suron reached out and grabbed him by the throat. The Global Guard made a choking sound and fell to his knees.

Still clutching the man's throat, Suron said, "You will not touch the CEO of Prevor Industries."

The Global Guard gasped for air, then made a louder choking sound. Suron had tightened his grip.

"Do you understand?" Suron said. "Nod if you understand."

The Global Guard nodded and Suron let go. The Guard gasped for air like a man who almost drowned.

Lek couldn't help but feel amused at the cocky Global Guard being so easily restrained by a man more than twice his age.

"Was that entirely necessary?" Mar said.

"Nobody will touch you without your permission or cause you bodily harm," Suron said. "Those are our orders from Mado Prevor himself."

"I like that man more every day," Mar said and chuckled.

The Global Guard stood up and stepped toward Suron so they were face to face. "The Leader will hear about this outrage."

"Yes," Mar said. "Please tell him my head of security restrained you with one hand after you attempted to touch me. That'll go over well with him. Now, we have business to attend to."

"Yes," Lek said. "The Leader will want a speedy response."

"Exactly," Mar said to the Global Guard. "You don't want to keep the Leader waiting, do you?"

Mar put her arm around Lek's shoulders, then they headed toward a door which Lek assumed led to her office. Both Suron and the Global Guard were behind them. As they crossed the threshold into the office, Suron said to the Global Guard, "You can't go in there."

The Guard grabbed Lek's shackles and said, "The prisoner is not to leave my sight."

Suron said, "Why is the prisoner here?"

"To meet with the CEO of Prevor Industries."

"He can go in there to meet with the CEO, but you can't. If that's a problem, then you'll have to return to the Leader and tell him you stopped the prisoner from completing his mission."

Mar said, "This meeting is above your pay grade, soldier, and there's no way in or out of this office besides this doorway. See for yourself." She waved the Global Guard into the office.

He stepped past Mar and Lek, walked around the perimeter of the office, then exited. "All right, but no funny business. I'll have to report this to the Leader, too."

"Please do," Mar said, taking a few steps further into the office, then pointed to the nervous receptionist. "This is Gols. He'll keep you company."

The Global Guard turned around and Gols smiled at him. During the interaction between Suron and the Guard, Gols had retreated behind the reception desk.

"Shall we?" Mar said to Suron who stepped into the office, and she shut the office door with the three of them inside.

"Why are you a prisoner in shackles, Lek?" Mar said, sounding exasperated. "Gols just told me you were on the way with an important message from the Leader."

"That's true," Lek said.

"But a little lacking in specifics."

"That's true as well," Lek said. "Why don't we sit down and chat?"

Mar sat behind her desk, moving a viewing screen to the side so she could talk directly to Lek who seated himself across from her. Suron stood behind Lek, making him feel uncomfortable. Lek turned around and said to Suron, "Please feel free to sit down."

"Don't worry about him," Mar said. "He's just doing his job. Now, what's going on?"

Lek told her about the Leader's ultimatum. He observed her as he spoke. She listened intently. She'd become good at not showing her emotions.

"That's disconcerting," Mar said. "I assume Linara doesn't know about this yet."

*It's so like Mar to worry about me when I just told her about Rajer's predicament*, Lek thought. "No, she doesn't, but I appreciate you asking," Lek said. "Do you know where Mado Prevor might be?"

Mar's eyes shifted from Lek to Suron who took a step forward and now stood beside Lek, looking down on him.

Suron said, "We'd rather not say."

"I understand you're not telling me because I'm GSS, but seems like we're in the same boat here."

"That may be true, Lek," Mar said, "but this is so much bigger than the both of us. There is so much more going on here that—"

Suron said, "Mar Jeps, I think you've said enough."

Then Suron opened the office door and called out, "Gols, can you come in here?"

Gols entered the room and Suron said to the Global Guard, "He'll be back out to babysit you in a moment." Then Suron shut the door.

Gols said, "What can I do for you, Mar Jeps?"

"I'm not sure," Mar said. "Suron?"

Suron told Gols about the Leader's message, then took up his position behind Lek again.

"That's unfortunate," Gols said, standing beside Mar's desk. "Sooner than expected."

Mar said in surprise, "Was this expected?"

"Yes," Gols said, starting to sound nervous again. "Mado Prevor likes to have all possibilities covered. I don't believe Rajer Jeps' difficulties or Lek Valsted's were figured into the equation, but the Leader being frustrated with Mado's absence and issuing an ultimatum for Mado to appear was foreseen. The thirteen-day deadline makes dealing with it tougher, but we'll work through it."

Suron said, "You've probably said enough."

"Enough?" Mar said. "What is he talking about? Work through what?"

Lek said, "I have no idea what's happening here. Are you going to comply with the Leader's demand? What about Rajer's situation? What about mine?"

There was a knock on the door. Suron said, "Gols, you want to take care of that?"

Gols said, "I will, and I'll alert Mado Prevor."

Suron opened the door for Gols then told the Global Guard they'd be out in a few moments and closed the door again.

"What are we going to do about this?" Mar said to Suron.

"We should discuss it in private," Suron said.

"What about Lek?" Mar said. "There's the private lift." She pointed toward the back of the office.

"Too dangerous," Suron said. "We don't want to stir up Vidor any more than we need to. The random number of days to the deadline is his way of saying he's in control now. Sorry, Lek Valsted, but you'll have to leave with the Global Guards. Probably shouldn't keep that one waiting much longer."

Mar said to Lek, "I'm sorry you got mixed up in this." She stood and came around the desk. Lek stood and Mar embraced him, holding him tight.

"That's what I get for being a good friend," Lek said and chuckled nervously. He noticed Mar wasn't amused.

"We'll see what we can do for you. Won't we, Suron?" Mar said and released her hold on Lek, kissing him on the cheek.

"Yes, of course," Suron said.

Lek said, "What should I tell the Leader?"

"Tell him I'll be in touch soon," Mar said. "If you see Rajer, tell him I love him." She patted Lek's arm and squeezed it.

"Oh, I almost forgot," Lek said. "Reach into my left-hand pants pocket. There's a memory wafer there."

Mar said, "Suron, be my guest."

Suron removed the wafer from Lek's pocket and handed it to Mar.

"What's this?" Mar said, turning the wafer in her hand.

"A little gift to use against the Leader. It'll protect the Movement from the Leader's purge. There's a document on there with an explanation of what the wafer contains."

"I don't know what to say," Mar said.

"Neither do I," Lek said.

Mar stepped forward and kissed his cheek again. "Don't worry. I'll do what I can for your family."

"I appreciate that. Good-bye and good luck."

"Thanks, I think we all need it."

Suron opened the door and Lek headed toward the lift with the Global Guard close behind. As the lift doors closed, Lek peered through the reception area into the office where Mar was staring at him. Their gazes met. She tried to smile for him, but it was awkward and sad. She didn't hide her emotions now and that brought home to him the bleak reality of his situation. He was doomed and everyone around him knew it.

As the lift descended, the Global Guard said, "Are we having fun yet?"

# MAR

Mar watched from her office doorway as the lift door closed with Lek and the Global Guard inside. Lek appeared lost. It saddened her that she couldn't do anything for him right now, then she sat down at her desk with an audible sigh. "Never a dull moment around here. I've only been back from Shamba for three days. Now this?"

"Don't worry. You'll get through this fine," Suron said.

"I'm not concerned for myself," Mar said. "You're probably used to dealing with casualties in your past, but in this case, we're looking at the death of a good friend and, of course, Rajer, and we've already lost a few along the way. Is there any chance of Mado getting back here in time?"

"In the military, I never liked losing men. I always saw my job as attaining the best results with minimum casualties and that's my job here, too," Suron said. "As for Mado, I don't see him returning anytime soon. If he'd gone to Shamba, we wouldn't be having this conversation. He'd just come back and deal with Vidor."

From the doorway, Gols said, "Suron is correct."

"You said Mado predicted this problem," Mar said. "Why am I not surprised? Did he make a vid to explain this, too?"

Gols stared down at the ground, shifting his feet back and forth. "Would you like me to get the vid for you?"

"Sure, let's see what's planned for me now."

Gols left the office and returned with a memory wafer in hand. "Shall I set it up for you?"

Mar held her hand out toward the viewing screen behind the desk. "Be my guest. Would you like to stay for the show, Suron?"

"One moment," Suron said, then walked to the back of the office, putting his hand up to his ear to activate his audio implant. "Are they gone?…Yes…Great work out there everybody…Head back to your regular posts…I have a meeting but I'll check in soon…Copy that."

Mar turned her desk chair around to face the screen as Gols inserted the memory wafer. When Suron returned from his conversation, the vid start-up screen displayed Mado sitting behind his office desk.

"All ready?" Mar said, glancing at Gols and Suron. "Let's get this over with."

Mado said, "Hello, Mar. If you're watching this, then I never arrived in Shamba after Breeze Celebration and for one reason or another I can't return to the Complex, either. My hope is you're watching this vid a considerable amount of time after Breeze Celebration. Maybe years later.

"I made this vid because I surmised the Leader might become impatient with my absence and lash out. He's a difficult person to keep in check and I've only become good at it after years of practice, so no one's blaming you for your current state of affairs.

"You're probably watching this in a state of emergency. In short, the plan ahead involves evacuating the Complex and bringing the contracted techs to Shamba for Project FoFu. Gols has a list. Each of these techs signed an employment agreement with full knowledge of this plan. Gols has digi-mails on a separate wafer to communicate with the remaining employees about their severance packages and confirm the accounts to send their final pay. Gols will coordinate this plan. He has been briefed extensively on the matter and understands the necessary logistics to move personnel and equipment to the caverns where the spaceships are being constructed. He can answer any questions you might have, so I won't go on here. Wel Warver will bring part of his security detail. When you and Rajer are settled in Shamba, Gols will provide you with a vid detailing how to proceed from there. I wish you the best."

The vid ended and returned to the start-up screen. Gols removed the wafer and joined Suron on the other side of the desk. They waited for Mar to speak, but she could only think of Rajer. If she ran away, his death was certain. On the other hand, she had the fate of Kodan civilization riding on her.

Mar turned her chair back toward her desk. "So you both knew about this?"

"Yes," said Gols and Suron in unison.

"I know Mado is the master of covering all options, but I assume he didn't know Warver would be murdered and from this vid, it doesn't sound like Mado thought Rajer would be on the verge of execution."

Gols looked up at the taller Suron who peered down at Gols.

"Don't all speak at once," Mar said.

Suron said, "You're correct."

"So I'm expected to leave and let Rajer die, Gols?"

Gols looked up at Suron.

Suron said, "Don't look at me. Answer her."

Gols said, "Well, the plan…"

"Yes," Mar said.

"…the plan didn't include Rajer being arrested. You're correct. It's a simple evacuation that's been slightly complicated by the Active Glass pane in the dome being non-operative now. That pane was designed for the evacuation, not Breeze Celebration. As a backup, Mado had tunnels dug from the Complex to outside of the dome. The logistics and timing will be problematic—"

"I don't care about that, Gols," Mar said, raising her voice. "Answer my question."

Suron said, "The question whether you're expected to leave and let your partner die is rather loaded, even for Gols to answer. First of all, he didn't arrange the plan."

"I understand that," Mar said.

"And of course, nobody wants your partner to die," Suron said.

"Then this plan is irrelevant because it no longer fits the parameters of our current state of affairs, so we need a new plan," Mar said.

Gols said, "Mado Prevor gave explicit instructions—"

"I don't see Mado here," Mar said, glaring at Gols, "and according to the contracts I signed, as the current CEO, I'm in charge of Prevor Industries and responsible for its continuing existence."

Suron and Gols looked at each other, and Gols shrugged.

Mar said, "You thought I wouldn't read those contracts after I signed them? I trusted Mado enough to sign them, but I wanted to know exactly what they said. And the one line that sticks out in regard to this conversation is 'The undersigned maintains all rights, privileges, and power over any and all corporate decisions in relation to Prevor Industries in all its aspects and subsidiaries.'"

Gols and Suron looked dumbfounded.

"Don't look so surprised," Mar said. "My son got his fotographic memory from somewhere, didn't he?"

Suron said, "Nobody is denying your intelligence, but this is a strategic plan. I agree with evacuating Prevor Industries before the Leader acts. Vidor didn't break down the Complex's gates after Breeze Celebration because of Mado's threat and his assumption that Mado was still on the planet. Those were the only reasons. If Mado doesn't appear, then Vidor has no reason to hold back. He'll bring the entire might of the Global Assembly forces, and if we survive, it won't be a pretty future for any of us. He'll hold all the cards."

Gols stared down at his feet.

"Gols?" Mar said. "I understand your loyalty to Mado's course of action, but do you truly think it's right to leave without seeing if I can save my partner or stop the assault on the Complex?"

Gols slowly lifted his head. "My job is following orders, not to make them, and these are the orders I was given."

Suron said, "Do you have an alternative plan in mind, Mar Jeps?"

"Off the top of my head," Mar said. "I would meet with the Leader. I'd tell him I know the WAEF wasn't shot down, and that Mado is off planet with my son. I'd tell him Mado is not coming back soon and he hasn't told me anything about where they're going. I think I'm assuming correctly that this threat is all about the lack of progress on the Global Assembly spaceship project. I'll tell him if our techs hit anymore snags, I'll communicate with Mado personally and see if he can come up with a solution. In response, I'd expect Vidor not to attack the Complex and stay the executions of Rajer and Lek."

"That's reasonable," Suron said, placing his hand on Gols' shoulder to stop him from quaking. "But Vidor is a man who lashes out at any slights. I know him well and I'm certain he's been in denial about Mado Prevor's disloyalty. He'd refuse to believe he was made to look like a fool by anybody. I bet he's been stewing on this since Breeze Celebration. When he does have the truth, his rage will be epic."

"But we need to play on the source of the rage," Mar said, pushing her chair closer to her desk. "Gols, are the recent setbacks on the government spaceship project real or the result of Mado's ruse to fund Project FoFu?"

"They're having the same problem with the cryo-units as Project FoFu."

"That's good to know. I probably should be more on top of the government project, now that I'm up to speed on Shamba. Does Mado have these setbacks scheduled?"

"Yes, but there isn't another one for a while. I was going to tell you when the date got closer."

"Good to know," Mar said. "Like I said, I'm assuming the recent setbacks at the Global Assembly project and Mado not being available to fix them is driving the Leader's anger. That's because his family means everything to him and he's concerned about their survival. I believe this plan will work if I couch my plea to him in a guarantee that with Mado's help, the Global Assembly project will move forward for the sake of his children."

Gols said, "That makes sense."

Mar said, "Suron?"

"Oh, I agree, I just think we need to keep Vidor's temper in the back of our minds."

"Good point," Mar said. "Gols, I assume the techs who have been flying back and forth from Shamba are the ones who would be evacuated there permanently—is that correct?"

"Yes, the majority of them."

"It'd be prudent to send those techs to the Shamba site or keep them there for now just in case my gambit with the Leader doesn't work. We should also prepare to liquidate our assets to avoid seizure so we can fund building the spacecraft in Shamba."

"I like all of this," Suron said, "but before we proceed with these details, do you mind if I blow some holes in your plan?"

"Yes, please do."

"Well, what if Vidor decides to arrest you at this meeting and invade the Complex, taking control of Prevor Industries?"

"Depending on where we set up the meeting, you could bring a security contingent that can suppress the Leader's men," Mar said. "I suggest we do it at the Plemso estate. If his children are there, then the Leader might be less inclined toward violence. Taking his arrogance into consideration, he'll probably be fine with holding the meeting there and not send his children away because he'll assume I'm clueless and will just come alone with you.

"Also, let's suppose he'll attempt a takeover of the Complex. We'll designate the day when I meet the Leader a mandatory holiday for all personnel not going to Shamba—scientists, administrators, excess security personnel, janitors, everybody. That way nobody gets arrested or hurt, and if the corporation is taken over and shut down, then we just pay the severances Mado mentioned. We should have cruisers waiting outside the dome at the end of the tunnel with all necessary materials ready to go and put all non-tech personnel headed to Shamba on standby for evacuation from the Complex."

"I like it," Suron said.

"Gols, you've been quiet. Care to weigh in?"

"I've been listening," Gols said. "It all sounds logical."

Suron said, "It covers most of the problems that might arise, but if you're arrested, who takes over as CEO? There's no real line of succession."

"These are unusual circumstances," Mar said. "Prevor Industries will cease to exist as a corporate entity if the Complex is invaded and all the workers are paid severance and the essentials are evacuated. If I'm arrested, then we'll need someone to help Rika oversee the project in Shamba.

Someone who can handle the monetary complexities of a massive project and is competent at juggling multiple tasks. Somebody who understands Mado's directives."

"Agreed. I think I know who you have in mind," Suron said.

Gols peered up at Suron who smiled down on him, then Gols turned to Mar. "You can't mean—"

"Yes, I do," Mar said, standing up and approaching Gols. "Who knows this corporation, this project better than you, all the nuts and bolts? You're the ideal person to take over. Your only task will be coordinating everything and making sure that the spaceships in Shamba are completed."

"I don't—"

"You don't think you're up to the task," Mar said. "Ever since I arrived, you've been running this corporation without me, so this should be simple for you."

Gols smiled. "I'm humbled and honored, Mar Jeps. I guess I never think anybody notices now that Mado Prevor is gone."

Mar chuckled. "I compliment you all the time. Maybe you don't listen. Seems like you've always got the next thing to do rattling around in that brain of yours."

"I don't know what to say," Gols said, "Of course, I'll do it."

"We're all set then. If we don't return or you don't hear from Suron or me by a specific time, then personnel and necessary equipment head down the tunnel," Mar said. "A few other tasks come to mind: make sure all corporate secrets, including how to reenergize the domes, are removed; destroy or relocate any sensitive experiments; back up all servers off-site and erase the ones on-site. If I forgot anything, I have no doubt one of you will think of it, but our most important role is getting as many spaceships as possible built in Shamba and ready for launch.

"And Gols, have you alerted Mado yet?"

"No, I couldn't with that Guard in the vicinity. I planned on doing it after this meeting."

"Well, let's hold off on contacting him until after I speak to the Leader about his ultimatum," Mar said. "Then I think both of us need to send Mado a transmission."

# Rajer

Rajer lay on his back on the bed in his cell. His eyes were closed and he kept recalling his visitation with Mar over and over in his head in a never-ending loop. Before they entered the simulation, he memorized her from head to toe: from her penetrating eyes, her inviting mouth and lips, the nape of her neck, the heave of her breasts, the curve of her hips, her strong yet sensual legs to her small, ticklish toes. He recalled the tone of her voice: The sincerity and love she possessed for him. He was a lucky man to have experienced this sort of attachment to a partner in his lifetime. He happened to be in the right place at the right time to be so fortunate. He knew men who had gone their entire lives without ever making such a connection. Not just physical, but spiritual. *For Powers-That-Be sake, I'm a lucky man.*

Rajer saw no reason to open his eyes to the white cell. He didn't need a reminder of his circumstance. He maintained no hope the Leader was ever going to let him walk free on the basis of his supposed deal, especially now that Mar had given in to his wishes. Lek's insight into the situation was most likely correct. Rajer's pending execution was a nice piece of leverage for the Leader to keep in his back pocket.

Then Rajer heard the Active Glass powering down. He opened his eyes and sat up to see Lek being shoved into the cell by a Global Guard. Lek flew forward and landed on his knees. The Active Glass went up again. The Global Guard glared into the cell with disgust and Rajer read the man's lips as he said, "Scum."

Rajer hurried to Lek and helped him to his feet. "This is a surprise—an unwelcome one, but a surprise nonetheless."

Lek said, "Not glad to see me?"

"I'm always glad to see you, but not inside this cell with me. What happened?"

"You happened," Lek said and shoved Rajer, who stumbled then fell onto his bed.

"Don't get any ideas about sharing this bed. You can have the top one."

"I'm glad you still have a sense of humor," Lek said, walking to the Active Glass wall and attempting to peer down the hall, left then right.

"I've tried that already. These cells are well designed. Can't see down the hallway at all. You should know that," Rajer said, walking up to Lek. "Truthfully, what are you doing here?"

Lek turned. There was a sadness in his eyes, a look of utter loss. "I wasn't kidding," Lek said. "You happened. The Leader wasn't pleased with the way I've dealt with you so he called for my execution, then ordered me to visit Mar with an ultimatum."

"How did she look?" Rajer said. "Is she all right?"

"After what I just told you, that's the first question out of your mouth? Not, 'That's horrible, Lek. How're you doing?'"

"I'm sorry, but you look like crap and you're in this cell with me, so I have a pretty clear idea already of how you're doing."

"Point taken," Lek said. "You mind if I sit down on your bed for now? I'm exhausted."

"Go right ahead."

As Lek sat down on the bed, he released a long sigh. It became clear to Rajer how lost and despondent Lek truly was. He'd known Lek for over thirty years and he'd only seen him this way once before when Linara was having difficulties giving birth. She was in labor and the med wasn't sure if the mother or the baby would survive. Fortunately, Mar stepped in and consulted with the other meds and everything turned out all right.

Rajer began to feel sad and responsible for the pain he'd inflicted on his friend. By tackling the woman at Breeze Celebration, Rajer had not only ruined his life, but Lek had put himself and his family in a precarious position by attempting to help Rajer, and now it appeared he'd pay for it dearly.

"I'm sorry," Rajer said. "I'm truly sorry for what I've done. I love you, man."

"I love you, too, but don't be so full of yourself. What finally put the nail in the proverbial coffin was Ador."

"Ador?"

"Yes, I went to his memorial service."

"Damn. I missed it."

"It was fitting," Lek said. "They named a lecture hall after him and there were some poignant speeches."

"Why was that a problem? The man is dead."

"That's why I thought it wouldn't be a problem. To be thorough, I even received permission from my director," Lek said, "I went to pay my respects, but that wasn't the main reason I was there. I went to tell Mar that you were alive."

"I don't know what to say."

"That would be a first."

"I mean, this is completely my fault, then."

"Yes, Rajer. You're correct. Your fault. I have no free will. I didn't put my family at risk by going out of my way to do something I thought was the right thing to do. Thinking I could get away with it was delusional," Lek said and chuckled. "You have absolutely no idea how much you owe me."

"What do you mean?"

"It doesn't matter. Forget that I said it."

"What did you mean, damn you?"

"I'm already damned." Lek stood, walked past Rajer to the Active Glass wall without looking at him, and stared out into the hall.

Rajer stayed put for a moment, soaking in the silence, and thought he'd leave well enough alone. Here stood his best friend, the man who was always there for him, who was now avoiding him in order to conceal a detail about their relationship. Rajer's curiosity grew. He searched his mind for what Lek might be referencing but came up with nothing. Finally, he had to know, so he strode up to Lek and tapped him on the shoulder.

"Can't you leave me in peace and let it go?" Lek said, not turning around.

"In this place? What else have I got to do? And since you've known me when has that ever been an option?"

"Powers-That-Be, you're an idiot."

Rajer grabbed Lek's shoulder and tugged to make him turn around, but Lek wouldn't budge. Then he stepped forward and leaned against the Active Glass wall so he was standing perpendicular to Lek.

Rajer said, "If I'm an idiot, I guess I should act like one." Then he began tapping Lek's shoulder, saying over and over again, "Tell me."

Lek began laughing and turned toward Rajer. "You're just proving my point."

"Maybe so," Rajer said, continuing to tap Lek's shoulder, "but you're locked in this cell with me and I don't have anything better to do than what I'm doing right now."

"I should've kept my trap shut." Lek marched back to the bed and sat down with his hands on his knees and stared at the floor.

"Are you going to make me chase you around the cell?"

"Yes, I am."

"So be it," Rajer said, crossing the cell to stand in front of Lek. "Now, what're you so reluctant to tell me, but almost blurted out before?"

"I almost told you because I was angry, but my being here is not your fault."

"That's nice to hear, but I'm going to continue feeling guilty if that's all right with you. I have to preoccupy myself somehow in here."

Lek looked up at Rajer. "Well, here it is. You remember being surprised by how poorly the loyalty part of your interview for the Budgetary Standards job went? And how you were still offered the position? Well, it went as badly as you thought. Nobody in the room monitoring your vitals or your voice analysis believed you were speaking the truth. I know, because I was in the room with the GSS admittance officer and her assistants. You failed with flying colors, but I convinced them afterward that the equipment was set to the wrong baseline and therefore the results were flawed. They bought it because the readouts were so bad, it had to be the equipment. The admittance officer was a newbie and I was a higher-ranking officer, so she believed me and passed you."

"You always knew I wondered what happened. Why didn't you tell me years ago?"

"I couldn't risk you or anybody else learning the truth. If word got out, they would have sent me to the same place I am right now."

"So why tell me now?"

"Maybe I want you to know how I've looked out for you over the years, how what I did to get thrown in here wasn't anything new, so maybe you should be more grateful and less irritating."

Rajer began to laugh. It started slow and built up from somewhere deep inside him as if a valve had been turned open all the way until he was laughing loud and hard and uncontrollably from the gut. At first, Lek appeared annoyed by Rajer's outburst, and then it was as if the same valve was opened inside him and he was laughing just as hard.

Rajer was laughing so much he ran out of breath, gasping for air, and Lek did the same.

Rajer said, still catching his breath, "You're hilarious."

"I guess I am," Lek said, then chuckled a bit more.

"You know you're the closest person I have in the world to a brother," Rajer said. "I love you and love the fact that you withheld that story until now. I know you said you didn't tell me to protect yourself, but we both know you were protecting my feelings too."

"You know me too well."

"That's true," Rajer said. "I've been meaning to tell you, when I was in the simulation with Mar, I told her—"

Lek leapt up from the bed and placed the palm of his hand firmly over Rajer's mouth so he couldn't speak, then leaned his head forward and whispered into Rajer's ear, "Everything we say in here is being recorded. That's why they threw us together. So from here on out let's confine the conversation to reminiscing." Lek removed his hand from Rajer's mouth.

Rajer whispered into Lek's ear, "Then why did you screw yourself by telling me the story about the interview?"

Lek placed both his hands on Rajer's shoulders and held him at arm's length. "You were annoying me," Lek said. "But seriously, my punishment before I entered this cell is death. I don't have anything left to lose and I thought it'd be best to tell you now since who knows when I'd get another chance."

"Well, at least we'll go out together."

"I'm not sure I can find any consolation in that," Lek said, sitting back down on the bed. "There might be a stay of your execution if Mado makes an appearance. Where is he, anyway?"

Rajer leaned forward and whispered softly in Lek's ear, "I have no idea."

Lek looked up at the ceiling and said, raising his voice, "He said he has no idea. See—I tried. Don't I get leniency? If not for me, then for my family."

Rajer shoved him.

"You can't blame a man for trying," Lek said. "For my family."

"No," Rajer said. "If anybody gets that, I do."

# ORN

A GSS guard pushed Rajer Jeps into the interrogation room and slammed the door shut behind him.

Rajer said, "Are these guards trained in shoving people?"

Orn was sitting at the table, facing the doorway. "Rajer Jeps, have a seat." He pointed to the chair across from him.

A broad smile formed on Rajer's face. "What took you so long?"

"You're cheerful for a man so close to execution."

"I wouldn't call it cheerful," Rajer said. "I'd say at peace. You may not be acquainted with that feeling."

"Sit," Orn said, raising his voice.

"If you insist," Rajer said, seating himself, then began tapping out a rhythm with both hands on the metallic table. Orn assumed it would be a short rendition and Rajer Jeps would stop soon, but he continued doing it with that smile plastered across his face.

"Stop that," Orn said, "or I'll break both your hands."

Rajer stopped and pushed out his bottom lip as if he were pouting. "It wasn't that bad, was it?"

Orn had seen this before. A prisoner feels like he has nothing to lose so he acts out.

Rajer said, "So why do I have the honor of this visit? I got a new roommate yesterday."

"Yes. I know about that."

"Of course you do. Did you come here to bask in the Breeze Celebration hero's glow?"

"Nobody's calling you that," Orn said, placing his palms on the table.

"I'm sure those people aren't in your social circle," Rajer said and peered down at Orn's scars. "I've been meaning to ask you about those scars. It must have smarted when it happened, huh?"

Orn chuckled. "It didn't smart as much as having the air squeezed out of your body in the execution tube will," Orn said. "Do you really think you're a hero? What you did was stupid. Heroism by the losers is seen as stupid from the winning side."

"You're already declaring victory."

"Yes, decades ago. Looks that way from where I'm sitting."

"One man declaring victory prematurely could be seen as delusional to another," Rajer Jeps said, scooting his chair closer to the table. "I have to say I'm enjoying this conversation more than I thought I would."

"Isn't Lek Valsted amusing you?"

"He's the best, but we've known each other for years and we've heard each other's stories more than a few times."

"Even the one where he helped you get your Global Assembly job?"

"Well, life is full of surprises."

"That's true," Orn said. "I never thought you had the balls to do what you did at Breeze Celebration. Roneh

Rayush must have really gotten under your skin. Your partner is quite the piece of ass for her age, but when you have a hot young thing rubbing against you and then you're betrayed, that's got to hurt." Rajer's arms were now crossed over his chest and he was holding himself, sitting back in this chair. Orn thought he was getting to him. "I mean, the way you lunged at poor Roneh, that was real hostility, but it's always the ones boxed up for years in a cubicle in a place like Budgetary Standards who are so easily emasculated. They just snap. And after Tetrick Vanderlord, Mar Jeps definitely traded down." Orn stopped to let that seep in.

Rajer sat there in the same position blinking, not saying a word, then he began snickering and said derisively, "Is that the best you got? I'd think someone of your expertise could come up with a better routine than that."

"Really? I wouldn't push it."

"I'll give you complete disclosure, because that's what you fellas are all about," Rajer said. "When I went after Roneh, I was angry. You're correct there. But it wasn't over some slutty advance she wouldn't let me consummate. I wasn't even particularly angry at her getting me drunk on Malrap. I was angry at myself for allowing her to drag information out of me, told to me in confidence, that might endanger my son."

"Stepson."

"Yes, have it your way. Stepson. You'd never understand why that doesn't matter anyway," Rajer said. "I felt like I'd betrayed his trust and she was the tool of the betrayal. Then

I saw her in the Arena and I knew she was up to no good, so I followed her and saw her remove a weapon from an unconscious guard, so I kept following her. One thing led to another and the rest is history, as they say."

Orn wasn't pleased with this interview. Rajer was too comfortable with himself.

Rajer began to pound out a beat again so Orn snatched Rajer's right hand and snapped his pinkie finger at the top joint.

"Dammit!" Rajer screamed in pain, grabbing his hand and peering at his finger bent in the wrong direction. "What was that for?" He continued moaning.

"I'm sick of your attitude. You've been in your hole too long, and you've forgotten you're a prisoner and sentenced to death."

"If I'm sentenced to death, why should I show you any respect?"

"That's a good point, and that's why I broke your finger. I wanted to remind you who's in charge here," Orn said. "You have plenty more joints on your fingers to break."

Rajer was still grasping his hand with the broken finger. "What do you want from me?" he said. "I don't know where you can find Mado Prevor."

"Why would you know that?"

"I have no idea, but your interrogators seem to think if they beat me enough, then I'll tell them something I don't know."

"That's just ridiculous. There's no reason for you to know the answer to that question. Mado Prevor is too smart to tell the likes of you."

"Your interrogators need to get the memo," Rajer said. "So, what do you want?"

"I want to know about Mar Jeps."

"I don't think you have a shot with her."

Orn chuckled and said, "Very funny, but it's making me wonder which finger I want to break next."

"What would you like to know about her?" Rajer said. "I'm well versed in the subject."

"The Leader wants Mado Prevor, but Mado isn't going to appear. That's the truth, although the Leader is convinced otherwise, and if Mar Jeps doesn't give him Mado, he's eventually going to take it out on her, her employees, and the population."

"Do you have a question?"

"Don't interrupt. That's your final warning," Orn said. "So, if Mado Prevor can't be handed over to the Leader, how do you see Mar Jeps dealing with it?"

Rajer took a long pause. He was resting his hand with the busted finger on the table like a wounded animal, attempting to minimize the pain by not moving it, then he reached over with his other hand and popped the finger back into the joint. He only groaned at the pain. Orn didn't think Rajer had it in him.

Rajer looked up at Orn, then smiled. "That smarted."

Orn said, "Do you have an answer, or do I have to break your arm this time—and not at a joint?"

Rajer rolled his eyes.

Orn pushed back his chair, scraping the legs across the floor.

Rajer held the palm of his undamaged hand out toward Orn. "Calm down," Rajer said. "I'm just gathering my thoughts."

"I'll give you to the count of six and then…" Orn said, sliding his chair back toward the table.

"Yes, you'll break something," Rajer said. "Look, I have no idea what Mar has in mind. When I lived with her, she was a med who went to work every day and cared for people. Now she's CEO of Prevor Industries. She's being threatened by the Leader of the planet, the man who issued the order to kill her son and probably her ex-partner, too. Another person might act in a vengeful way when the opportunity arose, but Mar is about the sanctity of life. If the Leader is asking for something that's not in her power to give and being stubborn and threatening people's lives, then I'm not sure how she'll respond with her newfound power, but don't underestimate her. She's brilliant and she won't back down."

"Yes, I've seen that firsthand," Orn said. "So, you're saying she's more dangerous than the Leader might foresee?"

"If by dangerous you mean acting in a way that won't be expected, then yes."

Orn pushed back his chair, not scraping the legs this time, then stood and leaned forward with two hands on the table, glaring at Rajer in silence. Orn waited. Rajer stared back at him. There was no fear in his eyes. If anything, Rajer was surprising Orn once again by scrutinizing him. This pansy from Budgetary Standards had been transformed. Then it dawned on Orn: this was Mar Jeps' influence on him.

Rajer said, "Can I help you with anything else?"

Orn laughed and walked around the table to stand beside Rajer.

"I'll tell you something, mostly because you'll be dead soon and the surveillance cams are off. When it comes to your beloved Mar, the Leader may be in over his head," Orn said. "Thanks for the revealing conversation."

# Vidor

Vidor was meeting with the Supreme Commander of Global Forces, the Head Director of the GSS, and the Lead Commander of the Global Guard when the intercom buzzed and his receptionist said Mar Jeps was on the line.

Yesterday, Lek Valsted had returned without a reply from her and she had decided to wait a day to contact him. He had to admit he was impressed by her mettle. His message had a time limit, so a less experienced person without an understanding of power and tactics would have been unnerved and called him as soon as Lek Valsted departed their office. Mar Jeps astonished him at every turn. He found it unpleasant.

Vidor first thought about placing her call on his comm's speaker so those in his office could hear how he handled her, then concluded it would be best to deal with her on his own. He didn't know what to expect from her and who knew what she'd say to him in front of his men. In his recent conversations with Mar Jeps, she'd shocked him with her audacity. Of course, Mar Jeps had spent years living with a Vanderlord, so he figured her lack of respect for his office and her tendency to speak her mind had evolved in that household.

Vidor decided to give Mar Jeps time to cool off, deflate any courage she'd mustered before she made the call to him. Maybe she'd question what she'd worked herself up to say. He told Kel to place Mar Jeps on hold.

He rose from his desk and rejoined his visitors on the couches. Head Director Rikin was wearing a Global-Assembly-blue shirt with a Global-Assembly pin, while Lead Commander Penat sported his black Global Guard uniform with the red GG patch over his heart. They were sitting on the same couch, while Supreme Commander Zy Bofort had a couch to himself. Ribbons covered the entire right side of his blue Global-Assembly uniform.

Vidor had known all these men for decades. They were as loyal as loyal could be. They'd been discussing the maneuver to purge the Movement and simultaneously seize control of the Prevor Industries Complex. The Head Director was tasked with arresting the techs from XAF-758 and those in charge of maintaining the power for each dome.

Vidor sat in an armchair at the head of the couches and said, "So, gentlemen, are we all on the same page? I want you prepared to move on my command. I expect your forces and your agents to be ready in six days in case our deadline gets pushed up."

Supreme Commander Bofort said, "We understand the order, sir, but we're uneasy synchronizing this planetwide purge action with the attack on the Prevor Industries Complex." He'd been a lieutenant under Vidor during the Separatist Revolts and they'd fought together through Vidor's toughest military campaigns. He replaced Supreme Commander Nar Falojin after the DOME riots.

Vidor said, "You aren't going soft on me, Zy, are you?"

"No, sir. My duty is the security of the planet, a duty shared by every man here. But this maneuver could be more safely actualized in stages, speedily moving the full might of our forces from dome to dome with a small forward strike team in each dome monitoring our targets so they don't escape, then finally moving on to the Complex. That way, we still strike every target on the planet without stretching our forces thin in a simultaneous planetwide attack." Zy always exuded confidence in his point of view.

"Do all of you feel this way?" Vidor said.

Both Head Director Rikin and Lead Commander Penat said at the same time, "Yes, sir."

Vidor said, "I wouldn't be where I am if it weren't for the three of you and your service to Koda. I respect your opinions. That being said, my reason for perpetrating this maneuver in this fashion is to demonstrate the might of the Global Assembly—the sheer awe of the attack will deter our enemies from opposing us in the future. I completely understand your concerns, but I believe all three of you can coordinate this historic moment in Kodan history and make this strike happen without a hitch. We outgun if not outman our opponents on all counts. Send me your coordinated plans of attack in the next few days and have your men on alert and ready to move. Do I make myself clear?"

All three men said, "Yes, sir."

"You're dismissed," Vidor said, standing up.

Head Director Rikin and Lead Commander Penat stood, saluted, and marched out of the room. Supreme Commander Bofort stood, then didn't move.

Vidor said, "Something on your mind, Zy?"

"Yes," Zy said. "May I speak freely, sir?"

"I welcome it."

"Although I completely understand your political and, may I say, theatrical reasons for such a maneuver, as Supreme Commander I feel I have to state again my apprehension regarding this attack. You know as well as anyone that recruitment has been dropping since the DOME riots, the one-child mandate, and the thinning of the population due to the dome Selection Process. Our forces aren't as robust as they once were. They're already spread thin, keeping the peace since Breeze Celebration, guarding Global Assembly offices and facilities across Koda. Honestly, my concern is for the safety and lives of the fighters we currently have in our forces."

"So is this concern about victory or the welfare of your soldiers?"

"Frankly, both. With our recruitment so low, our active soldiers are a valuable commodity."

Vidor took a few steps until he stood nose-to-nose with Zy, who stiffened as Vidor approached him. "Did you trust my orders when I was your commander on the field years ago?"

"Yes, sir."

"Were we not victorious?"

"Yes, we were, sir."

"When everyone else said I was misguided, did I not eliminate our opposition in the DOME riots?"

"Yes, you did, sir."

"I'm still your commander so I expect you to act on

my orders, otherwise I can find someone else to take your position. If you're not in your current position, then I don't see a place for you at all. You know what that means."

"Yes, sir. I understand, sir."

"I don't expect to be questioned again," Vidor said, raising his voice. "You're dismissed."

"Yes, sir." Zy saluted, backpedaled to the other end of the couch, and marched out of the room.

Vidor was agitated. Zy was one of his best underlings and he never questioned him. That was one of the reasons he was promoted to Supreme Commander. He thought about what Zy said concerning the thinning of Global Assembly forces and began to feel a twinge of doubt. Maybe he should call Zy back and hear a more detailed account of what he deemed dangerous about the maneuver.

Vidor walked over to the window overlooking the Global Plaza, reminding himself that he was the Leader and that his command of Global Assembly forces in the Separatist Revolts and his decisiveness during the DOME riots had gotten the planet this far. He respected Zy for being a commander who cared about his soldiers, but this was Vidor's army. He would do what he thought necessary based on his success in the past and Zy would follow.

The intercom buzzed—Kel reminding him that Mar Jeps was still on hold. Vidor told her, "I've got it," then sat down at his desk, pushed in his chair, and took a deep breath. He reminded himself of his anger at Mado Prevor. That was a good way to keep him on his toes.

Vidor picked up his comm and said, "Hello."

There was no answer.

"Hello," Vidor said again.

No answer.

"Mar Jeps, are you there?" He could feel his temper rising. *Would she have the gall to hang up on me?* Vidor thought. "Hello…Mar Jeps, are you there?"

Vidor took the comm away from his ear and was in the act of hanging up when he heard Mar Jeps say, "Hello…Hello…"

"Yes," Vidor said.

"There you are."

"Yes, I'm here." His voice was clearly full of anger.

"I had you on speaker while you had me waiting, then I walked out of the office for a moment to speak to my assistant and of course, that's when you came on the line."

Vidor didn't believe her. He thought she was toying with him. That's what he would do. "I believe yesterday's message was clear so why're you calling?."

"I'd like to discuss it."

"I'm listening," Vidor said, feeling more in control.

"I'd like to meet to talk about Mado Prevor."

"Again, I think I was clear on wanting him presented to me by my deadline."

"Yes, you were, but if we meet in person, I can explain Mado's current situation."

"Explain to me why I should bend to your demand."

"No matter how much you want him, Mado will be unavailable to appear in person. I believe I can clear up any misunderstanding," Mar said, "I can explain why not taking over Prevor Industries is the right thing for the Kodan people and the right thing for your family."

Vidor thought this was some sort of tactic on her part, but he'd play along. "Where would you propose this meeting take place?"

"Can we do it at your estate?"

"That's highly unusual since this will be official business."

"I understand, but your home is so lovely and calming, I believe for the good of the planet that it'd be best to have our little summit there."

Vidor saw how he could take advantage of her proposal. With Warver gone, Suron would never leave Mar Jeps' side. Arresting Suron and Mar Jeps at the estate would be easy and with Suron out of the way and not commanding the Prevor Industries security forces, invading the Complex would be simpler strategically. It might ease Zy's concerns. Whatever Mar Jeps was planning, he was positive he could outmaneuver her. "As I said, this is highly unusual, but this entire situation is unusual, so I'll agree to it."

"How about ten days from now?"

"I can accommodate that," Vidor said, thinking, *That'll give my people enough time to put the strategic plans together and get the forces ready.* "I'll have my receptionist set up a time on that date."

"I look forward to it."

Vidor put Mar Jeps on hold, intercommed Kel to set up the time for the meeting, then Kel told him Orn Shiv was here to see him.

# ORN

When Orn entered the office, the Leader appeared to be in a better mood than the last time he saw him. Orn wondered how he would take what Orn was about to tell him. He approached the Leader at his desk, clicked his heels together, saluted, then stood at attention.

Vidor said, "At ease, Orn. Just got off the comm with Mar Jeps. I'm having a meeting with her soon, and I'm going to find Mado Prevor. I assume you haven't found him."

"I haven't discovered him after another sweep of the planet so I'm more convinced than ever that my prior conclusions are correct regarding Mado Prevor's whereabouts."

"That he's on the WAEF with the Vanderlord boy?" the Leader said. "Absurd."

"That's actually not why I'm here," Orn said. "I suppose the Supreme Commander, Lead Commander and Head Director were here to discuss something important?"

"You'll hear about it officially today or tomorrow from the Head Director," the Leader said, then launched into telling Orn about the simultaneous planetwide maneuver to purge the Movement and seize control of the Prevor Industries Complex in detail. He was proud of it. Orn was knowledgeable about the Leader's purge idea because compiling the list had been the highest priority at the

GSS, but Orn was unaware this maneuver had been set into motion.

"So, you've chosen to act on your purge idea…now?"

"Do I hear criticism, Orn?" the Leader said. "Do I need to remind you who gives the orders around here?"

"No, sir. Of course not, sir," Orn said. "I just wondered if this is the best time to act on it."

"Oh, are you the Leader now? I didn't realize. Did you rise up through the ranks of the military, get elected three times to the Presidency, then assume your rightful place as Leader of the planet? Well, please, O great Leader, shower me with your wisdom. Tell me why this isn't the best time to act." He slammed his fist on the desk.

Orn didn't think anything he said now would get through to him, but he decided to try.

"As I said last time I was here, there's an unsettled feeling among the population around the planet that has persisted since Breeze Celebration," Orn said. "Kodans are still debating whether Yor Vanderlord's words were true, whether his vids were real. The media campaign to discredit them surely had an impact, but my hunch was correct about the way the undecideds were leaning. Have you seen the latest polling? It shows them swaying the wrong way. Greater than fifty percent of the population don't believe the Global Assembly counterpoints against Vanderlord's presentation."

"Greater than fifty percent?"

"Yes, 54.3% sir. That's based on a poll performed by one of our clandestine contractors."

"I haven't seen that poll. Dammit! Davik better not be holding it back," the Leader said. "No matter. My purge will put those numbers back in our favor. Just a matter of statistics."

"If you might indulge me for another moment?" Orn said. "I came here for another reason."

"May as well. You're already here."

"I appreciate that, sir," Orn said. "I spoke with Rajer Jeps this morning to obtain some sense of Mar Jeps' capabilities."

"That man is irritating."

"Yes, sir," Orn said. "But one thing he emphasized was not to underestimate Mar Jeps."

"You've mentioned that before," the Leader said, standing up from his desk and looking out the window. "Do you have anything else for me?"

"There's rumors about the Movement planning some sort of action on the heels of Vanderlord's presentation so they don't lose a foothold in the minds of the people," Orn said. "And there's been a steady increase in chatter—both digi-mail and comms—between the leaders of the Movement and their followers. They sound emboldened about something."

"What does this have to do with Mar Jeps? Are you saying there's a connection?"

"Yes, sir."

"Her involvement in the Movement is minimal at best."

"She has contact with her son's University colleagues. That's a clear connection."

"Minimal at best," the Leader said "Is this chatter just in Capitol City?"

"No, planetwide, sir."

"I've heard nothing about this from the Head Director."

"I've been doing my own research," Orn said. "You have him focused on your purge."

The Leader turned to Orn. "Exactly. And the Movement hierarchy will be arrested and disappear soon, so problem solved."

"If you'd hear me out, sir."

"Isn't that what I'm doing? I'm not sure what else there is to say and you're growing tiresome."

"Let's say we're underestimating Mar Jeps," Orn said. "One thing you taught me early in our relationship was never to underestimate the enemy."

"True, but that's taking into account the enemy's weaponry, manpower, and leaders."

"Yes, sir."

"In this case, we're talking about a woman who was a med just a short time ago with no tactical military experience and hardly any connection to the unarmed civilians in the Movement who are mostly pacifist intellectuals who we beat back easily at Breeze Celebration."

"What about Suron?"

"Now, that's an interesting point," the Leader said, taking a few steps toward Orn. "Kush was a fine strategist in his day, but he was mostly under my direction, so we can't give him too much credit for the victories he achieved, and that was a long time ago."

"Although I never liked him, he was highly competent in his role."

"Wasn't he under my overall command?"

"Yes, sir."

"So those victories were due to me, not him, correct?"

"Yes, sir."

"Anyhow, Suron is irrelevant since he'll be removed from the equation on the day when we take back the planet," the Leader said. "Anything else? Have we taken everything into account now? Your theory is farfetched, Orn. There's absolutely no evidence for any of this. I expect more from you. Now stop wasting my time."

"Yes, sir. Sorry, sir," Orn said. "One last thing—we have intel that Mar Jeps has traveled outside of the Capitol City dome. We have vidcam footage of her in the cruiserport at Mafanikio."

"So what? There's nothing in that backwater that can hurt us. She was there because of Prevor's Relief Foundation. I already know about it." The Leader took a few more steps so he was standing less than a meter from Orn. "I value your input, Orn, and that's why I've endured this get-together, but the purge will be the solution here."

Orn figured it was foolhardy, but he was going to take one more shot at stopping this mistake. The Leader had told him to be completely honest with him. "Yes, sir. That's one way of looking at it," Orn said. "The other way is that Kodans who are sitting on the fence and even those on your side will see a Leader attempting to stamp out dissent altogether. They'll ask themselves, 'Why would the Leader want to do that if Yor Vanderlord's facts were false?'"

"Are you saying my actions will make me appear guilty of lying to the Kodan people?"

"With all due respect, I'm saying your actions could give further credence to Vanderlord's presentation."

"Ridiculous!"

It was evident to Orn that the Leader had made up his mind. When the Leader was a military commander and Orn a young man serving as Colonel Plemso's attendant, he observed a leader of men who was willing to hear counterarguments from his officers and modify his own thinking to include other people's ideas. He was generous in obtaining promotions for his officers so they could follow him up the chain of command and remain by his side. When his officers were by themselves and Orn spied on them, they talked about how their promotions were self-serving so Vidor could use their skills in the next military campaign and take credit for the victory. There was a rumor that Vidor's father had hired a publicist to promote his son's military career because the media was full of features about the great military exploits of Vidor Plemso and his single-handed defeat of the Separatists.

As Colonel Plemso rose through the ranks and then was elected President, he began to believe this myth about himself. He forgot about the people around him and their impact on his elevation to the most powerful position on the planet. Now, as Leader, he thought it was solely his will and intellect that got him here. The danger was evident, but Orn could only do his job and perhaps the Leader would listen. Orn thought about how best to respond to the Leader calling his analysis "ridiculous."

Orn finally said, "I don't think so." He regretted the impulse the moment it came out of his mouth.

"You don't think so?" the Leader barked at Orn.

"I don't, sir," Orn said, backing up and sitting down in the chair across from the desk, hoping the Leader would feel less threatened. He perched himself on the edge of the seat, not committing himself to its binding fit. "Yes, sir. While I would never contradict anything you feel so strongly about, I'm concerned that the purge might trigger an incident like the DOME riots."

"I took my place as Leader because of the DOME riots. It was a good thing. That's why I rule now with unbridled authority, which is what Koda truly needs in this time of crisis. I'll never apologize for my actions."

"Yes, sir," Orn said, scooting further toward the front of the chair. "I just don't know if now is the right time for another move like that one. You're already Leader and that's not in debate."

"Damn right," the Leader said, approaching Orn. "So are you saying the Global Assembly forces with all their power might not be able to handle the rabble? That's what the Supreme Commander said. Are you siding with him? Did you talk to him as he was leaving the office?"

"No, sir. I didn't know the Supreme Commander felt that way. I would presume he has a good idea what his forces can and cannot do."

"And I don't?"

"The final decision is yours."

"Thanks for pointing that out."

"Nobody will contradict your final decision, but the Supreme Commander is your most competent military advisor and it couldn't hurt to listen to his counsel, but

I don't presume to be a military advisor."

"That's good because you stunk at it," the Leader said and chuckled.

"Whether my overall idea is farfetched or not, I feel strongly about the Movement being active and getting ready to act. If I wasn't concerned, I wouldn't have come here. I wish you'd take what I've said under consideration after what happened at Breeze Celebration."

"Are you saying what happened at Breeze Celebration was my fault?"

"No, sir," Orn said. "After Breeze Celebration, you said you expected the Powers-That-Be truth from me, not what you want to hear. That's what I'm giving you. It's all of our butts on the line if things go sideways and I have no doubt you'll make the right call, but please listen to the competent people you've surrounded yourself with."

"You want me to listen?"

"Only for the good of the globe, sir."

"All right, then. I'll indulge you. Bring me some solid evidence for your theory," Vidor said, poking Orn in the chest. "There'll be consequences for your insolence, though. Right or wrong, I'll put you behind a desk in the Mauan dome and your interrogation privileges will be taken away for an indefinite period of time for insubordination. Do I make myself clear?"

"Yes, sir."

"Off you go, then. You've got your work cut out for you."

# YOR

The day was nearing to navigate around the red dwarf and land at Terminus A-1. Yor and Mado still couldn't get the engine involved in the explosion to start up, and every conceivable answer to the vibration problem caused parts to break. Mado had the foresight to bring extra parts, but there were only so many.

Mado was always the optimist, but he stated they might be at an impasse. At less than full power with one engine down, they both knew the maneuver around the star might kill them. Mado began saying things like, "I've made it through worse than this," or, "We'll be able to fix this properly when we arrive at the way station where we can use the IPRB and have better quality metal…but we have to get there first."

That didn't fill Yor with confidence so, unbeknownst to Mado, he was spending time alone in the storage room, working out some solutions of his own. One was using a planet near the red dwarf for a gravity assist to slingshot them toward the star with additional momentum, then slingshot around the star. Yor thought it might increase their chances of survival. To get it right and convince Mado, he was applying his math skills.

Mathematics was one of Yor's strong suits. As a child, his great-grandfather tutored him in math for children far older than himself and Yor enjoyed it so much that

     *Howard Libes*

it became a secret hobby. While his University mates were out losing their minds at Malrap parties, Yor was obsessed by SEEDER-program mathematical workbooks his father removed from the Vanderlord estate. The books contained equations the SEEDER pilots were required to memorize and master for their voyages in case their computing devices broke down. Back then, Yor rationalized this hidden passion as learning more about the SEEDER program. Lately, he wondered if his great-grandfather had plotted for him to acquire this skill all along in case he ever found himself in outer space.

Then one day, in the midst of a calculation for the second slingshot, Mado intercommed and asked Yor to join him in the control room. He said something important required his immediate attention. When Yor arrived, the holo-device had been activated and Mado was staring out the control-room window. The red dwarf was now the size of a fist in the distance. Mado had put on his prosthetics.

"Everything all right?" Yor said. "Sounded like something important so I hurried and you're wearing—"

"It is," Mado said, not turning around. "It is. Sorry if I worried you. I was thinking about our approach to the star and the way station."

"I've been giving it some thought, too."

"I hope you're not getting cold feet."

"No, nothing like that."

Mado spun around to face Yor. "That's good to hear. I want to discuss this topic with you at great length, but first we have to deal with a comm from Koda."

"Is my mother all right? You want to do this in the living chamber?"

"She's fine, but considering the nature of the transmission, we'll need to execute it here," Mado said, moving to his left and revealing Gols on the control-room viewing screen. Yor assumed it was a paused vid. Mado walked to the screen, flipped a switch below it and pointed at the screen.

Gols said, "Hello, Yor Vanderlord. I hope all is well with you and Mado Prevor as you receive this message…"

Gols looked directly at Yor and smiled at him, and Yor realized Mado had finally rigged a two-way transmission.

Gols continued, "…and your voyage has been a safe one so far. Life is well on Koda, but we have a developing situation here which I need to inform you about. This is something we didn't foresee happening so soon, but as we've learned, plans don't always unfold the way we draw them up. Well, not we but you, Mado Prevor."

Mado said, "We have a time limit on these transmissions, Gols. Get on with it."

"Seems that the Leader has grown uneasy and incensed with your absence and has requested your presence over and over to no avail, and that has escalated into him threatening an incursion on the Prevor Industries Complex. I'm fully aware that your evacuation plan is in place to deal with this problem, and that part of the plan was getting your approval to move forward with it…"

"Is there anything we can do to stop this?" Yor said to Mado, who put his finger to his lips and pointed at the screen to signal Yor should wait for Gols to finish his statement. Yor noticed Mado had placed the prosthetics on his hands, too.

Gols continued, "…so I would be coming for your approval, but apparently Mar Jeps has her own ideas and wishes to supersede yours. She is the current CEO and has the right to do so, and I'm under contract as a Prevor Industries employee so I'm supposed to follow her orders. Instead of evacuating and falling back to Shamba, she wishes to negotiate with the Leader in person and come to a more peaceful outcome."

"Is she crazy? She must be out of her mind," Yor said. "She can't negotiate with that madman."

Somebody grabbed the cam. It moved until it landed on the image of his mother who said, "Listen here, young man, don't talk about your mother that way. I'm in full possession of my faculties."

Yor was stunned when he heard his mother speaking to him live. "Mother! It's so good to see you. How are you?"

"I'm well for a woman who is out of her mind."

"I'm sorry. I thought this was just a transmission from Gols," Yor said. "Mado, how is this happening in real time with no delays when we're so far from Koda?"

Mado said, "I've been releasing FBBs from the WAEF at specific intervals along our path."

"FBBs?" Yor said.

"Frequency Booster Buoys," Mado said. "I developed them for Project FoFu and XAF-758 so ships could have two-way communication without delay no matter their distance from one another along a similar route. I was bringing them to Shamba as the first prototypes, but they ended up out here with us. As you can see, it turned out to be a great test-run."

"You're full of surprises, Mado," Yor said.

"Yes, he is," Yor's mother said.

"I'm so happy to actually talk to you."

"Me too, but Gols said we need to keep this relatively short for security purposes."

Mado said, "Correct. The frequency modulation will only fool the GSS for so long."

Offscreen, Gols said, "Yes. Before I forget, I wanted to tell you that Commander Warver has died."

"How?" Mado said. "He was one of the strongest men I ever met."

"Poisoned by the government."

"Vidor is pulling out all the stops, isn't he?" Mado said. "That's sad. Warver will be missed, but Kush Suron is highly capable."

Gols said, "Yes. Colonel Suron has confirmed through his sources that the military is drawing up simultaneous arrests of the Movement's leadership as well as the plans for attacking the Complex."

"Well, that's something," Mado said. "I trust you, Mar. I've put you in control of my corporation and Gols has sent me intermittent updates on projects and financial reports demonstrating the fantastic job you're doing, but please tell me about this plan of yours."

Yor's mother talked about Mado's plan then launched into her own, which sounded fairly dangerous since she was placing herself at risk of being arrested or killed.

Mado's plan was simply to run away, while his mother's plan was assaulting the problem head on. This didn't shock Yor. She and his father were kindred spirits in that way.

Yor said, "I don't understand. Why can't you just escape to Shamba?"

"If I might interject," Mado said, "This is a brilliant gambit."

"Why take the risk if there's a safer way to deal with it?" Yor said.

Yor's mother said, "There's Rajer, for one thing. He's locked up at the GSS and sure to be executed. I might be able to save him this way. Did you forget about him?" She was annoyed.

Yor was embarrassed. He hadn't considered Rajer in the context of the conversation. "I'm sorry, Mother. You're correct, but there has to be another way to save him."

Mado said, "By my calculations, there's a high probability your mother can pull this off. Saving the Complex will give us more time to pump units out of the Global Assembly project and build as many ships as we want in Shamba. As the domes draw closer to failing in the next fifty years and the stakes get higher for the Leader, we can probably get more units than before out of him, too."

"Fifty years?" Yor's mother said, then looked down to where Gols was sitting. "Maybe it's time to show me that report."

"I will get you a memory wafer with a copy after this comm ends."

Yor's mother said, "I'm glad I won't be around to experience the end of the domes. That'll be a disaster of major proportions."

"You might be around," Mado said. "Gols, please give her the memory wafer explaining the box in the safe, too."

"Yes, Mado Prevor."

Yor said, "So are we done discussing this dangerous plan?"

Both Mado and Yor's mother said, "Yes."

"Do I have any say in this?"

"Yor, I love you," Yor's mother said. "I understand you're concerned about me. Maybe now you understand how I felt when my baby put himself in front of the entire planet on Breeze Celebration and challenged the Global Assembly."

"I see you've made up your mind and I get it. I'm not happy about it, but I get it," Yor said. "I understand about Rajer. How is he, anyway?"

"Dealing with his incarceration better than I expected," Yor's mother said. "I saw him a while ago. He's pretty proud about saving your life and I think that's sustaining him. By the way, I've had interactions with Kodans who praise your speech and are saddened by your loss. Thought it'd be good for you to know."

"We've got to wrap this up," Mado said, "A few things, Mar. I'm sure the Leader will want to talk with me. Just tell him that's impossible because of how far the WAEF has taken me from Koda, but he can send me a one-way transmission if he so desires. I also have a few thoughts about your plan, but I will send you a one-way transmission in the next day or so when I've had a chance to think about it more."

"We have seconds left for the transmission to remain secure," Gols said.

Mado said, "Gols, keep up the good work. Mar, I'll communicate again soon." Then he swatted Yor's shoulder with the back of his hand and pointed to the screen. "Go on."

Yor said, "I love you and I miss you. I have so much to tell you. I wish we had more time."

Yor's mother wiped away the tears streaming down her face. "I love you, Yor. You be safe out there. I know Mado will take good care of you. I love you." She blew Yor a kiss and the transmission ended.

Mado placed his hand on Yor's shoulder. "I know that wasn't easy."

"Why did you agree to her plan?"

"You heard me explain why."

"I know what you said, but the risk is just too damn high. This is my mother's life."

"It's no riskier than what we did at Breeze Celebration. Your mother was correct about that," Mado said. "By the way, Gols sent me a one-way transmission before this one with information about a new GSS study. Kodans' doubts about the Global Assembly's campaign to suppress the truth of Yorlik's discovery is at an all-time high. That's good news, right?"

"Sure, but the government hasn't toppled yet, has it?"

"No, not yet," Mado said, removing his hand from Yor's shoulder. "Remember, you have to start thinking long-term."

"So there's nothing I can say to change your mind or my mother's on this?"

"You can send her a one-way transmission and attempt to change her mind if it makes you feel better," Mado said. "I have more good news. I may have figured out why the engine isn't starting, so I need to get back to it."

# MAR

Mar read the Global Assembly Corps of Engineers report on the structural integrity of the domes. It was sobering. A half-century of research and development, quadrillions of units spent, yet expert scrutiny deemed that the life-span of the domes was less than a hundred years, probably closer to fifty—which was nowhere near the thousand years they were supposed to last. Mar was saddened and angry when she thought of how Tetrick's assessment of the domes was completely on target, and he was murdered for it. Mar didn't know how Mado got his hands on this report, but she was grateful to be reading it before her meeting with the Leader. She intercommed Gols to come into her office.

Gols entered as he always did: out of breath as if he'd run a long way to get here when his office behind the reception desk was no more than ten meters away. Gols said, "What can I do for you, Mar Jeps?"

"I was wondering how Mado got this report."

"From the Leader himself," Gols said, standing in front of her desk now.

"From the Leader?" Mar said, surprised at Gols' response. "How did that happen?"

"Mado Prevor heard through his sources in the Corps, many of whom worked for him in building this complex and remained on the payroll as informants, that a rather damning report had been drawn up on the domes. He'd already been working on the blueprints for the spaceships, but this report gave him another reason to think it was the right time to propose the spaceship project to the Leader. When the Leader gave the go-ahead, Mado asked for a timeline on completion of the project and the Leader gave him the report."

"This'll be useful for our meeting."

"About that," Gols said, "We know the summit is nine days away, so I was thinking it might be constructive to practice your presentation and maybe send Mado a preview. He's dealt with the Leader before and understands how to get through to him."

"That's brilliant, Gols."

"Really? Thank you. Would now be a good time to learn about the box in the safe?"

"Yes, please," Mar said.

Gols walked over to the framed promotional poster and swung it aside. Mar opened the safe, then Gols reached in and removed the silver metal box with the orange ribbon on the lid. Mar had been curious about this box since the first time she saw it. She had already looked inside. She couldn't help herself. The top lifted off easily, but there was a translucent seal around the opening with a similar smaller size box and memory wafer inside. The contents were beyond her reach unless she wanted to break the seal, and she didn't go any further to be respectful of Mado's wishes.

Gols closed the safe, swung the poster back in place, and handed the box to Mar.

Mar said, "So what do I need to know before I open it?"

"I was told the vid on the memory wafer explains everything," Gols said. "Are you all set, then?"

"I thought there was more to it than that," Mar said. "I guess that's all for now."

"Then I'll leave you to it," Gols said and exited the room.

Mar opened the lid of the box and stared through the translucent seal. *What could be so important?* she thought.

The seal ran about seventy-five millimeters down from the top of the box, creating what Mar assumed was an airtight chamber inside. She attempted to pry the seal up by working an edge with her fingernail, but no luck there. She kept a knife in her desk drawer for when she ate midday meal here, so she used it to puncture the seal, then sliced through it along the width and two sides of the box and rolled back the seal to create an opening. The scent from inside was familiar, but she couldn't place it.

Mar spun around in her chair, then stood and inserted the wafer in the side of the viewing screen behind her desk. She was expecting the start-up screen to appear with Mado's image, but it was black. *Stranger and stranger*, Mar thought. She pressed the start button on the screen and seated herself.

The screen stayed black for a few moments longer, then an image appeared: a wall of books about four meters from the viewer's cam. She couldn't make out any book titles before a person's torso appeared wearing a white button-down shirt and an old-fashioned brown vest. The person groaned as he lowered himself into the seat before the viewer. It was Yorlik. He looked tired and not his vigorous self. This was at the start of his aging acceleration. This vid was taken in the Vanderlord estate library and she realized the scent in the box was one she associated with Yorlik.

Yorlik said, "Hello, Mar…" He paused and took a drink from a glass. She could tell the contents were Malrap.

Mar was overwhelmed with emotion. It was so good to see him, to hear his voice as if he were alive again. She wasn't too shocked, though, because he never went away in spirit.

"Well," Yorlik said, clearing his throat, "if our plan is going correctly, then I'm speaking to Mar. I imagine you're surprised to see me. I'd estimate it's probably a decade or two since I left this body behind. I'd have to say it served me well. I saw and experienced things few Kodans can ever dream of. Partially that's because of the Rejuv Serum and the contents of the small box before you. Go ahead and open it. I'll wait." He realized the irony of his statement, laughed, and reiterated, "I'll wait." He pointed at the viewer's cam to make sure Mar got the humor, too, then he took a deep breath, exhaled, and closed his eyes.

Mar opened the smaller box to reveal another translucent seal, although this one had a tab so she could easily peel it back. Inside was a device resembling a respirator mask with a palm-sized canister connected to the front about a hundred millimeters in circumference and fifty millimeters thick. She turned the device in her hand. There were two more canisters underneath it.

Mar looked back up at the screen as Yorlik continued, "You're probably wondering what you're looking at. The mask and the substance in the canister constitute the Rejuv Treatment which kept me alive during the latter part of my journey." He held up a device matching the one in her hand. "This isn't unlike the respirator masks on Koda today, except this is more of a combination inhaler and respirator. It's calibrated to deliver the substance and oxygen from the room around you in a precise mixture. In addition to this vid, on this wafer are instructions on how to use it most efficiently based on a person's height and weight, and how not to abuse it. You can download those instructions onto your viewer. Each canister used properly should keep you alive for eighty to a hundred years beyond your normal lifespan. If I'm correct and I'm speaking to you twenty years in the future, then you're the perfect age to start the treatment, which will literally halt your aging process. In addition to the instructions is a breakdown of exactly how the substance works on a cellular level, its chemical makeup, and how I developed it from the soil of a distant planet. As a med, I know you'll want to see that part of my research before you imbibe. The other canisters are for Yor and Tetrick.

"You're probably asking yourself why you'd want this gift," Yorlik said. "Mado and myself have estimated that it will take twenty-five to thirty-five years to develop and build enough spaceships before launching and another fifty years to reach the habitable planet. Of course, that's if everything goes as planned. This gift to you is a selfish one on my part. I truly believe that with your brilliance and no-nonsense approach to life, you're the one to lead the Kodan people to their glorious new home, and I'd like you to see it along with Tetrick and Yor. Mar, I can't even express in words how wondrous a place this new planet is."

Mar could clearly see Yorlik's eyes light up as he mentioned the planet.

"Of course, soon I'll no longer remember it. That's why I'm recording this vid now, because my memory of the discovery will be erased which saddens me, and it's a paradox if you think about it. Once my memory is erased, I will no longer possess that memory, so I won't be sad not to have it anymore, so is it realistic to be sad on this vid about not remembering the memory in the future? I'm sure this is all somewhat perplexing on your end. Kind of like time travel for you and me since I'm talking to you from the past and you're in the future, although I'm not alive anymore, I assume.

"Sorry, I digress," Yorlik said, then chuckled to himself. Mar recalled him doing that often, as if Yorlik was telling himself a joke. She assumed this quirk in his personality was a remnant of spending so many years by himself in space. "Where was I? Oh, yes. This Rejuv Treatment was a miraculous breakthrough for me. Not only did it allow me to discover the viable planet, but it brought me back to Koda to experience life with my family, to witness Yor being born and growing into a brilliant child, to spend time with my grandson and you, to put together a plan to save my people against the resistance of the government.

It gave me time I otherwise wouldn't have had. I can't go into the details of how I stumbled onto the chemistry for this treatment, that would take too long. Let's just say my initial findings were unexpected and miraculous. I feel like I'm rambling. My mind does that a little more than usual these days.

"So, apart from what I said earlier about my selfish reasons for giving you this gift, I truly want you to have it out of my love and respect for you. I realize you've resented me at times. My arrival certainly complicated your life. I've watched from afar as you've held this family together while you excelled as a med. I know I've foisted this responsibility on you. I suppose it was received unwillingly, but I love and respect you for taking it on, and if I know you, you're doing an incredible job.

"For what it's worth, I want you to know that my regard for you far exceeds most of the individuals I've met in the close to two hundred years I've existed. I don't know any other way to say it."

A person in the room said something. Mar couldn't make out what was said, but it sounded like Mado. Yorlik leaned away from the viewer's cam and said, "I think that's something you'll need to handle yourself, my friend."

Then Yorlik moved back to the viewer and said in the sincerest tone, "I don't have any more to say. I wish I could answer the questions you undoubtedly have, but you can always ask Mado and he'll most likely have the answers. I'm aware you've had reservations about him in…this past, but I hope that's changed by your present. Good luck with the future."

Yorlik blew a kiss, then reached forward and the screen went black. Mar sat there staring at the black screen. At first, she was in awe at experiencing Yorlik again. She was amazed at his ability to execute impactful plans that reached so far into the future.

Old feelings emerged, too. Yorlik assumed because she was partnered with Tetrick that she'd want to be part of the Vanderlords' compulsion to lead the planet out of the crisis. He never asked her when he was alive. Now, this vid confirmed that Yorlik had the expectation close to twenty years ago that she would be the person who ensured his plan's success. *He knew back then I had no desire to walk in the Vanderlords' shoes.*

*But here I am.* Mar wasn't angry. After everything she'd experienced since Breeze Celebration, her feelings of being put upon were in the past. She was honored at being selected by Yorlik for possibly the greatest role in Kodan history and she wouldn't shirk from the duty ahead of her. *My life has always been about saving lives, hasn't it?*

Mar removed the wafer from the viewing screen and placed it in the drawer of her desk. She would look through the specs and instructions later. She opened one of the canisters and ran her finger through the substance, then closed it. She manipulated the canister connected to the respirator mask and figured out how to remove it, then she intercommed Gols to return to her office.

Gols arrived and said, "I just received that promised one-way transmission from Mado Prevor." He handed her a memory wafer. "What can I do for you?"

"A few things," Mar said, holding up Yorlik's custom-made respirator mask. "I need this replicated precisely without taking it apart or altering the settings in any way. Is there one person in the Complex who has those skills? This needs to be done with the utmost discretion and secrecy."

"I can think of a handful," Gols said, taking the device from Mar. "But one in particular has all the skills."

"Make sure he knows—"

"She…"

"Make sure she knows she is required to do this on her own and I need the final product a few days before the summit. The existence of this project will be destroyed and erased upon completion. A sizable bonus will be paid to this person upon delivery equal to twenty-seven days' salary."

"The person I have in mind has her own lab and works by herself. She personally assisted Mado Prevor on a few of his own projects."

"Can we count on her to keep this secret?"

"Definitely," Gols said, turning the device in his hand, looking it over. "Can I ask what it is?"

"Better you don't know," Mar said. "Handle with extreme care."

"You sound more like Mado Prevor every day." Gols chuckled.

"Thanks, I think."

"You said you had a few things for me."

"Yes," Mar said. "Can you get me a small bag of topsoil for the house plant in my penthouse?"

"Don't we have somebody who takes care of that?"

"I'd like to care for it myself," Mar said. "And get the First Lady on the comm for me, please."

# Yor

Yor was seated on a crate in the storage room. He was taking a break from his calculations. He added to the tally marks on the wall. It was 105 days since Breeze Celebration. Yor began thinking about his mother and the danger she was courting in her meeting with the Leader when Mado entered and said, "We've got a problem."

Yor was immediately engaged. Not only because of Mado's statement, but also because he'd never seen him in such an agitated state. Mado had taken off his prosthetics again and his Prevorian nostrils flared as he breathed heavily. Yor rose and walked over to him.

"What's the matter?" Yor said, placing his hand on Mado's shoulder. He thought of his great-grandfather telling him tales of his days sailing as a child.

Mado's breathing calmed and his nostrils stopped flaring. "That was alert of you."

"Thanks. I like to think I'm a good listener and learn from it," Yor said. "Now, what's the problem?"

"I've figured out the malfunction in the inoperative engine."

"Can we fix it?"

"Let me show you and explain," Mado said and strode down the hallway toward the engine room. Yor followed.

In the middle of the engine room, tarps had been laid side by side and on top of them was the portion of engine

 *Howard Libes*

four that had been damaged, removed, and replaced. The shattered part was puzzled together, then connected to the other damaged parts to configure this portion of the engine as it was before the incident.

"Is this what you've been doing all day when you told me to take the day off?"

"Yes. I had an idea why we couldn't get the engine started even after we replaced the parts and the reactor was feeding it power," Mado said. "It was easy to see once I pieced it all together. Sometimes visualization doesn't work and you just need to see it for real."

Mado pointed down to a place where the faulty metal in the power coupling had shattered like glass when it was subjected to the heat of the engine running at close to full power.

Mado said, "We know the metal is flawed here. How does that explain the engine not working? Tell me what you see when you examine the coupling closer."

"You mean the missing pieces of metal?"

"Yes, and where did they go?"

"We figured they blew into space during the explosion."

"A bad assumption on our part," Mado said, walking down the length of the engine, "because if you look closely at the parts on either side of the coupling, the power converter, and the combustion chamber, and at the way the metal is damaged, there's two different incidents."

"The shudder."

"Exactly," Mado said in that tone of wonder Yor knew so well. "The engine did blow out the engine nozzle, but then something caused it to blow back on itself."

"It backfired," Yor said. "So what caused it?"

"Precisely."

"I have a feeling you're going to tell me," Yor said, "but I'll conjecture it has something to do with the shards of metal."

"You're correct." Mado pulled two shards out of his pocket and fit them into the gaps on the coupling. There were still three missing.

"Where did you find them? Go ahead, regale me," Yor said and chuckled.

"We know the explosion happened when the metal in the coupling shattered. For some reason, the metal was flawed in this one but not in the couplings in the other five engines, so we decided to replace all of the parts on this tarp with our spares."

"Almost our entire inventory of spares."

"Unfortunately," Mado said. "And still the engine won't start. Power is flowing from the reactor to the converter, so the problem had to be further down the engine."

"You didn't."

"I did. I put on my spacesuit and crawled down the engine tube toward the nozzle, and I found these fragments jammed into one of the power rotors so it wouldn't turn."

"No way we could've known that. All the engine rotors generate excess power for the core and the engines overall. We'd never notice the drop in power output from a rotor not turning without the engine firing," Yor said. "So the shards shot up the tube in the explosion and got caught in a rotor, but that still doesn't explain why the engine won't start or backfired."

"You're correct again, my boy," Mado said. "You know the exhaust hatch which opens and closes over the nozzle to keep any debris from space or a planet's atmosphere getting into the engine tube when the engines aren't firing?"

"Yes, of course."

"The hatch has a safety feature. The engines won't fire up with the hatch closed."

"A reasonable feature."

"The hatch was a silly idea in the first place. The engine should've been designed differently. I don't know what your great-grandfather was thinking. There is no—"

"That's probably something for another discussion."

"Sorry, I'm just frustrated it took me so long to figure this out."

"You were saying the hatch has something to do with the engine not starting?"

"Yes, correct," Mado said. "When the explosion happened, one of the fragments lodged under the hatch, triggering the release. That caused the hatch to slam shut, so part of the blast from the explosion backfired into the engine instead of shooting into space. I could see the fragment jammed under the hatch when I was in the tube."

"I assume the hatch won't open automatically."

"Correct. I've flipped the switch more than a few times."

"So why didn't you just crawl up the tube and remove it?"

"Think, Yor. There's the series of rotors in the tube between us and the hatch."

"Right. Can't you just take the rotors apart and crawl past them, remove the shard, then reassemble the rotors?"

"Removing the rotors would mean breaking the seal on the bolts holding the rotors in place. Those rotors are the originals. I have no way to replace the bolts or any other portion of the rotors if they break. We'll need all the energy the spinning rotors manufacture in the power-core for maximum thrust when we maneuver around the red dwarf," Mado said. "Your great-grandfather's interdependent systems were economical, but inefficient."

"So what's the solution?"

"Spacewalk."

Yor said, "You have your suit—what's the problem?"

"You'll have to make the walk and the repairs," Mado said. "I'll have to work up the engine to see if it fires and calibrate the power output from here while you're out there. That way, if there's other damage requiring a spacewalk, you'll already be there. It's just a test. I'm not going to push the engines while you're strapped to the ship's hull."

"Why can't you do the walk and I'll do the other stuff?" Yor said. "I've never performed a spacewalk before except in the HGD and that was maybe once or twice."

"Have you ever worked up the engines? One mistake might mean one broken part we can't replace," Mado said. "You can practice weightlessness in the docking-bay airlock where I can turn off the gravity. That'll take some getting used to, but we don't have much time before we have to maneuver around the red dwarf and the engines need to be shipshape by then."

"Shipshape?"

Mado laughed. "A term I learned from your great-grandfather."

After a few days' practice, Yor stepped into the docking-bay airlock for the spacewalk. He wore his great-grandfather's spacesuit with a pack strapped to his chest containing the driver to open the hatch manually, the driver to unscrew the bolts holding the housing around the hatch in place, and a folded-up extension arm to reach in and remove any shards lodged in the outer rotors.

Mado said, "Are you ready?"

Yor was facing Mado at the docking-bay control console. "As I'll ever be."

Mado reached down to the console and threw a switch.

The inner airlock door slid closed and although Yor could see Mado's mouth moving through the window in the door, he heard nothing. Mado pointed at his right forearm. That's when Yor finally comprehended how nervous he was—he'd forgotten to activate the comm inside his helmet. He reached over and pressed the comm button on the right forearm console of his spacesuit.

Yor said, "Sorry about that."

"It's all right. Take a deep breath, and don't forget to magnetize your boots and switch on your helmet lights when you're turned toward the outer door."

Yor did as he was told and, with his back to Mado, gave him a thumbs-up.

"You've got it, my boy. I have all the confidence in the universe in you."

Yor didn't know what to say so he held his thumb up higher.

Mado said, "Remember the tether is to your right. It's only about fifteen centimeters from the doorframe. Opening the outer door now. Good luck."

Yor focused on the view of space through the outer-door window to focus himself, then the door slid aside and the open doorway was filled with stars. He stood there frozen, staring out at the abyss he was about to step into.

Mado said, "How you doing?"

Yor moved toward the threshold, making sure his boots caught the metal beneath him, then peeked outside and down.

Mado said, "Remember what I told you. Your first reaction will be fear that you're going to fall, but there's no gravity. Can't happen. Erase that impulse from your mind."

"I can drift away, though."

"True, but that's why you have the boots and the tether."

Yor walked to the right and flipped open the tether compartment. He pushed his finger through the hook inside the compartment and pulled a few times. The tether wouldn't budge.

Yor said, "When was the last time you safety checked the tether?"

"Thirty, thirty-six years ago."

"That doesn't fill me with confidence."

"You'll be fine. You have your boots, too."

Yor yanked on the hook again and the yellow tether came free and unraveled. He clipped the hook onto his suit, then grasped the ladder rung to the left of the tether compartment with his right hand and pressed the button on his spacesuit console to demagnetize his boots.

"Here I go," Yor said, maneuvering so that he had both hands on the ladder rung with his feet on a rung below. "Pretty awesome."

"Once you get used to it, you'll long for it," Mado said.

"Tether is clear of the door."

"Closing outer door. Remember I'm here if you need me."

Yor climbed the ladder until he reached the walkway, then magnetized his boots and stood up on the hull of the WAEF. He gazed along the hull's walkway to the engines, mesmerized by the uncountable stars. Yor thought Mado might be right about this being habit-forming.

Mado said, "I know it's spectacular, but you only have so much oxygen in your tanks and we have no idea how long the repair will take."

"You have a point," Yor said and began moving step by step toward the engines. He changed tethers, connecting the first tether to a ring by the second one so it wouldn't retract, and continued on his way. Engine four was in the path of the walkway, which made Yor's chore a little easier.

When he reached the nozzle for engine four, he attempted to turn the hatch's emergency release with the driver, but the hatch wouldn't open so he unscrewed the bolts around the hatch's housing and placed them in the pack. When he lifted the housing off, Yor raised the hatch with his other hand and the shard that had jammed it shut floated up and out toward space. Yor positioned the housing inside the engine nozzle and grabbed the shard with his free hand, then put it in his pack. With the hatch removed, he could clearly see the release mechanism.

Yor waved at the nearest outer-hull vidcam. He knew Mado was watching his every move. "Mado?"

"Yes, Yor. I'm here."

"The release is broken."

"All right. Put the housing back on and bring in the hatch. We'll repair it at the way station," Mado said. "How about fragments in the rotors?"

Yor maneuvered his body into the nozzle, still holding on to the hatch. "I see the two pieces but can't reach them with the extension arm—they're lodged on the inner side of the outer rotor."

"Then you'll have to crawl into the tube and get them. You'll need to detach the tether and be careful removing the fragments—if the shards are caught in there and you pull too hard, you could puncture your suit's glove. Use the pliers at the end of the extension arm."

Yor placed the hatch beside the housing, clipped the tether onto the ship, and crawled into the tube. He carefully did as Mado suggested. When he climbed back up the tube and poked his head out of the nozzle, the sight before his eyes made him gasp.

Mado said, "Yor?"

"Did you see that?"

"What?"

"You didn't see it?" Yor said.

"No. What was it?"

"I'll explain when I get back inside."

Yor put the hatch housing back and took the hatch with him. He walked halfway down the hull, then connected to both tethers, strapping himself to the ship while Mado performed a successful engine run-up.

Later, Yor was in the living chamber eating a meal when Mado asked him what happened on the spacewalk that made him gasp.

Yor said, "When I was climbing out of the engine tube, directly in front of me, I saw a spaceship that wasn't of Kodan origin, paralleling our course and I assume traveling at the same velocity as the WAEF. This ship was maybe half the size of the WAEF or smaller. It was round at the bottom with a silver dome on top of it. The bottom was lit with a white light and rotating back and forth while the silver dome remained stationary.

"Then the dome swiveled, revealing a sort of control-room window, and I saw two pilots. They were alien, but they didn't look like you. They had large, bulbous grey heads, completely hairless. No visible ears or nose, a lipless mouth and their two eyes were large and black. The faces were expressionless. One of them held up their hand, which had three thin fingers coming out of the palm. Then the bottom portion of the ship began spinning with increasing speed in one direction, and there was a blinding flash of light and the ship disappeared. At first, I thought I might've been hallucinating from lack of oxygen in the old spacesuit, but the gauges read normal."

"You weren't," Mado said. "How did I miss them on the cam? I turned away for seconds to start the calibration on the engine while you were in the tube. How long were they there?"

"From the time I poked my head out of the tube, maybe twenty seconds," Yor said, drinking down an entire glass of water. "Hard to say. Could have been less. Have you ever seen anything like that ship before?"

"Not the ship, but I believe I've seen the life-form in a craft typical of early space flight when I was with your great-grandfather. It was a crash site. If it's them, they've obviously advanced since I saw that ship. We never really knew how old the crash was."

"Right, you told me about them. I didn't make the connection," Yor said. "What do you think they wanted?"

"Who knows? Saying hello. Getting a look at us. Hard to tell. The universe is vast, and this is the second time we've come across them, so I'd say it's not the last time we'll see them," Mado said. "But right now, we have more pressing problems. Engine four is back online but like the other engines, it can't achieve full power. And we've got to circumnavigate the red dwarf."

"About that," Yor said. "I've almost got those calculations ready for you."

# MAR

While they were trying on dresses, Mar and Flomina discussed designers and what looked best on Mar. When they finished making their selections, Flomina exited the dressing room saying she needed a breath of fresh air. Mar followed a while later and found her garments in a clothing bag at the front counter. The proprietor said Flomina had purchased the items and left. Mar was beside herself. Shopping was only meant to be a ruse—she'd set up the date with Flomina to discover the Leader's plans for Rajer and foster Flomina as an ally.

Now, Mar stood on the sidewalk outside the dress shop. Suron and another Prevor Industries guard stood on either side of her while she gazed up and down the block for Flomina. She'd never visited Oedor Place before. This was where the wealthiest Kodans shopped. Many lived nearby in mansions which they paid extra in taxes to possess since the domes went up. They were only charged the levy to assuage any sign of favoritism by the Global Assembly after the DOME riots, and for people of their wealth, the expense was a pittance. Although many of the shoppers lived within walking distance, the cruiser lot was packed with the newest high-end models on the market. Just the wealthy showing off their net worth to their peers.

Mar's comm buzzed. It was Flomina. She told Mar she was feeling faint and peckish, so had walked to a bistro a few blocks away. She asked Mar to meet her there, saying Mar couldn't miss the bistro because the Leader's cruiser was parked out front.

As Mar strolled down the street flanked by Suron and the other guard, she passed a few well-known people she'd seen on various tabloid shows. She watched those shows when she desired brainless viewing after a difficult shift at the clinic. Yor and Rajer used to give her grief about it and she shooed them away, but that felt like a million years ago and recalling it made her sad. She needed to pull herself together before she arrived at the bistro.

Flomina was correct. The Leader's cruiser was difficult to miss. It was a Global-Assembly-blue military-grade cruiser with blacked-out windows, twice the size of the one that rescued Mar. Anywhere else on Koda there would've been a crowd of people attempting to get a glimpse of the First Lady or the Leader inside the vehicle, but they weren't an item of curiosity here. The Kodans on this street lived in the same world as Flomina and she was an equal instead of a person to worship for their wealth or fame.

Two of the Leader's security detail stood outside of the bistro. Mar had seen one of them on her recent visit to the Plemso estate. She told Suron and the other guard to wait outside, too.

Inside the bistro, Mar's senses were overwhelmed with rich odors she hadn't experienced in years. Her normal fare as a dome dweller was processed protein meals. They came in different flavors and brands, but when they were heated they all had the same nondescript scent. Here, she could tell right away she was smelling food raised for consumption or grown in the ground.

A hostess in her early twenties greeted Mar with exuberance and a broad smile. She was dressed in a fashionable light-green coverall outfit with cutouts in places, revealing her bare skin. The personal shopper had shown Mar this dress for her recent dinner at the Plemso estate. The cost far exceeded a restaurant worker's salary, but the establishment had probably bought it for the hostess. The garment fit her curves well. It was definitely a dress for a younger woman.

"The First Lady is waiting for you, Mar Jeps," the hostess said.

Mar wasn't surprised she was recognized. She had appeared on *The Lure* last night.

"Please follow me," the hostess said and turned on her heels. The back of the coveralls was cut away from her waist to her neck, revealing much of her bare back. As they passed through the bistro, Mar noted only half of the tables were occupied, but the empty tables were all set with white tablecloths, pink fabric napkins, metallic utensils, and yellow porcelain plates. Each table was decorated with a different-colored blossom in a clear vase filled with water as a centerpiece. The scent of cooking food grew stronger as she moved further into the building and Mar could hear the racket of the kitchen.

Flomina was seated in a back-corner booth, and she smiled and waved when she spotted Mar. Two security guards stood on either side of the table. Flomina scooted out of the booth. She was wearing one of the signature sundresses from her clothing line. Mar reflected on how Flomina had spent a great deal of her life training to appear beautiful. This time was no exception. She hugged Mar, smelling of a perfume emulating an exotic blossom.

Flomina said, "Sorry about this back booth. I'd rather sit by a window, but I'm condemned by the need for security." Flomina waved her arm at one of the guards.

"This is fine," Mar said. "Better to be safe."

"Although what's life without a little danger?" Flomina said and chuckled.

Mar thought of her life since Breeze Celebration and forced a laugh.

Flomina said, "Shall we sit?" She snapped her fingers at the hostess who scurried off. "I ordered you Eglew juice. I recalled how much you like it."

"It's a little early for Eglew juice," Mar said, "but I'm taking the day off from work, so why not?"

"That's the spirit. Let the fun begin," Flomina said, sliding into the booth as Mar sat at the place setting across from her.

"So glad you could make it," Flomina said. "Where is that waiter? I told him you were on your way."

"That's all right," Mar said. "I'm not in any rush." She lifted the decanter to pour herself Eglew juice.

"No, don't," Flomina said, a tone of annoyance in her voice. "That waiter isn't going to get a tip at this rate." Then, to one of the security guards, she said, "Go find that waiter, will you?"

The guard headed toward the kitchen without hesitation.

Flomina said, "My father always stated, 'You can't let the help forget they work for you.' I'm sure your father had sayings like that, too,"

"No, not really. We weren't affluent enough to afford help."

"I'm sorry—that must've been rough," Flomina said with pity in her voice.

"No, we made do."

"So brave. What did your father do for a living?"

"When I was growing up, he was a foreman in a plant manufacturing stun weapons. He started there right out of secondary school and worked his way up from the assembly line to foreman over twenty years."

"And look at you—a successful med and now head of a powerful corporation. They must be proud."

"We don't speak much."

"Oh, they're not in a dome?"

"They are," Mar said, "but the political views of my ex-partner created a rift between us that never healed."

"That's too bad," Flomina said as the waiter arrived with the guard towering over him.

The waiter was a young man, maybe in his early twenties like the hostess, with short-cropped blond hair. He wore a light-green suit. He looked scared.

"Where have you been, young man?" Flomina said. "Do you like your job?"

"Yes, First Lady."

"Then do it," Flomina said, pointing to Mar's empty glass.

The waiter's hand was shaking as he poured the Eglew juice and he spilled some on the white tablecloth. "I'll get that mopped up immediately," the waiter said, then, still holding the decanter, he turned to Flomina. "Would you like some?"

"I asked you for something else," Flomina said. "Do you remember?"

"Yes, yes, sparkling water. I was getting it when your man brought me back here."

"Are you blaming my guard? Were you heading to the market to get it?"

The waiter giggled nervously. "No."

"I specifically asked for Norian Sparkling Water."

Mar was aware of the scarcity of this brand. It hadn't been produced in at least fifteen years since catastrophic flooding wiped out the Norian coastline.

"Yes, First Lady. Right away," the waiter said. "Anything else?"

"No, go do your job," Flomina said and pointed in the direction of the kitchen.

The waiter walked a few steps until he was clear of the table, then ran toward the kitchen.

Flomina said, "Where were we?"

"I was saying—"

"You were talking about your poor parents and your ex-partner."

"Yes, they—"

"Partnering can be so difficult. I gave up a lucrative and fun-filled life of my own to be with Vidor. I have to admit, he did bewitch me with his personality—his confidence and charm—and other things, if you know what I mean," Flomina said, blushing. "My father warned me about Vidor. He warned me that once the novelty wore off, I'd see Vidor for who he truly was and I might not like it."

"Really."

"Yes," Flomina said. "My father was good friends with Vidor's father and watched Vidor grow up. Of course, I didn't listen. I'd become successful in my own right at a young age and thought I knew everything."

"If it's not too personal," Mar said, "what did he warn you about?"

"Vidor's narcissism and temper. The man is a bully," Flomina said, peering outside the booth. "This waiter is incompetent."

"Narcissism?"

"Oh, come now, Mar," Flomina said. "You're a med. I'm sure you've noticed my partner's narcissistic tendencies, but I can live with them. We don't spend that much time together except for Global Assembly events where I need to make an appearance. I'm usually busy apart from him, still running my own business and taking care of the boys, who are my greatest concern and joy."

"That's about the size of being a parent."

"That's the truth, isn't it?" Flomina said.

The waiter appeared holding a bottle of Norian Sparkling Water and a glass. "Sorry it took so long. Nobody orders this anymore, and the inventory was difficult to find in the pantry."

"Spare me the excuses," Flomina said.

The waiter froze in fear.

"Are you going to stand there or pour the water?"

The waiter snapped out of his daze, then pulled the cork and poured a small quantity into the glass he'd brought with him. The carbonation from the water floated through the air like a drizzle and Mar could taste the sugary spice of the water on her lips.

He handed the glass to Flomina, who barely let the liquid touch her lips. "I love it. A shame it's so rare." She held the glass out for the waiter to fill it.

When he was done, he said, "Would you like me to put it on ice or leave the bottle here?"

"If you knew your job, you would have brought the ice bucket with you. Just leave it," Flomina said and the waiter placed the bottle in front of her. "Is our order ready yet?"

"It should be out shortly."

"Well, get to it, then," Flomina said, clapping her hands together. "We don't have all day." The waiter ran off.

Flomina held up her glass. "Here's to a successful shopping adventure."

"And good company," Mar said, holding up her glass and joining Flomina in the toast.

"That flavor takes me back," Flomina said, looking at her glass. "As a child, we drank this at dinner almost every night. I haven't seen it in years, but when I noticed it on the menu, I couldn't help myself although the cost was outrageous. I guess that's what we get for this crisis."

"Yes, this juice connects me to my childhood, too."

"Funny how that works."

"You mentioned the menu," Mar said, looking around the table. "You ordered already? I probably should do that."

"Oh, I'm sorry, I ordered a few different dishes for the both of us while I was waiting for you. No need to concern yourself. I know you'll love them," Flomina said, then sipped at her water. She giggled and pinched her nose as the bubbles tickled it. "Where was I?"

"You were—"

"Yes, the boys, they are the light of my life and they make living with Vidor tolerable," Flomina said. "I'm sorry. That's a horrible thing to say. This is between you and me, right?"

"Of course," Mar said, taking a sip of her juice.

"I worry about his narcissism rubbing off on the boys. I can see it developing in my older one, Carz. The younger one is a darling. He's more like me. He's my baby. Well, who am I kidding—they're both my babies. I only wanted one child, but Vidor wanted two and now I'm glad I surrendered to his demand. I can't see living without my little one," Flomina said, taking another sip of the water. "I can't imagine how those boys might turn out if I wasn't around. Vidor acts like an animal trainer more than a father. I hear that's how his father treated him, which is why he acts the way he does. I try to get him to be more affectionate, but it doesn't come easily to him. He's constantly pushing them to study and do better at everything, which isn't bad in itself, but they need to play, too. Don't you agree?"

"Absolutely, Yor was always—"

"I knew you'd agree. Men like Vidor never under-stand that children need to be children. It isn't all about molding a boy into a hardened man. You know who understood that?" Flomina said, pointing at Mar, then went silent.

Mar had no idea. "Who?"

"Guess," Flomina said, peering outside the booth again for the waiter, shaking her head, then refilling her glass with sparkling water. "Would you like some?" Flomina held the bottle out toward her.

Mar searched the table for an unused glass. "I don't have a clean glass."

"Where is that waiter?" Flomina said, annoyed again.

"I don't want to make a fuss. It's not a big deal."

Flomina turned to the guard and said, "Go!" Then she said to Mar, "You should get what you want. That's what a place like this is all about and that's what we're here for."

A moment later, Mar heard the sound of footsteps running toward them. The waiter looked harried with the guard directly behind him. He was holding an empty glass wrapped in a cloth napkin. He picked up the bottle of sparkling water and began pouring.

"Half is fine," Mar said.

"Nonsense. Get your fill," Flomina said.

The waiter topped off the glass, then placed the bottle in the middle of the table and the glass in front of Mar.

Flomina said, "You only thought to bring one? Maybe I want some Eglew juice."

"I can go back and get—"

"Not necessary at this point," Flomina said with irritation in her voice. "How many tables are you working? This place isn't even close to capacity."

"I have—"

"I don't care. Just do your job. How close is our order to being ready?"

"Almost done."

"See to it, then. Go on." Flomina shook her head and mumbled under her breath, "Someone won't have a job at the end of the day."

She didn't mean for Mar to hear it, and Mar didn't say anything about it.

"So," Mar said, "who is this person who thinks children should be children?"

"Oh, yes. I was referring to your Mado Prevor," Flomina said. "Aren't you going to try your water?"

Mar picked up the glass and took a sip. The bubbles tickled her nose and the water completely quenched her thirst, cleansing her palate of the juice and leaving behind an aftertaste of sugary spice. "Whoa! That is better than I would've imagined. First time I've tasted it."

"Isn't it wonderful?" Flomina said. "I'm glad I could give you the opportunity. I hear there might be a hundred bottles left in the hands of collectors. I should hint to Vidor that this might be a good present for me…But yes, Mado Prevor always brought the boys the newest version of that toy you manufacture."

"HGD?"

"Yes, they love that thing. Vidor hates it. Mado attempted to explain the educational aspects of it, but Vidor made his mind up and that's that with him,"

Flomina said. "The boys adore Mado. Call him Uncle Mado."

"That's sweet."

"They adore him, and he helped us out quite a bit with the estate," Flomina said. "Although if I hear Mado's name around the estate one more time, I may have to strangle Vidor."

"What do you mean?"

"You don't know?" Flomina said. "Vidor is simply obsessed with finding Mado's whereabouts. He has men scouring the planet searching for him."

"I was aware he wanted to find him, but I had no idea of the extent—"

"Oh, my—it's Mado, Mado, Mado around the estate when Vidor is home, because Vidor feels betrayed. It's talk at the dinner table, at bedtime, in the morning when we wake up, and anytime in between. At one point, I threatened to take the boys and stay with my parents if he didn't tone it down."

"Again, I had no—"

"You don't know where he is, do you?" Flomina said, leaning toward Mar. "Do you?" There was a tone of desperation in her voice, although Mar saw through her poor acting and realized the Leader had put her up to asking her about Mado. That might have been why Flomina agreed to meet her for this outing.

"No," Mar said, picking up her glass of juice and taking a sip. "Mado left the corporation and doesn't want to be disturbed. He hasn't made his location known to anyone."

"I notice you have a nice tan," Flomina said. "Have you been traveling?"

Mar was sure now that Flomina was probing for a location. This was the Leader's doing. "I've been outside the dome, traveling for the Relief Foundation."

"Sorry, I'm being nosy," Flomina said. "You're a busy woman."

"Yes, I don't get much sleep."

"But if you knew where Mado was you'd tell me, right?"

"Of course," Mar said. "Let me ask you a question, if you don't mind?"

"No, please, I've probably said enough," Flomina said and chuckled. "Vidor chastises me all the time for going off at the mouth so please, go right ahead."

"Does the Leader ever talk about my partner?"

"Your partner…oh, the one who jumped that woman at Breeze Celebration to stop her from shooting your son?"

"Yes, he's in a GSS cell and I was wondering if the Leader ever mentions granting him clemency."

"Not a word. Nothing I can recall, anyway."

"If you hear anything, would you let me know?"

"I don't usually get involved in Vidor's affairs."

"Well, if you could put a word in—"

"Finally!"

The waiter appeared with another behind him. They were both carrying trays laden with three dishes apiece beneath domed metal covers.

Mar said, "How much did you order?"

"A little bit of everything. What we don't eat, the guards can take. I'm famished, though."

The waiters placed the dishes on the table and uncovered them with a flourish. Half the plates were full of various meats including one winged creature. The other dishes were organically grown substances, fried or in sauces. Mar was familiar with many of these dishes but hadn't seen them in years. She'd thought the dinner at the Plemso estate was lavish, but she recognized the head of a nearly extinct creature at the center of a meat tray. The rich scent and presentation of the entire assortment was overwhelming to Mar's senses. Her mouth watered.

Flomina said, "What do you think?"

"I don't know what to say."

"Do I know how to order, or do I know how to order?" Flomina said, pleased with herself. The waiters stood beside the table, one of them holding a fork and knife for the meats and the other a fork and spoon for the rest of the dishes.

"I don't know how I'll fit into those dresses after this."

"Oh, you'll make do," Flomina said. "Tell them what you want. Don't let it get cold!"

# Vidor

Earlier in the evening, Vidor started watching a recording of yesterday's edition of *The Lure* in his study. He thought it would be a good way to relax at home, but as the opening credits rolled, he saw Mar Jeps was a guest, appearing as CEO of Prevor Industries. Paresh asked her when Mado Prevor would take charge again.

Mar Jeps said, "Mado Prevor won't be back for a while."

Paresh said, "What do you mean by 'a while'?"

"I don't see it happening in the foreseeable future," Mar said and chuckled.

Paresh said, "He is quite the act to follow. Does that concern you?"

"No, Paresh," Mar Jeps said. "I have confidence in myself and the people who work for me." Paresh asked her why Mado Prevor left and she told him that his sabbatical was precipitated by the death of her son, after which Mado needed to sort some things out. Paresh attempted to broach the subject of her son and Breeze Celebration, but Mar Jeps said she'd rather return another time and discuss it. For the rest of her spot, she promoted the HGD upgrade about to hit the market and new products in development.

Vidor turned off the viewing screen. He acknowledged the true intent behind this appearance. Mar Jeps had confirmed that she was the woman in charge of Prevor Industries, laying the foundation for her imporance in Kodan society in case she was arrested by the Global Assembly. Her finger was on the switch for powering the domes and now everybody on the planet knew it. Her disappearance would create panic.

Vidor's mood became foul. He decided to stay at his desk, sip Malrap, and read the Supreme Commander's troop readiness report. He hoped this would cheer him up, but it didn't.

Vidor managed to lift his spirits by reminding himself that in five days, Mar Jeps would arrive here to persuade him not to invade Prevor Industries, but instead the Global Guards would arrest her in front of him. She'd never know what hit her. He smiled at the scene unfolding in his mind's eye and was confident he would figure out a way around her latest move on *The Lure*.

There was a knock on the door and Vidor closed his viewer. He glanced at his suit jacket, which was on the back of an armchair, but he didn't feel it was necessary for this meeting.

"Come in," Vidor said.

Joro Camtur entered. He had aged since the last time Vidor saw him. Joro's hair appeared to be thinning and his paunch was bulging a little more than usual. Joro was younger than Vidor, but Vidor was always in better shape due to his military training. He still ran in the mornings and as Vidor's father used to say, "There's nothing like good genes." Vidor always felt like he'd got a good draw in that regard.

"Come in," Vidor said again, "and close the door behind you."

Joro smiled and slid the door closed. "Strange being here when it's not full of people. Got your comm a while back—sorry it's taken so long to get here," Joro said. "How are you?"

"Things have been crazy," Vidor said. He rose from his desk chair and grabbed the carafe of Malrap, his half-full goblet from the desk, and an empty one for Joro. "Please have a seat."

"Being in this study always takes me back."

"You always say that," Vidor said, placing the carafe and glasses on the low table. He seated himself in the armchair across from Joro, then filled both goblets.

"Whoa!" Joro said. "I really shouldn't. My med told me to cut back on the Malrap."

"Just tell him it was an order from the Leader."

"All right," Joro said, chuckling. "Maybe I'll have some. You only live once."

"That's what they tell me," Vidor said, handing the goblet to Joro.

Joro took a small sip. "Ah! That's some fine Malrap."

"Yorlik had good taste. He was a worthy adversary too."

"I thought you despised the man."

"I definitely did although a soldier can admire his enemy. As you've noted, I drink his Malrap. I've surrounded myself with his library," Vidor said, then holding his arms out wide.

"He did like the finer things in life."

"That's undeniable," Vidor said. "Then I impulsively surrounded myself by you and Mado Prevor."

"Again, the finer things," Joro said and chuckled.

Vidor didn't laugh. He leaned back in his armchair and drank down half his Malrap while staring at Joro the entire time. "I wasn't joking."

"Am I missing something?" Joro said, taking a larger swig of his Malrap.

"Without a doubt."

"Please fill me in. Anything I can do to help."

"I've heard that line many times from you over the years," Vidor said, placing his goblet down on the table and topping it off.

"Have I disappointed?"

"You've always made good on your promises, and I have to admit that you're one of the reasons I am where I am today," Vidor said. "But it seems rather convenient."

"Convenient? I'm not sure I understand."

"Or maybe you do and you're smarter than I've given you credit for."

"Again, I—"

"Mado Prevor. This has to do with Mado Prevor," Vidor said, raising his voice. "He has seemingly disappeared after his prodigy defamed my administration in front of the entire planet and flew off."

"And you've dealt with Yor Vanderlord."

"Indeed, but Mado Prevor is nowhere to be found to answer for Vanderlord's treason, and he had the nerve to transmit a message threatening the Global Assembly and dictating how I should rule."

"I'm shocked. I didn't know. I don't know what to say."

"I want answers, Joro. You brought that man—Vanderlord's prodigy—into my life. I took him into my home and I trusted him, and this is how he repays me, how you repay me?" Vidor said, feeling his temper rising. "I want answers. The GSS has been searching for him, but he appears to have vanished off the face of Koda. Only one clue hasn't been examined thoroughly, because I told them I'd take care of it myself. Do you know how I intend to take care of it?"

"I don't, but I have a feeling you're going to tell me."

"Damn right," Vidor said, picking up his goblet and drinking down the entire contents in one gulp, then smacking the goblet down on the table so hard that a crack formed up the goblet's side. "Bringing you here is me taking care of it myself, and you should be thanking me. Some of my most accomplished GSS interrogators want a crack at you, but I told them, 'Joro is an old friend. He's been by at my side for decades, supporting me. I can't believe Joro of all people would do anything to undermine me.'

"You know what they said? They said, 'That's why he's so dangerous. He's spent years cultivating your trust, just like Mado Prevor, so when the opportune moment presented itself, he could strike the most harmful blow to you and the Global Assembly.' I argued with them. I couldn't believe it. Then they showed me the evidence," Vidor said. "I told them, if that's true, then I deserve an explanation in person."

Vidor picked up his goblet, noted the crack, and threw it against the wall directly behind Joro who raised his arms over his head to shield himself from the shattered glass raining to the floor. Then he stood up and fetched a clean goblet from the cabinet behind his desk. "Where were we?"

"You were going to ask me something regarding Mado Prevor. About some evidence that involves me."

"Right," Vidor said. He sat down, filled his new goblet to the top and took a healthy swig. "Right, so…" Vidor had lost his train of thought again. He probably shouldn't have been hitting the Malrap so hard before his appointment with Joro.

"You said Mado has disappeared from Koda," Joro said. "That sounds unlikely."

"That's exactly what I've been telling my people," Vidor said, raising his voice again and draining the rest of the Malrap in his goblet. Vidor thought, *That's my last one.*

"How could he have disappeared off the face of the planet?"

"One of my men believes he was on the WAEF with the Vanderlord boy when it took off and now…"

With his mind soaking in Malrap, Vidor contemplated telling Joro that the shooting down of the WAEF was a fabricated incident, and about Orn's theory that Mado was in outer space with the Vanderlord boy. He stopped himself short. Then he noticed Joro sitting there observing him and smiling. Vidor searched his mind for the last thing Joro said to him. He couldn't recall so he decided to take a different angle on the conversation.

"So I was shown the vid."

"What vid?"

"There is a vid of you and Mado discussing something before he boarded the WAEF on its way to the Arena. Aside from Yor Vanderlord, you were the last person to speak with Mado before he disappeared."

"Can I see the vid?"

"I have it somewhere on my viewer, but you don't need to see it to tell me what you discussed with Mado."

"We talked about the setup for the WAEF at the Arena. You're aware Mado requested the ramp—he wanted to make sure the arrangements were finalized."

"Yes, the ramp, the setup," Vidor said, attempting to collect his thoughts. "That was one of the things the GSS wanted to bring you in to discuss."

"Why?"

"They said there was no reason for the ramp unless Vanderlord knew ahead of time he was going to launch from the Arena after his speech. That you were aware of Vanderlord's Breeze Celebration plans and conspired with him along with Mado."

"All I know is what I was told to do. I had no knowledge of any scheme. Mado requested the staging and I complied, but I wasn't complicit in whatever he was planning."

"Don't confuse the issue with fancy legal mumbo jumbo, Joro. This is serious business."

"I understand." Joro took a few deep breaths through his nose and exhaled. He was starting to sweat. "Mado asked me to set up the staging a certain way, and as a Breeze Celebration organizer in charge of this specific detail, I made it happen. Nobody above me complained and the staging was built. There's nothing more to it."

"That's where you're wrong. There's more," Vidor said, picking up the empty goblet and tapping it on the arm of his chair. "GSS's lipreading experts translated your conversation with Mado." Joro's eyes moved back and forth from Vidor's face to the goblet he was tapping on the chair. Vidor thought he saw concern in Joro's eyes.

"And what did they discover?" Joro said, shifting in his seat.

"Am I making you uncomfortable?" Vidor said. "Why don't you tell me?"

"Hard to recall exactly."

"Come on, Joro," Vidor said, tossing his goblet directly at Joro who reached out and caught it with one hand. "You've always been one of the sharpest minds in the room. I remember you telling stories in graphic detail about events that happened years ago, so I'm not buying you failing to recall a recent conversation. You can either tell me or I can have the GSS pick you up and neither of us want that. I'm fond of you, Joro, and you know they won't be as nice as me."

"I appreciate that," Joro said, shifting in his seat again. "We talked about whether the ramp was ready, of course."

"Of course."

"I told Mado about the GSS agent who visited me, and that the man was kind of scary. I told him how the agent questioned me about the perimeter around the ship and didn't believe me about the radiation problem. Then I told Mado how the agent asked about the ramp and didn't buy that it was just theatrics," Joro said. "I asked Mado about Yor and he told me Yor was waiting for him aboard the WAEF. I complimented him on the restoration, how it was a long time coming and how it was a fantastic thing for my grandchildren."

"Sounds like you recall an awful lot. Can I have that?" Vidor said and pointed to the goblet in Joro's hand. Joro looked down at his hand as if he'd forgot the goblet was there, then tossed it in Vidor's direction. In his Malrap-addled state, Vidor didn't come close to catching it, swiping at the air, but it landed in his lap. "That story sounds about right."

"It not a story. It's the truth."

"I still think you know more than you're saying."

"I know your goblet's empty."

"I think I've reached my limit."

"So," Joro said, "it's been rough around the office since Breeze Celebration?"

"You don't know the half of it."

"I'd love to hear all about it, but it'll have to wait for another time," Joro said. "My son dropped me off and he should be arriving to pick me up right about now."

"So soon?"

Joro stood and slugged down the remainder of his Malrap, placing the goblet on the low table. "By the way, I know there was no vid of my conversation with Mado. Part of me understands you felt like you had to use that trick to ensure I gave you an honest answer. Another part of me is rather hurt that you thought you had to use it because you couldn't trust me to tell the truth."

Vidor stood and approached Joro.

Joro took another deep breath, then broke out into a cough he was unable to control. He placed his hand over his mouth and struggled to catch his breath, then began choking. He put his other hand on Vidor's shoulder and leaned on him.

Joro continued gasping for air and removed his hand from his mouth, noticing his fingers and palm were covered in blood. Vidor could see dread in Joro's eyes and placed his face closer to Joro's.

"You're right, Joro. Being betrayed hurts," Vidor said and swatted Joro's hand off his shoulder.

Joro fell to the floor and writhed there, choking until he stopped breathing and he was dead. Blood from his mouth was soaking into the carpet. Vidor would have to clean the carpet now. He kicked Joro's corpse. He searched Joro for his comm and deactivated it, then carefully broke Joro's goblet on the low table, throwing the shards in the trash.

While pouring another goblet of Malrap, Vidor told himself, "Orn really needs to work on that poison. It always settles to the bottom of the glass."

A few moments later, there was a knock at the door. He could tell it was Flomina.

Vidor examined himself to make sure he had no blood on his clothes, then he opened the door.

Flomina stood on the other side.

Vidor held the door open long enough for Flomina to see the body on the floor, then he exited the study, shut the door behind him, and locked it.

Flomina said, "Who is that?"

"None of your business," Vidor said, sipping from his goblet.

Flomina slapped him across the face. "This is my home, too."

"Yes, as you constantly remind me, but one of us has to liven the place up."

"You're an animal." Flomina slapped Vidor across the face again.

Vidor was stung by that one. "What of it?" Vidor said, stepping toward Flomina and wrapping an arm around her, then pulling her against him.

They kissed passionately.

Flomina grabbed his ass with both hands while they kissed, then pulled out of his grasp.

Vidor was aroused.

Flomina said, "Are you drunk again?"

"Yes, I've been a bad boy."

Flomina embraced Vidor, kissed him softly on the cheek, and whispered in his ear, "Poor baby."

Vidor embraced her back and bit her ear. She moaned. Vidor said, "I need to be punished."

"Do you?"

"I do."

Flomina bit Vidor's shoulder, breaking the skin. He needed her now. They released each other from their embrace and stepped apart.

Flomina said, "By the way, I had my date with Mar Jeps. She may know where Mado is but she's not saying, and I bought dresses and charged them to your personal account."

Vidor said, "You'll pay for that."

"I'm counting on it, but you'll be useless to me if you get any more drunk." Flomina snatched the goblet from Vidor's hand and slugged down the contents. She placed the goblet on the floor by the study door, then took hold of Vidor's hand. "Now, come to bed."

# MAR

Mar sat on the Vanderlord estate patio chair, gazing out at the lit cityscape sparkling in the distance. The summit with the Leader was in two days and she'd begun doubting the events she'd set into motion.

There was a knock at the terrace door. Mar didn't need to turn around. She'd asked Suron to meet her and left the apartment door open for him.

"Come on out," Mar said.

Suron walked up to the railing, taking in the view of the city. "I can see why you like it out here."

She surmised Suron had come from training for the summit. He was wearing his workout clothes: combat boots, dark-blue pants, and a tight dark-blue formfitting pullover with the Prevor Industries logo on the right side of his chest. He smelled of sweat. The more they worked together, the more he reminded her of a younger version of Warver. Not only in his loyalty to the corporation and his disdain for the Global Assembly, but also the way he listened to Mar's thoughts and freely disagreed with them. That last quality was one she required most often these days.

Mar rose and joined Suron at the railing. He was observing the city like a lookout, scanning the horizon. Always vigilant. She thought at first it must be exhausting, but as she became further acquainted with him, she understood this was second nature.

"See anything coming our way?" Mar said to break the silence.

Suron turned toward her. He was clean-shaven with short-cropped hair, as always. Ready for inspection. "You look tired," Suron said.

"Just what every girl wants to hear," Mar said. "It's true, though. I've been sleeping less and less these days. As you know, I've got things on my mind."

"I'm well aware," Suron said, turning to look out at the cityscape again. Mar watched him as he spotted cruisers heading in their direction, then veering off.

"When you escorted me to meet with the First Lady, you said you hadn't seen Mado's latest transmission and read my digi-mail about the plan for the summit. I was wondering if you've had a chance yet. We're coming up on the date."

"Yes, I did. Sorry I didn't get back to you earlier about them, I've been preoccupied practicing with my men," Suron said. "When I received your comm asking to meet this evening, I went through them again."

"I'd like to know your opinion of how it all looks."

Suron turned toward Mar and took a step forward, towering over her. "Permission to speak freely?"

"Of course."

"As I've mentioned before, I served under Vidor for many years, and although your plan has merit and is tactically sound, I don't believe you completely understand the vicious, egotistical individual you're facing."

"Yes, you've mentioned that before," Mar said. "I think I have some idea, but you're saying you're concerned for my safety?"

"That's my job."

"Is it? I didn't have a clue."

Suron remained stony-faced, showing no sign he realized Mar was kidding.

Mar said, "Is there any way you think the plan could be better?"

"It's kind of a quandary."

"How so?"

"I completely understand why this is the alternative to running away, but losing you would be a horrible blow to this corporation and the future of the Kodan species. Gols would do a competent job, but he lacks the ability to think creatively, which is what you've done the entire time you've been here and what you're doing with this plan."

"I appreciate it, but running away isn't an option anymore, so what can you suggest to make the plan better?"

"I like it, but part of me wants to bring more men and overwhelm whatever Vidor has in store for us. Another part of me thinks going with the small, quick unit we discussed earlier is best. I've been working with my men on both scenarios, assuming we'd have this conversation."

Mar said, "Warver told me to trust my instincts. What do your instincts say?"

"Yes, he always told me that, too."

"So?"

"Go with the smaller force," Suron said. "Vidor will assume you're just coming with me. He'll underestimate you. No offense."

"None taken. In this case, in many respects, it's to our advantage."

"So, if he brings any Global Guards, it'll only be a handful," Suron said, "I'll focus on the smaller force in the time I have left."

"I already told Flomina we were bringing a small security contingent so she'll be expecting it," Mar said, taking a few steps back from Suron and looking out at the view. "Do you like Mado's idea of a planetwide diversionary tactic?"

"Very much so," Suron said. "It's smart and I wouldn't expect anything less from him. I assume you've moved forward with it as you noted in your digi-mail."

"I have," Mar said. "Gols is also helping me put something together that might be a game changer in my negotiations with the Leader. Something to tip him toward agreeing to our terms and putting us in a stronger position in the future if he reneges in any way."

"Can you tell me what it is?"

"Not sure if I'll get it together in time. The tech is having some issues with it," Mar said. "It won't have any impact on your job whether it succeeds or fails. It's just a little something to appeal to the Leader's vanity and his desire to stay in power for as long as possible."

"If you don't think it will affect the security detail, then I don't need to know any more, and if you think it'll play on Vidor's ego, then it sounds like a winning idea."

"Flomina confirmed leaning on this strategy the other day," Mar said. "I'm disappointed my outing with her wasn't more fruitful, but I think we did some bonding. I'm just concerned that her asking about Mado shows the Leader is one step ahead of us."

"He certainly has more experience with these sorts of confrontations, but I believe your plan has the right elements."

"Let's hope so," Mar said. "My last meeting with him didn't go well."

"I'd advise against drinking anything. You don't want to get drunk and I wouldn't put it past Vidor to poison you."

"Duly noted," Mar said, "I really like your playacting idea, too. The Leader will think you're just a subordinate who I bully. And it'll gives us the opportunity to act on the circumstances as they happen and gain the upper hand."

"I think we can pull it off well. The signal is easy and Vidor will have no idea," Suron said. "Anything we haven't covered? It's getting late."

"There's one more thing I've been meaning to ask you," Mar said. "Have you thought about which cruiser we'll fly over there? I don't want to come off as too militaristic with the armored cruiser, while the red one seems more suitable for social visits."

"Prevor Industries has more than two kinds available in the fleet and I've already picked one that addresses the concerns you just mentioned. It's fast and armored, and I'm outfitting it with some necessary defenses and comms. It'll carry the men and their weapons plus you, me, and the pilot. So, in answer to your question, we're all set."

"What color is it, though?"

Suron cocked his head and said, "I don't see—"

"I'm kidding, Suron," Mar said and chuckled. "Sounds like you've got it handled. Good night."

**ON THE DAY OF THE SUMMIT, AS THE PREVOR INDUS-**tries cruiser approached the Plemso estate, Mar removed her comm from her pocket and activated it.

Sitting to her left, Suron said, "You're doing that now?"

Mar didn't say anything as she waited for the comm to connect.

Flomina answered, "Are you almost here?"

"We're approaching the estate now. See you soon."

"The boys and I are looking forward to it."

"Me, too," Mar said. The comm ended. For an instant, Mar started thinking about the implications of today's meeting going wrong, then stopped herself. *Like surgery*, she thought, *I have to remain focused and confident.*

Suron said, "What was that?"

"Flomina asked for a heads-up as we got close," Mar said, repositioning the silver-metal case at her feet on the floor of the cruiser.

The cruiser slowed, spun through 180 degrees, and hovered over the landing pad.

"Ready yourselves," Suron ordered the four security personnel in the cruiser, one of whom was sitting to Mar's right and the other three behind her.

Suron leaned forward and said to the pilot, "We're a go." Then the cruiser began descending to the landing pad.

Mar felt her stomach tingling with nerves.

Suron said, "You ready, Mar Jeps?"

"As I'll ever be," Mar said. "I just hope I've learned from my mistakes."

"If anybody's got this, you do," Suron said and patted her shoulder like he might have done in a past life as he entered a battle with a soldier who'd never experienced it before. It didn't really comfort her, but she was heartened to have a combat veteran by her side and ready to back her up.

The cruiser touched down and the three guards behind Mar emerged as the cruiser powered down. Two stationed themselves at the front of the cruiser and one stood beside Suron's door. The guard to Mar's right opened the door beside him and jumped out, then closed the door and positioned himself outside the door. Each guard put a hand behind their ear and spoke.

Suron listened on his audio implant and said, "Copy that."

Mar didn't recognize any of the guards, but they were on the Prevor Industries payroll and handpicked by Suron for this assignment. They were all tall, strong men, wearing brown coveralls with the corporate logo over their right breast. Each had a handheld stun weapon secured to a belt around their waist and carried a hi-tech stun rifle, a new model the corporation had developed but not yet marketed to the Global Assembly. Suron and his men appeared ready. Mar hoped she'd live up to her role, too.

"All clear," Suron said. "Ready to disembark?"

"I believe so."

Suron put his hand behind his ear and said, "Ready to disembark."

Suron slid open the door beside him and Mar followed him out of the cruiser carrying the case. The air was filled with the scent of flowering trees. Davik Atmar scurried up to greet them, observing the four guards taking up a new formation: two flanked Mar and Suron and two stepped behind them.

Davik Atmar said, "Looks like you brought company, Suron. You know how the Leader feels about surprises."

Suron said, "He'll get over it."

"We'll see about that. Sorry to hear about Warver. I had a lot of respect for the man."

"Thanks, Davik," Suron said. "He always spoke fondly of you. No matter the company you keep."

Davik Atmar forced a smile. "Well then, shall we go?" He turned and headed toward the renovated Vanderlord estate cart. "Not enough room for everybody, I'm afraid."

"We'll make do," Suron said.

Davik Atmar looked a bit jumpy. He wasn't full of small talk like last time.

Mar sat beside Davik Atmar. Two of the men flanked the cart beside him and Mar and the others took up flanking positions at the rear of the cart. Suron sat in the back with his rifle drawn, pointed to the rear.

As the cart began moving forward, the guards jogged alongside. Mar always knew that violence was a possibility, but these regimented guards and Suron's earnestness brought it home to her. Davik Atmar peered back and forth and to the rear at the guards running beside the cart. His left leg was twitching up and down. He saw Mar observing him and forced another smile.

Mar forced a smile back at him and tightened her hold on the case in her lap. She inhaled deeply, hoping the forest scents would take her mind off her nerves which only grew worse as the cart exited the canopy of trees and the green lawn spread out before her. She spotted the Leader standing at the railing of the terrace observing the procession coming toward him. She clutched the case to herself with one hand and waved to the Leader with the other. She noted he was wearing a suit. Mar had worn a simple sundress, far less formal than her outfit for their previous meeting.

The Leader stood frozen at the railing, holding on to it with both hands. He continued observing until they were halfway along the path to the terrace steps, then he slammed one of his hands down twice on the railing and disappeared from view. Shortly after, Mar heard the sound of breaking glass. Davik Atmar flinched and the cart swerved slightly. His leg twitched faster. Mar grew concerned. Maybe she shouldn't have come here with heavily armed guards. Maybe she was exacerbating an already dangerous situation, but there was no turning back now.

When they stopped at the terrace stairs, Davik Atmar said, "Would you like me to take the case for you?"

"No, I've got it," Mar said. "Thanks for asking, though."

Davik Atmar climbed out of the cart followed by Mar, holding tight to the case's handle. The guards surrounded Mar with Suron standing beside her.

"Well," Davik Atmar said, observing the guards and Suron. "Here we go, then. Follow me."

Davik Atmar led the way up the stairs. Suron walked

beside Mar with two guards in front and two in back. A few steps before they reached the terrace, Davik Atmar darted up to the top and scurried off to the left, then Mar heard the distinct high-pitched sound of stun weapons powering up. That caused the Prevor Indus-tries guards to activate their rifles, which emitted a low hum that wouldn't have been audible to anyone more than a meter away. Suron stepped in front of Mar. Her heart raced.

When they reached the terrace, the guards reconfig-ured seamlessly, two of them flanking Suron on either side with Mar behind him. She spied the scene through a space between Suron and the guard to his right.

Three Global Guards were standing beside the Leader with their weapons drawn. They were large, burly men. One had a deep scar across the side of his face and another had "GG" tattooed on his neck. They were all dressed in black Global-Guard uniforms and looked like men to whom violence came easy.

The Leader said, "I'm disappointed you'd bring vio-lence to my home, Mar Jeps."

Suron said, "This security detail of yours is out of the ordinary, Vidor. Global Guards don't usually protect the head of the Global Assembly."

When Suron said "Vidor" and "head of the Global Assembly," Mar noted the Leader stiffened and practically snarled. Suron refused to call him Leader.

The Leader said, "No…the Leader…the Leader doesn't usually…but looks like my impulse was correct here."

Mar said, "Suron, please keep to your job, which doesn't involve speaking for me." She stepped through the space between the guard and Suron, who moved forward to stand at her side.

"Yes, Suron," the Leader said, appearing pleased with Mar's reprimand.

Suron's face was frozen, expressionless. He didn't intend to give the Leader any satisfaction by reacting to Mar's statement.

Mar said to the Leader, "I have to say, I'm disappointed you've brought heavily armed Global Guards to our meeting at your home. Do you have something in mind other than discussing our problems? What are your intentions?"

"I believe the time for words is over." The Leader raised his right arm, signaling the Global Guards who aimed their weapons. "My intentions are—"

"Yes," Flomina said, standing in the doorway of the estate with her two boys beside her. She wore a sundress much like Mar's. "What are your intentions for our guest, Vidor? In front of our children, in my home."

"Flo, take the boys inside," the Leader said, raising his voice.

Flomina yelled back at him, "What are these thugs doing here?"

The Leader said, "Funny you should ask. I was just telling Mar Jeps my concerns about her guards."

"I wasn't talking about them," Flomina said. "They're obviously her corporate security contingent—my father travels with a similar group of men. It's standard procedure to bring them along and she already told me about them. I'm talking about these thugs on my terrace. I want them gone. Where's our usual guards?"

"On break."

"Well, call them back from their break and get these thugs out of here."

"These aren't thugs. These are highly decorated members of—"

"Do I look like I care? Get rid of them. Now!"

Flomina and the Leader stared at each other and an awkward silence fell over the terrace. The boys giggled. They were sporting shorts with cloth shoes. The older one, Carz, wore a Global-Assembly-blue pullover with "Capitol City Military Academy" on the front while the younger, Minok, had a solid red pullover.

The Leader said to the boys, "You two go inside."

"They'll stay right here with me," Flomina said. "Where's Davik?"

Davik Atmar stepped out from behind the Global Guards.

"Davik," Flomina said, "escort these individuals off my terrace and tell our regular guards their break is over."

Davik Atmar looked over at the Leader who let out a groan of resignation.

"Are you deaf, Davik?" the Leader said, "You heard her, but keep them close by." Then he said to the Global Guards, "Go with him." They powered down their weapons and Davik Atmar began walking toward Mar. She and Suron stepped aside and the Global Guards followed Davik Atmar past them and down the stairs.

The Leader said, "Now that's out of the way, you can take the boys inside, Flo."

Flomina chuckled. Anger spread over the Leader's face.

"I'll do as I damn well please, Vidor," Flomina said. The boys giggled again. "You two watch your step if you want the gift from Mar Jeps." The boys ceased laughing as if Flomina had hit a switch.

"What gift?" the Leader said.

"May I?" Mar said, lifting the case.

"Please do," Flomina said, approaching Mar, who carried the case to the table. The children stood in place, unmoving. "Come on, boys." They dashed to their mother's side.

Mar opened the case and handed Carz an HGD device with one headset and gave another headset to Minok.

"What's this?" the Leader said.

"What does it look like, Vidor?" Flomina said.

"I'm getting a little fed up—"

"Yes, yes, I've heard it all before," Flomina said. "We'll be out of your thinning hair in a moment."

The Leader turned on his heels and poured himself a goblet of Malrap.

"Starting early, I see," Flomina said. "Anyway, what do you boys say to Mar?"

The boys said in unison, "Thank you, Mar Jeps."

"You're very welcome," Mar said.

"Very good," Flomina said. "Now go play out on the lawn. You've spent too much time inside today."

Carz said, "Can we take this with us, Mother?"

"Of course," Flomina said. "But stay clear of those men down there, please. You can use the power outlet in the lawn at the edge of the woods. Now, come here and give your mother a hug before you leave." Minok hugged her immediately, while Carz looked sheepish and reluctantly gave her a quick hug. Flomina held Carz by his arms and laughed. "I know it's a bother to show affection to your mother as you get older, but you'll always be my baby boy." Then Flomina kissed him on the forehead. Carz glanced over at Mar, embarrassed.

"Yes, Mother," he said. "Can we go now?

"Yes, go," Flomina said. "Love you."

Carz ran down the stairs.

Minok said, "Bye, Mother, love you." He hugged Flomina again, then he waved to Mar and followed his brother down the stairs.

Mar said, "He's a sweet one."

The Leader said, "She's spoiled them rotten with her affection."

"They're my babies, Vidor, and if you knew better, you'd show them a little more of it."

Mar said, "They grow up so fast."

"You'll never understand," Flomina said to the Leader.

"I understand all too well," the Leader said. "Now, can we get back to our business?" He took a healthy swig of Malrap.

Flomina hugged Mar, then stepped away and examined her from head to toe. "You look hot in that dress. Doesn't she look hot, Vidor?"

"That's a little inappropriate," the Leader said.

"Oh, right!" Flomina said. "You're deciding what's inappropriate now?"

Mar said, "Thanks for the recommendation on the dress and the fashion advice in general."

"You're most welcome. Let's do midday meal and shopping again soon," Flomina said. "Vidor, you be nice to this one." She winked at Mar.

"Your wish is my command, dearest," the Leader said sarcastically.

"It better be," Flomina said, then she pointed at the corner of the terrace where the wall was stained with Malrap, below which was shattered glass. "And don't forget to have someone clean up your mess."

"Yes, dear," the Leader said even more sarcastically and they both laughed.

As Flomina approached the house, one of the regular security guards exited and held the door open for her. She waved goodbye to Mar and disappeared inside the building.

The guard said to the Leader, "Davik Atmar told me to come out here."

"Yes, station yourself in your usual spot," the Leader said and gulped down his remaining Malrap.

Suron tapped Mar on the back twice, then gripped her forearm. "How about that? Looks like we have the advantage. It would be silly to send us away now too."

Mar turned to Suron, "Yes. Why don't you go now, too? Meet you back at the cruiser."

Suron appeared surprised, then leaned toward Mar and said loud enough for everybody else on the terrace to hear, "I don't think that's a good idea."

"Take your men," Mar said in an angry tone. "That's an order."

"This isn't what we talked about," Suron said, sounding alarmed.

"We'll discuss this insubordination later," Mar said. "Now go. That's an order." She pointed toward the stairs.

Suron looked perturbed. "All right, men. You heard the boss. Let's move out." Then Suron said to Mar, "I hope you know what you're doing," and led the four guards down the stairs.

The Leader was delighted at the interaction he'd witnessed.

"So?" Mar said. "May I sit?"

"Please do," the Leader said. "Would you like something to drink? I have some of that juice you like."

"No, I'm fine," Mar said, shutting the case, seating herself, and tucking the case beside her chair.

The Leader poured himself another half-goblet of Malrap and sat down across from her. "So, what's going on between you and Flo?"

"We went shopping for dresses. Fashion is definitely her expertise," Mar said. "I like her a lot—she's smart, sassy, and quick-witted. I like a person who speaks her mind."

"She certainly is all that," the Leader said, taking a sip of his Malrap. "Although to be honest, I think you've befriended her to keep me off balance and at bay."

"I'm not sure what you mean."

The Leader cleared his throat, then put his glass down on the table. "And what is it you've given my boys, exactly?"

"Your boys are adorable," Mar said. "The gift is the newest unreleased version of the HGD. Flo was saying how the boys were looking forward to the next upgrade, so I thought I'd bring one for them. I know a few people over at Prevor Industries."

"They love that thing," the Leader said, enunciating the word "thing" with disdain.

"It doesn't sound like you're fond of it."

"Not at all. It's a child's toy and a device for losers who want to escape from the real world. It's mindless entertainment. I'd rather they were sitting in my study reading Yorlik the Great's books than plugging themselves into that thing for extended periods. I told Mado the same when he gave them their first one."

"I appreciate your point of view. I didn't have that problem with Yor, though. He always had his head in a book." The Leader rolled his eyes at the mention of her son. "We've updated the device and I've opened a whole new division to utilize the tech for job training in all fields including meds. The one I've given the boys has fabulous new additions. too."

"You should have told Flo before you exposed them to anything inappropriate for their age."

"Please," Mar said. "Remember I raised a child of my own. The HGD I gave them is uploaded with age-appropriate simulations including one for a cruiser pilot and one where they maintain a cruiser. It's less technical than the adult version where they'd learn how to do actual maintenance—rewiring, replacing parts."

"I did talk to Mado about military applications, but

he refused the idea. He said the Great man would never have agreed to it and neither would he."

"Yes, that's something we can discuss if you're not arresting me today."

The Leader laughed, then gulped down the remainder of his Malrap. "Where did you get that idea?"

"Oh, come on," Mar said. "I'd be remiss to expect you to treat me as an equal. That's not your style, but at least show me some respect by not lying."

"An old friend—or at least someone I thought was a friend—once told me that respect is earned."

"I agree with your friend. True respect is earned through trust and honesty," Mar said, acting like she was fixing her hair to cover-up the activation of her audio implant so Suron could hear what was said. "Maybe that time is upon us? What do you say?"

Suron said to Mar over her audio implant, "All is secure down here. We appear to be on schedule. I haven't received word, but Davik got a comm and panicked so I let him go. Maybe stall a little more."

The Leader said. "When do you mean? Now?"

Mar said, "Maybe I will have that Eglew juice." Mar fiddled with her hair again and deactivated the implant.

The Leader grunted and stood up. He poured a goblet full of juice from a carafe next to the one with Malrap.

Mar said, "You know, when we were shopping for dresses, Flo told me she thinks you and I could work well together."

"Did she?" the Leader said, placing the full goblet in front of Mar. "Anything else before I sit down?"

"No, this is wonderful," Mar said. "I told her in order for us to work together, we'd need to be honest with one another, yet here we are and you've already lied to me."

"Some would say lying is a matter of perspective," the Leader said, looking out over the terrace railing, then turning and hurling his glass at the house. It shattered on the wall above the head of the guard who dashed away from the fallout.

"Something wrong?" Mar said, standing and peering out onto the estate's lawn. At the bottom of the terrace stairs, where the cart was parked, the Global Guards were on their knees, their arms restrained with zip-tie cuffs, surrounded by Suron and the Prevor Industries security guards. The Global Guards' weapons lay on the grass behind Suron. There was a burned spot on the lawn where it had taken a stun blast. It seemed like their playacting got the desired results.

Over near the wooded area, the Plemso boys sat on the grass, hooked up to the HGD, oblivious to what was happening nearby.

The Leader said, "This is an outrage."

"Are you telling me you had no plans for these Global Guards to arrest me today, then invade my corporate complex?"

"What you've done here is—"

The mansion's door flew open and Davik Atmar came rushing out to the Leader, carrying a viewer.

The Leader said, "What is it, Davik?"

Davik Atmar stumbled over his words, making no sense.

"Out with it!" the Leader said.

"Maybe this is something I need to tell you in private," Davik Atmar said, looking suspiciously over at Mar.

"I don't have time for your tomfoolery. Tell me what's caused you to come crashing out here or I'll throw you and your viewer off this terrace."

Mar said, "Yes, Davik. Please tell us."

"All right," Davik Atmar said. "We've just received a comm from the Supreme Commander—he requests a termination of today's plan and a redeployment for crowd control and possible riots globally."

"Riots?" the Leader said. "Have you lost your mind? What are you talking about?"

"May I show you?" Davik Atmar said, placing his viewer on the table and opening it.

"Go ahead. This better be worth the interruption."

"Yes, Davik. Go right ahead," Mar said.

Davik Atmar looked at Mar, then over at the Leader. He appeared confused.

The Leader gazed at Mar with derision, then said to Davik Atmar, "Are you waiting for an invitation?"

As Davik Atmar activated the viewer, Mar walked behind him and the Leader to gain a better vantage point. A viewing-channel news show was playing with the sound off. Two announcers were speaking—a woman wearing a purple and green polka-dot dress, and a man in a green jacket, a red shirt, and a purple tie. Both sported Global Assembly pins and their demeanor was one of concern. Across the bottom of the screen, a headline read MASSIVE MARCHES MENACE DOMES. Then the image cut to a reporter accompanied by the words 'Anga City—Mlimoan Dome' in the bottom right-hand corner of the screen. He was standing on a sidewalk, pointing to the street behind him where a wall of people were marching —men, women, children—carrying signs reading *We Want The Truth, No More Lies, Is There A Planet?*, and *Where is Yor?* Then the broadcast cut to a shot from a cruiser hovering above the city, showing a continuous line of marching demonstrators packing a four-lane street for ten blocks with more coming up behind them and streaming toward them from other parts of the city.

The Leader poked at the viewer's screen. "What is this?"

"It's what I was trying to tell you, sir. It's why the Supreme Commander asked to redeploy the troops."

"Because of one damn dome?"

"No, sir," Davik Atmar said, his voice shaking. "It's happening in all nine domes. The turnout you see in the Mlimoan Dome is indicative of what's happening in every dome except for three where the turnout is slightly smaller the other six. The Supreme Commander is concerned that if violence breaks out, the military won't be able to contain it with their personnel spread out over all the planet. He said he needs the entire military at his disposal so he can prevent a disaster anywhere on the planet if the demonstrations get out of control."

Davik Atmar pressed a button on his viewer and the sound came on. The viewing channel personalities were saying pretty much what Davik Atmar had just told the Leader about the planetary situation. Behind them, images appeared in succession of the marches in each dome, taken from the viewpoint of a hovering cruiser. The streets in the downtown areas of all the domed cities appeared to be overflowing with demonstrators.

The Leader slammed the viewer shut with a crunching sound. Davik Atmar gasped.

The Leader said, "Don't be such a baby, Davik. You can get another one."

"I…what…" Davik Atmar said, closing his eyes to compose himself. "What would you like me to tell the Supreme Commander, sir?"

"Obviously, tell him, the Lead Commander, and the Head Director to cancel all planned actions for today and redeploy forces to deal with any problem areas." To Mar, the Leader said, "I have to do everything around here."

Davik Atmar picked up the viewer to the sound of rattling parts inside and tucked it under his arm. "Will that be all, sir?"

"Yes," the Leader said. "Go do your damn job."

Davik Atmar raced into the mansion without shutting the door behind him. The guard walked over and shut it.

The Leader said, "Sorry about Davik. Where were we?"

"I was talking about respect and lying. I was talking about how those Global Guards were ordered here to arrest me," Mar said. "And while we're being honest, you might as well know I'm aware that the plan to arrest me and take over Prevor Industries is part of your unrelenting quest to locate Mado Prevor, so you can ensure the spaceships get built because the domes will fully fail in fifty to eighty years due to your incompetence in the management of their construction. You planned all of this, even though last time I was here I told you we'd help build the ships."

The Leader stared at Mar, shaking his head back and forth, then he mumbled something under his breath.

"Excuse me," Mar said. "I couldn't make out what you said."

"If you must know, I said, 'Orn was right about you.'"

"What did your attack animal say?"

"He said I shouldn't underestimate you."

"I'd be flattered if it came from a less despicable person."

"Orn does have his charms," the Leader said, sounding satisfied with his underling.

Mar was disturbed the Leader would find anything about that monster amusing.

The Leader said, "So, if we're attempting to be honest here, should I assume you knew about these protests?"

"Yes, although the turnout exceeded my expectations. I guess Kodans still want to think their own thoughts."

The Leader kicked the leg of the table, almost knocking over Mar's drink. She glanced at the lawn. The children were still immersed in the HGD and the Global Guards were now sitting on the grass, chatting with Suron's men. Suron noticed Mar observing them and nodded to her.

Mar said, "Maybe now we can sit down and work out our differences—or at least the ones that would cause you to arrest me and occupy my corporation."

"You mean Mado Prevor's corporation," the Leader said, holding out his hand for Mar to seat herself first.

"Maybe we should start there. I am CEO and majority shareholder in trust at Prevor Industries, so it's my corporation to run now," Mar said, sitting down in the same seat as before. "Oh, and yes, I know you didn't shoot down the WAEF because Mado is in outer space with my son heading to Powers-That-Be knows where."

"Well, I guess I did misjudge the situation." The Leader walked over to the carafe of Malrap, filled a goblet, then seated himself.

"As far as Mado is concerned," Mar said, "I've communicated with him and he's not returning to Koda anytime soon, so you have to deal with me when it comes to Prevor Industries and the spaceship project."

"I'd like to talk to him about putting someone different in charge of the project."

"That's not possible."

The Leader slammed his fist on the table. "Why not?"

"Because of what I just told you about my status at the corporation," Mar said. "From here on out, you'll have to deal with me, and that's final."

"I don't like it."

"You have a problem working with me?"

"You've just demonstrated I can't trust you."

"And you can trust Mado after everything he's done?" Mar said. "You've proven that I can't trust you, either, so why don't we start building trust between us with a mutual agreement?"

"What do you propose?"

"Let's say taking over Prevor Industries is off the table. You could kidnap the necessary techs for the spaceship project, but that would be a waste of time. You know as well as I do that Mado is the intellect behind the tech in those ships. He's more than proved it judging by the failure to make headway in his absence. If we hit any snags in the project, I can reach out to Mado and see if he'll apply his genius to the problem. If you do decide to take over the Complex, Mado won't cooperate and the ships won't be completed."

"So I'm supposed to trust you'll get the project done?"

"Yes, you'll get your spaceships before the domes collapse. Mado has informed me that building the spaceships is a twenty-five-year project, and that's if they can mine the necessary resources in that time to finish the ships while fighting the atmospheric conditions. I'm thinking thirty-five years is a more reasonable estimate, but we'll see how it goes."

"You didn't answer my question. Why should I trust you'll get this job done?"

"We'll set up a timeline toward completion and establish goals for finishing certain stages of the project. If we can't find the resources or are slowed by unforeseen circumstances then we revise the timeline," Mar said. "That way you can keep an eye on the progress."

"That sounds fair so far, but—"

"I have other stipulations. You won't punish people for today's march. There won't be any purges, and no more arresting people for speaking their minds or executions for the collapse of the domes. I'll be keeping an eye out. If laws on the books are truly broken, by all means enforce them."

"See, this is where I draw the line. Telling me how to run my government. That placed our relationship on the wrong footing before and now you're doing it again."

"I'm just asking you to be reasonable. Let Kodans think their own thoughts. If you're so afraid of public discourse, then maybe you aren't ruling well."

"Are you saying I'm unreasonable? Governing isn't so simple."

"If you break the rules I've just set, then the same punishments apply. I'll instruct my techs not to reenergize the domes and you'll have a greater crisis on your hands. The spaceship project will halt, and maybe I'll release the report on the structural integrity of the domes. Plus, I have your list of all the members in the Movement you were going to purge today and memos from you directing the purge and telling the GSS to compile the list. I'll release that information, too. You can't stop all of those things from happening at once."

"This is blackmail. How is trust based on blackmail?"

"I don't see how asking you to rule ethically is a form of blackmail," Mar said. "And if it helps you swallow these demands, then do it for your children's sake so your family will have a future."

The Leader took a sip of his Malrap, then put the glass on the table and stared into it. Mar could tell he was considering her deal, but she assumed he was also pondering how to swing things to his advantage.

The Leader said, "I'm not sure why I trust any of this, but for the sake of my children, I'll consider tempering my actions, although that's never been my strong suit. I still refuse to comm you every time I need to make a decision about a dissenter in the Movement causing problems for my government. I am the Leader."

"I don't know what to tell you. Find an advisor with a little more compassion. How about Davik Atmar?"

"That fool?"

"Then I don't know who. That's something for you to figure out."

"Is that it?" the Leader said. "You don't want anything for yourself, like a place on one of the spaceships?"

"That's funny," Mar said. "We'll probably both be gone from this existence before those ships are finished, but I do want something for myself."

"Ah! So much for ethics."

"I want you to pardon my partner and Lek Valsted."

"But you just said you want me to enforce the laws. Sounds hypocritical to me."

"I don't think I'm asking too much," Mar said. "You did tell my partner you'd pardon him."

"Seems like you want things both ways," the Leader said. "As far as Valsted is concerned, the punishment is already underway so I can't help you there. I'll have to think about your partner. He did break an important law that keeps our government intact, but I like to think I'm a man of my word, so I'll take it under consideration."

"Good to hear."

Then a mischievous look came over the Leader's face. "I do have something to ask of you as part of this agreement since you've asked so much of me."

"What is it?"

"Whenever I request, I want you to appear by my side at Global Assembly events including Breeze Celebration. If you deny me, then this entire agreement is null and void."

Mar couldn't think of anything more odious than standing by this person's side and lending support to his regime, but if this would save Rajer's life and help Project FoFu move forward, she would swallow her disgust. "I don't see a problem with that as long as it's not an execution."

The Leader grimaced. "All right," he said, sounding disappointed. "I'll need to deliberate on all these points. It'll take me a few days to get back to you."

"I guess I can live with that," Mar said. "To sweeten the agreement, I have something for you." Mar lifted the case from the floor, set it on the table, then began to open it. The guard hurried toward them, but the Leader waved him away.

Inside the case, a hidden compartment contained the duplicated Rejuv Treatment respirator mask, a memory wafer, and one of the metal canisters. She removed all of them from the case and laid them on the table.

"What is this?" the Leader said.

"This is the way the Great man stayed alive all those years in space," Mar said. "Mado was keeping it under wraps. Yorlik called it Rejuv Treatment and regular dosing completely halts the aging of a person's cells. I've read the science on it and in the short time I've had it in my possession, I've done my own research and seen the cellular results. It's sound. And we were both there when Yorlik landed."

"If it's so sound, why isn't Yorlik sitting here right now?"

"I can only assume he wanted to age normally when he returned here."

"He was such a do-gooder. Unbelievable," the Leader said. "So why are you showing me this?"

One by one, Mar pushed the respirator mask, the memory wafer, and the canister toward him. "It's all yours. The instructions are on the wafer. There's enough material in there for you to live thirty to forty years beyond the normal Kodan life-span and there's more where that came from if our relationship goes well."

"And why are you giving me this?"

"So you can live to see your children grow up, so you can meet your grandchildren and maybe even your great-grandchildren. You might see them leave Koda, and if you can live healthily enough to be placed in a cryo-unit, maybe you'll even reach a new planet. This stops aging but it doesn't protect against diseases, so maybe cut back on the Malrap."

"You didn't answer my question," the Leader said. "You're good at that. You should be a politician."

Mar laughed. "Take this as a gift given in good faith and hopefully you'll agree to pardon my partner."

"There it is," the Leader said with a self-satisfied smile.

"So you'll agree to all the terms?"

"As I said before, I'd like to think things over."

Mar held up her glass. "Here's to agreeing in the next day or so."

The Leader lifted his glass and drank. Mar raised the glass to her mouth, tipped it slightly without the juice reaching her lips, then placed it back on the table.

"Now I need to be on my way," Mar said. "Give my regards to Flo." She picked up the case and hurried down the terrace stairs. When Suron spotted her, he gathered his men to meet her.

"How did it go?" Suron said as he walked beside Mar down the path toward the cruiser with the guards surrounding her.

"Seems like a success, but I'll never fully trust that man," Mar said. "Tell you more when we're in the cruiser, but I need you to find out what's happening with Lek Valsted."

# LEK

"**G**et a move on," the Global Guard said, shoving Lek in the direction of the dome's exit door.

There were hundreds of doors like this one around the border of each dome. They were installed for maintenance and emergency procedures, and the codes to open them were known only by higher-ups in the Global Assembly. They weren't guarded for three reasons: The codes were a fiercely protected secret; anybody who managed to bypass the code system and break out into the hostile environment beyond the dome walls was considered suicidal; and if anyone entered the domes from the outside, the door sensors would trigger alarms at the GSS.

The Global Guard shoved Lek again. Lek would have preferred walking to the door with dignity, one foot in front of the other, but he was aware it was the Guard's way of humiliating him. This was the same Global Guard from the Prevor Industries visit and he'd told Lek on the way over that he'd requested this detail. For a moment, Lek thought about overpowering the guard and running away, but in truth, he'd never be able to survive on the run forever even if he did manage to subdue the Global Guard, who was younger, twice as large, and a head taller. Consequently, Lek resigned himself to his fate.

As he approached the metal door, Lek noted a man standing beside it who looked vaguely familiar. He had dark, coiffed hair and wore a white button-down shirt with one button open at the collar, black pants, and polished black shoes. He was possibly in his late forties, early fifties. Lek could tell right away the man was GSS by his disgusted stare. GSS recruits were taught to do this at the Academy to demean the enemy, and this man did it better than most.

The Global Guard continued to shove Lek until they stopped in front of the exit door and the man said, "You're relieved, soldier. I can take it from here."

The Guard unlocked Lek's shackles and saluted the man, then turned around and marched off. The man continued to stare at Lek's face as the Guard's footsteps faded into the distance. Then his gaze shifted to Lek's hat and he knocked it off Lek's head. Linara had given Lek the hat on the day she and Ara visited him at the GSS. Lek's final request had been to see them one last time.

The visitation took place in a GSS interrogation room. Lek had been waiting there, wearing his white prison coveralls, when Linara and Ara entered. They wore identical multicolor polka-dot dresses and Linara was clutching a wide-brimmed hat. A GSS guard closed the door, then stood there blocking it.

Linara told Ara to stay where she was for a moment and not follow her. She walked up to Lek and threw the hat at him, which bounced off his chest to the floor, then she smacked Lek as hard as she could with an open palm across the face. Ara screamed and began crying. Lek presumed this was Linara's best shot since she swung from her hip, but he was so numb from the ramifications of this moment that he barely felt the sting. Over Linara's shoulder, he saw Ara with both hands covering her mouth, bawling, tears streaming down her face.

"How could you?" Linara said, staring into Lek's eyes. "How could you?" She began to weep and Lek followed suit as they embraced, then Lek felt Ara hugging his leg. She was still crying. He reached down and placed one arm around her back and pulled her up against him. Eventually, they all stopped crying and stayed in that position for an indeterminate amount of time until the guard said, "Let's wrap it up."

They separated and Lek bent down to Ara. "Just remember I love you, and when you get older, you'll appreciate I was trying to make the world a better place. Your mother might be angry at me for a long time and your lives won't be easy, so you be a good girl and help her the best you can. And please leave the door open a crack for me, my beautiful blossom."

"Always," Ara said. "I love you, Papa."

Lek held out his arms and Ara jumped into them. He lifted her up, kissed her on both cheeks, and held her tight.

"Time's up," the guard said. "I won't say it again."

Lek lowered Ara to the ground, bent over, and kissed her forehead.

Linara handed him the hat and said, "I told them it was mine, but I brought it for you." She approached Lek to embrace him one last time but the guard tugged her away by the back of her dress.

"Time for you to go now," the guard said, placing both his hands on Linara's shoulders and guiding her toward the door.

"Let go of her," Lek said, grabbing one of the guard's arms. The guard released his hold on Linara and pushed Lek hard in the middle of his chest. Lek flew backward. His head struck a wall and he fell to the floor. He was disoriented as he watched the guard herd Linara and Ara out the door, shutting it behind them. Lek clutched the brim of the hat in his hands.

Now, Lek reached down to pick up the hat but the man smacked his hand away. The back of the man's hand was severely scarred. Lek immediately recognized him from GSS legend and Rajer's description.

Lek stood up straight and said, "Were you sent here by the Leader?"

"No," the man said, reaching down to pick up the hat and tossing it into the distance. "I asked for this assignment. Think of it as an exit interview." The man chuckled. "Seriously, I was curious to meet the traitor who would give up a promising career for nothing."

"Nothing?" Lek said. "Somebody like you couldn't possibly understand why I did what I did."

"I've heard that story before," the man said. "Please illuminate me regarding your stupidity. Why did you do it?"

"Friendship and love."

"Weak reasons to die," the man said. "I prefer loyalty."

"I presume you're talking about loyalty to the Global Assembly. I bet you don't have many friends," Lek said, spotting where the hat lay in the distance.

"Never had time for such frivolity."

"It's a lonely way to live."

The man tracked where Lek was looking and said, "Don't concern yourself with the hat. In your sentence, the Head Director stated you must leave the dome without anything to protect you from the environment outside. I suggested you leave naked as a matter of mercy to quicken your death, but the Head Director said we needed to demonstrate some sort of decorum."

"Yes, by all means, we must uphold decorum."

"I thought it was absurd, too, but he's the Head Director."

Lek understood this might be the last conversation he'd ever have in his existence, so he was curious about something. "Can I ask you a question?"

"Why not?"

"Do you truly believe everything the Global Assembly does is for the good of the Kodan people?"

"The good of the people?"

"Maybe I should restate the question. Do you believe everything you're asked to do for the Global Assembly is correct?"

"Do I believe it?" the man said. "I'm a soldier given orders and I follow them."

"So you do whatever the Global Assembly tells you to do, no questions asked?"

"One hundred percent."

"Don't you ever question how the Global Assembly acts toward the citizens they're supposed to serve?"

"I serve the Leader and the Global Assembly, and Koda's citizens exist to serve them, not the other way around."

"I guess that's the difference between us."

"And that's why you're about to exit the dome," the man said. "Step in front of the door."

"I'm not in any rush."

"Step in front of the door."

Lek moved toward the door, then gazed over his shoulder at the hat, thinking about his final embrace with his family. He observed the man typing the code into the pad, then recalled him standing in the distance as Lek conferred with Mar on the day of Ador's memorial. Now he realized the man was here to finish the job he started. Nothing less.

The metal door slid open, revealing the chamber leading to the outside door. It was about a meter wide and two meters in height and length. A powerful stench emanated from it.

Lek placed his hand over his nose and pinched it. "What's that smell?"

"That's from the poor saps who decide to stay in there instead of leaving the dome. They die from starvation and their rotting corpses are found later. Their stink lingers." The man smirked at Lek.

"Well, I guess this is it," Lek said. "What's your name, anyway?"

"I don't think that's relevant. You'll be dead in a few moments."

"I'd like to know the name of the last person I talk to before I die."

The man continued smirking. "Sure, what does it matter? My name is Orn Shiv."

"Good-bye, Orn Shiv."

"Go on," Orn said and shooed him into the chamber.

Lek sighed and stepped into the chamber. The door slid closed behind him. The stench made him dry-heave a few times as he walked up to the outside door, which was solid metal like the one behind him. A light went on above the outside door, then an ear-piercing horn sounded six times and the door slid open.

Sweltering heat rushed in and the air burned Lek's nostrils and throat. He thought about staying inside the chamber, but if he was going to die, he didn't want to spend days contemplating his decisions while he starved to death. He'd rather the end come quickly. He held his breath like he was diving into the deep end of a pool, then stepped out of the chamber as the horn sounded again and the door closed behind him.

Outside, the scorching wind felt like he'd stepped inside a blast furnace. The entire landscape in front of him was greyish-brown and dead. The soles of his feet inside his cloth prison shoes felt like they were burning. He touched his face and it was already blistered. He couldn't hold his breath much longer, so he decided to take a small breath through his mouth, and he began coughing. Gasping for air, he fell to his knees, which began to burn through his prison coveralls when they touched the ground.

Lek thought he heard a cruiser above him, the engines increasing in pitch as it landed a short distance away. The sun was so bright he couldn't focus ahead for long, and he was too weak to get up and search for the cruiser.

Lek decided to relinquish himself to dying. He couldn't see any shelter to hide from the environment.

The pain throughout his entire body was excruciating. He just needed to take a few deep breaths and his life would be over. He thought about Rajer and was glad he tried to help him. He thought of Linara and Ara and how much he loved them. He pictured them, wanting their images in his mind as he took his final breath.

Then a person appeared in front of him, wearing a breathing apparatus and a suit like a deep-sea diver.

The person held out their hand and said, "Lek Valsted? Mar Jeps sends her regards."

# MAR

After her meeting with the Leader, Mar decided to take the next day off. At midday, she sat on the couch in the penthouse, basking in the silence, taking a break from reading *Power Over the Future*. She told Gols to leave her alone except for an emergency or a comm from the Leader.

So when Mar's comm buzzed, her heart raced and she stared down at the device, wondering if she was ready for what the Leader might say. Gols was on the other end of the line. "The Leader is on the comm and you may want to turn on a viewing channel."

"Which one?"

"Any one." The nervous tone of Gols' voice scared her more than usual.

Mar leapt up from the couch and switched on the viewing screen, and at the same time she told Gols to connect her to the Leader.

"Hello, Mar Jeps," the Leader said before she could say anything.

On the screen, a female viewing-channel host was sitting in front of a desk, saying, "…and now let's go to the Capitol City GSS building." The next image was a male reporter standing at the back of an auditorium. People were seated in rows behind him, facing the other way. The reporter said, "We're here at the Capitol City

GSS execution hall to witness the execution of Rajer Jeps for aiding the terrorist Yor Vanderlord in spreading his malicious propaganda and assisting him in escaping Breeze Celebration. Roneh Rayush, the heroine of Breeze Celebration, will assist in the execution."

Mar went cold. She said in a panic to the Leader, "What are you doing?"

"I'm calling to discuss our conversation and to relay my conclusions about the agreement you proposed."

"I meant…I'm watching a viewing channel right now…what are you doing?"

"Oh yes, I was going to ask if you were watching," the Leader said, clearing his throat. "As for your proposal, I agree to all your blackmail presuming you live up to your end of the bargain, but I'm executing your partner."

The reporter said, "Looks like the execution is about to begin."

"Why are you doing this?"

"Oh, it's starting," the Leader said.

The vidcam shot of the reporter cut to Roneh Rayush standing to the left of a Global-Assembly-blue execution tube, smiling. She was dressed in a Global-Assembly-blue dress with a Global-Assembly pin. The dress was tight-fitting. They wanted her to look sexy. They'd also changed her hairstyle to expose her face and make her look stern. The vidcam panned right and zoomed in to the tube's small window where Rajer could only be seen from the neck up. The rest of his body was inside the tube. He appeared to be smiling, which Mar found puzzling. Maybe he was attempting to show courage or contempt.

"Why?" Mar said. The panic in her voice had turned to anger. "I've extended your life with the Rejuv Treatment. Why wasn't that enough?"

"Yes, that was nice of you, but what kind of Leader would I be if a citizen breaks his Loyalty Oath and I let him go free? You're the one who said I should enforce the law. I only told your partner I'd consider a pardon, and maybe you thought I was more compassionate or I'd worry about what Flo might think, but that's not our arrangement. I do my job. She doesn't interfere, and she reaps the benefits of being partnered with me. Isn't that right, dear?"

Mar heard Flomina say over the comm from a distance, "Sorry, Mar. I like you, I do, but Vidor is correct."

Then the Leader continued, "You do have some things hanging over me like the power source and your stolen intel and of course the spaceship project, but since you sweetened the agreement with the Rejuv device, I have all the time in the world to wait for you to die, then I can go back to my old ways. I did some research and discovered your grandparents passed in their mid-seventies so I only have to wait twenty, twenty-five years and I can go back to arresting and executing whoever I want when I want since you won't be around anymore to enforce our agreement. And if you have your own Rejuv device, I'll wave goodbye from my spaceship as the dome collapses around you.

"I want you to know—I want you to remember every single solitary day for the rest of your life—that this execution is a consequence of your blackmail. You get everything you want except what you really want. I will expect the timetable for the spaceship construction on my desk in twenty-seven days.

"Oh, and by the way, I have an official Global Assembly event coming up. The invitation is in your digi-mail and I expect you in attendance by my side or there will be further consequences."

Flomina said, "Looking forward to seeing you, Mar."

"Enjoy!" the Leader said and the comm disconnected.

Mar dropped her comm and remained standing in front of the viewing screen. The vidcam had pulled back from the closeup of Rajer to show a nondescript man to the right of the tube wearing a Global-Assembly-blue suit and a Global-Assembly lapel pin. The man read aloud from a digi-tablet, "On this day, the Leader of the Global Assembly, the honorable Vidor Plemso, has decreed the life of Rajer Jeps forfeit for crimes against Koda. May the Powers-That-Be watch over him."

The vidcam panned left to a two-shot of Roneh Rayush, standing closer to the tube now, and Rajer's face in the window. Roneh Rayush was handed a palm-sized box with a red button on it. Rajer's eyes shifted to the box. He was alarmed. People being executed were usually given a final opportunity to renounce their acts, but they either didn't trust what Rajer would say or this was part of Mar's consequences. It looked like Rajer hadn't been told about this twist—Mar could see the confusion in his eyes. He yelled, "Wait! Wait! Wait!" but nobody cared or could hear him from inside the tube.

Roneh Rayush stepped closer to the tube, looked directly into the vidcam, and said in a triumphant tone,

"For the good of the globe," and pressed the button. The vidcam panned right and zoomed in to the portal. Rajer was terrified as all the air was slowly evacuated from the tube. His breathing became labored, then his eyes opened wider and he said, "I…love…you," and the life went out of his eyes. The vidcam pulled back slightly. Below the portal, a monitor installed on the tube displayed Rajer's heart and brain activity. Both had flatlined.

Mar turned off the viewing screen and fell back on the couch. Memories flashed through her mind: The first time she and Rajer met on a date at a café in the Old Quarter; the first time she realized she loved him and wanted to be with him forever, dancing with him at one of Ador's parties; snuggling on their couch together and falling asleep with the warmth of his body against hers.

She wept while staring at the blank viewing screen and felt cold and empty. Mar didn't know how long she sat there in that state before she curled up and fell asleep in exhaustion.

---

**MAR AWOKE WITH GOLS STANDING BESIDE THE** couch. She had a blanket draped over her.

Gols said, "I'm so very sorry, Mar. My deepest sympathies."

Mar forced herself to sit up and rubbed at her eyes. "How long was I out?"

"A few hours. I came in earlier and dropped off the blanket," Gols said. "I was surprised you didn't give the order to evacuate the Complex. Do we need to evacuate the Complex?"

"No, Gols. No. No need to evacuate."

"I don't understand. The execution was part of his ultimatum. If the Leader isn't invading the Complex, why did he do that?"

"He said consequences."

"Consequences?"

"That's what he said."

"So he agreed to everything but—"

"Yes."

"The man is a monster."

"Yes, he is."

"So what now?"

"Everything moves forward as planned."

"Can I ask you a question?"

"Sure, Gols, why not?"

"What was that device you had our tech replicate?"

"Oh, that," Mar said. "Just between us?" She didn't know why she asked him. Gols was one of the few people on Koda who she trusted implicitly.

"Of course."

"That was part of what the Great man called his 'Rejuv Treatment.' That device and a specific substance halted his aging until he stopped taking the treatments."

"So am I correct in presuming you gave them to the Leader since you took them to your meeting?" Gols said. "So that monster is going to outlive us all?"

Mar pointed over at the open bag of topsoil she'd requested from Gols, leaning against one of the potted plants. "I don't think so," Mar said. "That's what he received in place of the real substance."

# YOR

Yor and Mado couldn't find a solution to operate the engines at full power. The poor quality of the metal in the parts continued to hamper their efforts. Every time they pushed the engines past three-quarters power, signs of catastrophic failure loomed, although a few of the engines seemed sturdier than the others.

Mado decided to consider a strategy for making it around the red dwarf involving Yor's mathematical calculations, although he defined it as "high risk." The plan involved the WAEF reaching maximum velocity at three-quarters power during the planetary gravity assist, then lowering the output of the most vulnerable engines while keeping the remaining engines at three-quarters power and slingshotting around the star using the extra momentum from the gravity assist.

Before Mado began evaluating the math for Yor's maneuver, a transmission arrived from Koda and a somber day was spent mourning the passing of Rajer and Joro, who was missing and presumed dead. Mado spent a portion of the next three days working on the equations. When he was done, Mado told Yor he was comfortable with the strategy, but he recalculated for a different trajectory so they wouldn't get too close to the star. Mado's concern was overburdening the WAEF's heat shields, which hadn't been restored or safety checked before Breeze Celebration.

Yor said, "So when you say you're comfortable doing this, what does that mean?"

"There's always the probability that something like this will fail, but I'm sure we'll be fine," Mado said, heading over to the food replicator and punching in a code.

"I don't believe you."

"Why not?"

"Just the way you're acting," Yor said. "Feels like you're withholding something." Yor walked over to Mado and stood directly in front of him.

"What makes you think that?"

"I've seen you act this way before. You're being evasive," Yor said. "Coming over to the replicator in a sort of rush for your Gleckos—your comfort food. You didn't really answer my question. Then there's your tone of voice and the fact that you're looking over into the corner instead of directly at me."

"I see you're using your mother's skills. Reading me. She'd be proud."

"And you're being evasive again," Yor said. "Out with it."

"What would you like to know?"

"What is the probability this maneuver will fail?"

"I think it's best you just know that it might succeed."

"Why do you always do that?"

"Do what?"

"You know what! We've discussed this so many times, but you always fall back into this behavior. Why is it so hard to treat me as an equal and tell me the whole truth? Is it because you and my great-grandfather went out of your way for years to hide the truth and keep me in the dark until I was deemed ready? Are you concerned that if you tell me the truth at this point in my life with everything that's happened over the past year that I won't be able to handle it? Or is this some Prevorian way of communication that requires me to pry the truth out of you?"

"That's funny."

"I don't find it funny."

"No. I thought what you said was funny, because it's probably a little bit of all those things but mostly the first one."

"Well, stop it!"

"What do you want me to say?"

"The entire truth when I ask it instead of what you're doing now."

"I meant, what do you want me to say about our current situation?" Mado said as the replicator beeped. "There's a better chance this maneuver won't be successful. More can go wrong than right. I reached this conclusion using a multitude of factors in my calculations, including the conditions in which this craft was stored when it was in Global Assembly possession, the time it's already spent in outer space with equipment it was never meant to bear strapped to its hull, traveling at speeds it was never meant to go, and the flaws in its original design."

Yor burst out laughing.

"Now, I don't see anything funny in what I just said. It's serious. There's a good chance we'll die."

"I'm laughing because I love it. That might be the first time I've ever heard you answer a serious question from me in a tone where it's obvious you're not holding anything back."

"I kind of like the way it felt, too."

"That's great," Yor said, patting Mado on the back. "Now please continue doing it."

"I'll do my best."

"Mado, I've never seen you do anything less."

"That is my way."

"It is…it is." Yor placed his hand on Mado's shoulder. "Now, about that dying part. How do we stop that from happening? Is there another path to the station?"

"We've already committed ourselves and there's no way to avoid the star's gravity anyway."

"I still think my original calculations will work."

"I don't believe so. As I said, the heat shields aren't up to it."

"You always preach the importance of having options."

"In this case, we're out of them."

"All right. I'll bow to your experience," Yor said. "So how can I help in the preparations to increase the probability we'll live?"

"I have a checklist."

"Let's see it."

Mado walked over to one of the viewers he'd installed in the living chamber for the museum staff and pulled up a list containing 124 items.

"This is the list?" Yor said. "You were going to do all this by yourself so I wouldn't know about the danger?"

"No. I was going to prep you for some sense of danger, but probably not so directly, then ask for your help."

"Well, let me know the tasks you think I can handle competently and I'll take care of them."

"That was my plan." Mado pulled a memory wafer from the breast pocket of his shirt, inserted it in the side of the viewer, and typed into the keyboard. Different screens raced by, then Mado handed the wafer to Yor. "There's your list. Good talk. Get to it. We have fifteen days."

***

**WHEN THE TIME FOR THE MANEUVER ARRIVED,** Yor strapped himself into the seat at the rear of the control room and began to fret about each of the forty-one chores Mado had given him. He wondered if he'd missed anything. Maybe he forgot to tighten a screw. Maybe the power-flow wasn't consistent to the automated onboard navigation system and the circuitry was faulty. Maybe he didn't run enough simulations to catch problems with the power converter for each engine.

Mado gazed over his shoulder at Yor from the pilot's chair and said, "Don't do that."

"Do what?"

"You're wondering if you successfully completed the list I gave you."

"How did you…?"

"I read your mind, of course."

"I didn't know—"

Mado laughed. "Just kidding. I've been through this before. Space Travelers are taught in training not to second-guess ourselves on the verge of danger, which is natural, because it will throw our focus off and increase the likelihood of failure…So don't do it. Now, let's count down from six."

Mado turned back to the control console and Yor began counting down with him from six, then Mado stopped at three. He turned around and said, "By the way, if it makes you feel any better, I double-checked the work I gave you and it was all done correctly. Now, let's start counting from the top again."

At the end of the countdown, Mado flipped a switch, igniting all six engines at three-quarters power. The sudden acceleration pinned Yor to the seat, and the g-force almost caused him to pass out. Mado lowered the radiation shield on the control-room window. The ship's automated onboard navigation system was controlling the WAEF now to ensure there were no mistakes during the maneuver. Mado insisted he could perform the task without the ship's automation, but he trusted the system to detect any emergency in the ship's workings quicker than he could and make the necessary course corrections.

Yor felt the increase in g's as the gravity assist began. Mado had told him that he should embrace what was coming, which would be frightening his first-time. Mado would be fine given his experience and Prevorian physiology. He turned to Yor, attempted to smile, and said, "Here we go."

Yor began to think about the family and friends he'd left behind on Koda but was unconscious before his thoughts went any further. When he regained consciousness, the red star filled the screen of the starboard cam. He could tell by the roar of the engines that at least half of them were running at low power as Mado had planned, but he was concerned when he noticed Mado was steering by hand. Obviously, something had happened while he was unconscious which caused Mado to take control from the onboard system. Mado had both hands on the steering mechanism, struggling with it, leaning in to it so the ship would hold its course. Yor imagined Mado was exuding strength far beyond the capability of any Kodan.

Alarming noises were emanating from Mado—squeals, warbles, yelps—interspersed with words in a language Yor assumed was Prevorian. Mado peered at the navigation system, then at the screen with the red dwarf filling it, then at the navigation system again. Yor swore the ship was constantly being pulled closer to the star since it looked brighter on screen moment by moment, and Mado's unsettling noises increased in volume and shrillness.

Yor was frightened, and he decided it was time to take action. He learned that the artificial gravity was off when an errant screw floated by him. He reached up and grabbed a ceiling handhold. A series of them had been installed so the crew would still be able to move around the control room if the gravity generator failed. He unfastened his harness with his free hand, then grabbed the handhold with it. He made his way across the control room, fighting against the g's, until he stood behind Mado. He held on with one hand and began flipping switches on the navigation computer with the other.

Mado turned his head while still struggling with the steering mechanism. His nostrils were flaring. "Yor, what do you think you're doing?"

"Looks like we're losing to the star's gravitational pull," Yor said. He finished flipping switches. "Any other systemic issues I should know about?"

"No," Mado said. "You're correct about the problem, but pushing the engines further than three-quarters is too dangerous."

"Then we need another option, so I'm saving us. I hope." Yor punched the button to complete the entry of his maneuver. A light appeared on the control console with a switch below it. "Punch it, Mado. Trust me."

Mado turned to the console.

Yor said, "Just wait till I get to my seat." He worked his way back and buckled himself in.

Mado turned to Yor and said, "I have faith in you," then took one hand off the steering mechanism and flipped the switch.

The ship's automated system took control again and all the engines fired online at three-quarters power. Mado let go of the steering mechanism. The WAEF rattled violently, as if it was about to come apart bolt by bolt. Yor gripped his harness with both hands, closed his eyes, and felt as if he might lose consciousness again.

Time passed and the ship continued to rattle. Fear filled the pit of Yor's stomach. He'd never believed in a higher power, but he prayed now: *Powers-That-Be! If I get out of this alive, I will be a better person and do whatever needs to be done to save my people, above and beyond what I've already done.* When he heard all the engines power down, Yor opened his eyes and felt like he could breathe again. Mado was calmly flipping switches and pressing buttons with both hands. The viewing screen displayed the aft cam. The star was still large, but behind them.

Mado turned around in his seat and said, "We barely made it, but we made it and that's what matters. And you don't have to keep those promises."

"How did you…?"

Mado laughed.

Yor said, "Let me guess. You've been through this kind of thing before."

"Life-threatening dilemmas, yes," Mado said. "That was a close one, though. We should reach our destination shortly. The gravity generator is back on—I had to turn it off for more power during the maneuver—so feel free to undo your harness and stand when you're ready. Just take it easy. Your legs might be a little unsteady."

Yor unbuckled his harness and said, "Probably more than a little."

"And by the way, fantastic job. You saved us."

After the WAEF landed on A-1 beside the SEEDER program way station, Mado explained what had gone wrong. When they attempted to navigate around the star, lack of power caused the ship to be pulled closer to the red dwarf than planned and the hull temperature was nearing catastrophic. Given the high probability of irreparable damage to the ship and their deaths if they got any closer, he decided to make a last ditch effort to save them by taking over the steering since there was no time to reprogram the automated system.

"But you had already programmed in the solution

to our problem. Hadn't you?" Mado said. "The engines could have exploded."

"It was more of a course correction using the star's gravity, but someone told me to always have options," Yor said. "So I worked on a few after you told me that we might die."

"We came close," Mado said. "I was making promises, too."

"I heard. Didn't understand a word of it, but I got the gist."

Mado extended the docking-bay walkway to the second-floor entrance of the way station and they climbed into their spacesuits. Twenty-five years ago, the Prevorian spacesuit Mado had used during his travels with Yor's great-grandfather was left inside this station. Mado designed and built his new suit over the years, which had been stowed away before Breeze Celebration. Mado put on his helmet and sealed himself inside, activating the oxygen system and the helmet lights. Yor did the same.

As they stood inside the docking-bay airlock, Mado closed the inner doors from the console there. They magnetized their boots and Mado threw the switch on the console and the outer doors opened to the walkway. Yor followed Mado to the station and through the round walkway windows, he observed the barren planetoid landscape pockmarked by meteor strikes.

He noted this was the first time he'd visited a planetoid. He'd also experienced a gravity assist to slingshot around a star and performed a spacewalk. In his wildest dreams, he'd never thought this would be his life. This was his great-grandfather's life, but he was loving it.

Mado unlocked the way-station door using an inter-face on the forearm of Yor's spacesuit and they stepped inside the outpost's airlock.

It was pitch black inside the station when the inner airlock door opened. As they'd planned earlier, Mado headed across the floor by himself. His helmet lights illu-minated a few couches and control consoles. Yor waited just outside the airlock with his helmet lights on. The floor layout appeared to be one big room. In his studies, Yor had read that these early stations were stocked with bare essentials for the SEEDER-program crews while the search for a planet occurred. Once the viable planet was found, more elaborate outposts would have been built along the path to the planet as rest stops to accommodate travelers on the way to their new home.

The overhead lights flickered on and Yor found him-self standing in a large room with a staircase in the middle leading down to the first floor. The area around the stair-case was outfitted with couches and recliners like those in the WAEF's living chamber and between the windows, the walls were lined with consoles and viewing screens. Mado stood in the middle of the room by the staircase and waved Yor over to him. Yor turned off his helmet lights and joined him.

Mado said, "Keep your helmet on—it'll take a while for the air to be breathable. Until then, let me show you what's downstairs." Mado pressed a few buttons on a console at the top of the staircase. The lights turned on downstairs and Mado waved for Yor to follow.

Halfway down the stairs, Yor stopped. He was overlooking a storage room, filled to the brim. He didn't recognize many of the items, but before Yor could ask about them, Mado began pointing, saying, "That's the engines your great-grandfather and I fashioned for the WAEF from my spacecraft. That's the field generators we mounted on the WAEF allowing us to travel as fast as we did. There's the IPRD. Those are the barrels of soil from the lava planet your great-grandfather used to extend his life-span, and that's my pod to return home."

"Return home? To Prevor?"

"Yes, Yor. The time is nearing for me to go home, and on this voyage, you've proven yourself worthy to command the WAEF."

"Really? Doesn't feel like it."

"It'll feel like it when you do it."

Then the entire station shook.

Yor grabbed the staircase's railing. "Does this planetoid have earthquakes?"

"That wasn't an earthquake," Mado said, hurrying up the stairs.

When Yor caught up to him, Mado was gazing out a window at a larger version of the spaceship Yor had observed on his spacewalk. It had landed a short distance from the station. This ship's radius was maybe forty-five meters and it was about four stories tall. A doorway appeared in the craft's smooth metallic dome and a ramp extended from the doorway to the ground. Yor and Mado watched together for a while. Nothing emerged, but a message in a language unintelligible to

Mado was transmitted and repeated in a recorded loop over a speaker system.

Yor said, "What do we do?"

"I'm going to see what they want. The message doesn't sound threatening. You stay here."

"I'm not letting you go alone. How do you know whether the message is threatening or not? You have no idea what they're saying."

"I've done this before, Yor. Nothing to worry about."

"Nothing to worry about? I don't believe you."

"All right. You're correct. There's something to worry about. There's always something to worry about."

"We don't know who they are or what they're intending."

"True, but I didn't know your great-grandfather, either. I took a risk meeting him," Mado said. "They're more technologically advanced than both of our civilizations. If they wanted to harm us, they'd have done it already and we wouldn't be having this conversation."

"If you go, I go."

"Your priority is Koda. No matter what happens. I have faith in you." Mado put his hand on Yor's shoulder and closed his eyes. Yor was overcome by Mado's confidence in him. "Everything will probably be fine and I'll return shortly." Mado reached inside a pouch on his spacesuit and handed Yor a memory wafer. "Just in case, this is the plan. I was going to show it to you today, and I still might. If I don't return, then do what you have to do."

Mado headed down the stairs. Yor wanted to run after him but let him go. Once Mado's mind was made up, there was no stopping him. Moments later, Yor watched Mado walk across the planetoid's surface to the alien ship and head up the ramp. When he was inside, the ramp retracted and the doorway disappeared, leaving the spaceship's dome whole again. The bottom portion of the ship lit up and began rotating back and forth and the ship lifted off without a sound. The landing gear retracted, then the bottom of the ship began spinning with increasing speed in one direction. There was a blinding flash of light, the way station shook, and the ship vanished. Mado was gone.

**HOWARD LIBES** has been a writer for over 30 years and is a graduate of the University of Oregon Writing Program. He edited the 2,300-page manuscript of *If They Move…Kill'em: The Life and Times of Sam Peckinpah* by David Weddle (Atlantic/Grove Press) and worked as a collaborator—writer and interviewer—on *Among the Mansions of Eden: Tales of Love, Lust, and Land in Beverly Hills* by David Weddle (William Morrow/HarperCollins). He has been a freelance writer for many publications, including *Los Angeles Times Magazine*.

Currently, he is tapping into his lifelong obsession with science fiction and writing the SEEDER series. *When All Else Fails* (Happy Mistake Publishing), the first book in the series, was released in 2017.